WEALTH

A MALLORY O'SHAUGHNESSY NOVEL

Volume Three

PSALM 119:14   *I have rejoiced in the way of thy testimonies,
as much as in all riches.*

Paula Rae Wallace

Order this book online at www.trafford.com
or email orders@trafford.com

Most Trafford titles are also available at major online book retailers.

Printed in the United States of America.

ISBN: 978-1-4269-4468-0 (sc)
ISBN: 978-1-4269-4469-7 (e)

Our mission is to efficiently provide the world's finest, most comprehensive book publishing
service, enabling every author to experience success. To find out how to publish your book,
your way, and have it available worldwide, visit us online at www.trafford.com

Trafford rev. 10/22/2010

www.trafford.com

North America & international
toll-free: 1 888 232 4444 (USA & Canada)
phone: 250 383 6864 ♦ fax: 812 355 4082

Credits

Permission for cover map courtesy, Arkansas State Highway and Transportation Department

PREFACE

JOB 28

1. *Surely there is a vein for the silver, and a place for gold where they fine it.*
2. *Iron is taken out of the earth, and brass is molten out of the stone.*
3. *He setteth an end to darkness, and searcheth out all perfection: the stones of darkness and the shadow of death.*
4. *The flood breaketh out from the inhabitant; even the waters forgotten of the foot: they are dried up, they are gone away from men.*
5. *As for the earth, out of it cometh bread: and under it is turned up as it were fire.*
6. *The stones of it are the place of sapphires: and it hath dust of gold.*
7. *There is a path which no fowl knoweth, and which the vulture's eye hath not seen:*
8. *The lion's whelps have not trodden it, nor the fierce lion passed by it.*
9. *He putteth forth his hand upon the rock; he overturneth the mountains by the roots.*
10. *He cutteth out rivers among the rocks; and his eye seeth every precious thing.*
11. *He bindeth the floods from overflowing; and the thing that is hid bringeth he forth to the light.*
12. *But where shall wisdom be found? and where is the place of understanding?*
13. *Man knoweth not the price thereof; neither is it found in the land of the living.*
14. *The depth saith, It is not in me: and the sea saith, It is not with me.*
15. *It cannot be gotten with gold, neither shall silver be weighed for the price thereof.*
16. *It cannot be valued with the gold of Ophir, with the precious onyx, or the sapphire.*

17. *The gold and the crystal cannot equal it: and the exchange of it shall not be for jewels of fine gold.*
18. *No mention shall be made of coral, or of pearls: for the price of wisdom is above rubies.*
19. *The topaz of Ethiopia shall not equal it, neither shall it be valued with pure gold.*
20. *Whence then cometh wisdom? and where is the place of understanding?*
21. *Seeing it is hid from the eyes of all living, and kept close from the fowls of the air.*
22. *Destruction and death say, We have heard the fame thereof with our ears.*
23. *God understandeth the way thereof, and he knoweth the place thereof.*
24. *For he looketh to the ends of the earth, and seeth under the whole heaven;*
25. *To make the weight for the winds; and he weigheth the water by measure,*
26. *When he made a decree for the rain, and a way for the lightning of the thunder:*
27. *Then did he see it, and declare it; he prepared it, yea, he searched it out.*
28. *And unto man he said, Behold, the fear of the LORD, that is wisdom; and to depart from evil is understanding.*

Thus far with Mallory:

DAZZLING Finds Mallory O'Shaughnessy destitute and desperate following the death of her beloved daddy. Trusting the Lord, she encourages her mother, Suzanne to trust in God, too. Dangers assail as she realizes that her humble little frame house in Pike County, Arkansas, sits atop lamporolite diamond pipes. Who is trespassing? Why has the Faulkner family showed up? Is her beloved childhood friend, David Anderson going to be God's choice for her life's mate?

TREASURES takes Mallory into new adventures and dangers as she relocates to an elegant mansion in Dallas, assuming the reins as CEO of DiaMo Corporation! New friends and fresh experiences take her from the realm of dreamy-eyed arm-chair traveler to actual exploration of far-off exotic locales. Perils beset as she finds the Lord faithful beyond all measure.

TABLE OF CONTENTS

Chapter 1: WORKLOAD

Seventeen year old Mallory O'Shaughnessy wakened while her room was still dark. Overtaken with exhaustion, and with some strong drugs still in her system, she had gone to bed early. Now, she was awake, feeling refreshed, although the hour was early. She guessed it must be associated with jet lag. Stretching lazily, she pushed up her pillows, reaching for her lamp and Bible at the same time.

She turned to the book of Genesis. Since her father's death the previous January, she had skipped around haphazardly in her Scripture reading: at first, seeking for comforting passages; then later, passages dealing with the Biblical sites in Turkey. Now, she decided it was time to begin at the beginning of her Bible, and discipline herself. Besides, she was planning to begin her career, today, as a college student majoring in Geology. She intended to square all of her course work by the infallible Word of God, beginning with the Genesis account of creation.

Genesis 1:1 In the beginning God created the heavens and the earth.

Of course, she had committed the first verse to memory in grade school. She read on, quickly reading four chapters. The time span, according to her timeline, was from B.C. 4003 to 3875, through the "fall of man" and Cain's killing his brother. The narrative in Genesis moved along quickly. She turned to her Proverbs chapter, twenty-six, and copied verse thirteen about a slothful man, and his lame excuses for not getting busy doing what was necessary. Even though it was Saturday, after being gone for twelve days, she had plenty to do.

She was excited about it though. Her hazel eyes danced with excitement about the tasks she needed to accomplish. Finishing praying through her journal, she made a to-do list. It helped her prioritize, and she could see progress as she scratched through completed tasks.

She finished bathing, sliding into the big, terrycloth, Turkish robe and pointed slippers while she dried her hair and did her makeup. A light tap on the door preceded Diana's poking her head in.

"Come on in," Mallory urged. "Have you had any coffee yet?"

"Of course! I brought you a cup, too. You're up early."

Mallory laughed. "Yeah, 'Early to bed, early to rise…'. I couldn't stay awake last night; then I couldn't stay asleep this morning. I have lots to do today. I think I'm going to the office right away. You think anyone will mind?"

"I hope no one does. They shouldn't. You certainly provided everyone with a wonderful time! Over all," she added, remembering some extremely tense moments.

Mallory laughed agreement "Yeah, over all! I'm dying to open all my packages, but I'm making myself do some work first. You were right about the shopping! I'm not sure how stuff will work in my office; maybe I'll hire someone to put it together."

"M-m-Mm!" Diana cleared her throat loudly.

"You have too much going on already! I wasn't hinting! But, if you're insisting-"

"I insist! I love that kind of thing! I didn't see all you bought, but I've been kind of formulating a plan! And plans for more jewelry and clothing designs!" Diana's eyes sparkled with excitement. "I need to get out of here, so you can finish getting dressed, get to the office to do your work, so you can come to Tulsa next week and help me with mine. You think your aunt and Herb are planning to get married?"

"I don't know. I'm kind of disappointed that none of the unsaved people got saved on the trip."

"As far as we know, they didn't," Diana corrected her. "It's a heart thing. At least they got a lot of good exposure to the gospel. I'm going to go see if my family's waking up. See you downstairs."

She exited, leaving a void and a light hint of fragrance.

Mallory dressed quickly in white, to save decision making. White sandals, gold jewelry, she was ready.

Nearly everyone was poolside eating breakfast. Mallie carried a plate of food inside. The morning was already warm; a prelude to Dallas summertime! She picked up her stack of mail, sorting out junk as she enjoyed melon and berries. There seemed to be quite a bit of first-class mail, mostly from people she didn't know. She opened one, which appeared to be a fan letter from some wacko! Sighing, she wondered if that was what the others were. She shoved the stack aside and smiled as her mom joined her, bringing her a plate of Eggs Benedict.

"Is Aunt Linda still here?" she asked.

"Probably," Suzanne responded. "She's probably sleeping late. Diana said you're heading to your office. Erik and I are heading home! I should go in to my office, too. Roger's paying me well, and I haven't done much yet. Erik's eager to get updates on all his bad guys. Are you going to tell us how you ended up back in Turkey?"

Mallie smiled enigmatically. The group had done fairly well not grilling her.

"Can't tell you what I don't know, Mom," she replied, chipper as always.

Suzanne shook her head in amazement. Surely her daughter knew some of what had happened to her!

Mallie bid goodbye to everyone who was up, then was spinning down the long drive in her Jaguar. Top down, she couldn't help thinking about her episode with the baggage handler and Diana's Louis Vuitton full of expensive jewelry! She knew David wanted her to get rid of the convertible! David again! Why couldn't she get him out of her mind? No one from the Anderson family had been at breakfast. She wasn't sure if they were headed home early, or still sleeping in! She didn't want to say good-bye to David. The Faulkners probably would really mean it now about six months apart! That was why she just had to stay busy. She checked her mirror. One of her security SUV's was staying with her.

With Mallory gone, her houseguests began departing.

Her cell rang just as she settled behind her ornate, inlaid desk. Erik Bransom! She answered as usual, calling him neither Erik, nor Mr. Bransom. "Whazzup?"

"Mallory, I had a message on my phone. The governor's office doesn't have your number, but they've been trying to get in touch with you to do a publicity shoot at the *Crater of Diamonds*. They want you to come there and tell everyone that the *Park's* safe."

"Me?" Her voice was a startled question. Then she laughed. "Wow, I don't know! I've never been there! My dad wouldn't let me"

"You haven't? He wouldn't?" Bransom couldn't believe it.

3

"No, Sir! I guess he was afraid I'd find a diamond, and the *Park* personnel would verify it; then I'd know I really had been finding diamonds all those years! That's all I can think of now, for why not. I'd like to go and at least see that perfect diamond that's on display. I can't guarantee anyone's safety. I mean, I know they've ramped up security since Martin's crime spree! But still, if you have something valuable, you have to know someone will target you if they know about it. What does Mom think?"

Erik put Suzanne on. As usual, she told Mallory to make her own decision.

"When did they say?" She couldn't believe the answer! "Monday"! Nothing like notice! But she could get stuff done today, go to church tomorrow, then go to Murfreesboro on Monday, and then start the Geology!

"Tell them ok. What time Monday?"

"That they didn't say. I'll call back and ask, then I'll call you right back."

Mallory was already regretting saying she'd involve herself, even before her mom called back to say they wanted to start going over script and stuff at eight, sharp!

She hung up from her mom and called Diana's cell. She should probably let them know she was going home, so they could spirit David away someplace.

She was mildly surprised that Diana was less than thrilled about the whole publicity thing. Daniel took her phone, telling Mallory not to agree to anything like that again without checking with him. She was trying to keep from crying. She had asked her mom; Erik had good sense; if he saw a problem, he wouldn't have called her about the opportunity. Fighting tears, and trying to sound like she had a good attitude, she ended the call as quickly as possible.

⚓ ⚓

David sat next to his dad during the chopper flight home. Tammi had tried to chum it up with him, figuring she could whine about not seeing Larson, and get sympathy from him. He didn't want to talk about it! Or listen to her right now!

"Some trip, huh?" his dad asked.

"I thought I'd never see her again! It was my fault!" David's voice was a haunted whisper. "How could I have forgotten to tell Bransom about that car casing her? I've been pretty rude to both Bransom and Faulkner about her security! Then, I mess up even worse!"

He dropped his head into his hands in utter dejection.

John thought his son had acted like a smart aleck to the two men, but his heart still hurt to see him humbled. Smartest people in the world had to be seventeen year old guys! His lips twitched, realizing who his son had inherited that trait from.

Having Mallory back was a miracle! She had continued humming the "Angels" song, sleepily, during the flight. Then, this morning, he had heard her whistling, "My Lord Knows the Way Through the Wilderness". He hadn't heard the chorus in so long, he had forgotten about it. Like everyone else, he was curious to know what had happened. Bransom didn't think it was the Lord, or angels. He thought it was special agents, or something! The pastor knew it was the Lord! No telling who His instruments were!

David thoughtfully left his dirty clothes for his mom to do up, telling her no rush; he could get them after church the next afternoon. Hopping into his truck, he roared away. He figured all of the work at the camp was probably washed away. He wondered if any of the diamonds remained in the little unprotected house. He had a lot on his mind.

⊰ ⊱

Erik Bransom ate lunch with Suzanne, then went to the FBI office while she went in to her office. A thick dossier rested on his desk. Ahmir's information on Oscar and Otto. The English read a little funny; evidently someone had just pushed a computer button to translate from Turkish. Still more information than he had assembled thus far. He rubbed his face with both hands. Suddenly sleepy, he brewed coffee and jogged around the small space. He wondered idly how much weight he had gained on the trip. Pouring a mug of the steaming brew, he returned to his jigsaw puzzle. None of the pieces fit! The Charles River hadn't yielded any bodies; although it had hidden the luxury car for several months. So, was Ryland never in it? Faking a death wasn't that easy. Delia's P.I. wouldn't have been that easily fooled. Had the Malovich brothers executed the guy, having the body removed recently, so that a murder charge couldn't get filed? Did they have connections in Iran? Or was the kidnapping of Mallory totally unrelated to the previous incidents? Maybe she had never actually been removed from Eastern Turkey. He shuddered! He didn't think it was angels! But the odds of getting her back had been pretty small!

Mystified by all the new data, he turned his attention to the sheaf of photos from Oscar's computer. The one of David and the girl with the baby continued to trouble to him. He scanned her face into the computer to search for her identity. He nodded off, and the computer dinged with the ID hit. Sylvia Marie Brown. Address in Dierks. Refilling his mug, he switched off the coffee pot and the computer and headed to his agency car.

"Hey, Suze," he caressed her name when Suzanne answered her phone. "I'm heading up to Dierks to run an address. May make me a little late for dinner. Why don't you meet me at McKenna's at seven."

Her voice sounded worried. "You aren't doing anything dangerous by yourself, are you?"

"Promise to be careful!" He kissed into the phone.

As he approached the tiny town, he wished he had a less conspicuous car. He laughed to himself; that was nothing new. Probably any car would stand out to the small, close-knit community, but the big FBI car shouted, "Official"! He rolled into the city limits, anyway, the guidance system directing him to turn right on a small gravel side-street. Immediately on his right, he saw the small apartment complex stairs, visible in the picture. His gazed traveled around, taking in the other buildings, the cars and trucks parked along the street. He guessed he had been afraid he might see David's truck. Suddenly, he wondered what was wrong with him for even checking into this! He had plenty of pertinent sleuthing to do, and he was wasting time and gas running down Mallory's "friend". He castigated himself for being as much of a voyeur as Melville, snooping around into what people were doing, when it was none of his business. He didn't know why he felt a need to either verify or disprove David's explanation. He wasn't Mallory's dad, or really even her stepfather. He hadn't even been much of a dad to his own three girls. He blew his nose noisily, continuing slowly along the block. At a stop sign, he braked, looking both directions. He could see his quarry, moving toward him, trying to get back to her apartment with a few groceries, a twenty-four pack of beer: and now it looked like she had two babies. Pushing the double stroller through sand and loose gravel along the edge of the street looked pretty tough. He knew from her background that she was unmarried; he wondered idly who the dad was, or the dads. He crossed the intersection, realizing she had to have noticed the car. After turning back onto the two-lane blacktop, he pulled in at a convenience store and sprinted inside for more coffee.

This was where she bought her beer and groceries; he wondered if the store clerk would recognize David, but he didn't ask. Suddenly, he felt uneasy as he scanned around the Saturday afternoon crowd making up the customer mix of the moment. Campers and fishermen passing through, locals dining on the small-town fare the station offered. He pretended to shop for a pair of sunglasses, surveying the area behind him in the mirror on the display. Pulling out his phone, he speed dialed.

"Hey, Summers, where ya at?" he questioned when Ivan answered.

"I'm in Dierks! Watching your back for ya! Suzanne called me! You know how to stir up trouble! I'll say that for you! I don't have much man power available up there, either, so I called Morrison. He has a couple of Forestry LEI guys on the way! Even so, I don't think we can get these guys into custody with what we got!"

"I'm not sure what you're talking about," Bransom confessed. "I'm just up here spying on a local beautician. Then I stopped for coffee, and someone was messing with my car."

"Yeah! Stay inside the station. There's a big can of worms! I can't tell you all of it on your cell phone." Summers disconnected, seemingly enjoying ordering the Fed around for a change. Bransom was just relieved he was there, and curious to know what "the can of worms" was.

⇥ ⇤

Mallory fought back the desire to cry and tackled some of the documents that had accumulated for her attention as the CEO of the DiaMo Corporation during her absence. Disappointing her guardian and his wife bothered her.

Time flew by; she was suddenly starving. She closed her system and headed to the outer office. Darrell Hopkins and a couple of other security guys jumped up, ready to accompany her.

"A courier brought this for you," he announced to Mallory, extending an expensive-looking vellum envelope and a flat box. The envelope was addressed to her, and the letterhead announced that it was from the *Israeli Diamond Council*.

She gave her security head a quizzical look, and he shrugged his shoulders. Slitting the envelope neatly with an opener from Marge's desk, she pulled out a formal invitation to visit Israel to view their diamond facility! Leaving Thursday! First class tickets on El Al! Guests of the Israeli government! Her hands shook. She had wondered if it was Israelis who had helped spirit her out of her recent predicament. Now this? Immediately on her arrival home? They didn't want her to discount her diamonds to the Turkish merchants! It didn't say that! She just knew! She had been pretty sure she would have to tell the Turkish host, "No", anyway. The pricing structure was just too fragile! Everyone on the inside of the industry knew that!

Intrigued, she opened the plain vellum box to find a red, velvet, hinged box nested within. Opening it, she gasped with awe! Must be a bona fide invitation from the *Diamond Council*, alright! Nestled within the red satin of the box, sparkled the most amazing diamond necklace she had ever imagined!

"Looks like we're on our way to Israel next week," she announced decisively to Darrell. He nodded; he'd pick who else was going with them. He was relieved that Janice Collins was in!

Mallory suddenly wasn't sorry that she had agreed to do the *Crater of Diamond* Publicity thing without the Faulkners' blessing. She knew he was worried about her security. She wasn't asking them about Israel, either! Time for her take control of her own security and employees. She was issuing orders to Hopkins non-stop on the way home, like she had done it all her life. She picked up her aunt to take her to dinner, then called Herb, asking him to take the jeweler's position and accompany their corporate entourage on the Israel trip!

With that worked out, she rewrote her Chemistry paper: *Water Buoyancy in The Dead Sea*! With the paper sent to Tom Haynes, she opened her Geology course, reading the first five chapters of the *Introduction to Geology* textbook.

She absolutely loved her life!

Chapter 2: WONDERMENT

Herb Carlton drove home Saturday evening, his thoughts on Linda Campbell. Troubled thoughts, though. At first, their common bond was to hold out against the Christians. Then, he had just loved being in her company. Upon arrival back in Dallas, she had given him permission to call her "sometime"; she was worried things were moving too fast. He guessed he really was too old for her. He was fifty-eight, almost twenty years her senior. He sighed. He had lived through heartache and disappointment before. At least she had made the exciting trip even more fun, giving him someone to sit with on the coaches and at meals.

He always closed his shop on Sundays, but he went in to view the damage he was sure it had suffered in his absence. He took the cello and one of the violins with him. Cassandra Faulkner had bonded with the other violin; it really did have an exceptional resonance; so Daniel had purchased it for her. Mallory was going to use Cassandra's discard, to begin her lessons. He priced the two instruments, carefully filing his receipt for the purchase from the Istanbul pawn shop, and entering the instruments on his inventory. He checked the sales receipts and loan papers from the transactions of the previous two week's business. Merc had done okay. Herb was trying to shake off the loneliness when he heard the key turn in the lock; then the bell dinged as someone entered the front.

A handsome, slender young man approached him.

"Son, how do you have a key to my store?" Even as he asked, he was wondering if Merc had hired the kid, giving him his own key.

"Grandpa, you weren't gone that long." The cute kid laughed, showing dimples and strong, even teeth. Short, light brown hair, cut close, was spiked up, and muscular arms showed from a clean tank top.

"Samuel?" That was the only person it could be! His oldest grandson, but his countenance hadn't looked so happy for years.

"Yeah, it's me. Can you believe I got a haircut? And a shave?"

The laugh again, like when he was a little boy. It was more than a haircut, though! He was transformed! The sullen, angry adolescent was gone! Herb continued to stare at him in disbelief.

"Are you okay, Grandpa? Maybe you should sit down!"

Samuel had shown him nothing but disrespect and surliness for the past five or six years; now his eyes registered a genuine concern.

"I'm fine," Herb responded, afraid he might break the spell someone had cast on the boy. "A little hungry; you want to come to McDonalds with me? If you don't, it's fine," he hurried to add. Just because Samuel was worried didn't mean he wanted to go hang out with an old guy.

"Yes, Sir, I would like that. I want to hear about your trip. I have plans for later, so I came by to check on everything."

Herb bought! Boy, did he ever! Samuel put every bite of it away, too! Merc and Nell always complained to him they couldn't keep the boys filled up.

Herb even had a little appetite back. He had been so upset about Linda- But Samuel's emerging from his "phase" was a real lift.

Samuel threw the trash away, then checked his phone and pulled his keys from his jeans. "Sounds like a great trip. Dad said you met a lady; why aren't you telling me about her?"

"Nothing to tell. Why aren't you telling me what really happened with you? You're not the boy I left here a couple of weeks back. It's more than just a haircut. You've never said, 'Yes, Sir', and 'No, Sir' to me in your life! You entering the military?"

The cute infectious laugh again! His grandson met his gaze, amazed.

"Actually, I never gave the military a thought before! I've been so anti-establishment. That may be a pretty good idea."

"It isn't!" Herb said quickly. "Don't tell your mom you got it from me! I'm not trying to put bad ideas into your head."

"That isn't a bad idea; I'm just trying to work out what I should do with my life."

"A couple of weeks ago, all you cared about was your music and playing games, coasting through school. You gonna tell me why the change?"

"I can't! Dad made me promise. He doesn't want you upset with us."

The thousand piece jig-saw puzzle turned into a clear picture, and Carlton shook his head, amazed! He was more familiar with the Scriptures than he had admitted to Linda. Albeit, only the Old Testament. He suddenly remembered a passage about "running into a house to escape from a bear, to be bitten by a snake". That was what happened to him. He had avoided making a decision for Christ, the Messiah, for the whole trip. To run home and be met with it again. He laughed, but tears were rolling.

"You accepted Jesus." His voice was soft, not a question, but a realization. "Are you the only one?"

"No, Sir, all of us! At first Dad didn't want to, because of being Jewish. It's been confusing to all of us. I don't want you to be upset, Grandpa, but Jesus does fit the prophecies about Messiah. I wasn't supposed to tell you."

"So your plans later, are for going to church? You better get going so you won't be late. The store really looked good. I'll call your dad later and tell him so. Thanks for joining me." He pulled out his own keys.

Samuel pulled away toward home; Grandpa didn't seem mad. He hadn't threatened to disown them all. He had said he was going to call and compliment Dad about keeping the store.

Herb headed up 278 toward Murfreesboro. If he was going to make Faith Baptist in time for church, he needed to hurry.

⊰ ⊱

When Mallory returned from her office, she allowed herself to attack the purchases that had arrived from various places in Turkey. She slashed and ripped at unbelievably strong tape and packaging. Everything was intact! Rocking back on her heels, she surveyed her treasures in wonder. Like Christmas in May. Actually, Christmases had never yielded this much treasure! Except that Daddy had been alive! That job finished, she pinched on a big piece of bubble wrap, and watched Boston play, while she and Dinky attacked another pizza!

She was letting Dinky out when her security buzzed, announcing the delivery of two more packages. Wow! She still needed to decide where to put what she had already opened. To her delight, the two packages were from Delia, hostess gifts for Mallory's hospitable trip.

"Oh, she didn't have to do that," Mallie was moaning as she tore into yet more packing! She squealed with delight! Two of the cutest outfits! Both linen, of course! One outfit was sunny orange, similar to her Easter dress! The tone was slightly less vibrant due to the linen's color absorption.

11

It featured a short-sleeved pull-over sweater with a slim, vented skirt. Nestled next to it was a pair of matching, soft leather, high-heeled pumps and large, flat, clutch. A small, flat box housed a jewelry set of Diamonds and Madeira Citrines; choker necklace, earrings, and ring. The other ensemble was yummy lime, a suit similar to the gray tweed with the ruffles, only short-sleeved, with hot, Dallas summers in mind. It was matched with strapped, high-heeled sandals and a soft, slouchy bag. The jewelry, of Lemon Quartz and Diamonds shimmered with exquisite color and superb craftsmanship. Mallory loved the colored stones! Of course, Diamonds were her thing; but, "Why limit your options when God has provided so many?"

She had been excited all afternoon and evening at the prospect of the Israel trip. These new outfits would be perfect to take along. She wondered if Delia could have known about the trip. A smile of wonder crossed her face. No, only the Lord, preparing the way for her, as He always did!

She had some calls to make that she had been putting off! Now, it was getting late. She called the Faulkners to apologize about the publicity thing on Monday and the misunderstanding. Then she dropped the bomb on them about the sudden travel plans to Israel. She was doing a good marketing job on Daniel about it when he broke in, laughing.

"Okay, okay." he surrendered "Wow, that was something about Erik, wasn't it?"

"What do you mean? What about Erik? I was calling mom and him next."

"Well, he was tracking down-um-some girl at a little town called Dierks; guess she's connected somehow to Melville and a Federal Judge. Summers and some of Morrison's buddies rescued him from some serious stuff."

Mallory was quiet. "Some girl at Dierks~you mean Sylvia?" She was trying to figure out what Daniel was saying "Why was he checking on her? Did she do something?"

"You know her?" Daniel was surprised.

"Well, I found her! Looking for someone to give me a decent haircut. So, I loved the way she cut my hair, but I felt sorry for her. You know, she had a baby and no husband. She was having a hard time making it. I told David about her, but I didn't know he would get so involved and go totally off-road, trying to 'help her', or whatever. How's she tied to Melville, and I don't even know what a 'Federal' judge is. Is Mr. Bransom okay?"

"Yes, but it's a good thing your mom was worried and called Summers to back him up. As it was, they had to let the Maloviches and their cohorts go back into the woodwork. They didn't want a big shootout at the convenience store."

Tears were trying to escape. "So, you're telling me Oscar and Otto and some other gangster types are in western Arkansas instead of Eastern Europe? Do you think they were really in Turkey this past week? Do you think they hired those two guys to kidnap me?"

"Yes, I think they were there. The fact that they're back in the U.S. shows that they must have come back to make sure your uncle's body doesn't get found. They seem to think they can come and go as they please, as long as they appear before the same judge: Sylvia Brown's mother! Col. Ahmir hasn't been able to connect the brothers to the guys who kidnapped you in Dogubeyazit, or any of that smuggling route into Iran. An invitation to visit Israel seems a little coincidental: do you think Israeli operatives smuggled you back into Turkey?"

"I really wouldn't venture a guess."

She let it go at that, ending the call so she could call her mother. They were just leaving from McKenna's when Mallory called. She talked briefly to her mother about the trip to Israel. In view of Oscar Melville's being back in Pike County, she was having doubts about doing the publicity thing at the diamond mine on Monday! But then, Murfreesboro was her home! She had been there before Oscar Melville ever came on the scene! She was going! She called Darrell Hopkins to alert him to the situation. He could double up security, or whatever he needed to do! But safety was still from the Lord!

She breathed a prayer, "Lord, thank you for watching out for Erik, and all of us! Please keep keeping us safe. Help all the bad guys to get saved, or get thrown in jail. Please don't let Martin get loose. And please, don't let David love Sylvia!"

She phoned Kerry, who answered right away. He had heard about the Arkansas episode, already. He was surprised about the Israel trip, and even more surprised that Mallory was insisting he accompany her. She quickly outlined her theory, that they wanted to be sure she wouldn't discount her diamond prices to any buyers. She wanted Israeli attorneys to tutor him in some of the legal aspects of the industry.

He glanced at the clock on his mantle, a miniature reproduction of the one at Izmir. Late enough for Sabbath to be over, but maybe early enough he could call Jacobson, a senior partner with his firm. He told Mallory he'd call her right back, if he found out anything from his superior. If he couldn't, he'd just talk to her at church in the morning.

Mrs. Jacobson answered. Kerry never called their home, but Jacobson's cell was turned off. Apologizing for the family interruption, he quickly explained the reason for his call to the senior partner.

"Israel!" Jacobson's voice filled with reverence and awe. "My dream! Why are you living my dream, Larson?"

"Miss O'Shaughnessy's going, and she wants me to get filled in, too, about legal areas I don't know enough about. Maybe you would be more qualified to accompany her. I mean, there's no doubt you're more qualified–"

Jacobson laughed, a somewhat rare event. He knew Larson's face was flushing with embarrassment. "Yes, undisputedly, I am more qualified. You're still green as the grass. Maybe Jewish lawyers can teach you something. You still have a light week in court, miraculously. Make plans for going. Are you certain Miss O'Shaughnessy doesn't need more of a legal team?"

"She probably does," Kerry agreed. Traveling with Jacobson wouldn't be any fun, but the purpose of the trip wasn't to have fun, anyway, he reminded himself. He phoned her back.

Chapter 3: WELLSPRINGS

Mallory missed seeing her friend Callie at Church, so she gave her a call. Callie's excuses: she was still trying to get over jet lag, and spending time with her mom.

Mallory didn't really think those reasons for missing church were good enough; she thought Carmine would attend church if Callie asked her to, and if Callie were more determined to be faithful. Mallie was kind of bummed out about it, having hoped Callie could go to lunch with her someplace. Of course, Kerry invited her along with him and his group, but she declined his offer. No use in antagonizing Tammi and David needlessly. The lonely feeling descended again. No Daddy and Mom, nor her friends from her Arkansas church. Sighing, she decided she really needed to go home for lunch and do some school work anyway. Her Monday was going to be eaten up doing the *State Park* publicity, and she was leaving for Tel Aviv on Thursday.

Purchasing fast food, she hurried home, slipped into her bathing suit, and ate her lunch floating lazily on an inflatable raft. "Not bad," she admitted to herself laughingly. The Texas weather was scorching already, and it was only Memorial Day weekend. Being wet made being outside tolerable. From the raft, she surveyed the lovely architectural lines of her home and the colorful riot of the landscaping. Vibrant stripes and florals of the lawn furniture yielded a lovely resort look, like she couldn't have dreamed of eight weeks previously. God had certainly filled her life with beauty! And so had her father, Patrick Shay O'Shaughnessy, tutoring her into a spiritual maturity beyond her seventeen years, while developing a small inheritance and diamonds into an amazing estate for her.

She toweled off and set her laptop beside her on a cute awninged glider. She had always loved the derelict-looking porch swing at her old house Finally, it had collapsed, pulling down part of the weakened ceiling. No wonder the ceiling gave way! Her father had been stashing more and more heavy diamonds in it.

She accessed an e-mail from Mr. Haynes, apologizing for his and his wife's conversation the previous week in Istanbul. Finished with that, he asked if she were planning to take a summer vacation and resume her senior year in the fall.

Her heart leapt at the chance for a break! Then, she stopped herself. Yes, she was planning on summer vacations. Her family had never taken any. The previous summer, they had finally enjoyed four days at Galveston; now, Mallory realized, because of the prospect of Diamonds' being washed downstream into the Gulf of Mexico! Before the Israel opportunity had presented itself, she had already agreed to visit Shay and Delia in Boston, where they looked forward to showing her the historical sites of American history: planning to take her, too, to Fenway Park to watch the Red Sox play New York. Her eyes danced with anticipation at that.

But even with the exciting plans, there was no reason to delay her course work. She wouldn't want to do it when fall came either!

Dinky had pushed his way out to join her. She scratched his head, giving him the remnants of her lunch. He tried to give her hand a grateful lick, and she reminded him.

She responded to the e-mail that she would prefer to keep 'plugging away at it'.

⚎ ⚎

Donovan Cline, surprisingly, was upset, too, about Callie's missing church, grumbling to Carmine that she should be a positive force in Callie's life, now that he had granted her more access to their daughter.

It made Carmine furious! "You take her when you go out drinking with your buddies, and you're saying I'm a bad influence?"

Realizing she made a good point, he didn't argue.

"Just encourage her to go, maybe you can go with her," he suggested.

"Me! Go to church? Why don't you go with her?" Carmine was still terrified about her standing with God! If He really did exist! She wasn't sure! But Callie was sure of it; and she was a genius!

"Maybe I will!" Cline fired back. He ordered Callie to hurry and get dressed, then dressed up, himself. Within forty-five minutes, they were on the road toward Murfreesboro, Arkansas.

⊰ ⊱

Mallory finished reading some of her course material. Her brow furrowed with puzzlement as she read an assignment in English lit, *Beowulf.* She wondered to herself if forging ahead into her senior year academics right now was a huge mistake! But she knew it wasn't. She was glad for all the footnotes and explanation of all the archaic language in the selection. The *King James Bible* wasn't hard to read and understand at all, compared to this! She answered the questions at the end of the piece and sent them on their way before going in to change back into her church clothes.

She was dying to wear the new outfits from Delia, but she resisted. She needed something special for the TV interview and for the trip.

Callie still wasn't there for Sunday night, but Mallie did find a fun group to go with afterwards for dinner. She figured she should go straight home. Even with the helicopter, she would have to be up really early to be in Murfreesboro by eight. But, Pastor Ellis' two older kids were home from college for the summer, and she joined their family, and Kerry, and Max, and a few others she was becoming acquainted with. Several of them expressed concern for Callie, and it was a nice time.

⊰ ⊱

Lana Anderson began the prelude as the church was beginning to bustle with activity. Ivan Summers came in, without Janice. She had relocated to Dallas to join Mallie's security. She would be with her in the morning when Mallie came to promote the *Diamond Mine.* Erik and Suzanne waved as they entered. Then the Haynes came in; and Brad Walters, without Janet and the twins. John was greeting people in the back when Herb Carlton showed up, seeming more bashful and out of place than ever. John shook his hand energetically, and Tammi invited him to sit with her and David. That was amazing, in itself! That Carlton showed up! And Tammi's radical change! John was still feeling dazed by that when Cline showed up with Callie!

"I know," Cline spoke gruffly. "The proverbial walls will probably fall down!"

"They probably will," Anderson agreed. "Thanks for coming though! Herb Carlton just went in, and he's sitting with David and Tammi."

"Carlton, huh? Took him for holding out a little longer!"

John Anderson was amazed! "Yeah," he agreed. "I figured both of you that way."

The pastor knew the two men still weren't saved, and he was shocked to see both men in his little church

Callie and her dad joined Carlton and the Anderson kids.

Neither Cline nor Carlton responded to the invitation, but Pastor and Lana both exclaimed to them how welcomed they were, inviting them to join a group going for late dinner at Hal's lodge just a few minutes outside of town. Cline begged off for himself and Callie, but Herb tagged along.

Seated at a large table at the restaurant, John asked the pawnshop owner how his business fared in his twelve day absence.

In a hushed tone, Herb explained his grandson's total change in countenance and demeanor; then he related that his daughter-in-law, Nell, received Jesus after talking to Diana Faulkner at the hospital where Nell worked as a nurse's aide.

Lana was listening to the story in amazement, remembering the night at Saltgrass when Diana had dealt with Nell over the phone. During the entire trip to Turkey, none of them even realized Nell and Carlton were related. Nell and the pastor of the church in Hope had already gotten her four sons and husband to receive the Lord and get into church!

"So, what about you, Herb? John's eyes held the other man's gaze earnestly. "Are you ready to decide?"

"I do not think so," Carlton responded slowly, weighing his words carefully. "I am seeing wondrous things, but there is much I do not understand. You have written a booklet on *Jesus and the Prophecies of the Messiah*. Is that not correct? How is that book available?"

"I'll go grab you one," David offered smoothly. "I can grab one out of the church office and be back before the food gets here."

He was out the door before Herb could protest.

When David returned with the book, the quiet seeker insisted on buying it. After finishing a cup of soup, he excused himself to return to Hope

Mallory was in the air by five a.m., heading eastward toward the *Crater of Diamonds State Park*. She had slept fairly well, for being so excited. When she landed, there was a tight knot of people from the news media and the governor's office. Another bunch represented her support group. She was amazed! Her mom and Erik! Her pastor and his family-no David, though. Herb Carlton was there; longing to see the perfect diamond on permanent display in the museum. Another helicopter touched down, GeoHy, and Diana was there! Stunning as always, she wore a gorgeous blue, evidently also magically produced by Delia. Similar to Mallie's vibrant lime, yet different, and very definitely maternity, it coordinated with stunning jewelry of London Blue Topaz and Diamonds in white Gold.

The anchorwoman approached, evidently miffed that Mallory looked so elegant at such an early hour. She started right off with an arrogant demeanor, giving Mallory the impression that it was going to be a very, very long day!

Evidently some of the park rangers had been vying for position to be in front of the cameras. Mallory had always pretty much liked them all when she ran into any of them in town. A big guy named Hank was the one who would "interview" her about the *Park's* safety. They ran through the script, which almost guaranteed safety to Diamond-hunters. Mallory wasn't sure that was totally honest, trying to point out that even with all of the safety measures put into place for her, she still had experienced some 'close calls'. Regardless of the state of Arkansas' efforts to prevent further incidents like the Martin Thomas murders, people still needed God and their guardian angels. Hank laughed that he could see her point; they basically wanted her to say what they told her to.

Diana interrupted the tenseness of the moment by inviting Mallory to have a donut and some coffee.

Hank took advantage of the break to show Carole Lee Whitfield, the Little Rock news personality, and her camera crew around the *Park's* visitors' center, pointing out the D-flawless, 1.09 carat Strawn-Wagner Diamond; and also showing what the natural, uncut stones from the *Park* looked like.

Diana revised the lines. "*The Crater of Diamonds State Park* has been a fun and safe family destination since its founding. It is always the goal of various law enforcement agencies to safeguard the American public. This is one of the foremost goals of all Arkansas state agencies, including the Ranger service at all Arkansas State Parks. Sadly, there are always predators like Martin Thomas. Because of this, each citizen is also responsible for his own vigilance and safety. It is certainly the intention of the state to provide every safeguard possible, while also the individual responsibility of each citizen to exercise wisdom and discretion."

Carole Lee seemed nearly as resentful toward Diana as she did to Mallory. Diana, the "people person" could usually win people over to herself quite easily. Carole Lee wasn't tumbling.

Actually, the difficulty wasn't a personality conflict so much as a philosophy conflict! With Carole Lee and her humanistic views clashing with Biblical values, there was definitely tension.

Mallory looked good in the monitor, radiant and direct. With the filming of the testimonial for the Park completed, Carole Lee was supposed to conduct an interview with the newly wealthy Arkansas diamond heiress/celebrity.

Seated at a table in the snack bar, Mallory seemed poised and relaxed, her friends seated at nearby tables. Other Diamond tourists crowded around, trying to view the event, and get on camera, if possible.

Carole Lee began firing a barrage of questions, evidently aimed at tripping the teenager up. With amazing poise and humor, Mallory responded, cute and witty, seemingly enjoying the verbal duel.

Finally, pulling her papers with her questions into a stack, and smacking them huffily on the table to even the edges, she met Mallory's gaze with one final attack.

"You're only seventeen and you have all the answers! Don't you?" The Andersons weren't sure if it was the sunny lemon quartz haloing her throat, shimmering softly, or if it was just Mallory's special glow. She flashed a dazzling smile.

"Yes, Ma'am, I do!" Mallie's courteous reply. "All in one incredible, slim Volume!" Pulling a small Bible from her handbag, she held it up victoriously.

The camera cut away!

Chapter 4: WORRIES

David was in Hope on Monday morning, pricing Jeeps. They were expensive, even used. And he barely had any money. His mom and dad and Tammi all had checks from DiaMo when they got back from Turkey. David thought he was a corporate officer, too. But there was no check waiting for him. The other checks were big, too. Now, he wondered if Mallie had cut him out! Or if his hefty check got lost in the mail. He didn't want to ask Mallie, or Faulkner. He didn't want to seem ungrateful for his new pick-up by looking at the Jeeps. Just many areas of the camp property were inaccessible to it. Jeeps featured four wheel drive, but you could still tear them up. Maybe he should check out an ATV. He went to McDonalds for lunch to think about it. While he ate, he accessed headline news on his phone. There was a story about abused and underfed horses! Which gave him an idea! Not to adopt one of the starved animals! But to get a horse!

Of course, every kid usually dreams of having his own horse, and he had been no exception. So had Mallory and Tammi. He called Brad to share the idea with him. Even as he waited for the guy to answer, his mind was charging ahead. Horseback riding might be a fun feature of the camp when it became operational. And, he and Brad could ride over the entire property; some of which wasn't fenced yet, due to the accessibility issue. When Brad didn't answer, he left a message, then he bought a local paper to study the want ads.

Of course, there were horses listed for sale. He just really didn't know that much about buying one. Brad called back, excited. He knew horses, and he knew a good trader. He was amazed about his and Janet's checks from DiaMo! He promised to shop around for several good animals.

21

David headed north toward Murfreesboro and the camp site farther to the north. He began to cry, not about the money; well, maybe kind of that, too! But because of Mallory's seeing that picture Melville had shot of him. It wasn't what it looked like! The tears flowed more freely. He wasn't drinking beer with Sylvia! It wasn't his kid! He wasn't sure Sylvia knew whose it was! He was trying to help her: had even given some of his hard-earned savings for groceries! He was mad she had used his money to buy beer! But you couldn't tell that by looking at the picture! And Mallory saw it on the trip! He could still see the rosy, tell-tale spots on her cheeks, her eyes blazing angrily into his!

He didn't want her money! He wanted her!

Why should he even bother going to the camp? He thought he was on the payroll for overseeing it! And the new ministry headquarters building! Maybe he needed to find a job. His confusion and anger were firing his rebellion! He stopped himself. Why was that always his response to life? So far, it had only ever gotten him into trouble!

Punching the stereo on, he turned up his gospel music and started talking to God, pouring out his heart full of worries. "The trip was tons of fun; now he didn't know when he would see her again! And, if she hated him! He was finished with high school, and he wasn't sure what to do. Even if he did have a job with the camp and other building projects, he was planning to start getting a degree! In what, though? He was learning to fly, but that still wasn't really a life's calling, was it? Right now, he really didn't want to go into the ministry! Was that being rebellious?"

He pulled in a long, shuddering breath. He needed to talk to his dad.

When he reached Murfreesboro, he drove to the church! His dad's car wasn't there. His mom's car and Tammi's Mustang were at the parsonage, but when he went in, nobody was home. He vaguely wondered where everybody was. He splashed water on his face and chugged a tumbler full of milk, before charging back out toward his truck. He waved at the mailman as he saw him approaching, and waited for him.

"Hey, David," the postman greeted him. "Guess your girlfriend held onto your check for a couple of days. Here ya go."

He was leaning out the window to hand the envelope to the pastor's son.

David walked over to receive the piece of mail. Dumb little town! Everyone knew everybody's business!

Thanks, Bill," he said, trying to maintain an even, friendly tone.

"My name isn't, 'Bill'," the letter carrier corrected, puzzled.

"I know," David laughed. "We've always called you that because you've always brought us so many bills!"

Going back inside, he turned on the television. There probably wouldn't be much on but soap operas. He slit open the envelope! Strictly nice! Signed at the bottom, Mallory E. O'Shaughnessy! He sat down, dazed, studying the scrawl. Gone the big loopy, high-school-girl-style penmanship. Was that just this past fall? The colored gel pens, with hearts dotting the *i*'s?

Losing her dad had grown her up. He was suddenly overwhelmed with gratitude at still having both of his parents in good health. This check alone would be enough to pay for four years of college! Well, not some ivy league school, but that had never been big to him, anyway. For now, he planned to 'get a horse' and some groceries and put the rest in savings where it would gain some interest.

An ad came on the TV, trying to lure viewers to tune in to the Little Rock station for the five and six o'clock news broadcasts. Mallory's picture flashed on, briefly, and was gone. Wow! When he thought she couldn't possibly look more gorgeous, she surpassed herself! He was glad for a glimpse of her, but he didn't want her to be on TV! He wanted how it was! When every guy in the world wasn't seeing her and writing crazy letters like he had seen at her house on Saturday. He idly wondered if Faulkner knew she was getting weird fan mail. He needed to stop being so critical of Mallory's guardian. After all, he, himself, had failed her with the kidnappers in Turkey.

His cell rang, and it was Brad, calling to say he had located a couple of great-looking geldings. They were about thirty minutes away, so David agreed to come check them out.

What an answer to prayer. Thirty minutes before, he was worried how embarrassed he would be to tell Brad he didn't really have any money for a horse. Now he did. He could check out the deal and be back in plenty of time to watch both newscasts.

He was pretty sure his mom and dad had been at the *State Park* all morning, watching Mallory and the film crew. It seemed that they could let him in on a little more information about her. At least the Lord had led him to his house, and to turn on the TV to catch the commercial. He wondered if his parents would have told him about her appearances on the evening news.

❧ ❧

The horses were beautiful! David realized his emotions had been all over the charts all day! Now he hated to admit it, but he had fallen head-over-heels in love! With a horse! He rode it around the pasture a couple of times, and didn't want to get off! Only Mallory and the news story could have motivated him to dismount. The fact that Brad was nearly as emotional about the animals helped, too. He had already rented a double trailer to move the animals to a stable leased nearby. He planned to settle the horses in, then get to the feed store. They would need tack, too.

David listened to Brad, dazed. He tried to explain that he needed to get to the bank and deposit his check; then he was pretty sure it might take a few days to fund. Brad had already written the checks for the horses, trailer, and stable, telling David he could pay him back when his money funded.

David returned to his mom and dad's with his heart lighter. It seemed like whenever the separation from Mallory grew greater than he could bear, the Lord did something else special for him, to focus his mind elsewhere. Owning his own horse was a dream come true! A dream he had nearly forgotten about! But the Lord hadn't!

By the time he returned to the parsonage, his family was home, and Diana was with them. Stunning in a rich blue with sparkling jewelry the same color, she looked pretty out of place in the humble little house. Since she always looked so perfect, David was always surprised how nice she was.

"Did my mom and dad fill you in about Herb Carlton and the nurse's aide, Nell, that got saved?"

Her countenance registered surprise. "No, she responded. "How are they connected?"

John was chagrined that in the busy events of the day, he hadn't thought about telling Diana the new developments from her witnessing. He nodded to David to finish his story.

Tears sparkled in her eyes. All the news was so wonderful it was hard to grasp! After Nell's decision, she had managed to pull her husband and all four of her boys into the Kingdom with her! And, into the baptistery. And Herb was her father-in-law, who had despaired for his son's marriage and his four grandsons. The Lord had made such a difference in Samuel, the oldest, that Carlton had driven to Faith for church, and was reading, seeking for answers for his own life.

Suddenly, David wondered if Diana was there to make sure he couldn't see Mallory on TV; instead, she found herself a cup of coffee. She plunked onto the sofa, which was even more worn out than it looked. Managing not to spill the beverage, she laughed, pretty sure she was stuck there until Daniel arrived. He pulled in a few minutes later, bringing pizza from Hope. Not sure Mallory would make the Tulsa news, they had all traveled to Arkansas.

The pizza was good, and the houseful of people was a fun group, but the news story was disappointing. After filming until mid-afternoon, the crew got enough tape of Mallory to edit and splice until she was saying exactly what they wanted. The camera focused on the Strawn-Wagner, the *Park's* attractive entrance, a few diamond-seekers sifting dirt. Mostly, it was Carole Lee, filling the lens, filling the air time with chatter.

"Maybe they'll show more at six," Lana commented. Lana and Diana took turns, filling David and Daniel in on all that really happened, and on what Mallory really said. It made David mad when he heard about how rude the anchorwoman really was, and how poised and funny Mallory had been in dealing with her and her questions. Lana laughed, trying to describe the expression on Carole Lee's face, when Mallory told her she had all the answers to life's problems in "one incredible slim Volume".

Daniel Faulkner laughed. It sounded like Mallory! And she was right! Still, he was finding that life was complex and confusing, at times. Even if you did know your Bible! Like when you have a kid that's eleven, and she thinks she's in love!

At six o'clock, Mallory's story didn't show at all, with no explanation, although it had been hyped in commercials all day.

David was disappointed; well, they all were. He didn't like the anchorwoman anyway, her opinions and sarcasm. A rank liberal! She had wasted Mallory's time, and been rude, besides.

"Yes, Mallory's time was wasted," Diana commiserated with him. "From our view; of what we thought was supposed to be accomplished. But by Mallory's surrender to the Lord, she accomplished His purpose! If God desires for her words to reach every ear in America, He can accomplish that. Maybe His purposes were accomplished, though, by the people hearing her, who were there."

David nodded agreement. But he was already deciding to help God out. If he could get his hands on some of the footage, he could get it into cyberspace. He was amazed at himself. Earlier, he was jealous about her making local television; now he planned to send the interview around the world. Well, only if the Lord didn't stop him.

When the party broke up, everyone headed separate ways. The Andersons assumed David was heading back to the camp property. He cut up toward Malvern and hit 130 east toward Little Rock. Time to go dumpster diving! He had no plans for trying to gain entrance to the station. His bet was that the catty woman had thrown out the tape, rather than archiving it! He hoped so! He prayed so!

◁ ▷

From the filming appointment, Mallory and her mom drove around Murfreesboro, first past the original DiaMo mine location. Mallory was amazed! Great idea. The company that purchased the valuable property had leveled it off, leaving the trees, brought in topsoil, and planted a fast-growing grass. It would cut down on erosion and make it harder for casual observers to see Diamonds lying on the ground. Good way to try to hold the stones in place while the company operated within the court system. Mallory was certain they must be planning on mining the acreage as soon as they could finagle a way around the environmentalists.

Next, they went to the land recently purchased byDiaMo, next to the church. No cars there, then, she had seen David's truck go by. She was busy, though. Her mom sat in the car, doing some work and making some business calls. Mallory was familiar with the vacant property, having played there often throughout her childhood.

She had insisted to Kerry Larson, Daniel Faulkner, and Pastor Anderson that it would be a poor location for the new ministry headquarters. Daniel had told her that the creek just ran across the back, but really, the whole acreage was low-lying. Often times, the creek would lap right up to the back corner of the church building next door. The same with the recently acquired DiaMo land. But there were diamonds here!

She was thinking about the verse in Job 28, about dried-up river and creek beds. She knew the manner in which flood-waters deposited Diamonds as they bounced them downstream. It seemed like the stones, with high specific gravity, should be trapped in front of boulders. Actually, though, large stones and boulders created eddies, which then carried the gems around, dropping them into pockets behind the barriers.

Using a trowel, she scraped at top soil, trash, and dry leaves, digging down into some of the areas where the physics of water and gravity could possibly have deposited a treasure! The weather was warm, and she was wearing her gorgeous new outfit from Delia, including the pastel leather heels. Hardly mining gear! When she could get on her knees, it was easier. Still, not one to give up, she continued the search. Then, she found one! Yes! No? Yes? It was nice sized, but it was different looking! A Pink?

Probably the majority of Pike County diamonds were colored, browns mostly. Smart marketing had given those value in the jewelry industry, when once they would have been relegated to "industrial". The yellow ones were valuable, with the value increasing accordingly with the depth of the color. But if this were a pink~ She slid it into a plastic gem jar. It was pretty; something to take with her to Israel!

Chapter 5:   WAILING WALL

Mallory and her entourage: Kerry Larson, William Jacobson, Herb Carlton, and Linda Campbell; with Darrell Hopkins and Janice Collins heading security, arrived at Ben Gurion International Airport early Saturday morning where they were met by government representatives for transport to Jerusalem. With its being the Sabbath, the ancient city was quiet. After checking into the King David Hotel, they were met by a tour operator who walked them along the *Via de La Rosa*, the Seven Stations of the Cross, ending at the *Church of the Holy Sepulcher*. Jacobson had opted out of the Christian tour. Kerry explained to Mallory that non-Catholics recognized *Gordon's Calvary*, a different site, as the place of the crucifixion, burial, and resurrection. Still, beginning at the palace of Caiaphas, the high priest; then the ancient Antonio Fortress where the Roman soldiers garrisoned, they realized they had to be on the spot, or very near, where Jesus had actually endured the mock trials and scornful treatment of the mobs. They viewed gambling games carved into the stone floors of the ancient military complex. They were awed at being there! Even Herb and Linda succumbed to the wonder.

In the Arab quarter of the city, they were exposed to the local, favorite, fast-food; Falafels! Actually, pretty good! When they returned to the hotel, Mallory sought out Mr. Jacobson. She had learned that Sabbath ended at six p.m., and then they were all to be dinner guests at eight-thirty with some notable government and Diamond industry people.

With a humble spirit, Mallory invited the Jewish attorney to be her teacher, explaining she was only seventeen, with pretty much of a rural USA background. Some of the Jewish customs, such as Sabbath elevators, already had her perplexed. She thought her understanding of the Bible would be enough. Now, she realized that being here would most definitely make much of her Bible clearer to her. But she realized that diplomats received coaching, so surely she needed it even more. During her recent tour of Turkey, she hadn't been as aware of 'Culture Shock' as she already had been in Israel. Maybe, because there had been so many Americans traveling together, and not interacting that much with the Turkish people.

William Jacobson was happy she asked. He always had to remind himself she was only seventeen! She acted older and wiser. He gathered the rest of the group together, trying to give an overview of the culture and beliefs. One of the things he emphasized was the fact that their dinner was going to be in a *Meat Restaurant*. Kosher dietary laws required not having *meat* and *dairy products* at the same meal, or in the same restaurant. He carefully explained to Mallory that even though she took her coffee white, she shouldn't request cream or creamer. Something Kosher would be offered. No cheeseburgers, no butter for bread. If you wanted milk products with your meal, you ate in *Fish Restaurants*. At breakfast, where milks, cheeses, and yogurts were staples, there would be no meat. Of course, there wasn't any ham, bacon, or other pork products at any of the Kosher establishments.

The group listened in amazement, glad Mallie had asked.

Back in her room, she changed into the most beautiful garment she had ever seen compliments of Diana! A long, slender, watered-silk gown, in a mystical, sea-green mist, it fitted in gracefully at her slender waist, flaring out to a broad, self-ruffle at the hem. The bodice featured short, puffed sleeves, and a straight, square neckline. Sparkling Diamonds in white, blue, and green circled her throat and shimmered in dangles from her ears. No bracelet, but her Diamond ring from her daddy circled the ring finger on her right hand.

With a gentle brush of glittery eye shadow repeating the color of her eyes and gown, a hint of bronzer on her cheeks, her lips stained with the cinnamon lipstick, softened with gloss, she looked stunning. Luxurious coppery hair cooperated with her efforts to clip it upwards, and she pulled a few wisps loose. Sliding her feet into silver, strapped, high-heeled sandals, she slid her room key, her iPhone, and a few other essentials into her matching watered-silk evening bag and headed for the lobby to meet the limousine.

Herb Carlton was amazed at her elegant taste, stating his opinion emphatically.

Mallory laughed. "Wish I could take credit for it, but believe me, being ready for a 'State Dinner' at a moment's notice isn't anything my upbringing prepared me for. The Lord had it all mapped out in advance for my daddy to meet and Daniel and Diana, and involve them in my life. I never even thought to ask about the itinerary, to think about what to bring for each occasion. I've never worn a formal before because I never went to school dances."

She cut herself off, blushing as Carlton continued to ogle her fixedly through his glasses. She knew he was captivated by the Diamond necklace, but still-

It was an incredible piece: the pale greens and blues mingling into curling waves, tipped with foam of sparkling, colorless stones, set in white Gold, with drips of ocean spray and Diamond droplets here and there. Mallory didn't know how Diana got it. She kept saying she hadn't found anyone to move the jewelry designs off her drawing board. Mallory had offered Mr. Carlton the job, but she wasn't sure he had given her a straightforward, 'Yes', yet.

Jacobson, Linda, and Kerry joined them, and they moved toward the waiting limo. A few minutes, and they were at their destination. In the elegantly appointed hall, Mallory took in every detail with interest. Lovely table linens: Delia would be impressed. Sparkling china and crystal! Lots of pieces of silverware! She was totally fascinated by the centerpieces, with each table featuring unique carvings, skillfully cut from various melons, fruits, squash, and vegetables, combined with cut flowers.

A woman who was imposing despite her short stature and chubbiness introduced herself to the Americans. Lilly Cowan, she had a high position within the Diamond Council. Poised, tough, but good-humored, she took charge of the group as if they seemed in desperate need of oversight by her. Walking with a definite limp, she escorted them to their places at a head table, ordering them all to sit down, so she could. She plopped down, immediately indicating to the table steward, her desire for wine. Mallory and Kerry declined it as graciously as possible. Carlton, Linda, and Jacobson nodded, yes.

"Oh, but you should try-" Mrs. Cowan's dark eyes sparkled mischievously. "Israel has the finest grapes, the finest wines!"

"That's what we've heard," Mallie agreed. "Everyone who has ever come here has come back saying you have the best strawberries, tomatoes, and oranges, too. My mom grows tomatoes! I love them, but the grocery store ones the rest of the year are hard and flavorless. My mom cans delicious tomato juice!"

"I would like your mother," Lilly agreed. "I like you!" As if to prove her words, she gave Mallory a noisy smack on the cheek.

Insisting on the wine seemed to be forgotten.

Members of the Israeli Knesset presented themselves, teasing and joking with Lilly, shaking hands with her guests. Mallory kept rising courteously, trying to remember names and make small talk like Diana did so well.

Lilly watched observantly. The girl's Diamond necklace was really superb and imaginative; the fancy, colored stones were a little on the expensive side. The more intense the color of fancy Diamonds, the more valuable they were. But, these soft, muted tones blended together to truly resemble ocean waves and match the color of the dress and the girl's expressive eyes. The ring she wore was incredible, even to the woman who dealt in exquisite stones day after day! Quite the amazing young lady!

The meal began with the presentation of appetizers. Mallory watched Mr. Jacobson carefully, since he was both American and Jewish. Maybe he could steer her clear of goat brains, or anything else weird. Her falafel from earlier had worn off, but she was unsure what the presentations were. Then soup, salad(not her definition of salad), entrée, dessert. The dessert was the best part, brought with coffee, and she remembered not to ask for milk. No alternatives were offered, so she sipped it black. With the seven-layer chocolate cake buried under chocolate-dipped strawberries, the coffee tasted good. The meal was enjoyable, with the dessert's being the high point.

Mallory had never been anyplace where wine and liquor flowed like they did here. She and Kerry continued to refuse any of it. Herb had sampled his initial glass of wine; Linda had a second glass. Jacobson continued to accept wine, refusing the harder liquor. And Lilly became more and more talkative as the meal progressed.

With the meal finished, the crowd dispersed. Many people, both men and women, came by, telling Mallory they would see her the next day, or the next." Welcome to Israel! What did she think?"

Her responses were becoming automated. For one thing, she had been awake for a very long time. For another thing, she had a headache! Finally, her right wrist had been bothering her, and all of the shaking hands was causing it to hurt worse.

Everyone who hadn't left was queing (getting in line) to load onto coaches. Lilly unceremoniously yanked Mallory along with her, her group trying to keep up, as they cut through the crowd. Pulling Mallie to the front, she indicated for her to hop onto the lead coach, first. Evidently, Mallory was the guest of honor, but you still had to elbow for your place. When she hesitated, waiting for a hand from Kerry, Lilly gave her an unceremonious boost. Tripping on her dress, she finally managed to fall into a seat, where Lilly plopped down next to her.

"Excuse me, Mrs. Cowan, do you mind if I talk to my client for a minute?" Kerry interrupted. He thought she minded, but at least she moved, and he took her place beside Mallory.

"You okay?" he asked, concerned.

"Just jet lag," his client responded. She guessed that was part of it. She hadn't been home from Turkey for a week, before hopping on another jet for this trip. And, she hadn't recovered from the last trip! She had hurt her wrist falling down the hillside at Pamukkale when she thought she saw Oscar Melville! Then, she was pretty sure her head had really thumped around in the trunk of her kidnappers' car before she regained consciousness, after being chloroformed. After regaining consciousness, she had tried to brace herself from some of the bumps. She was bruised everywhere, and the bruises were still getting darker. She felt stiff and old for her seventeen years!

"Where are we going? Do you know?" she asked him.

"To the Diamond headquarters, but I'm not sure how late they plan to keep us."

"Probably all night," Mallory responded gloomily. "They rested all day."

Kerry laughed. "A day of rest doesn't sound like a bad idea. I always think I should try it sometime."

"No kidding," Mallie agreed. "If you like it, suggest it to Mr. Haynes. Have you ever read *Beowulf*?"

"Not since the beginning of my senior year in high school. We keep telling Haynes to go easy on you."

"You do? Wow! Wonder how rough he'd be if you weren't telling him that."

Before the coach brakes finished their hissing halt, Lilly had Mallory by the hand again, dragging her off the coach as unceremoniously as she had pushed her on! She was certainly a dynamo! Mallie couldn't help liking her.

"What did your lawyer want?" she demanded.

Mallie was stunned by the blunt question. Not knowing how best to answer, she met Lilly's gaze.

"Is he your boyfriend? Why did you bring lawyers with you?"

"He isn't my boyfriend. My father retained him to represent my corporation. He's a good corporate attorney, but none of us really know the Diamond business. In Turkey, the jewelry merchants wanted us to agree to undercut the pricing structure. I wanted him to maybe get with some attorneys here about corporations and Diamonds. Does that make sense? Well, Kerry was just on the twelve day trip to Turkey, and he was afraid the senior partners wouldn't want him to come overseas again so soon. When he called Mr. Jacobson, it was his dream to visit Israel, so we brought him, too."

"And you are a strong Christian?" Lilly had nodded as Mallory spoke.

"Yes, Ma'am. I got saved when I was seven, and I've been a member of a really good Bible-teaching church ever since. We loved actually seeing sites in Jerusalem earlier today."

Lilly Cowan was relieved. The heiress' bringing her attorneys with her was a good move on her part, but it had caused some consternation amongst the Israeli hosts.

꼭 ⊱

Suzanne and Erik gazed with wonder at Mallory's e-mail! She seemed to be taking Israel by storm! Looking positively stunning, smiling from pictures with Lilly, the mayor of Jerusalem, the mayor of Tel Aviv, and members of the Knesset, she sparkled! From the Diamonds, the glitter makeup, but most of all, from an inner radiance.

Suzanne was relieved that her daughter seemed to be emerging from the clouds of grief that had overshadowed her since January. Still not six months, though; she was aware that Mallory's grief was still far from healed.

She figured Mallie had already sent the e-mail to the Faulkners, but she forwarded it to them, just in case. She was sure Mallie's gorgeous clothing and jewelry were from Diana. Suzanne had more respect for Patrick now, than she ever had. Unclear exactly how he knew Daniel and Diana, she had to give him grudging credit for his farsightedness about Mallory, and about a lot of things.

"You sending it to the Andersons and the Sanders?" Erik questioned.

She wasn't going to, even though she was really proud of her. Erik didn't have to coax her very hard

⚬ ⚬

David was catching up on his checking account and e-mails in his dad's study when the e-mail came through. Wow! No one told him she was going to Israel, and here was an e-mail from the King David Hotel business center. She had already been to the Roman soldier place, and a *Church of the Holy Sepulcher*. It was late Saturday night there, when she sent the update. She and Kerry were planning to go to church and take communion at the *Garden Tomb*. After that, they were going to the *Wailing Wall*. He was jealous! She and Kerry?! He thought about calling Tammi, so she could be miserable, too; but she would see the e-mail soon enough. He wondered if any of his family would have told him Mallie was out of the country again. He thanked the Lord for letting him see the correspondence, then he e-mailed the pictures so he could get color prints made-in Hope! In case he wasn't supposed to have the pictures, he didn't want the photo lab in town blabbing it all over.

He accessed another on-line site! Of Mallory at the *State Park*! He had done a good job of finding the discarded film and sending out her truthful message. He played the video again, of her pulling out her Bible, triumphantly proclaiming the truth that it held answers to any problem life could throw at you. He enjoyed the startled expression on the anchorwoman's face as she frantically motioned for the cameraman to cut away.

⚬ ⚬

Diana viewed the e-mail forwarded from Suzanne with satisfaction. Her designs looked fabulous on Mallory! Despite her years as a Christian, the Lord still surprised and delighted her by His marvelous ways! Mallory's friendship was already so special!

The sites in the Holy Land looked and sounded incredible! She and Daniel had discussed the possibility of the Christian pilgrimage. Not that it was necessary to increase your standing with the Lord, but something enjoyable to help visualize and understand more of the Bible! A brief shadow crossed her face as she thought about Daniel, and how fearful

34

it made her for him to travel beyond US borders. She thanked the Lord again, that the recent travel to Europe and Asia hadn't affected him.

She guessed her thinking about him had caused him to materialize, because he had come in looking for her.

"Thought you were coming right out to swim with us," he began. "Good thing I came to set you free from this vicious computer! I'll fight it for you!" Carrying a large fork from the grill, he feinted toward it threateningly.

She laughed. "Watch out, Don Quixote! Go tilt at windmills before you ruin expensive electronic equipment! I'm checking out how much Mallory is helping my designs."

He viewed the monitor. "Looks to me like it's the other way around; your designs are helping her."

"Oh, you're so nice," she squealed in delight. "Race you out to the pool!"

⊰ ⊱

Mallory and Herb Carlton jolted wide awake with interest as they toured the Diamond facility. There was a multi-media presentation to begin with, explaining where Diamonds originated. A quick course in "evolutionary Geology." Mallie wasn't sure how she would ever get truth straightened out from evolutionary myth. Yes, they were Carbon! Yes, they were formed by heat and pressure, then spewed upwards in volcanic upheavals! (Maybe) No, they weren't millions and millions of years old!

The video also showed a brief overview of the sorting and selling structure.

At the close of the film, they toured the facility, actually watching Diamond experts studying stones, cleaving, cutting, polishing!

Herb had seen it before, of course. He was interested in finding out more from Diana and Mallory what exactly they had in mind for his position in their company. He had hesitated to tell the two ladies what the cash outlay would be for what they were talking about, that would enable him to make the jewels they were visualizing. He figured once they saw the list of what it would take just to get underway, they'd drop him and the entire idea. Too bad; because the entire concept took his breath away! That he might finally realize his lifelong dream!

At the end of the tour, they exited through the retail jewelry store, where Lilly encouraged Mallory to "Take her time and really shop around." One of the key slogans seemed to be, to *make Israel green!*

One of the head-jewelers joined them in the store, complimenting Mallory's jewelry, and asking her if the stones were from Arkansas. She didn't think so, because she had never heard of anybody's finding blue or green there.

Opening her small evening bag, she withdrew the gem jar with the Diamond unearthed the previous Monday.

Pulling the jar apart, the Israeli expert held the stone, turning it over, then studying it with a loupe.

"It looks definitely pink! Color can be tricky to assess in uncut material. This was found by your father?"

"No, Sir, I found it, just this week. We sold the first property, the one where our house was, and where I grew up. This is from acreage DiaMo has purchased since then."

Even as she spoke, she was slightly troubled that this man, all the way in Israel, seemed aware of the small DiaMo Corporation deals! Of their practically being forced to sell the valuable claim for the sake of their endangered employees. Her gaze had met Darrell Hopkins', and she could tell the same thing had occurred to him. Did the Diamond cartel use gangsters like Oscar and Otto to help them achieve their goals?

The thought flitted through her mind of... "Spiritual wickedness in high places," and she suddenly wondered who she was really dealing with! Immediately, she was comforted by the realization that the Lord knew, and no one could oppose Him, and win!

Her eyes traveled around the brightly lighted store, sparkling with tempting jewelry pieces! Maybe everything wasn't as beautiful as it all appeared to be on the surface!

The jeweler returned the stone to its jar, handing it back to Mallory reluctantly, his gaze meeting Lilly's.

Mallory shivered with a sudden chill. Surely, they wouldn't kill her for it, would they? Everyone knew she was here, officially. That was at least some comfort! Erik Bransom had been upset at Suzanne's becoming a target for thieves, just the previous month! Mallie's thoughts returned to Martin Thomas. He was just one of a long line of people who had killed for Diamonds. Gazing at the pink Diamond for a long moment, she dropped it back into her bag. It hardly seemed worth that much!

Back in the limousine, Kerry held his hand out silently to Mallory for the stone. She slipped it to him obediently, trying to keep the driver unaware of the switch. In the lobby, they parted company, exhausted.

In his room, Kerry loosened the cover on the vent and stashed the diamond. Hardly brilliant! He couldn't think of anything better. Banks were closed, and the safe at the front desk really seemed like a big announcement! He wished Mallory hadn't brought it; probably so did she! They all still had a lot to learn! Their personal security seemed adequate for the five of them, but add a high-value Diamond, and the entire dynamic changed!

⊰ ⊱

David called Daniel Faulkner about the diamonds that he had discovered in the ceiling of Mallie's old house. Alexandra answered since everyone was in the pool, and she had scrambled out the fastest to grab it. Sounded like they were having fun! David could hardly wait until his mom and dad's new house was finished, with a pool and all kinds of luxurious amenities.

Daniel's voice was pleasant as he picked up. "Hi, David, what's going on? Have you seen the pictures of Mallory in Israel?"

"Yes, Sir," David answered courteously. "I was in my dad's office checking my e-mails and bank statement when it came in. She looks great! How long is she supposed to be there?"

Faulkner laughed. "That I'm not sure about. They're returning soon, I hope. Evidently, Mallory dug up a nice pink diamond on Monday afternoon and took it with her so she could show the Israelis a sample. Kerry said they've been a little bit nervous since. The Israelis seem to know everything about DiaMo. Now, Kerry wonders more than ever who was behind the kidnapping of the employees.

"I'm sure they do know all about DiaMo," David asserted. "It's their business to know! You know they have operatives all over the world. Politically, of course, but you can be sure they keep tabs on everything that could affect their nation economically, too! When Diamonds are involved, there are always lots of rumors and stories flying around."

Daniel was pretty surprised by David's grasp of the situation. "I heard you and Brad got horses," he changed the subject. "If you get a chance, maybe you should look into finding a few more. It was a great idea! Maybe you could get a couple of little mares and a pony. We're always looking for places to ride. Is there room at that stable to board more, until we get stables built at the camp? The corporation is reimbursing your and Brad's money. You really do need them to help you oversee all the land, and you're taxed on less when things aren't in your name."

"Don't reimburse me. I want *El Capitan* in my name. He's mine!" David hadn't intended to sound so passionate, but he really didn't care.

⊰ ⊱

At breakfast in the hotel on Sunday morning, Kerry was relieved that no one had attempted to break in to any of their rooms. He and Mallory both carried Bibles. She was dressed in a vibrant, sunny orange, with matching gemstone jewelry shooting sparkles. Herb, Linda, and Mr. Jacobson were planning to take the entire tour, including *Gordon's Calvary*. The limousine took them through the streets of Jerusalem, then wound outside the walls, up the *Mount of Olives,* driving past the *Garden of Gethsemane,* then pausing for a photo shoot, amongst a jumble of tourists and their coaches. They were looking across the *Kidron Valley* at the sealed up *Eastern Gates.* Arabs, with automatic weapons paced back and forth on the wall, aware of the prophecy about the Messiah's promised return through these gates!

"When Messiah returns, those guards and their weapons won't stop him," Kerry chortled triumphantly.

Tears streamed down Mallie's face. "No kidding!" she agreed. The morning was cloudlessly beautiful with a playful breeze. She didn't want to get back into the car to leave. She was sorry they didn't have time to actually visit the *Garden of Gethsemane.* Still, to be in Israel, able to see this much, was more than she had ever actually expected to do! Oh, she had dreamed! Actually, she had dreamed of touring Europe: England, France, Switzerland, Italy! God's choices were better, and maybe she would still someday see the other places. *Gordon's Calvary!* Their driver let them out, and they walked a short distance, mingling with pilgrims from many lands. Flowers danced, vibrant and colorful, and Mallory saw the tomb entrance as she had seen in photos. Carved into the face of a cliff; there was no "stone" there to roll back and forth, but a small door closed off the actual tomb. Six days a week, pilgrims could actually enter the *empty tomb.* On Sundays, it was closed. Folding metal chairs were set up in the garden facing it, and the "congregation" were all taking places. They sang several familiar hymns themed to the grave and resurrection. Tears flowed down Mallie's face again, as she detected foreign languages mingled with the English lyrics she was singing. Christians from around the world, who loved Jesus! There was a sermon about the resurrection! "He is not here. For he is risen, as He said. Come, see the place where the LORD lay.." The service closed with Communion! Jacobson, Herb, and Linda declined.

Following the service, they joined their driver for one last site. *The Wailing Wall.* They had all seen it on the news before. Mallory had always been confused, because Jesus had prophesied that there "wouldn't be one stone left on top of another" of the Temple of His day. It had seemed to Mallory that with a western wall of the Temple still standing, the prediction hadn't been totally fulfilled. Now the guide was explaining, not only about the western wall, but also quite a bit about King Herod. Always trying to firm up his grasp on power, he had ordered baby boys killed at the time of Jesus' birth. Also, he had rebuilt and expanded the Temple in an effort to curry the favor of his Jewish subjects. Always building massive projects in an attempt to get himself a name, he had rebuilt the Temple far larger than the original one. In order to make his large project possible, earth work had been necessary. He had enlarged the peak of Mt. Zion by filling in earth. The western wall, or *Wailing Wall,* was constructed as a retaining wall to hold the fill dirt in place. It had never been part of the Temple.

When they entered the enclosure, the ladies were directed to the "women's side", and the men, who were required to cover their heads in respect, went to the side designated for them. Mallie observed everyone around her curiously. Many people wrote out their prayers, pushing the rolled up missives into cracks between the massive stones. Some wept, some rocked, some stretched heavenward, some bowed. Some sat silently, Bibles, Torahs, or prayer books open on their laps. She was thrilled to be here, but even more thrilled that God had always heard and answered her prayers when she called to him from her little house in Arkansas! And from her old tractor there! That any time she paused to draw near to Him, He drew near in response. She didn't write a prayer to push into a cranny! She didn't need to!

Chapter 6:   WAYSIDE

On return from Tel Aviv, the group deplaned in New York City where they met Daniel Faulkner at the bank to retrieve the valuable Diamonds that had been stashed in a safety deposit box en route to Turkey.

Daniel produced his key and ID, and the entire group went in with him to remove the gems. Herb removed his scale from his battered case to weigh the stones and was perplexed by the difference of the weight compared to that deposited three weeks earlier.

The discrepancy troubled Larson and Faulkner, who had taken oversight for the dazzling wealth. They requested to see the branch manager, who was annoyed at the suggestion one of his employees could have broken protocol. Their system was foolproof! It had to be, or no one would risk depositing their valuable items and documents. He went over the system for their benefit.

Without leaving the secure area, Kerry phoned Bransom for his opinion. Kerry was an attorney, and William Jacobson, a senior partner in the firm, but they weren't sure what to do legally to determine if a theft had been committed.

In view of the bank's secure system, Herb thought the only place for the Diamonds to have been removed from the sock, would have been during the cab ride. Hopkins, Larson, and Faulkner all took offense at that suggestion. They were nervous about carrying a fortune in Diamonds around New York City! They certainly hadn't taken them from Kerry's briefcase, removing some for themselves, in view of a New York cabbie!

Carlton simply insisted the stones had been weighed and the weight verified before the three men had left the jet with them. Now, the weight was nearly twenty-five carats less. Daniel was the sole renter, holding the only key. He could have gained access at any time during the previous three weeks.

"Except, that I was with everyone in Turkey for twelve of the days. My presence in Tulsa since we got back can pretty well be verified. Maybe you can subpoena the bank for security footage of who might have opened the box."

"Well, a lot of people knew about the diamonds," Bransom reminded them. "Those stones were the ransom Mallory's kidnappers were demanding for her release. I don't see how they could have gotten any of them out of the deposit box. I mean, if they could, why wouldn't they have taken them all? You sure your scale hasn't gotten banged around and knocked out of kilter?" he directed toward the jeweler.

"Has a special case; made to bring along. I don't think it's the scale. I think the largest stones are missing," Herb responded, definitely, and sadly.

Mallory was tired. She agreed with Carlton that some stones were missing. She was as certain the three men in question hadn't taken them as she was that she hadn't. She asked Bransom if the FBI could get the bank's security video, then decided to get back on track with the original plan.

Herb noted down the new weight of the diamonds, verified it with the members of the group, then with a bonded and insured courier. The Diamonds would arrive in Dallas the next day. They hurried to board the GeoHy Gulfstream to return to Dallas, themselves.

Mallory helped herself to a big slice of New York style pizza and a diet Coke, glad to be back in the good old US, eating unhealthily! Mixing meat and dairy!

She tried to show her pictures to Daniel Faulkner; she could tell that the missing Diamonds had him concerned. Kerry was worried, too; his ability to practice law would be at stake if he were found guilty of criminal charges. Since Mallory knew it wasn't any of her associates, her mind was working on who else could have robbed them.

Her thoughts kept coming back full circle to the Maloviches, and Sylvia Brown's recent connection to them. And Sylvia's mother, Antoine Martine, who had recently become a Federal Judge. Mallory thought the name sounded made up. But how could you get to be a Federal judge without using your real identity? She was puzzled.

❧ ❧

Tammi's sixteenth birthday was at the end of May, but her party had been delayed a couple of weeks by the trip to Turkey. Ordinarily, she wouldn't have been so gracious, but something nearly miraculous was transpiring in her life. David bought her a gentle little mare, deep brown, with a white star on her face, presenting it to her after she got her drivers' license and finally took possession of her new, yellow Mustang. She loved the horse, stroking her softly and naming her, *Star*. She was excited at the prospect of driving to the camp in her own car, to go horse-back riding with her big brother.

Mallory wasn't at the party, but she had sent her gift with Erik and Suzanne. A *Precious Moments* about being friends. Tammi was moved to tears by it, with no complaints that Mallory didn't get her something big and expensive.

She rode with David back to the stable, and they had a good talk. Tammi was worried about the missing Diamonds, with even the hint that Kerry might be accused. She hadn't fallen apart about Kerry's accompanying Mallory on the Holy Land trip. The only thing she really said about it was that she hoped to visit there some day. The pictures made it seem pretty special.

At the stable, David taught her how to saddle *Star*, insisting that she go through the process several times. She wanted to learn, and she was excited. She said almost exactly the same thing David had realized, "That she had nearly forgotten her dream of owning her own horse! But the Lord hadn't."

He brushed tears from his eyes quickly, hoping she wouldn't notice. She noticed, and her eyes teared up A really cool thing, too, was her budding friendship with her big brother!

⚜ ⚜

Mallory was glad to be home! Every time she left and came back, it seemed more like "home" to her. Dinky went crazy when she came in, and she went outside with him and played for over an hour. She was playing ball with him, but at the same time, she was practicing throwing with a deadly accuracy, mostly left-handed. Since her right wrist still bothered her, she used the opportunity for improving her aim with her left hand.

She was still pretty pleased with herself for "having nailed a rabbit" with a rock, as it had zig-zagged away from her as fast as it could go. Her mind returned to her reluctant rescuers. They had seemed to think her rabbit-killing was the result of "luck". She wondered if they had really eaten it after they had salted and dried it. She knew from her Bible reading that rabbits were considered "unclean" by Jewish people. But, if they were covertly in another country, they would give themselves away by adhering strictly to their own customs.

Most of the time, it bothered her that she had blown up the house where her captors had held her for part of a night. She had already freed herself and taken off in the only car! Probably, her killing the occupants of the house was murder, unnecessary. She guessed her main motivation for it was fear that they could call someone else about her escape, who would come help them recapture her. They had threatened to sell her to be someone's wife. Tears stung her eyes. She hadn't heard little kids, but she had been aware of toys strewn around. She tried to halt the agonizing thought process.

More mail was stacked up, and she had formulated a plan for what to do about it. Some of it was lunacy, many pleas for money. Daniel and Diana had warned her about it before the first envelope arrived. It went with the territory of having a lot! Everyone thought you owed it to them, to share! Some of the stories were incredibly sad! Most so incredibly sad, that they were hoaxes! Mallory's plan was to put Marge in charge of it. She wasn't a real great "people" person, but she was really more capable then her first impression had indicated.

Of course, Mallory tithed, and Kerry was setting up a foundation for charitable causes. Besides propagating the gospel, Mallory had a special feeling for law enforcement officers wounded in the line of duty, and for the dependents of those who lost their lives. There was a lot of heartache and poverty in the world. She couldn't help everyone! They all needed salvation, anyway, and then they would have the Lord for their help.

Reluctantly, she opened her curriculum. She had received a *B* in Geometry! Yes! It was her worst grade! Her paper on *Water Buoyancy* had received a ninety-six. Biology was finished, American History, American Lit. She sat dazed! Her junior year was over. She was finally a mighty senior! Not to be on campus! And, she was a college student at the same time! She couldn't understand why, but she loved the Geology!

The Geology chapter brought her thoughts back to the missing Diamonds. She called her mom and talked to her for a few minutes about her most recent trip, and about what had gone on while she was out of the country.

Finally, Suzanne laughed. "So you basically need to talk to Erik? Why didn't you say so?"

"Mom, I like talking to you. And, I did miss you on the trip. And I don't call you much because I know you're busy. I just wondered if the FBI got surveillance or any more information from the New York bank."

Suzanne laughed again. "I'll have him call you as soon as he can. He's on-line now, chatting with Col. Ahmir, so I'm sure he'll have some new information for you. I don't know about the bank; are you sure some of the Diamonds disappeared?"

"Yeah, Mom. Mr. Carlton's sure. That's why he weighed them to begin with, the accountability thing! Keeping track of them! I'm about to go to bed; do you think Erik can call me in the morning?"

"He's grabbing my phone now. Sleep tight, love you."

"Hi, Mallory," Erik greeted as he grabbed the phone from Suzanne. "I just got updated from Ahmir. Things have been interesting there! They found a very sophisticated smuggling pipeline. They can't say so, but they think the Iranian government must have known about it; maybe helped excavate it. Of course, now, the Islamic Republic is decrying it, saying how many Turkish smugglers they have rounded up. We have you on satellite imagery. Your fireball made you easy to spot. From it, we ran forward and backward. Looks like you had an interesting journey." She detected amused curiosity. She knew she was at liberty to tell part of the story, but she wasn't ready to.

"Do they have any evidence that Oscar and Otto entered and exited the country?" she changed the subject. "I'm still interested in the details of your trip up to Dierks."

He was amazed! Touché! He was still humiliated about his fiasco and Suzanne's sending Summers to bail him out. After his talk to David about going in without backup, then he had done the same thing! Of course, he hadn't figured driving by a girl's apartment would develop into a fiasco! That was the thing though! You just never knew!

"Evidently the Maloviches didn't enter or exit Turkey legally," he replied "Doesn't mean they took the Iranian route. That would be convoluted, even for them. All that coastline, wouldn't be easy to come ashore unseen; but, it wouldn't be impossible, either. I have received some information from the bank. Faulkner did sign in to the safety deposit area last week. That's hard for me to believe, though. I mean, the guy strikes me about as honest as any man I've ever met. Then, if he isn't as honest as he seems, at least he would be smart enough not to go sign his name on a line to steal stuff. He knew the Diamonds were weighed, although not properly inventoried. We're changing that, too. The rest of the Diamonds falling out of your little old house have oversight on top of oversight to eliminate any further shrinkage."

Mallory was relieved to hear that. They were all finally starting to "get it" about the ease with which the stones could disappear.

She knew Daniel Faulkner hadn't been back to the bank. Someone had to have forged his signature! But, then there was the problem of ID! Easy enough, though, if there were a sophisticated gang behind the theft. Fake ID, but how could they have gotten his key?

"You there, Mallory? You fall asleep?" Bransom's voice bringing her thoughts back to the conversation.

"No, Sir," she laughed. "Just lost in thought. What's the latest with Martin Thomas?"

"Interesting question. Haven't checked on him in awhile. I better do that first thing in the morning. Then I'll let you know."

"Okay, sounds good. Thanks for everything, Erik."

She meant to say it; although it still sounded strange. Her mom had found a really great guy! She sat still for several minutes, thinking about Erik Bransom and his entrance into their lives. What a miracle! And, so were the Faulkners! She loved all of them! If she couldn't have her dad, she had other treasured people in her life!

She watched most of the news before faling asleep. The Rangers won, and Boston lost! She could almost see David gloating! He sure was cute though!

Awake early because of jet-lag, she sat up and read her Bible. She was finishing the book of Genesis. It felt good to get her Bible reading and her life back into order. While she ate breakfast, she prayed through her journal. Christians were mandated to pray for the "peace of Jerusalem", but she had never been careful about doing it. She hadn't always prayed for America, although Pastor Anderson had always preached that it was the duty of citizens to do so. Now she jotted the reminders carefully into her notebook. She added Lilly's name to people she was wanting to see receive the Lord. Then she prayed for Shannon, Donovan, Carmine, Aunt Linda, and Mr. Carlton to make their decisions for Christ.

Janice Collins phoned her to ask her what her plans for the day were, so she could arrange security. Mallory was impressed. Actually, she had a plan, and she went over it with her security agent.

Her first agenda item was a swim. She had only been in her pool twice, so far. Now the hot Texas morning made the appeal even stronger. Under Janet's watchful eye, she swam several laps before going in to get ready for her day. She loved her relaxing Jacuzzi, but opted instead for a quick shampoo and shower. She dressed quickly in a white eyelet short -sleeved suit, embroidered in brightly variegated thread, then accented it with multi-color Sapphire jewelry. It all looked really cute together! Blow dry! Make-up, white bag and sandals! Time to get her nails done soon! Not today, though!

Her cell rang. It was Diana, and she answered eagerly. Diana, just finding out about the missing gems, was worried about Daniel's being implicated and about what Mallory thought.

Mallie did her best to assure her friend that they would get things sorted out, telling her she'd call her if she found out anything new. She had to go, her other line was ringing.

It was Erik! Before he had opportunity to call about Martin Thomas, the Little Rock FBI office had phoned him to inform him the kid was dead! Not before he had critically injured a deputy who was transferring him to a competency hearing! Bransom listened sadly to the details of the incident. Didn't sound like the deputy had much of a survival chance. He relayed the information to Mallory. She was pretty stunned by the news, but it was hard for her not to be relieved.

Janice was trying not to be ecstatic! Thomas was the craziest criminal she had ever dealt with. She called Summers. He was glad Thomas was out of the way, too; but he knew the deputy and his family. The three of them joined in a quick prayer meeting for the injured lawman.

After delivering her accumulation of mail to Marge, she checked on the status of DiaMo Corp. business. Nothing that had to be dealt with today! After going over some instructions with her office staff, she was off again. By early afternoon, she was in Hope. She went to Sanders Corp. first, to see her mom and give her some Israel souvenirs. Her first visit to her mom's workplace since Suzanne had resumed working for Roger.

"Wow! Nice office, Mom! This is a change from your old desk and chair of the early days!"

Suzanne laughed. "Yeah, not bad! I still can't believe your father arranged your penthouse suite of offices! This is like a broom closet in comparison! I still can't fathom that Patrick did all that!"

Mallory's laugh rippled. "I can't believe it either, and I think I had more confidence in him than you did."

She and Janice accompanied Suzanne to the cafeteria. It was beautiful, and the choices sent out tantalizing aromas. They all made selections and were enjoying the lunch when Beth and Roger entered with Constance and her new baby. Mallory jumped up to go check him out. He was adorable, chunky, and starting to really smile. She cradled his soft head against her cheek! He was so sweet she didn't want to turn him loose. Finally, she relinquished him back to his grandpa.

From the Sanders Corp., they headed to Erik's office. He showed her the fax of Daniel Faulkner's signature sent from the bank. He had a couple of agents trying to make sense of the video. The signature looked like Daniel's, but handwriting analysis wasn't possible from a copy. Erik allowed Mallie and Janice to watch the video.

Actually, business was slow for deposit boxes at the small branch bank. Mallie asked one of the agents to find out how many boxes were usually rented out in a month. She wasn't his boss, but she was pretty cute, so he called their liaison person at the bank. Most of the boxes were unrented; that section of the banking business wasn't exactly the briskest.

They resumed the video. Nothing-nothing-nothing! Then, within a thirty minute period, five people inundated the lone bank officer! Three renting boxes! Two accessing the boxes they had recently rented!

"Okay!" Mallory sat upright, excitement dancing in her eyes. "There's the diversion! Sudden business overwhelming the one employee!" Her eyes were riveted on the events unfolding. The sixth customer, a woman, signing in to access her box! She had big sunglasses on and a cute hat pulled down on her brow. The black and white images were poor quality, but if they were in color, Mallory would almost be willing to bet the girl had multi-colored hair! Sylvia Brown, again?!

Bransom checked the date on the video with the one on the paper signed by Faulkner. They didn't match.

"It doesn't matter," Mallory insisted. "She dated it wrong on purpose, so if anyone referenced the date of the signature with video, they wouldn't correspond. "But how could she sign *Daniel Faulkner,* a guy's name, without raising questions?"

Bransom frowned. Mallory was smart, but he wasn't convinced. He didn't want to raise the ire of a Federal Judge for no reason. He couldn't tell why Mallory was so convinced it was the same girl. And how would she have gotten the key?

He placed a call to Jed Dawson, and Mallory and her contingency headed back to Dallas.

Mallory's thoughts swirled. She wasn't sure why she had wasted so much time trying to track down two or three stones. In the industry, losing a few was an inevitability. She was convinced the girl in the surveillance was Sylvia. Now she wondered, if, in fact, she had been the one to seek out the stylist! Or was it the reverse? Mallory had found the business card and traveled to Dierks for haircuts. Then, when David had showed up with the stylist at church, Mallory had stopped using her. Mallory had thought she was becoming friends with her stylist, but when Mallory greeted her at church, offering to sit with her, Sylvia had acted really hateful. Evidently she felt she and David were an 'item'! Maybe they were!

But why would the small-town Arkansas girl travel all the way to New York City to steal a few Diamonds from DiaMo? Was she trying to cast doubts on Daniel and his good name? The Diamonds were valuable! Taking all of them would have netted them infinitely more! She sighed! Maybe they assumed the stones would never be missed; that seemed the most logical! If any of it was logical!

And Martin Thomas! Dead! She had never lost a class mate before! Someone her own age! She wondered if there would be a funeral. If there were, she should attend. But she hadn't ever been to many funerals, none since her dad's! Tears clouded her eyes.

She called Herb Carlton. She wasn't sure why he wasn't accepting her and Diana's offer. The most obvious reason was that he was happy with his life and his pawn shop, and he really wasn't interested. That was certainly his prerogative! She guessed she was having a hard time dealing with rejection! He didn't answer, and she left a voice-mail.

"Hello, Mr. Carlton. Mallory O'Shaughnessy. Just one more call about hiring you to help us with our jewelry designs. If you really aren't interested, do you know anyone else just like you that we could hire instead? Do you have a clone somewhere? Maybe a twin brother? Why do bad guys like Oscar and Otto come in pairs? And there's only one of you? I can come to Hope tomorrow and give you more details, or you could come to my office. If you have someone to recommend, please tell me about them, not them about us." She left both phone numbers.

She sat back and closed her eyes. The freeway was busy! Lots of eighteen wheelers, and she was glad to let someone else drive. She put on a headset and turned up her music. She wondered what was developing about the Andersons and their ministry headquarters and recording studio! And the camp! More calls she should make! The next thing she knew, she was home.

❧ ❧

David was early for church on Sunday morning, checking the ancient air conditioning system, and making sure there were paper towels, soap, and TP in the little restrooms. He whistled without realizing he was. He could hardly wait for the worn little set of buildings to be totally refurbished. He needed to meet with his dad. Maybe they could this afternoon. His dad didn't like extra stuff on him on Sundays. But David was leaving for Tulsa following the evening service so he could meet with the architects early in the morning. He started coffee brewing in the little workroom.

Tears came to John Anderson's eyes! He could see David's pickup before he even pulled into the little gravel parking lot. He texted Lana! "David's already here." He knew that would help ease her mind. Tammi had been up early, too, helping with breakfast and the dishes, and styling her younger sisters' hair. What a blessing. He quoted:

> *III John :4 I have no greater joy than to hear that my children walk in truth.*

He walked in, singing in his loud baritone, slightly off-key, and David came out to meet him. They hugged, then David stood back to survey his dad in amazement. He guessed he had never seen his dad look good. His 'Sunday-best' had always basically been a pair of black twill pants, usually faded, a white dress shirt, occasionally new, but often worn and frayed. A short polyester tie, and a black sport coat, or suit jacket, or whatever it was, from sometime back in caveman times. Never big enough. His long bony wrists had always shoved out past clothes that looked like he had long-since outgrown them.

His dad looked better than Daniel Faulkner! He knew that was really saying something! But it was the truth! He had never really thought about his dad looking bad, until now, with the comparison!

Evidently his dad had visited the custom tailor! He stood there in a gray, glen-plaid suit with a slight sheen to it. The pants actually broke into cuffs that revealed sharp-looking, new, black, leather loafers. A brand new French-cuff shirt, revealing a monogram on one cuff sparkled with the Gold and Diamond cufflinks. The handsome watch from Mallory wasn't evident, nor the Mont Blanc, but David was sure his dad was wearing the watch and the high-end pen nested in his breast pocket. A silk twill tie in black and white diagonal stripes coordinated with a black pocket square! And his nerdy, parted, greasy, swirly hairstyle was gone, too!

"Excuse me, Sir, have you seen my dad around anyplace?" he laughed when he could finally find words.

John laughed self-consciously. "You think it's overkill?"

Erik and Suzanne, entering, heard most of the conversation.

"Overkill!" David laughed. "Looks great!" Then the inborn mischief couldn't resist.

"I mean the Diamond cufflinks make you look like a riverboat gambler. You should definitely give them to me."

The pastor looked at them with a frown of genuine concern. "Didn't Mallory give you a pair, too?" he queried seriously.

"Yeah, she did. But two pair are better than one! Just kidding, Dad."

David visited with the Bransoms. Usually if anyone would mention something about Mallory, it was one or the other of them. And, they were both pretty cool! David hadn't heard about Martin Thomas. Like Mallory, it was a lesson in mortality for him. He had worried about Thomas getting to Mallory, especially after he had nearly managed to pull off an escape.

When his mom arrived and his little sisters and brother, all dressed up in new stuff, he figured he should probably work in a shopping expedition for himself, too. Now, he wished he had something as sharp as his dad for his meeting with the architects.

In the afternoon, he met with his dad about some of his ideas for the church plant renovation. John was determined to stick with red. David thought beiges and earth tones would look better. Different seasonal flowers would dress it up, and purple flowers wouldn't clash with red. It would look nicer for weddings, too, and the bride's colors and bridesmaids' dresses.

John argued that he didn't do that many weddings.

David responded that the nasty-looking red might be the reason why. And, a lot of the church kids were just now growing up enough to be thinking about weddings.

The meeting ended with John's being determined to accompany David to the meeting with the architects. To his surprise, David didn't argue with him about it. David was actually relieved. His place in Mallory's corporation was a grow-up-quick experience! He wasn't sure he could handle it. Partnering with his dad was kind of a dream-coming-true for him, anyway. They both returned to the parsonage to grab a nap before the service, so they could make the late-night drive together.

David tried to concentrate on his dad's sermon, not because it wasn't a good sermon. His dad was his favorite preacher of the many he had heard. But, he would turn eighteen soon, and he still couldn't tell what God's will was for his life. He knew it was take one day at a time. Be obedient to the tasks of today. God won't show you your next ten, twenty, thirty years in a crystal ball.

" His will: be faithful in Bible-reading and prayer, be respectful to your parents, keep up schoolwork, work on the building projects, take flying lessons." He was making notes on the bulletin; he hoped his dad would think he was taking sermon notes. He wanted to stay right and marry Mallory. If not Mallory, some really exceptional Christian girl to serve the Lord side by side with, bringing up Godly children. He couldn't think of anyone else who would fill the bill.

He still hadn't heard much of the sermon, but he moved to the altar on the first note of the invitation. A sour note! The new piano was in tune, but his mom still wasn't the best pianist. He knelt. He had a burning desire to know! Patrick's talk to him about Proverbs chapter nine had suddenly caught hold of him! He couldn't afford to waste the time the Lord had for him, wandering aimlessly in wrong paths, squandering not only his own life, but the lives of those God had ordained for him to help. Tears poured down his face! Tears for Martin Thomas! He remembered the times he had jeered cruelly at the misfit boy! What might have been the outcome if David Anderson had been the Christian he should have been? Not the *Pastor's Son* he should have been! Just the Christian he should have been. The Holy Spirit gave him peace. He needed to settle his Christianity issue before he could ever decide if he was called to preach. Whatever his vocation or calling in life might be, he needed to be a steadfast Christian, first and foremost!

Following the service, David and his dad bought large coffees and headed toward Tulsa. John offered to drive first, offering David the options of sleeping or watching a video in the back. Still awed by the features of the awesome vehicle, David laughingly declined both choices in favor of sitting in the front and visiting.

After chatting about numerous things, David asked what the status was of his mom's getting a fur coat.

John chuckled. "I never thought about anything like that, we were so broke! Of course, now we could easily afford one. It's sure a loaded issue, though!"

"Why, Dad? Because of animal rights activists? Why is it suddenly immoral and reprehensible to wear fur, when so many issues that are clearly wrong by the Bible have no outcry about them whatsoever? It's mostly envy, don't you think?"

"I guess it's more complicated than that: things usually are. Of course envy drives lots of wrong stuff. But many people have been carefully educated by the media, and the powers that be, to genuinely believe the fur industry is wrong. People are convinced that animals are needlessly tortured to death, or trapped in awful traps! Of course, people around us are trapped in cruel situations, or the clutches of sins and bad habits, and there's no outcry about that. People should always be more important than animals. God put animals here for our enjoyment. He made the first skin -garments to cover the nakedness of Adam and Eve. Of course, that must have broken their hearts, too, since the animals were given to them to care for. Now, they saw the lambs sacrificed to cover their sins. Death entered the world at that time, and man's seen its destructive forces for the millenia since. Animals have died since that time, for food, for clothing, just for sport. They don't have souls, but people like to believe that they do. I mean, many animals have lots of intelligence, and they seem to be affectionate and have "personalities" although that's a stretch, since the word "personality" comes from the root word, "person"."

David laughed, "What do you think about Mallory's dog?"

His dad cut him a sideways glance. "What do you mean?" he asked cautiously. But his eyes were twinkling, and a grin was breaking across his face.

"You reconsidering your position on reincarnation? I mean that dog's spooky, Dad!"

John laughed. "The dog isn't spooky; she found him where someone had tried to dump him at the shelter. She prayed for a dog, and the Lord provided her with one."

"So, what about Mom's coat?" David returned to the subject.

"I don't know. People might stop tithing." He figured he wouldn't be able to ride far with his son without ending up in an argument.

"Yeah, I know, Dad. Figured that would be on your mind. But the Bible doesn't say, 'Tithe as long as the pastor's wife doesn't have a fur coat'. Christians are supposed to tithe because it's obedient! And it's the way to have God's blessing on them, too! I mean, when Mom had on her new Easter dress, Charles Tate said, 'See, I tithed, and the pastor's wife got a new dress'. I told him Mom got the new dress because she tithes, and that his tithing should get his wife new dresses. I think you should preach more on tithing. People don't really seem to understand it."

John laughed. "David, tell me you didn't really say that to Charles. The members complain that I mention giving as much as I do. Many of them 'get it', a lot of them don't want to 'get it'. It's a work that has to be mixed with faith. If you believe the Bible is a miraculous book and its promises are true, it's easy to tithe. Otherwise, it's a real sticking point."

"Well, Patrick gave the money, and Mallory would want mom to have one. You should go ahead and get her one."

"Well, it's summer. If I get her one now, she'll die of heat stroke cause she won't be able to resist wearing it. Maybe by next winter, I can get my mind wrapped around it. Did she put you up to this?"

"No, Sir. When Diana Faulkner started talking about it on the flight to Turkey, I thought her interpretation and 'doctrine' were way off-base. But, she really knows her Bible! And she knows God!" He started to cry.

"I mean, you've taught me the most about Him: you and Mom! But, I never grasped that He is so Artistic, and Creative, and Kind! Somehow, I missed all that!"

"The Faulkners have been eye-openers for me, too. You know, the Bible says to 'behold the goodness and severity of God'. I've been more prone to emphasize His severity. Not a bad thing! But the Bible says 'the goodness of God leads us to repentance'. I want my ministry to become more balanced. I love what she pointed out about the *Lady in the Wilderness* with linen, silk, embroidery, gold, cashmere, leather and fur. God did ordain a difference between the genders; then we fuss at our wives for liking feminine things. It's easy to grumble when they like the jewelry store windows better than the sporting goods."

"Yeah," David agreed, stretching. "That's the cool thing about Mallory. She likes hardware and sporting goods stores."

John laughed. "Yeah, you stick with that thought!"

They stopped for burgers and a chance to stretch; then David jumped into the driver's seat. Back on the freeway, he continued, "Seriously, Dad, you need to get mom a coat now. Summer is when they go on sale."

"You know that how?" John was curious. Surely Lana had looked into it and coached him.

"Because of all the ads in the newspaper. All the fur salons are advertising great deals that include 'cold storage' for the rest of the summer. What's 'cold storage' and what does 'fully-let-out' mean?" he finished.

"You're asking me?" John laughed. "You're the one who seems to be 'in-the-know' about all this. Wake me up when we get there."

He was snoring so fast David could hardly believe it. But his dad always could conk out fast. He turned on some music. He loved driving the freeway at night. And he had lots to think about.

"Easy on the gas, David!"

Grinning, he eased back on the accelerator.

His going forward in the service had helped clarify some things for him. He had been trying to see too far down the road. The Bible actually cautioned against trying to do that. Just one step at a time, one day at a time, on the way with Jesus. Follow the path one day at a time without veering off course (to the right hand, or the left). As you did that, awesome things occurred along the wayside. He was excited about spending a night at a big-city hotel, but relieved his dad was along.

After the meeting with the architects, the building projects he was to oversee would be farther along the path to reality. When he had leisure time, he could ride *El Capitan*, and, although Tammi planned to find a job, she could also come ride with him as much as possible. He felt peace. Just trust God, even if you can't see it spread out before you like a quilt! Just take one block at a time!

Chapter 7: WISDOM

Mallory was finishing her devotions on Monday morning when Diana called her.

"You didn't tell me your wrist was bothering you," Diana plunged in with a good-natured accusation.

"Well, I think I sprained it, and I think it's getting better," Mallory responded, trying not to sound too defensive. "If it isn't a lot better in a couple of weeks, I'll call a doctor."

"In the mean time, you can't practice your piano or start with the violin."

"Well, I have plenty of other stuff to do. I'm not sure learning violin was such a good idea anyway. I haven't had time to play the piano."

"I have an appointment for you at an orthopedist here at four this afternoon. Hurry and get ready so you can meet the chopper at ten. I'll meet you when you land, and we can have lunch together and work on some designs until your appointment. Better hurry!"

Mallory could tell it was an order, but she didn't mind. They couldn't fuss at her about her schoolwork if they were demanding that she be here or there: do this or that! Could they? Suddenly she was aware that they were going to demand a lot of her! She closed her Bible and hopped into whirling bubbles. So much for her nails today, too. She dressed quickly in a fragile, pale, mint green outfit that she had actually found for herself. Well, with the Lord's help! She put a green amethyst slide onto her Omega, then added the delicately-colored jewelry to her earlobes and wrist. Her diamond ring from her dad and her elegant watch completed her jewelry choices. Grabbing metallic gold sandals and handbag, and her sunglasses, she joined Janice and her day's security detail for the quick ride to the chopper pad. They were Tulsa-bound before ten.

While they were in the air, Herb Carlton returned her call. He was willing to meet with her today about the position she had offered him. Frantically, she wished the day weren't already so full. Trying to sound calmer than she felt, she coolly requested for him to see her the next day in her office in Dallas. To her amazement, he agreed. She finished arranging the appointment and phoned Marge to enter it into her calendar. Her spirits soared. Maybe he was more interested than he seemed. She opened a massive Geology textbook. She had it online, but had purchased the heavy book anyway. She reread some of the chapters, highlighting parts with yellow. For some reason, she could see it in her mind and retain it better this way. She was a Bible high-lighter, too.

She greeted Diana with a hug. Wow! Did she look cute! Finally, she looked expectant enough that Mallory thought she might have noticed, if she didn't already know. She was wearing a beautiful silk suit, blue and white print, reminiscent of the famous Iznik tiles in Turkey. Mallie gasped with amazement.

"Tell me I don't really look like a kitchen backsplash! Daniel said I do!" Her blue eyes were alight.

Mallory laughed. "Ooh, that's mean! He didn't really, did he? I think it adapts gorgeously! Did you find out what you're having?"

"A boy! Jeremiah's happy about it, although he knows he won't be a playmate any time soon. The girls are just excited about a baby."

"I might have to come steal him. I finally saw Roger's grandbaby. I hate to admit it, but he nearly lives up to the hype! He's sweet!"

Diana agreed. She had received a picture of Mallory tenderly snuggling Baby Anthony.

"Where are we?" Mallory questioned curiously. She had been engrossed in her studies when the chopper landed. They were actually in downtown Tulsa, rather than the suburb where the Faulkners lived.

"Daniel's office is here," Diana responded brightly. She indicated the building that towered impressively above them, before they ducked into an intriguing Bistro on the street level.

Janice accompanied them inside; the two guys posted themselves unobtrusively outside the front and rear doors of the establishment. The maitre d' showed them an alcove, and Daniel scrambled to his feet to greet them. John and David Anderson rose, too.

"Hi, Honey," Daniel greeted, "Look who I found wandering the streets of downtown Tulsa. They just finished meeting with Amos Sullivan about plans for Patrick's projects. Hi, Mallory, good to see you. Erik called me about your theory regarding the missing diamonds. Guess that's kind of on his back burner."

"It may be. He has more pressing stuff about the Maloviches, plus actually some cases that don't involve us at all. Then Col. Ahmir is using him as a consultant. I called Delia about hiring a private investigator. She does that a lot, when stuff happens that the police don't have manpower for, or interest in. I mean, my dad only pulled out gem-quality stones, so those were all nice. The biggest ones were the ones taken! But they weren't the highest value of the bunch, by far. I think Sylvia Brown took them. I don't know why she would, or how she got your key. Kerry and Darrell are feeling the stress, and I know you are, too. That's the main reason I want to find out."

David was studying the menu. Every time he thought he wouldn't get to see Mallie again for a long time, something would happen. At least it wasn't like the ordeal when Melville had tried to strangle her. He had almost lost her then! Then again, when she had been abducted in Turkey.

Everyone turned in their orders before Diana asked how the meeting with the architects had gone. It had gone great! The firm, Sullivan and Mason, had designed the skyscraper they were sitting in. Their preliminary plans for the ministry headquarters and the Bible camp were amazing! When the church received it's facelift, it, and the ministry building, would be the most exceptional-looking edifices in Murfreesboro!

A laugh escaped from Mallie. She was sure the architects were good, but Murfreesboro didn't offer much competition in the beautiful-building category.

"Pastor, you're quiet, today," Diana observed. "How were your services yesterday? We work really hard on our class, but you know how singles are. They must stay out late on Saturday nights. They promise us they'll come, but then they don't get out of bed."

He nodded vacantly. "What does 'fully-let-out' mean?" he blurted.

Diana looked at him blankly, not sure they were talking about the same thing.

"About fur coats," David explained. "The ads say they're 'fully-let-out'. Were they little, and they alter them to make them big?"

Diana's laughter bubbled. "No, that isn't what it means. It's the way the furrier takes a pelt that's short and wide, and makes it long and narrow. They slash the skins diagonally into thin strips, adjust them over slightly, and make many seams that the hair hides. There are miles of stitching in each full-length coat that's 'fully let out'. My coats are in storage, or I could pull up the lining and show you. Are you getting one for Lana today?" She was curious and excited.

"I don't think so," John answered slowly. "I figured I had until winter to mull it over. Then David said the prices are best in the summer. That makes sense, I guess. You said yours are in storage; does that mean 'cold storage'?"

"It does. Heat isn't good for them! And they should never be stored covered. At the end of each season, I have mine cleaned, glazed, and stored. Are you thinking about mink?"

"What else is there?" John was confused. He equated 'fur coats' with 'mink coats'.

"I guess you want to surprise her with one, but the best surprise isn't to buy it and give it to her. Have her fly in tomorrow to meet you here. Daniel and I will meet you both and go with you, or we'll just give you a couple of business cards of furriers in town. There are so many kinds of fur, and so many styles. She should try them on and find out what she likes"

The pastor looked more confused than ever.

Daniel made a pretense of coughing to cover his laughter. Diana had been a little annoyed the previous month, when he had gone shopping with the Andersons, after they got their passports. That had been followed by a hilarious conversation later that night about Diana's learning to shop when she first arrived from Africa. She knew that was what he was thinking about. She had been a quick study! Now, she planned to help the Andersons spend their money.

They ordered their food. Delicious-sounding, gourmet sandwiches graced the extensive bill of fare, but Mallory chose soup.

David was surprised. Patrick O'Shaughnessy had always seemed to think he was *Saint Patrick,* and that he could save Ireland all over again, if he and Mallory and Suzanne ate enough potatoes. It was cheap, too. That was why Mallory always went for the meat any chance she got! He didn't say anything, though. Any more, he found himself pretty tongue-tied in her presence. The pale green set off her lightly-tanned skin to perfection.

"Tell us about your horse," Daniel invited as soon as they had prayed. He dipped a chip into guacamole, focusing his interest on the teen.

David was surprised. "Well, some of the terrain at the camp property is nearly inaccessible. I thought about a Jeep or ATV. Then, I accessed news headlines, and there was a story about horses. I bounced the idea off Brad; he loved the idea. His brother-in-law breeds the German Shepherds, but he knew of a ranch with some good stock. So, we each found a gelding. I named mine *El Capitan*. Then, I got Tammi a little mare for her birthday; she named her *Star*.

Mallory listened, slightly chagrined. David Anderson had trumped her again! He knew it, too!

Daniel nodded thoughtfully, and David continued.

"Brad's looking into more horses and tack. The architects drew prints for a stable to go up right away, concurrently with the main building. We actually want to get going right away with some day camps. Dad's a bow hunter, and he wants to have an archery range and teach archery. Then we can get some ping pong tables and horseshoes.

"And get batting cages, and put in a ball diamond!" Mallory added excitedly. "Maybe we won't have a gym right away, but we can put up some baskets, maybe some tether balls!"

"Yeah, we can do that even this summer! Bring kids out for fun, then preach to them!" David's voice was excited. "Tammi was going to look for a job, but I can give her one helping out with everything! Maybe there'll even be things Jeff can do! He's big enough to be bored with summer vacation and start getting into trouble."

John nodded. David's enthusiasm was a wonder for him to behold. And the ideas were great! John had figured it would take a couple of years to fulfill Patrick's dream for the property. Maybe not! Something to be said for the impatience of youth!

"Mallory, when did you hurt your wrist? Why didn't you say anything?" Daniel asked her, changing the subject and pulling her into the conversation.

She laughed. "Well, I fell down the mountain at the *Cotton Castle*, but it didn't seem to be hurt that badly! Erik fussed at me for going off by myself! Like I intended to! So, that kind of hurt my feelings. Then, the bus blew up, and Sammie was hurt! Then, I really hurt it worse climbing out of my little prison the big blue car took me to. I thought it was getting better again, but then it bothered me a lot when I kept shaking hands with people in Israel."

"Well, we need to get you patched up so you can start violin. *The Maestro* comes every Tuesday afternoon. Means you're coming to Tulsa every week."

Her gaze met his. He was serious. She was pretty sure there was no room for argument.

"Every Tuesday afternoon starting when?" She was pretty sure what the answer was going to be, but asked anyway.

"Starting tomorrow. You may as well spend the night. It's going to be kind of late by the time you see the doctor."

"I'm interviewing Mr. Carlton at my office tomorrow. Maybe I can start violin next week. I'm not sure I can even hold the violin or the bow right now, anyway."

She could feel the color flushing her cheeks. She didn't want to argue with him! Especially since she was pretty sure she was going to lose! And, in front of David!

Diana saved the day. "You <u>are</u> interviewing Mr. Carlton? That's wonderful! What's the deal with him and your aunt?"

"That, I'm not sure about! I just decided to try one more call. I'm glad I did. I can't figure out what his hold-up is. You want to come help me persuade him?"

"No, might seem like we're ganging up on him. I'll pray about it, though. You can still spend the night tonight and go to Dallas in the morning for the interview, then come back here for the lesson. You won't be needing to be able to hold the violin for awhile. *The Maestro* probably has a different approach than you're expecting, anyway."

Something about the way she said that made Mallory more nervous than ever. She wished she had never mentioned learning another instrument!

She glanced at David, and he was grinning from ear to ear. She resisted the temptation to stick her tongue out at him. He could be <u>so</u> annoying!

"What do you think, Pastor?" Diana had returned her attention to Anderson. "Are you bringing Lana here tomorrow to shop for a coat? I mean you all could look in Dallas, but there are several fur salons here that are pretty great!"

"Not tomorrow. I still have too much to think about." He avoided her eager gaze. He wanted to talk to Mallory about it-alone! She sure always managed to be busy. Patrick had really been sly to involve the Faulkners in her life. They were going to demand that she be everything she could be! It was amazing! He couldn't keep from smiling to himself. Mallory didn't seem to be particularly happy about it at the moment!

꿍 ꕷ

John called Lana as they neared Murfreesboro, asking her to load up the other kids and meet him and David at Hal's. He had driven half-way while David slept; then they had switched off. He was pretty sure the Faulkners hadn't planned for David to be around Mallory again so soon. It was like the Lord kept overriding their attempts to separate the two. John was relieved about the entire situation. Kept him from having to play the heavy with David. He inwardly thanked the Lord.

At Hal's, they all ordered the Chicken Fried Steak, Monday's special. It was fun; the kids evidently couldn't think of anything to fight about. David shared his ideas about beginning day camps right away. When he mentioned that Tammi and Jeff could help him, they both jumped at the chance. Tammi offered to go on-line as soon as she got home to order some of the sporting goods equipment. With the meal complete, David headed toward the camp property. He made a stop first, though, to pick up a newspaper. He needed to find someone to teach him to play the violin!

꿍 ꕷ

John sent the little kids in Lana's car with Tammi and opened his passenger-side door for his wife. She hopped in, slanting him a cute, curious, sideways glance. He thought guiltily that she was probably expecting this maneuver to be so he could surprise her with a coat.

"You seem happy," he ventured before sprinting around to the driver's side.

"I usually try to seem happy," she laughed as he turned the key in the ignition. "I usually am happy. I thought the dinner was great! I didn't have to cook and wash dishes! Not only were the kids not at war, but they were actually being nice to each other! What's not to be happy? How was the architect? Does David still seem okay?"

He winked at her as he reached for her hand. "David seems great, the building plans look fantastic." He told her that the church and ministry buildings were going to be the best looking buildings in town, and she laughed harder than Mallory had. He pulled in at the site where their new home was taking shape. The pool and hot tub were being excavated.

"It's going to be a lot to keep up," she observed. "The kids are excited about all the fancy stuff, but they won't be so crazy about helping with all the maintenance."

"They aren't going to be doing it, and neither are you. It's amazing the words of Jesus about 'the more you have, the more trouble it all causes you', a loose paraphrase, I know. More insurance, more security, more upkeep and maintenance: more worries!" He laughed. "Guess life throws problems at you whether you're rich or poor. I don't know if I want you to have a job at all. You've worked so hard. I mean you'll still have the job of being my wife and the kids' mom. Those are pretty big jobs, and you do so great. I thought about having you be the secretary for the ministry. Now, I think I may hire other people. Maybe we should look for a couple to work with the youth and music."

"You think Tom Haynes will go for that?" She frowned worriedly.

He helped her out of the car, and they walked around the spacious new home. It was really going to be something! Beyond anything he had ever dreamed of! He had already asked Diana how to hire trustworthy live in help. She was a people person, and she had sources when it came to hiring.

"I don't think Tom and Joyce will be a problem any more." His voice held a sudden resolve. "I just love this big, kitchen area. It's going to be so bright and open. We can have people over when we want, and who we want. But you'll have caterers and all kinds of help. When we don't want anyone over, we'll be able to say so. Won't that be a nice change?"

She smiled a searching smile. "It will be, but I haven't minded how things have been. As long as you and the kids are okay, I'm happy." She couldn't imagine how the Haynes could ever cease to be a problem.

In the deepening twilight, they returned, walking hand in hand to the car.

≒ ⊱

Otto Malovich returned his field glasses to the case and moved stealthily back into the woods edging the Anderson's property.

≒ ⊱

The orthopedist sat taking a lengthy history. "Where did Mallory fall? How far? From how high? How did she catch herself? How did she subsequently worsen the initial injury? How exactly did she climb from her confinement?"

62

She answered the best she could, but there was some information she was not going to divulge! Although his information was sketchy, he deduced that the trip to Turkey had been quite the adventure! His eyes traveled from the *Iznik Tile* motif of Diana's suit, back to Mallory. Being from the Middle East, himself, he was aware of constant intrigue. The type of enclosure the girl described was pretty common. He wondered how she had managed to escape with only a sprained wrist, and not a broken neck. Both ladies were really cute and fun; he hated to see them go. He was concerned about the sprain! A break might have been easier to correct. He wanted the teen to play the piano again, and learn the violin. He immobilized the wrist and scheduled a follow-up appointment.

Closing his office door, he made a phone call.

⊰ ⊱

John Anderson kept checking his rear view mirror. Someone had been trespassing at the site of their new home. He shivered. Until now, he had deluded himself into thinking his family was safe from the criminal activities that surrounded Mallory. After all, Adams had only been ready to shoot Tammi because she had showed up at the O'Shaughnessy place instead of Mallory, by mistake. But, if he and his family hadn't been targets, initially, they were now. He had been naïve! No, stupid! He hustled Lana inside before going out to the garage to bring in his hunting bow and arrows. The corporation had tried to insist that he, Lana, and Tammi, get licensed for handguns, and carry a weapon at all times. He paused, glancing up and down the quiet, small-town street

He gazed at the neat little parsonage. Church members painted the exterior every two years. He was pretty sure that all the white paint was what kept the old, wood-framed house propped up. They never made improvements to the interior, inferring that the kids would just ruin everything, anyway. Well, that wasn't the opinion of everyone! Just Joyce Haynes! Who was always the most vocal!"

Now, he wondered what had been wrong with him, to be so cowed by her! He felt like he had abdicated calling the shots for his own family. Joyce Haynes had been running his church and his family long enough! He wondered if Tom was miserable being her puppet. Maybe he agreed with her. Who could tell?

He glanced into the living room. Lana was crocheting, and Tammi was on the computer ordering equipment for the camp. Jeff was building

Legos, and the little girls were watching a "princess" movie. His heart burst with pride!

He locked the doors, a first! Then checked the windows. Even dead-bolts installed would smash easily. The house was old and flimsy. He had always known it would be a tinder-box to a flame. Tears rolled down his cheeks. Good thing Patrick O'Shaughnessy had cared about his family! He had certainly let them suffer to maintain the status quo!

He couldn't figure out if he had been doing the right thing, for the sake of the Gospel! Or just taking the course of least resistance. He guessed it really didn't matter now. He climbed the steps to his office. Turning on a lamp, he opened his worn Bible. He tried to read, but his thoughts wandered. He and David hadn't known Patrick had hired *Sullivan and Mason* on Faulkner's recommendation, or that they would "run into" Faulkner leaving from the appointment.

He was trying to make up his mind about a fur coat for Lana. He had no idea how many times he had read his Bible from cover to cover. He loved it! It was his guidebook; had never failed him. He smiled to himself thinking of Mallory's sunshiny testimony before the newswoman. Only seventeen, but she had all the answers in 'one slim Volume'!

"Lord, it doesn't just say, "Yes, buy Lana a fur coat, or no, don't! A fur coat, a mink coat; I don't even know what I'm talking about. I know all the brand names and prices of boats, and guns, and sporting equipment. I know cars and sports stats. I'm way behind on stuff that resonates with Lana. Thank You she's been such a good Christian lady and wife, anyway. Thank You she loves You and lives to please You. Please give me clarity of thought, and help me overcome my preconceptions to find Your mind on this!"

When he prayed that, he was amazed!

Chapter 8: WORKMEN

Mallory loved being around the Faulkners. She hadn't packed for overnight, but the guest suite she had stayed in before now seemed to be her space. The products and cosmetics she used had magically materialized on an adorable dressing table. Everything necessary for a sudden stay seemed provided for. She thought for an agonizing moment that maybe "her house" in Dallas was a trick. Maybe they planned to hold her prisoner here, yet. She laughed at herself. If this were a prison, it wasn't half-bad. At the thought of being imprisoned, her thoughts returned to a freezing-cold, nasty, little patio, secured by an aluminum ball bat. She tensed, remembering, the jangling each time her captors dropped the bat into place, or removed it. Tears jumped to her eyes, unbidden. She could still hear a woman's voice, spitting out the word, "Twalot", as she had pushed a plastic bucket out into the depressing space.

Mallie dabbed her eyes delicately with a linen handkerchief, then checked her reflection in the spotless mirror. Waterproof mascara still in place. The suite was done in soft mauves, the walls covered in fabric, the bathroom laid in stone tiles that marbled the color softly. Mallory wondered curiously what the stones were, wishing she were already a Geologist, able to identify any stone that came her way. Laughing at herself, she turned on her laptop. The only way to gain such knowledge seemed to be the tedious, one-step-at-a-time, hitting of the books! She was engrossed in her work when Diana spoke softly to her through the intercom, to come eat dinner.

She hurried out to join them. Daniel was just removing steaks from the grill; Diana and the kids bringing out the side dishes. Mallory realized guiltily that she should have been helping. Before she could apologize,

Daniel was blessing the food. Then, they all settled in around the table. She knew they were working hard to make her feel like she wasn't an imposition. They could monitor her from the distance, if they chose to. She began to relax, but she was still embarrassed that Daniel cut her steak up for her while Diana dressed her baked potato. She felt like a baby on their hands while they waited for the advent of their new addition.

"Have you picked out a name for the baby?" she questioned. "I mean the new little, baby. I know my own name."

Diana laughed. "Hey, you're helping us get back into practice. Don't worry about it. I like *Xavier Michael*. Daniel isn't sold. What do you think?"

Mallory liked it! No! She loved it! She adored the way Diana spoke her children's names, caressing each syllable. Alexandra, Jeremiah, Cassandra, and now Xavier. She pronounced the *x* slightly, so it didn't sound exactly like a *z* sound. Mallory also loved the way Daniel affectionately cut all their names down to one syllable nicknames: Di, Al, Jer, Cass, Zave. That was the only thing she heard them argue about, and it was pretty funny. She could tell they were about to start. Their banter was always good-natured, but she still tensed, remembering the years of hearing her parents battle it out. She would fall asleep, thinking the arguing was over, just to hear it start back up! Best two out of three, best three out of five! Never a winner! Only pathetic loss!

"Yeah, I like *Zave*! At least everyone in his class won't be named that! I'll get dessert." He winked as he escaped his wife's mock-anger.

He reappeared with a fresh strawberry pie. Diana cut and served, and someone else appeared with espresso drinks. Then they all sat and visited until the vibrant landscaping disappeared into blackness.

The kids were already going through the motions of preparing for bed, but as Mallory entered the house, she could hear beautiful strains from a violin. Something incredibly poignant and sweet. A classical piece she couldn't identify.

"Cassandra, are you getting ready for bed?" Diana was mounting the stairs resolutely as she spoke. The five year old was having a problem obeying.

Cassandra had appeared at the top of the stairs. "I'm not sleepy. I have to practice. *The Maestro* comes tomorrow, and this has to sound good. I want to keep practicing."

Daniel had followed his wife. He wasn't sure why. She was a better disciplinarian than he was. He just thought his smallest daughter looked adorable, standing there with her violin in her hand on one hip, and the bow in the other hand on the other hip. Her lip was out, and her whole stance shouted defiance.

"Cassandra, give me the violin, and do as you were told." Diana held her hand out, but Cassandra backed away rather than complying.

"Come on, Cass. Mind Mommy." Daniel's encouragement was weak, but surprisingly, the small girl handed the instrument over, bursting into angry tears of defeat.

Diana placed the instrument carefully into the case and snapped the fasteners. "Get your pajamas on and brush your teeth. If you don't obey, you won't see this again until you do."

She watched, amazed! Cassandra could move fast.

The other two kids always needed the usual threats, bribes, whatever, to get them to practice. Cassandra was certainly the opposite. Since Herb Carlton had found this violin, they couldn't get it away from her. She was a prodigy, making her parents fearful. Their goals for their children were to develop them into all they could be. Discover their gifts and talents; demand good grades; encourage them along to discover and tap into their giftedness.

Now, they were doing the same thing with Mallory; Patrick had wanted them to encourage her to 'try her wings' in as many areas as possible.

But Cassandra's special gift!

When Diana turned to face Daniel, she could see the same fear and confusion mirrored in his handsome features.

⊰ ⊱

Mallory was up early, dressed, and on the helipad by five: forty-five, having arranged for her own transportation. She needed to get geared up for the interview with Herb Carlton. Since she had never hired anyone before, she had hoped to discuss his offer with the Faulkners. The episode with Cassandra had obviously shaken them! You didn't expect kids so cute and little to be capable of being so obstinate. She needed to clear her mind of the Faulkner's drama, have her devotions, and figure out her own plan.

She read four chapters in Exodus! The perfect reading before meeting with an artisan like Mr. Carlton. She read again about the workers God had prepared to execute His exquisitely thought-out designs for the Tabernacle, its furnishings, and the priestly garments. He had filled them with wisdom and knowledge for weaving, embroidering, working in precious metals, cutting and setting gemstones. She gazed critically at the renderings pictured in her Bible. She loved the photographs of Ephesus the Bible featured, but these drawings left much to be desired, in her humble opinion. She smiled to herself. The text explained that God had filled men with the spirit of wisdom and knowledge to cut gemstones and engrave them. But the picture just showed a hodgepodge of rough, odd-shaped and sized rocks smacked into rows on the Breastplate of Righteousness. It didn't even look nice, let alone like the exquisite, jeweled object it was! She read her chapter in Proverbs, and finished praying through her journal just as the chopper touched down on the rooftop pad at DiaMo. Extra requests in her journal were added for Cassandra-and Xavier!

☩ ☩

Herb Carlton, driving toward Dallas for his meeting with Mallory, was slightly chagrinned that Merc and Samuel had insisted on accompanying him. Merc was reading his Bible; Samuel, listening to something on his iPod, so it wasn't like they were bothering him. He just hoped he could lose them before his interview, so it didn't look like he was so insecure he couldn't face a teen aged girl by himself. They had never been at all interested in his store, now they seemed worried that he might sell, change directions.

He didn't know about, Linda, either. When she decided to cool their friendship, he had tried to go along with it. He had felt kind of like it was a strain to be around her again, in Israel. Although, such a trip! Such an opportunity! He was fearful of his future! Afraid to make drastic changes, yet more afraid not to.

His cell interrupted his reverie. Frowning, he checked the caller ID. Some kind of international code. Not a number he knew.

"This is Herb," he answered.

"Herbert, Darling! Lily! You are finally going to stop being cagey and accept Mallory's position? How are you such a stupid man?"

"Stupid to be cagey? Or stupid to accept?" As he tried to regain his composure, and banter back, he was wondering how the Israeli Diamond Council higher-up knew his business, or why she would care.

"Ay-ay! Stupid to be cagey! Stupid _not_ to accept! What are you waiting for? You aren't growing younger!"

He laughed. Their group who had met her in Israel couldn't help being both offended and amused by her bluntness.

"The pink stone! What is happening to it, Herbert?"

He shook his head, amazed. Evidently she had decided that was enough 'pleasantries': she could get to her point.

"I have no idea. I haven't seen it again since Israel. I'm not a polisher, Lily. I don't envy whoever cuts that one. I don't have the nerves for it. I never did have!"

A mirthless, staccato laugh. "The spoils don't go the fainthearted, Darling. You saw the stone! Tell me what you saw in it," she pursued.

"Are you in Israel?" he was suddenly curious.

"Don't try to change the subject on me!" She called him something; and it wasn't 'Darling' again! "I use that tactic myself; it doesn't work on me! I asked you a question!"

He sighed. "I saw the "Heart", of course." He guessed that was what she was after. Most diamond cutters liked the classic gem cuts. Round, brilliant cut; then marquise. Square cuts were harder to facet for sparkle, so jewelers liked round stones in square settings if a bride wanted that look. Romantic brides liked 'heart-shaped'. Ah! How cute! But they weren't respected industry-wide! Pear cuts were acceptable, if that was the best cut for a raw stone to save as much carat-weight as possible. He figured Lily was setting him up, and that whatever answer he gave would heap her scorn on him.

"Maybe you are less of a wimp than I thought! You are right! There is a beautiful, big, rosy heart in there. You think eight, nine carats, finished? Don't let anyone ruin that gem, Herbert, Darling!"

"Lily, I told you, I don't know where it is. It's probably listed for auction. It's out of my hands."

"It isn't listed at auction! Take Mallory's job! It's a honey! In answer to your question, I will see you soon. You better marry Miss Linda, or I will have to chase you down, and marry you, myself!" the laugh again, and the connection broke.

Merc closed his Bible. "Why don't you let me drive now, Dad?" he suggested. "I think I can do the Dallas traffic better."

Herb pulled onto the shoulder to comply. His son's driving had always scared him, but Merc finally seemed to be getting a boat-load of sanity. Into his forties, it was past time! Herb was trying to credit it to late in the game maturity, rather than admitting his son's salvation was working such a drastic change. Then, Merc's beginning to mature, had affected Samuel,

Nell and the other boys so amazingly! Sighing, he had to admit that was more of a stretch than the Salvations' making such a marked difference. Switching places, they reentered traffic.

Merc whistled cheerily, and Herb asked Samuel to pass him up a couple of the heavy catalogs he had brought along. As they neared Dallas, Herb suggested that his tag-alongs go eat lunch and come back for him after the interview.

Samuel was hungry, but he and his dad both wanted to be in on the interview process.

"Let us come with you, Grandpa," he wheedled.

Usually, the grandsons could get their way, but Herb was genuinely perplexed by this behavior. "Why are you so interested in my business, all of a sudden? For years, I couldn't get you to relieve me in the shop for an hour or two. Why do you care if I sell it, or get a different job?" His resentment was directed toward his son.

"We know that, Dad. You've worked hard, and you've kept our family going when Nell and I couldn't make ends meet. I guess it makes us insecure to think the store might be gone. What if you take this job, and then they let you go, for whatever reason? The store's at least some security for you."

"And for you, too!" Herb stormed. "You don't care about my retirement! Or what happens to me! You're worried about yourselves!"

Merc's concerns were the same things that worried Herb. That Mallory and the Faulkners would ask him to sell his business to devote himself to theirs! That they would back out when they realized the outlay their dreams would require!

"You're right, Dad," Merc had responded. "We just want to hear what she has to say. We know how much you've always wanted to make jewelry! We just think she might take advantage of knowing that's your dream. We want to help in the store and make your life easier. I guess we haven't appreciated all you've done for us until the past few weeks."

Herb met his son's gaze. It was more gratitude than he had ever expected to receive. He looked them both over, head to toe! They both looked fairly respectable.

"Okay, but keep your mouths shut and let me do the talking!"

When they found the address, a parking valet approached their car.

"Good morning, Mr. Carlton. Miss O'Shaughnessy's expecting you. I'll park your car for you!"

Mallory stood in the lobby of her office suites, ready to greet her head jeweler. She wore a soft, ivory, hand-crocheted, linen dress, and she had selected a pearl 'dog-collar' necklace that circled her elegant throat with five strands, fastened in front with a decorative yellow-gold and diamond flower clasp. Classic, pearl stud earrings accented with diamonds; her watch; and two rings completed her polished look.

Herb awkwardly introduced his two uninvited family members, but Mallory greeted them warmly.

"I have a luncheon set up in the conference room. I hope you're hungry. I didn't really tell you not to eat first." She was leading the way, then paused graciously to indicate the three of them precede her into the attractive room.

"What's with the suitcase? You planning to stay in Dallas for a few days and get started right away? I hope. I hope!"

Herb met her gaze. "I do not believe I would be that presumptuous. I brought some catalogs to show you some of the equipment I think might be necessary for start-up. Merc thought pulling a suitcase would look better than lugging up armloads of heavy stuff."

Mallory flashed Merc a smile. "Why don't you bless our food, Mr. Carlton, and we can load up our plates?"

A new Christian, he prayed awkwardly and briefly, but Mallory thanked him, then fixed herself a plate. She spread mayonnaise on one of the sandwich rolls, took some chips and fruit. Whatever she felt like she could manage somewhat gracefully with only the use of her left hand. She was aware of time clicking quickly by, wondering if she could call the Faulkners and beg off on the impending violin lesson until the following week. Pretty sure not!

The spread looked appetizing. Not being sure how observant Mr. Carlton was of dietary restrictions, she had ordered deli-sliced roast beef! Mayonnaise and mustard! No cheese or butter. She suddenly wondered anxiously what was in mayonnaise.

Carlton sat down directly across from her, and she leaned forward.

"Why don't we start by your telling me what your reservations are? Obviously, you have some."

"Does he have to sell the shop?" It was Samuel.

Herb shot him the look about who was to do the talking.

Mallory glanced at the teen and returned her attention to Herb. "Is that really one of the things keeping you from saying, yes? No, you won't have to sell. I actually don't exactly want to hire you as an employee of

DiaMo. What kind of company is your shop? Are you incorporated? Maybe you can reincorporate more broadly, and DiaMo can contract with your corporation for the jewelry design and manufacture. That way, you can earn more without raising your tax liability, I guess. You probably understand that better than I do. Kerry Larson told me you need to hire your own attorney and tax people, but it should be beneficial."

Herb sighed sadly. No wonder he hadn't been able to make her worry about expensive start-up costs! She was serving that ball back into his court. She could contract with his jewelry corporation! Except he didn't have one! Not much possibility of his getting one, either! No way he could raise capital like that! He sat there stunned. He shouldn't be wasting her time! Eating her luncheon! If he hadn't always helped Merc and Nell, he might have some savings! But not enough for a venture like that!

Merc realized the same thing, humiliation rising, making him want to lash out at little-rich-girl! Sitting there, telling them to retain their own attorney, tax people! Somehow, he remembered his dad had told him to keep his mouth shut, so he sat with his head ducked down, waiting for some miraculous escape.

"What's wrong now?" Mallory realized communication had died again. "Talk to me, Samuel," she addressed him mischievously.

He opened the suitcase, removing the top catalogs, opening where they were dog-eared down.

"This is some of the equipment necessary for making jewelry. You need to melt the metals, and lots of stuff. Grandpa has the expertise you're talking about, but we don't have any of this. Then, he would need inventory, of platinum, gold, gemstones."

"Well, I know that," she responded. "We've been working on that, and it's nearly ready. I have to hurry back to Tulsa by mid-afternoon, but we have time for me to show you the facility, if you're interested. Are you interested, Mr. Carlton? If you are, Kerry Larson is ready to set you up with an attorney friend of his to rework your business structure. That means you can hire anyone at your discretion to work for you. Of course, we'll have a confidentiality clause, and your employees would abide by it when they work on our designs."

Mallory threw her plate away. She was hungry, but eating and talking, and favoring her right wrist hadn't worked. Samuel grabbed another sandwich before they moved to the helipad for the hop to a new, unmarked warehouse complex.

꠸ ꠹

Daniel Faulkner had been aware of Mallory's early departure, but he didn't leave for his office according to his normal schedule. He and Diana had talked and prayed until the early morning hours. Now, Diana was finally sleeping. He carried his Bible to the music room so he could read it without disturbing her. Taking a sip of hot coffee, he let the Bible fall open.

"I know Mallory was right about its having all the answers, Lord. Please make Your will so plain we can't miss it. We have to do whatever glorifies You, and what's best for Cassandra and her special gift. Help us to do what will be right for Al and Jer, too, and for Mallory. And, Lord, bless David and the Andersons."

He leafed through the Psalms. Tears filled his eyes, yet again. So many of the Psalms were addressed to 'the musician' or 'the chief musician'. That was Cassandra! Poised to take the world by storm, if they could just set her free!

"But, Lord, she's still so little!" he moaned. He hoped the Holy Spirit was helping him pray. That was what the Bible promised. That whenever life was too bewildering to know what to pray, that the Spirit of God prayed with groanings that didn't yield themselves to the realms of speech.

He dried his eyes! They were red and swollen from weeping and wiping at them. When he and Diana had ended their season of prayer a few hours earlier, they had agreed it was time to let Cassandra pursue her dream. Neither of them were ready. For some reason, they had hoped to delay the inevitable. Now, they were in agreement that they could no longer delay talking to *the Maestro* about the course to pursue.

꠸ ꠹

Herb let his gaze meet his son's! Wow! What a plant! He was sorry now, that he had underrated Mallory so badly. Almost to the point of a missed opportunity to fulfill a life-long dream! And something he could grasp without being forced to relinquish his store! The whole thing was beyond belief! He wouldn't be an employee, but the CEO of his own corporation. His mind was already working on people he knew who would jump at the chance to help him create beauty from raw materials. Mallory's company, bearing the expense of the legal work and tax counsel his incorporation would require, in return for a small percentage of his stock.

He looked around him again, moving into the vault where the valuable jewelry components would be kept, where there were rows of smaller, state-of-the-art safes. If someone tried to burglarize the place, they might manage to drill one of them. Maybe to find little to nothing! It would take a while to penetrate the vault; then, each smaller safe would present a new dilemma. In the meanwhile, there would be alarm on top of alarm, and some other anti-theft measures.

Mallory smiled brightly. "Hope you like it. I really wanted your input, but I couldn't get you to commit. I need to get to another appointment now, but make a list of anything else that will be necessary. Kerry's here for you, and he'll get you with a colleague to work on the papers before you go back to Hope Thank-you for coming."

"Ah, time for your first violin lesson," Carlton smiled. "*The Maestro* is going to make you a musician?"

"Guess that's the plan," she responded as amicably as possible. She wasn't sure how crazy she was now, about the whole violin, thing! And she couldn't stand everybody knowing her business and talking about it! Maybe she would make the non-disclosure agreement really broad-brushed! Like Donovan Cline's were!

"Who knows? Maybe I'll be another Cassandra!"

Carlton's face became even more serious. "They must let her give her light! Does not your Bible say to 'let the light shine'?"

"The *Light*, meaning Jesus! It isn't talking about little girls with violins!" Angry tears had rushed to her eyes! She couldn't figure out why his remark frightened her so! She always found it amazing, how unsaved people knew enough Bible to be dangerous, but missed the Truth!

"Make a list of whatever is still necessary. As soon as the incorporation is filed and the non-disclosure agreements are in place, I'm eager to show you some of our designs! Of course, you have wanted to create your own designs! That's the marvel of this set-up! You're your own man to hire as many people as you need for both of our businesses."

Kerry ushered the three Carlton generations into one of the Suburbans, and Mallory lifted off toward Tulsa.

Chapter 9: WEEPING

Kerry Larson accompanied the three Carltons to meet a colleague, before returning to his office. He had quite a bit to accomplish prior to leaving for the day. William Jacobson paged him to come to his office, and he hurried to comply. When the senior partner offered him a seat, it made him more uneasy. Not having a choice, he sank into the proffered chair.

"Larson, we didn't know Miss Henderson was Donovan Cline's ex-wife when we started the vetting process. It didn't even turn up in our background check! You know any reason why not?"

Uneasy, Kerry met Jacobson's gaze directly. "No, Sir. I didn't know it, either, for a long time. I guess she was just trying to kick him out of her life as far as possible. You don't think she misrepresented?"

Kerry was nervous on Carmine's behalf. She had worked hard to get to where she was! Surely this firm wouldn't begin the disbarment procedure before she even got her shingle out! He knew his 'poker face' wasn't in place at all. He surveyed the other man, misery etched in his every feature.

"Well, we thought we were going to hire her to replace Tremont. But, if she studied law to fight Cline, we don't want any association with either one of them. Call her and tell her to put feelers out wherever she can. Maybe she should be prepared to leave the Metroplex. Take care of it, Larson."

It was an order, Jacobson's attention returned studiously to the brief before him! The junior partner was dismissed.

Kerry moved dazedly toward reception. He wasn't sure how he could break the news to Carmine. The firm had nearly promised her. She thought she was just waiting for Tremont to empty his desk and move on.

"Any calls while I was out, Sarah?" he questioned. He wasn't sure what he was hoping for: maybe a call from Carmine that she didn't want a position here, after all.

"No, Sir. A fax came to you from Daniel Faulkner, but Mr. Jacobson grabbed it, and said he'd take care of it

Kerry was mystified. He wasn't the Faulkner's attorney; he wondered if it was something related to Mallory. Why would Jacobson grab his stuff? He always delegated downward.

Sarah continued, "It was some paperwork about Cassandra Faulkner's going to Israel to play her violin with their symphony orchestra. Sounds pretty prestigious!"

She was a nice grandmotherly lady, and Kerry like her. He was glad she had offered up the information; he had been afraid to ask!

He managed to gain the solitude of his own office! Life could sure be a roller coaster! They had finally nailed Herb Carlton down! A victory! Then Carmine's dream was getting doused with cold water! Little Cassandra? Israel? Why had Jacobson grabbed the documents intended for him? He was reaching for his Bible when Sarah buzzed the intercom, her voice, modulated, professional:

"Would you like me to get Miss Henderson on the line for you?"

He forced his own tone to match hers. "Yes, Sarah, thank you."

⊰ ⊱

With his corporation paperwork signed and sent to Austin, Herb was on his way back to Hope.

Mallory had given him liberty to keep his pawn shop, run it, start up a jewelry manufacturing company; suddenly he was overwhelmed. He was only one man. He could only be one place at a time. He thought of selling his modest home: it was too small for Merc's family. Then, he could rent an apartment in Dallas. He was once more filled with misgivings. How could he oversee his store? It was open long hours, always with his putting in the necessary time. Employees had stolen from him or been unreliable. Now, Mallory had told him to hire a whole slue of people. It had sounded neat! Now, it sounded impossible! He would fail Mallory and her expectations. His store would go under, too, with his attention divided with something else.

"You're still worried, aren't you, Grandpa?" Merc was snoring in the passenger's seat, but evidently Samuel had been watching him in the rear view mirror. "Can I finish high school on-line like Mallory, and work for you? I can watch the shop a lot of the time. I really want to learn the jewelry business."

Herb's heart lightened. Samuel was different since his decision for Christ! Sounded like his grandson's life's-work decision was made! Perfect! Herb was grateful for every young person who entered the military! He was relieved that wasn't in Samuel's plan.

He prayed right there, racing along on Interstate-Thirty among the eighteen-wheelers, for Jesus to come into his heart and be his Messiah!

⊰ ⊱

Daniel wakened Alexandra and Jeremiah at the normal hour. Sleepy, they were as unenthusiastic as usual. Then, they started in with their usual complaints when they realized Cassandra was being allowed to sleep.

"Look kids, just get dressed for school, and I'll talk to you at breakfast. Your little sister had a late night."

"Yeah, Dad, cause she cried and carried on when she was supposed to go to bed. You should get her up! She deserves to be tired!" Jeremiah's words of counsel.

"Hurry and get dressed. See you at the table in thirty minutes." He refrained from arguing with his eight-year old son. At breakfast, he could go over some things with both of them, together.

"Where's Mama?" Alexandra looked around the breakfast nook eagerly. Her mother was always up early: singing, whistling, taking pictures of sunrises. With a flash of insight, Alexandra felt a sudden sense of dread.

Her dad had concocted home-made Belgian waffles with fresh whipped cream and sliced strawberries. Pretty special, but usually reserved for one Saturday a month. Never on a weekday. And usually he was at breakfast dressed to perfection. He was in his robe.

Alexandra took the seat Jeremiah had pulled out for her, trying not to cry.

Daniel poured their milk and sat down at the head of the table. "Why don't you bless the food, Jeremiah?"

Trying to control the quaver in his voice, he managed a prayer. Their house was always happy, but his dad's eyes looked like he had cried all night. Jeremiah couldn't figure out if his mom had lost the baby, or something. Or, if everything was just disrupted because of Cassandra. He met his sister's gaze.

77

"You guys, hurry and eat. Frances will be here soon to start your lessons." Both children complied. The breakfast was good, and they were hungry. But they were worried. They removed their dishes from the table and returned to their seats as their dad opened his Bible for devotions. He read:

John 21:21&22 Peter seeing him saith to Jesus, Lord, and what shall this man do?
Jesus saith unto him, If I will that he tarry till I come, what is that to thee? Follow thou me.

He closed the Bible and leaned forward. "Kids, everyone we know has advice for us about your little sister. We know you think she gets by with too much, and we're hard on you. We do try to be as fair as we can, while at the same time, recognizing your different needs and temperaments. You know the verses I just read are Jesus' answer to Peter when Peter wanted to make sure John wasn't going to be treated preferentially." He paused, searching their faces. Agonized, worried little faces. "Mommy's fine. We just talked about stuff and prayed until pretty late, so I wanted to let her sleep. You two are both good musicians and violinists. Even better than that, you're both good Christians and great kids. Mama and I are proud of you both. We expect you to keep being great kids and great Christians, regardless of what your sister does. That's what Jesus was saying. Whatever other people do or don't do, is immaterial for us. We are just responsible for our own actions. We follow Jesus according to His will for us, without worrying about what others are, or are not doing. Pretty hard for grown-ups to do, so I know we're asking a lot from you."

Al and Jer exchanged glances, but neither one attempted their usual opinions.

Daniel thought he had been hearing movement from upstairs, and Diana appeared. She was in the big Turkish terrycloth robe, unusual for her, too, to come to breakfast before dressing. Cassandra appeared behind Diana, and she looked adorable, wearing a dressy orchid dress, her hair pulled back into a tight bun.

"You're all dressed up this morning," Daniel noted jovially, picking at her as she passed him for her place.

"I wanted to look like this. I hope they come for me today."

Diana was cutting a waffle on the plate in front of the little virtuoso, but she paused to meet the little girl's gaze in consternation.

"Hope who comes for you today?" Daniel's voice was puzzled and alarmed.

"The violin people. I keep praying for them to come get me."

Diana caught the look Alexandra had shot to Jeremiah, but said nothing. Tears stung her eyes.

"When violin people come for you, then what happens?" She tried to make her voice bright and interested.

The little girl tried not to sound huffy. She thought it should be pretty obvious.

"Then I go with them. And we all play our violins all the time, and it's really, really pretty. Everybody's really good. If I ask Jesus in my heart, do my prayers get answered better?"

"Diana took her seat, beginning to section a grapefruit for herself, waiting for Daniel to answer the theological question.

"Well, Cass, I guess they do, but that's not the real reason why we should ask Jesus into our hearts. We ask Him because we need Him to take all of our sins away." He was trying not to cry, and it didn't help when she took a bite, getting whipped cream all over her face, and bouncing a strawberry slice down the front, and onto the puffy skirt of her Easter dress.

She was so little!

Cassandra watched anxiously as Diana dabbed the mess away and she still looked okay.

"I want to ask Him in then."

She confounded her parents so totally. Recently, she had rebuffed them defiantly whenever they brought the 'Salvation' subject up.

"So He can wash away your sins?" Daniel needed clarity.

The thunderclouds rolled across her small countenance. "I guess so, and so I can get prayers answered better."

Frances arrived, and Daniel jerked his head at the two oldest kids to follow her up to the classroom.

"Cassandra, you're little, but you can't just go someplace else with other people and escape problems. Maybe Jesus doesn't want 'violin people' to come get you and take you to a perfect place. You have to face problems, and work things out. Mommy and I are trying to find you another teacher that can take you even farther than *the Maestro* has. We want to work out a schedule so you can practice lots, but still eat and sleep when we say, too. We aren't trying to be mean to you, when we insist you pick up after yourself or take you to church. We do want you to invite Jesus in. Are you ready?"

She said she was, so Daniel led the prayer, and she repeated it, not in baby talk, but definitely in a little-girl voice.

She prayed: "Dear Jesus, please come into my heart today, and forgive me of my sins, so I can go to Heaven some day and never go to hell. In Jesus Name, amen"

After repeating it obediently, she added. "And please make them come for me today."

Her parent's eyes met above her head. Most of the time talking to the walls seemed to do more good than talking to their kids. Diana smiled into her husband's eyes. She still wouldn't trade anything about her life.

⊰ ⊱

Carmine wasn't answering her cell. In one way, Kerry was relieved. He dreaded breaking the devastating news to her. But putting it off was an emotional drain, too. And Jacobson wouldn't wait long before he checked on the status of the situation. He quickly finished the tasks that he could only do from his office. Heading his Porsche north on the DNT, he glanced at his watch. Maybe he could talk to Mallory before she reached Tulsa.

A couple of rings, and her reassuringly professional voice answered, "Mallory! What's up, Kerry? Did you get Carlton squared away?"

He hesitated. He wasn't sure why he had called her. "Yes, Ma'am, the Carltons are on board. The son was hoping to be an officer, but I'm not sure Herb totally trusts him."

That was the information she needed, although it wasn't really a pressing thing. No use in his crying to her about his law firm and Carmine. Mallory was his client, not his shrink.

"Something else of your mind?" she questioned. Tammi Anderson seemed to have calmed down about the professional bond she had with the attorney. And Mallie wasn't certain David cared who she talked to, but it made her nervous just to chat.

"Do you know anything about Cassandra's going to Israel to be a violinist with the symphony?" He figured she did, and she could alleviate his concerns.

The silence shouted at him across the distance. He could hear the rotors of the DiaMo chopper, but Mallory's calm voice wasn't coming right back with a logical explanation. His anxiety deepened. He was trying to think if he had abused attorney-client privilege by saying as much as he already had. He guessed not. He wasn't Faulkner's attorney. He knew Clint Hammond, who was. If there was a contract about their little girl, why hadn't they faxed it to their own counsel?

Finally, Mallory had responded. "No, I haven't heard anything like that. I'm just about to arrive in Tulsa for my first encounter with someone they all call *the Maestro*. I have a sprained wrist, but Diana said he wouldn't have me try to play right away. Guess he has some strange teaching method." She stopped herself. She wasn't sure how much she should tell Kerry Larson about Cassandra. She had witnessed quite a scene the previous evening when she had stayed overnight at her guardian's, leaving her feeling deeply troubled all day. Then Herb Carlton's strange comment had made her doubly sad. Made her wish she could turn back the clock, have her daddy, and the simple, quiet life they had enjoyed, back. She blinked rapidly, the tears sparkling on her long eyelashes.

"I don't really know anything, Kerry. Why don't you call Daniel?"

⧓ ⧓

After Cassandra's decision to ask Jesus into her heart, she finished the waffle and asked for another. Not surprisingly, she was starved. They hadn't been able to get her to eat much for the past several days. All she wanted to do was play her instrument! Non-stop! Now it was nestled into its case at her feet. Daniel disappeared to shower and dress, and Diana refilled Cassandra's milk and her own coffee. Sitting back down, she reached over and gave her daughter's hand a little pat.

"Daddy's waffles are sure yummy, aren't they? When you finish eating, are you going to play for me some more? Mommy loves your music."

"Huh-uh," she responded.

Diana was mystified. They worked hard at having the children answer with *Sir* or *Ma'am*. Cassandra knew her response was unacceptable, but lately, they had been letting discipline slide to maintain somewhat of an even keel. Cassandra was just so much different than her siblings. For one thing, she bruised if you just looked at her too long. When they paddled her, she always looked like she'd been beaten mercilessly. That was the Biblical answer for disobedient behavior, but it had never seemed to work with the little musician. Cajoling her and wheedling weren't working either. She was turning into a total tiny tyrant! Diana sighed.

"I mean, 'No, Ma'am'," Cassandra amended her response of her own accord. She could get in a good mood and comply when she got her way.

"You aren't? Mommy likes to listen to you. You really do have a gift, Cassandra." She hesitated searching her child's eyes. "Why aren't you playing? Maybe you should go potty."

Cassandra's obsession with practicing sometimes made her refuse to stop, even for that, causing her to have 'accidents'.

"For your information," Cassandra was responding importantly! She sounded like Daniel.

"When the violin people come for me, I'll play my violin with them. And, I'll remember to use the bathroom, and mind my manners. I can't play right now, because if I have my violin out when they come, I'll have to put it back away too fast! I might break the strings."

Tears had flooded Diana's eyes again. She was at a loss.

"Well, do you want me to bring you some toys, so you can play with them while you wait? Cassandra, what if no one comes for you today?" She didn't want to start her daughter into raging hysterics again.

"No, thank you, anyway, Mother. If I'm playing with toys, they'll think I'm a little kid. I'm praying for Jesus to help them come."

Daniel reappeared, showered, and cologned, in dress slacks with a polo shirt under a sport coat.

"Hey, why isn't my little musician making music?" He grabbed his little daughter, bouncing her around, and planting a kiss on her cheek.

"Father!" Her little voice was indignant. "Don't get me all messed up!" She pulled free, patting at her bouffant skirt.

"Hey, you better call me, 'Daddy', if you know what's good for you. What's with this *Father* business?" He was forcing his voice to sound light and teasing.

Her big blue eyes met his, serious, almost insolent. "I'll go wait for them in the monitor room. I can see when they get to the gate." She picked up her case and walked away, leaving them standing totally perplexed.

Hurrying to their suite, Diana showered and dressed quickly in a green, silk, maternity suit which coordinated with a cute dive-scene sweater inspired by a family photo. Hair! Make-up! She slid her feet into metallic gold sandals and transferred the contents of her handbag to a matching one. Skimming gracefully down the marble staircase, she retrieved one of her jewelry boxes from an artfully concealed safe, and clasped on an exquisite set of emerald and gold jewelry.

She found Cassandra still seated in the security room watching the monitor fixed on the front gate.

"Mother, you didn't tell them not to come?" the voice was worried and petulant.

"No, Baby. I've been getting dressed. I haven't called anyone. I hope Mallory's interview with Mr. Carlton is going well, but I haven't even called her. I brought you an extra set of violin strings. You're really good about not breaking them. These should hold you for awhile, and I'm sure *the violin people* always keep plenty of extras handy, anyway. Would you like to color while you wait?"

"No thank, you. I'll just keep watching. What time is it? Why don't they come faster? I prayed."

Diana pulled a kitchen chair into the tight space. "It's ten-thirty. Honey, Daddy and I talked until late last night. When *Maestro* comes this afternoon we're going to ask him where the best people are, and start looking for a place where you can get your questions answered, and learn more violin, and be happier. I don't think anybody's coming for you today, though. You want to change into something more comfortable so you can practice until lesson time?"

Daniel had come looking for them.

"Father, they haven't come for me yet," Cassandra complained.

"Well, good for them they haven't! I don't want anyone coming in here carrying my kids off! See why all this security's in place? If anybody tries to come for my little girl, they'll have to fight me!"

He started jumping around, guarded by his fists. "Put 'em up! Put em up!" he mimicked the 'cowardly lion' in the *Wizard of Oz*.

Cassandra dissolved into giggles of delight.

"You're so funny, Daddy. I'm really going to miss you. Look! Here they come!"

❧ ❧

Carmine Henderson was aware of the fact that Kerry Larson was trying to be in touch. The calls had filled her with misgivings. If Jacobson & Rawlings were finally approving her position, the official word wouldn't come through Kerry Larson. She made her way to her aging car and pulled out toward Kerry Larson's. If he had bad news, she wanted to look him in the eye and find out what had happened! Something that would doubtless have something to do with Donovan! She forced tears back and pulled up beside his home just as he was approaching and his garage door rose.

He was talking on his phone, but he hopped from the sports car, smiling acknowledgement of her. He indicated for her to precede him as he unlocked the door, and she entered his spacious, granite-countered kitchen. She settled onto a kitchen stool, and he went past her, disappearing. She gazed at her surroundings angrily! Enviously! All the appliances were top-of-the-line. He was barely more than a kid! Of course, she had had all this at one time! And better! The only problem with it was that Donovan Cline had been part of the deal! Now, she wished she hadn't come to Kerry's home. He had done so much for her! He wasn't the enemy!

He returned to the kitchen, studying a couple of papers which had arrived on his fax machine. He dropped them on the counter in front of her before pouring himself his usual tankard of iced tea and pouring a diet drink for her.

"What's this?" she questioned curiously. Hope was soaring that he was just wanting to bounce something off of her. Maybe her position with the firm wasn't doomed. She could get so negative and down!

She looked it over, puzzled, returning her gaze to her colleague.

"Lilly Cowan, an Israeli Diamond Council official, showed up in Tulsa, Oklahoma today, to pick up the Faulkner's five year old daughter. Cassandra's kind of a violin prodigy, and I guess the Israeli Symphony sent Lilly for her. She brought this contract. Daniel's attorney was out of the country, so Daniel sent it to me to look at. Since I was out of the office, Jacobson looked it over and told Faulkner to go ahead and sign it and let Cassandra go."

Kerry was struggling to speak, and his voice was charged with emotion. "I guess it's okay!" he continued. "Seems like Daniel and Diana were under pressure, that if they loved Cassandra, they wouldn't stand in the way of her becoming all she's capable of being. You know, the paperwork promises the Faulkners can write, call, and e-mail all they want, and travel to Israel and see her perform. I guess I'm just shocked that I never knew they were even considering anything like this! And now it's done! And she's on her way! Lilly was all right, I guess, for diamonds. Think she's harder than they are. She doesn't seem like a real caretaker for a five year old."

Carmine returned his gaze. The five year old was a demon on the violin! And, she could just be kind of a demon. Carmine had enjoyed helping entertain the little ones on the Turkey trip. Cassandra was adorable and talented, but Carmine thought she was a little out-of-control. It was easier to give her her way, than to cross her. She returned her attention to the so-called contract. She thought the wording was alarming.

"I guess she'll be okay. I'm sure Daniel will really stay on top of everything. As long as they get to talk to her all the time, they can make sure she's okay. Maybe she can really progress and be ready to come home soon." The tone of Kerry's voice didn't sound as upbeat as he hoped.

Alarm bells whanged out a discordant symphony in Carmine's brain. The paperwork sent a chill through her. Tears rolled down her face.

"What's wrong?" Kerry took the sheets from her hand, looking the document over again.

It looked okay. The Faulkners were going to retain full access to their daughter. With their money, one of them could go to Israel every couple of weeks, if necessary. Mallory would be traveling there occasionally for DiaMo.

"I like what it says," he began.

"Me too," Carmine shrugged. "Sorry if it makes me think of my ex-husband! It's what it doesn't say, that scares me!"

"What it doesn't say~" Kerry was at a loss. "What doesn't it say?"

"The Faulkners can call as much as they want! Doesn't mean anyone will answer! They can e-mail! No guarantee of response. Write letters? Who knows if Cassie will get them, or if anyone will help her write back? This says nothing about remuneration for her performances. You know she'll be a cash cow! She's so cute and talented. Who gets the ticket revenue she's bound to generate? It says 'the Faulkners can make plans to visit Cassandra in Israel at any time'. Make plans? They can plan all the trips they want to! Knock themselves out! They won't be allowed into Israel."

Before Larson could even absorb her words, his cell rang! William Jacobson! He answered, moving toward his office and pulling the door closed.

⊰ ⊱

Lilly Cowan arrived at the Faulkner's home in a black limousine. Her driver introduced her through the security system at the gate. Cassandra was ready to run, jump in, take off with anyone. She acted like she was going to start her usual theatrics when Daniel grabbed her.

"Be quiet, Cassandra!" Diana ordered. "*The Violin People* won't take you if they think you're real naughty. This may not be them. Just be quiet and listen while we find out who this is, and what they want."

85

The maneuver worked, but Daniel was getting tired of having to 'play his daughter's game' just for the sake of peace.

Diana invited Lilly in. Since she and Daniel hadn't yet begun to try to place their daughter, they were both amazed at Lilly's mission. The woman had begun with a high-pressure pitch. The Faulkners couldn't be so selfish as to try to keep their daughter and her talent for themselves.

Diana's head jerked up, and her blue eyes flashed a warning look.

Uncowed, the woman continued. They were cruel to thwart Cassandra's sensitivity. She went on, revealing knowledge of stuff they thought was their private, family business. All they could think was that perhaps Mallory had divulged information during her visit to Israel. But they really didn't think Mallory knew the of the problem until the previous night.

Diana, always gracious, had caused a lovely luncheon to materialize. "Well, Mrs. Cowan, we appreciate your concern." Diana was choosing her words carefully. "I appreciate your insights. We don't want to squelch Cassandra's desire to become a musician and a violinist. She is a gift from God to us; but when He gives a lot, He requires a lot. We think He wants us to nurture our children in their unique gifts, but also nurture them into well-behaved Christians. We are trying to balance Cassandra's giftedness with the responsibility that comes with it."

"Maybe you should set her free, and allow her to choose this Christianity-business for herself, later on, if she wants to. Who is there in Tulsa, Oklahoma, who can develop her talent? Are you trying to deny that she is frustrated and unhappy here?"

Lilly's voice dripped scorn. "I have brought a contract! Look at it! Send it to your attorneys if you wish. Israel is the perfect place for your daughter. Surely, you should consider your daughter's happiness more than your own!"

Daniel could hardly stand to hear any of it. He took the papers from her, moving to his office to fax them to his attorney. Then, worried the fax might get pushed aside, he phoned the law office. Clint Hammond was out of the country! He usually was out most of the month of June. Anguished, Daniel knew that anyone he revealed this to, would be opposed to it. He faxed a copy to Kerry, but was relieved he was out. Jacobson looked the contract over, and based on his love of Israel and his being enamored with Lilly Cowan and her position, he had thought it seemed like the greatest deal in the world for the diminutive violinist.

Having received a legal opinion, and figuring he had stalled as long as possible, he loped back down the sweeping stairs to the dining room. The 'contract' worried him with its vagueness, but the entire situation seemed to be the direction he and Diana had sought into the early morning hours, as well as a dramatic answer to little Cassandra's prayer.

Cassandra sat chomping on chips, taking everything in through wide, blue eyes.

"Honey, Clint's out of the country, so I tried to bounce it off Kerry. He was in court, so Jacobson looked it over. He thinks it's one of the greatest opportunities anyone could ever hope for." He was having a hard time keeping his voice steady.

"Mrs. Cowan, this isn't anything we take lightly. Cassandra has been frustrated, and she and we have both been praying. We feel you must be the Lord's answer to our prayers."

Lilly Cowan tried to keep her scorn from showing. She didn't care about answers to prayers. She just wanted to get the child, hop back aboard the private plane, and get her to Israel. She waited, annoyed, while they took Cassandra aside privately to make sure she was ready to leave home for a while, and to explain how far she would be going.

Nothing could dissuade the child. The tears of both parents didn't seem to move her at all. After a few minutes of good-byes, they asked her if she wanted to tell her brother and sister good-bye. She didn't.

Diana returned to Lilly, who was making an inroad into a plate of cookies.

"She wants to try it. Give me a few minutes to pack her up. What all will she need? She has a special blanket. She's trying to act too grown up for toys." Diana was making an effort to hold herself together and send Cassandra away with all she would need.

"None of that is necessary. We must go! Israel will provide the girl's needs."

"Okay, well 'the girl's' name is Cassandra." Daniel's heart was breaking, regardless of the resolve they had decided upon at three o'clock in the morning. This ice-cube woman couldn't even refer to his little girl by her name? Only their certainty that this was God's will, was shoring him up.

They stood in the high arched entrance, watching their small daughter carry her violin to the waiting limo. She smiled lovingly at her 'deliverer', trying to slip her small hand confidently into Lilly's. The woman rebuffed the trusting gesture! Then, the limo sped down the drive, and Cassandra was gone!

Daniel and Diana sagged together, both bursting into sobs. About everything! About Cassandra's determination to leave home regardless of their pleas. About Lilly's rejection of their daughter's gesture. About the awful void left because one of their children was gone!

Diana was drying her eyes, and trying to be thankful. If it was God's will to take their five year old, at least he hadn't called her to Heaven! She was still alive! Maybe her talent would bring praise to Him around the world! Probably Lilly's hard heart was what Cassandra needed. Cassandra could pretty well charm when it helped her attain her objectives. Maybe she was about to meet her match. Diana didn't want her child treated cruelly, but Cassandra seemed to think anyone was cruel who crossed her. They had prayed often for wisdom and guidance. They were convinced this was the answer. They were already painfully aware that it would be heart-breaking, and that they would be harshly judged!

Chapter 10: WORTH

Kerry Larson broke the news to Carmine about her future with his law firm. She was disappointed, but hardly surprised. He had gone to pieces about Cassandra worse than she had about her career setback. When he told her Jacobson's suggestion that she might need to move away from Donovan Cline's sphere of influence, she merely nodded.

She wasn't sure she could hold on long enough to go through another lengthy process. Now that she could see Callie, moving away was the last thing she wanted. She thought longingly that she wished God would help her like He did her Christian friends.

Kerry invited her to follow him to a restaurant, joining him for dinner. Carmine was enough older than he was, that he hoped Tammi wouldn't think she was a romantic interest.

Carmine just hoped she could reach wherever they were going before running out of gas. The needle was below empty when they arrived at one of the premiere steakhouses of the Metroplex.

Once seated, he started in again about Cassandra and the Faulkner's decision. He had the contract with him, and Carmine's analysis of it had him in a panic. Earlier in the afternoon when Mallory had suggested he phone Faulkner, he had done so. His friend had been too emotional to really talk, and he had basically told Kerry to mind his own business.

That was before Carmine had seen the unseen! Now, he was really worried.

He ordered steaks for both of them before continuing with his diatribe.

Finally, Carmine interrupted to suggest he be less judgmental without knowing all the facts.

He felt totally rebuked. She was right! He was the Christian who knew his Bible. She wasn't even saved, and she was more on track than he was. She went on softly, explaining how people had maligned her for not trying harder to fight Donovan for Callie. Her eyes sparkled with tears, but she managed to keep from crying. For seventeen years, she had done the best she could for her daughter. She confided to Kerry that she had been certain her former spouse would have had her killed had she created problems for him. She still wasn't in any position to make accusations against him.

Kerry nodded. She was helping his perspective, but the Faulkners' situation didn't seem the same at all. When did Christian parents start throwing their five-year-olds to the wolves, just because they threw a few tantrums? Or just because they were talented? Or whatever the reason was. Faulkner's numb words; maybe he could explain it sometime.

They were finishing the special house salad when William Jacobson and his wife passed them on the way to their table. After seating his wife, Jacobson returned for a word with Kerry, who rose cordially, waving to Mrs. Jacobson and conversing with his mentor. Jacobson was curious about whether Larson had dealt with Carmine about the firm's change of heart. He nodded toward her, then noticing the Israeli contract lying beside her plate, met Larson's gaze, concerned. He wasn't sure Kerry should have shown it to her.

"So, we have quite a little protegee!" Jacobson exclaimed jovially. "Invited to join the Israeli Symphony Orchestra! I can't wait to hear her perform! Mrs. Jacobson and I love the symphony!"

"Yes, Sir, I know you do. You are quite a patron," Kerry complimented sincerely.

Since William had okayed the Faulkners to sign the papers, Kerry was hesitant to point out Carmine's concerns to him. He probably wouldn't care, anyway. If Cassandra's talent were developed, he might not care whether her parents could stay in her life or not. And maybe Carmine's fears were groundless. Maybe her experience with Cline had left her jaded and distrustful of everyone forever.

"I see you have viewed the contract. I'm not sure why that was necessary." His voice was a crisp accusation, spoken to Carmine, but intended for his junior partner.

"I have seen it, Sir," she replied. "Perhaps I shouldn't have; but I have. I'm concerned about what may really happen to the Faulkners and their daughter. Maybe my experiences with my ex-husband have me bitter, but these promises to the Faulkners sound like things Donovan used to promise me. Like a dummy, I always fell for it."

She went on to explain her misgivings, pointing out the problems already mentioned to Kerry.

Rather than being offended, Jacobson asked Kerry's permission to join them for a moment. He blew his wife an apologetic kiss. She was used to his career demands, and she smiled back.

"Did the counselor here give you the news I told him to deliver to you?"

"Yes, Sir. He did. Of course, I'm very disappointed, but I understand."

Jacobson had placed his half-lens reading glasses on his nose, peering at Carmine over the top of them, readdressing the contract.

"I hope you are incorrect, and the Faulkners will still have as much communication with their daughter as they want. Maybe you are bitter, but you seem to have quite a bit of shrewdness because of it. Maybe you are still what our firm needs. Kerry Larson, here, is way too nice and too trusting. Maybe, if you will still consider Jacobson & Rawlings, you will be tough enough and distrusting enough to give us a better balance. Can you begin right away?"

Carmine sat wordlessly, momentarily stunned! She hadn't prayed a prayer to God. She had idly thought about how He would render aid to the Christians she knew.

She felt like she had totally come to the end! And He had graciously stepped in! She wasn't yet familiar with:

Ephesians 4:20 Now unto him that is able to do exceeding abundantly above all we ask or __think__, according to the power that worketh in us.

But God had responded to her thoughts when she was too distressed to formulate them into a prayer.

Finally recovering enough to meet William Jacobson's gaze, she nodded mutely.

"Nine! Ron Rawlings will go over your benefits and responsibilities. You ready to hit the ground running? Hope you're wrong about the little girl." He rose to rejoin his wife.

By the time Mallie arrived at the Faulkner estate, a palpable dread had settled around her, heavy and oppressive. She had tried to force the episode of the previous evening from her mind. Then, Mr. Carlton's strange, unsolicited comment had rattled her further! She had refused to discuss anything with Kerry. Her small-town upbringing and her dad had created within her, a strong aversion to gossip. Her wrist hurt, she was dreading *the Maestro,* she was afraid little Cassandra would be gone! And she missed her daddy!

Janice and Darrell shooed her into a vehicle at the helipad, and in a couple of minutes, she was at the high, arched entrance of the Faulkner estate. Louisa admitted her, leading her into the amazing kitchen.

A delicious aroma had met her at the front door. Now, in the kitchen, the delicate scents of spices lured her in farther. Daniel and Diana both seemed to be creating at the same huge pot.

"Hi, Mallory," Diana greeted. "Have a seat." She indicated a tall bar stool next to the kitchen counter, which gleamed with a glossy-finished, ebony wood from Diana's beloved Africa. Diana bent, pulling crispy loaves of bread from the oven, before leaning across the counter toward the girl.

She took Mallory's face in her two hands, gazing for long moments into her eyes. She dropped her gaze momentarily, then reestablished eye contact before beginning to speak. "I thought this would be easier to explain to you.". She thought she was cried out, but the tears were still fighting to free themselves. "Mallie, Cassandra's on the way to Israel." She bit her lip.

Mallory stared in disbelief, waiting for her friend to continue. Diana had never called her by the shortened form of her name before. She was such a stickler for every syllable, usually. Mallie kind of liked it; it sounded affectionate.

"We know most people will never understand why we allowed her to go, and that some people will judge us harshly. We're sure people will criticize us to you. We didn't send her because she caused us problems, or because we didn't know what to do with her anymore. We know that's what people will say. That's what it looks like. Well, first of all, Cassandra really wanted to go; with *the violin people,* was the way she viewed it. But, we didn't send her with Lilly because she wanted to go. I mean, when do you let your five-year-old make her own decisions?" She laughed a mirthless laugh.

Mallory was struggling. She was pretty sure Kerry's opinion of the Faulkners had taken a tumble already. She was trying to listen openly and fairly, herself.

Diana's voice continued through Mallie's mental fog.

"We have tried to make every moment count with all of our children, preparing them for the day when they fly from the nest. We always assumed they'd at least be eighteen. But in the Bible, that wasn't always the case. Samuel was barely past babyhood when Hannah took him to serve the Lord." She continued through tears. "Some of the kings of Israel and Judah were barely six or eight years old when they took up the mantle. I guess we want to tell you, that we feel this is what the Lord has for Cassandra! That He has given her this gift; He has used us to get her grounded, and He has asked us to surrender her earlier than we ever imagined."

Mallory's beautiful features looked anguished. She was too honest to acquiesce, to simply say she understood. She was trying to. Her gaze traveled beyond Diana to Daniel, who had finally ceased stirring the pot's contents, to face her. His countenance was ravaged-looking. A dreadful silence hung with the spices in the air.

"I know it's a lot to grasp," Daniel finally spoke. "Al and Jer will be down in about fifteen minutes. They don't know yet. They've been pretty upset about Cassandra, but they won't like this at all, either." He sighed. "You may be in for more Faulkner family drama. Sorry to pull you into this when you have sorrow of your own to deal with." He patted her shoulder as he passed her to pull a cute Canakkale pottery soup tureen and bowls from a cabinet.

Louisa appeared with the violin teacher, who made his way to the soup kettle, lifting the lid, and sampling, as if he were the head chef. Introduced to Mallory, he surveyed her warily. She shook his hand, left-handed, sizing him up curiously. He slightly resembled the pictures she had seen of Albert Einstein: gray hair shooting out crazily, piercing eyes beneath wild eyebrows. She wasn't sure he was wearing any teeth. He looked like he might have debuted with the *1812 Overture*. She figured he looked to be nearly two hundred.

Daniel ladled the fragrant soup into the tureen as Diana expertly sliced the fresh loaves into identical, perfect slices. Draining the liquid from some steamed clams, Daniel placed them into a matching dish, moving everything to the countertop. Evidently, the soup was a clam chowder, but since the shellfish were tougher than the toothless *Maestro* could manage, the other diners could add clams as they wished.

The food smelled so good, and her guardians and everything they did held her so captivated, that Mallie nearly forgot to be miserable. Having given up on eating her lunch while interviewing Mr. Carlton, she was suddenly ravenous. She was relieved that Daniel had taken the pressure off about an immediate response regarding Cassandra.

With hands washed, and the chowder dished generously in front of them, Daniel blessed the meal. *The Maestro* didn't like the prayer: he never did. He took a noisy slurp, then sopped a slice of bread. Evidently the Tuesday evening tradition was to make soup for the toothless teacher, then commence the four violin lessons. Mallory was picking up on the fact that this guy had been Daniel's teacher when he was a little boy.

Partway through the meal, Alexandra asked where her little sister was. She had thought maybe Cassie was napping late, but she knew her small sibling never wanted to miss any time with her teacher.

The Maestro rested his soupspoon in his bowl, fixing his attention on his host, evidently curious about the same thing.

"Well, Al, your little sister left late this morning for Israel with Lilly Cowan. They invited her to be a violinist with the symphony orchestra there." Daniel was struggling to keep his tone upbeat.

Alexandra met her brother's gaze. They always did that. If they couldn't really tell each other what they were thinking that way, they at least did a convincing job of making their parents think they could. Before the two children had a chance to respond at all, *the Maestro* broke into loud sobs.

Daniel and Diana knew their little prodigy was teacher's pet; but they had assumed it was he who had placed the wheels in motion about their daughter and the Israelis! Their gazes met in consternation. If *the Maestro* hadn't made the Israelis aware of their child, who had? Shaken, Daniel excused himself to refill the tureen with more of the rich, hot soup.

It was delicious, so everyone ate more. Mallie, hesitant to add the clams to the first bowl, added one for a 'try me' bite. It was a little tough and gritty, but not just awful. Her grandmother and Shay had told her excitedly that they planned to take her to a chowder place when she came next month to visit them in Boston. More bread! Everything tasted wonderful, but the remainder of the meal was marked by perplexed silence.

With a final slurp from *the Maestro*, Alexandra launched from her place to clear away the dirty dishes. Diana served Lemon Meringue Pie, dividing the fluffy creation into six perfect pieces, plating them expertly. Cups of coffee for the adults, milk for the children. Out of habit, Diana poured three cupfuls. This was going to be an ordeal.

⊰ ⊱

David had sought for a used violin in newspaper ads and Little Rock pawn shops. They were expensive. He had placed a large sum of his DiaMo check into savings, keeping out a chunk for daily expenses. That was getting gobbled up fast. He couldn't figure out why he didn't just forget about the whole thing. He was taking flying lessons, working full-time on the building projects, practicing at the gun range, going to church every time something was going on there! And, he was doing college coursework.

After begging the Lord for definite guidance, he had walked into the meeting with the architects, to feel an assurance that Architecture was for him.

Still, the nagging voice about learning to play a stringed instrument wouldn't stop.

He reigned in on *El Capitan*, dismounting at a site that was particularly picturesque. From his saddle bag, he drew his Bible, a thermos of milk, and a couple of bologna sandwiches.

After thanking the Lord for the lunch, he opened his eyes to gaze around the rustic setting. He wiped sweat with his sleeve and replaced his cowboy hat. Biting into one of the sandwiches, he opened his Bible. He read a chapter. He had already had devotions in the morning, something that was a comparatively new habit for him. Difficult to start, he now loved it so much, that stopping was hard. He took another bite and chugged some milk. The day was hot, but he had settled in the fragrant shade of a stand of pine trees where an occasional breeze wafted around him.

"Lord, if You want me to learn to play an instrument, please make it clear. I probably just want to do it because Mallory is. We've always been such rivals. Help me not to do wrong things, or even right things for the wrong reasons." He read the story in the book of Judges about Gideon and his fleece.

"Lord, here's my fleece, so I can know. You know I have a lesson scheduled tomorrow with that guy at two o'clock. If you help me to find a reasonably priced violin before then, I'll keep the appointment and see what he thinks. If nothing develops, I'll cancel and forget it."

Finishing his lunch, he remounted to return to the construction trailer. "Anything new going on I should know about?" he questioned Brad as he slung his hat onto a worn sofa.

"Nah. Just that things are going pretty good. Oh, Herb Carlton dropped by and left something in a box for you. I set it in your truck so it wouldn't get buried in here."

Curious, the kid loped out to his pickup. He could hardly believe it; the violin Herb had picked up in Istanbul! Standing there, surveying the gift in amazement, David Anderson was once more overwhelmed by the Lord's dealings with him. Evidently, he was supposed to, at least, give it a try.

He showed up thirty minutes early for the lesson, but Mr. Perkins greeted him congenially, inviting him into the cramped modular home. David shook hands, presenting the money for the first lesson. The cost had seemed steep, but now he was convinced the Lord was with him in the new endeavor.

The musician asked if he already knew any music. He did, just a little, having taken piano for a while, and the trumpet for band class. He liked to sing, sometimes accompanying himself on guitar. He felt sheepish, expecting the guy to throw him out on his head. Instead, Perkins ushered the student into what would have been a front bedroom, but was a cramped music room which housed a small spinet piano, and an assortment of instruments.

Mr. Perkins explained that violin required more musical knowledge by far than was required for strumming chords in a guitar accompaniment. David nodded his understanding. The guy was pretty nice, actually. Not sarcastic of a novice, but a willing and able teacher.

Perkins pulled a guitar from a case, requesting his new student to sing something for him.

Surprised, David strummed across the strings. A little out of tune. He adjusted the pitch, listening intently. Feeling pretty intimidated, he began singing "The Old Rugged Cross".

Perkins was impressed. The kid had perfect pitch. A little western-y, and wearing cowboy clothes "You wanting to fiddle or play a violin?"

❧ ☙

John Anderson spent much of Tuesday still thinking about the whole luxury lifestyle he was confronted with. He laughed. The Lord must have a sense of humor. The conundrum he was facing was probably the last thing he would have ever figured he would need to sort out.

He had grown up with a good dad and mom, and a nice-enough little sister. Not rich, but never feeling any kind of pinch, either. He had dutifully attended Nebraska State, majoring in Economics, hoping to enter the conservative political arena. Just before graduation, he had attended a *Campus Crusade* meeting. Tears came to his eyes. Sometimes it was just good to look back and remember. Even now, he knew some of his pastor friends gave that organization a bad rap. He could see the point his friends made, but God had used that ministry to step into John's life and introduce Himself. The tears rolled freely. God had changed his direction that day, and soon, the young zealot felt called to preach.

His parents didn't understand then, and they still didn't. They didn't disown him, or anything. There was just a difficult gulf now, between them. His parents didn't agree with what he was doing or how he was rearing his family. He had been broke when he graduated from NU and enrolled in a small Bible college.

He had been broke ever since. Not just 'even' broke; but 'in the hole' broke. He smiled through the tears. Lana had enrolled in the Bible college at the beginning of his second year. Breathtakingly beautiful, but he watched her for several weeks before he even attempted to talk to her. Well, for one thing he was a little shy, and she was intimidating! Also, with his call to preach, he figured he should marry someone who would be 'spiritual', to be a credit to his ministry. He laughed aloud now, thinking how he figured God would 'stick' him with someone hideously ugly. As he had watched Lana, though, he could tell that her love for the Lord was real, and that her countenance radiated joy that came from knowing Him. They became good friends, and when he graduated, they married.

God met their needs, giving them a place on a church staff in Lincoln. David, Tammi, and Jeff, were born then; insurance covering much of those expenses.

When the senior pastor of that church retired, he helped John candidate for Faith Baptist. The salary was pretty small, but the parsonage helped, and they did okay. He figured they still owed for the doctors and hospital stays for the two little kids. Feeding seven mouths, buying clothes, shoes, coats, all added up. They were in a deep hole when money began showing up in their account.

Now they had money! It was hard to get used to, really. Patrick had left money for the family, for an unbelievable new home, for totally refurbishing the church plant, and for constructing a ministry headquarters with printing and music recording capabilities. The endowment provided for continued maintenance of the three properties. Part of the organization was non-profit, but part was to develop into a profitable business, already organized by John's new attorney and CPA.

His thoughts returned to his wife, and the 'fur coat' issue. He remembered Diana, her laughing blue eyes alight, trying to talk him into it. Take Lana, and let her pick her own? He never had any idea what the prices might be of fur coats. If someone had asked him six weeks previously, he probably would have guessed ten thousand dollars, just because he thought that was a lot of money, and he thought fur coats cost a 'lot of money'. And when he thought of fur coats, he assumed they were mink.

He opened the newspaper, and, to his surprise, there were several furriers in Little Rock. The coats varied in styles and types of fur. Jackets cost less than full-length coats. Some of the ads were for garments with fur-trim, some were female mink, some were male. Diana had told him the male pelts were by far more luxurious and shiny. "Of course," he crowed to himself. Prices ranged across the spectrum. Most of the coats featured in the ads were far less than his 'ten thousand dollar' guess.

He considered his gun collection, squeezed from the meager family income through the years. He was fifteen years behind! He sprinted out to his car.

⚜ ⚜

The Maestro stayed for the lessons, only because of the new student. His heart was broken that the Israelis had spirited his little genius away from him. He wanted to learn more from Daniel, but they were both too emotional. Mallory had definitely captured his attention. He demanded Diana remove the immobilizer so he could view the wrist for himself. He had fired his usual barrage of questions at the girl, and she had actually answered quite satisfactorily. She seemed to have a sense for music: what *the Maestro* sought for in prospective students. If someone began telling him 'they just loved violin' he would go into a rage. He wanted students who loved 'the music', and who realized that violin was the best way to express 'the music'.

Sitting in the Faulkner's music room, he had insisted Mallory play the bass clef score to a classical piece. Listening to her sight-read the intricate piece, he felt like she possessed both passion and gift. She would do well with violin, provided her wrist healed properly.

He left at the usual time, carrying away the rest of the chowder, bread, and pie. The GeoHy check always arrived the first of every month when checks were generated.

Daniel and Diana returned to the music room after escorting him to the door.

"Well, what do you think?" they asked Mallory in unison.

"Wow! Quite the personage!" She hoped it was more subtle than saying, "quite the eccentric"!

"Well, you scored a hit with him!" Diana's voice came, light-hearted, and impressed. Then she grew serious. "You know, it's amazing! You have such talent and ability. Not surprising the devil has been trying to kill you! He has gotten in some good licks, by hurting your voice and then your wrist. He wants to quiet all of our songs."

"Let's have a prayer meeting." Daniel was dropping to his knees between Alexandra and Jeremiah as he spoke. Mallie slid from the piano bench, and Diana knelt next to her husband. It was quite a meeting! They prayed for Mallory's voice and wrist; for Cassandra and Lilly; for the diamond operation; the designs; the Anderson's ministry and business; the law enforcement and security personnel; unsaved friends and relatives; Diana's family, the Prescotts, serving the Lord in Africa. The prayers were filled with pain and joy. All five prayed, then joined in a concert of praise.

Mallory sat, listening carefully, head tilted to one side. Daniel was good on his violin. Finally he transitioned into a classical piece Mallory didn't know the name of. Poignant, bringing tears to her eyes, for some reason it reminded her of the Jewish people and the Holocaust.

Diana responded with a deep-toned dirge on the cello before giving her husband a light rap with her bow.

"Happy tones! Happy tones!" she reprimanded mildly. After a few more hymns, she told Alexandra and Jeremiah to get ready for bed, and they scampered obediently up the stairs.

"It's getting late, Mallory. I hope you're planning to spend the night. Did you get enough to eat?" Diana was always caring for her, and Mallie nodded gratefully.

"Come on upstairs while we pray with the kids and tuck them in. Be prepared for a scene," she warned as Mallory accompanied her up the curving marble stairway. "I'm surprised the children have held up so well, but they'll have plenty to say now, I'm afraid."

To their amazement, Al and Jer didn't say a word. Prayers completed, they both kissed both parents, told Mallory good-night, and hastened to their separate areas.

Mallory felt a little awkward being in the Faulkner's bedroom suite, but felt strangely like she was becoming more integrated into their lives. Kids tucked in, Daniel excused himself to the den to watch a golf tournament; Diana drew Mallory toward her design studio.

"I don't know what to make of the kids' response," she confided "Lately, they've told us off for everything we've done! Maybe they've been even more angry with Cassandra than we knew."

Mallory sank onto a straight chair next to a big drawing-table, running her fingers caressingly along a beautiful piece of fabric. "I think they're kind of scared to say anything," she observed. "Alexandra really jumped up to clear the dishes away, and I thought they both kind of hopped to everything all evening."

Diana met her gaze, her brows knit together at Mallory's assessment. Then she laughed.

"Cast out a scorner, and the simple will beware." She loosely quoted a verse from Proverbs, the best she could remember it. "Well, whatever works! Tell me about Herb Carlton."

Diana listened to Mallory's recounting of the interview and the set-up for the jeweler. It was brilliant. All the different corporations and the tax advantages afforded by the model. Of course, she felt really gratified about Nell's salvation, and Samuel's transformation. God was doing amazing things! Rather than working on designs, they chatted until late.

Finally, Diana suggested the exhausted girl turn in, asking to accompany her to Dallas in the morning to get the jewelry designs launched.

"Are you okay?" Mallory questioned from the door, before heading to her suite. "I still don't understand why Lilly Cowan came for Cassandra, or how she even knew about her."

Tears spilled down her cheeks. "It didn't come from me."

"I know, Mallory. We actually thought it was Jim, but he was truly shocked. We'll be hearing more from him, I'm sure.

"Jim," Mallory repeated blankly. "No wonder he prefers being *the Maestro!*" A giggle, and she disappeared.

Diana sat quite a while after Mallory's departure. What a treasure the girl was! She was happy beyond words at the way the Lord had sent Patrick to them, and then Mallory! She was thankful for Daniel! What a treasure! And for their three children. She was trying not to dwell on Cassandra, but realized the jet must have reached Tel Aviv by now. Detachedly, she was wondering how her daughter and the powerful woman were hitting it off. Might be some fireworks there.

She thought about the Anderson family, Shay and Delia, Carmine and her new position, Herb Carlton. What talents and abilities. What wonderful gifts and personalities. Tears filled her eyes for her three miscarried babies, even as the little one she carried stirred within her.

"Lord, thank-You for all you've done for me. Please bless Cassandra. Don't let her be afraid." Then she laughed softly as she moved toward the light switch of the spacious studio. "Maybe she needs to be a little bit scared. Thanks for scaring Al and Jer, too. And don't tell Daniel I called them 'Al and Jer'."

Chapter 11: WAGES

David Anderson spent the morning with Tom Haynes, his former high school principal, getting squared away to pursue his career in Architecture. Mr. Haynes had begun this conversation with David the same way he had begun every conversation throughout their tempestuous relationship. "Does your dad know about this?"

David had been working on curbing his sarcasm since his surrender to the Lord a couple of months previously.

"I guess he kind of does. I've been bouncing so many ideas off of him that I probably have him confused. If you're wondering, I don't know if I'm called to preach."

"Okay, why Architecture? No use in my setting all this up, and your spending your money, if it's just a whim. It's a pretty tough course with lots of competition once you get your degree."

Tom Haynes usually had a feel for the students he mentored! What their interests were, their academic strengths. David possessed the IQ for anything, something which helped him coast lazily through his high school career. Now, studying his high school transcript, Haynes could see that David had never taken any of the drafting classes offered by the small school.

His gaze met that of the young man seated across the battered desk.

David leaned forward, his dark eyes intense. He didn't want to try to sound spiritual for the man who chaired the deacon board at Faith Baptist. Sometimes he just felt worn out from always having to explain himself.

"I know, I've wanted to be everything! Policeman, fireman, coach! Those kind of top guys' lists; don't they? Oh yeah, and a fighter pilot, too, off a carrier!" He laughed before continuing.

"Since Patrick O'Shaughnessy's little talk with me, I've been doing some soul-searching. His talk was from *Proverbs 9*, about choosing either the wise path, or the path of the simpleton; about wasting the life God gives you, chasing things you think will make you happy, but that just squander the time and gifts the Lord gives you. So, I've been begging the Lord to show me His will."

Tears sprang to his eyes. "When Martin Thomas died, I realized I was a terrible Christian in front of him. I know the Lord wants to build me into a better Christian before He can use me in ministry. I don't know why, but I love the site plats and blueprints for the various building projects I've inherited." He laughed, telling Mr. Haynes how he felt like a big-shot, bringing the drawings to school, unrolling them in the cafeteria, he and Tammi showing off.

Haynes listened intently, his fingers steepled in his usual posture. He nodded.

"Then, all of the really ancient buildings in Turkey were amazing to me. Those city walls in Istanbul! Here, there's a trend to tear down stadiums and buildings that are more than fifty years old." He laughed again, his intense, dark eyes sparkling as he warmed to his subject. "I don't think I want to try to build the world's, next, tallest skyscraper, necessarily. I think it would be interesting to help restore Venice from the onslaught of time, or the Tower of London. Or even help save buildings from America's heritage." He finished by mentioning the Antonio Fortress in Jerusalem, solid after more than two thousand years!

"Okay, David, I'm sold. Sell your dad. I'll research everything out and have you ready to go, once I hear from him."

David rose to his feet, extending his right hand across the desk. "Yes, Sir," he responded evenly. "Thank you for your time."

Haynes continued to sit at his desk for long moments after David's boot steps died away. It only took him a few minutes to access a course of study. He figured he would be hearing from his pastor fairly soon.

David hopped into his truck, amazingly good-natured. If Architecture was truly God's will for his life, he should get his dad's opinion and blessing. As he headed toward the church, his phone rang.

"David," he answered. Caller ID told him it was Kerry Larson. "What's up, Larson?" he questioned.

"Well, I just got off the phone with Mallory. She nailed Herb Carlton down to become her master jeweler to get their jewelry designs into production as soon as possible. She used a pretty ingenious scheme. I mean, for a seventeen year old! She is catching onto everything fast."

David listened, always starved for information about her, but then worrying about everything he heard, too.

When David didn't respond, Kerry continued. "Guess Carlton's hold-up was whether he would need to sell the pawn shop. You know how most of corporate America is." He paused again.

"Guess, I don't, Larson. This is David Anderson! If you aren't talking about Murfreesboro High School's football offense, I'm probably not following you."

Larson laughed. "Sorry, you sound like me a few years back. I'm from a little town, too, and football was my life. Well, what I meant by Corporate America, in this context, was the way they treat employees. I mean some are better than others with their benefits, but most wouldn't tolerate a guy like Herb wanting to hang onto anything as demanding as his shop is. Most don't encourage any 'moonlighting' at all. So, Mallory actually didn't hire him as a DiaMo employee. She asked me set him up with an attorney and CPA, to form his own corporation. Then her corporation will contract with his corporation for the jewelry manufacture. The paper work was a little convoluted, since DiaMo already built the manufacturing plant. Carlton rents the facility from Mallory, but he hires all his own employees. DiaMo funded some of Carlton's startup costs for the incorporation, professional fees, and everything, in return for a small share of Carlton's stock"

David was relieved the plan wasn't too complex for him to follow. The plan was pretty amazing. Carlton's store would show more profit with the extra deductions allowed by incorporating. Then, he was bound to build earnings from making the jewelry designs.

"She instructed me to find an attorney and CPA for you in Little Rock, to turn you and your endeavors into a corporation, too. Be easier to do in a couple of months when you turn eighteen, although a surprising number of CEO's are younger than eighteen."

David chuckled to himself. Evidently Mallory was at work to keep the taxman from getting too much of the salary she was sending him. Astounding! Maybe he wouldn't mind having a corporation own *El Capitan*! As long as he owned the corporation!

⊰ ⊱

By Wednesday morning, Cassandra's absence had settled heavily on her brother and sister. Alexandra burst into tears when she realized her mother was planning an excursion to Dallas with Mallory.

Daniel, planning to golf, but feeling his own pain, and everyone else's, forsook the idea. He sent Alexandra to Dallas with the girls and headed out with Jeremiah to spend some guy time.

Diana carried a small portfolio of some of her jewelry sketches, humming softly as they alit from the chopper to enter the secured jewelry facility. Herb Carlton was there ahead of them, smiling, welcoming them with coffee and a light brunch. Once again, he had been unable to lose his two shadows. Merc and Samuel both stepped forward to shake hands with Mallory, meeting Diana and Alexandra for the first time.

All three men were amazed by Diana! She looked positively stunning in a sunny-yellow, silk suit. Her little girl showed a marked resemblance, surveying them through serious, gray eyes. Filling plates with the appealing food, they entered the conference room. Herb took his place diffidently at the head of the table.

"First employee you need should probably be a secretary," Mallory laughed, glancing around. "We really need minutes for this meeting."

Since Merc was secretary for his motorcycle club, he volunteered. Noticing his heavy tattoos, Diana wasn't too surprised he was a bike enthusiast.

The first order of business was the CDAs (Confidential Disclosure Agreements). They surveyed some pretty standard ones, prepared by Kerry, and the three men signed. This completed, Diana faxed copies to her attorney in Tulsa. Since he was out of the country, one of the partners returned an approval within a few minutes. Then all three parties signed contracts with *Carlton Jewelers, Inc.*, hammering out the details for the production and delivery of the jewelry designed by Diana and Mallory.

The food grew cold as they eagerly shared their ideas: the sparrows, the chess-pieces, the *Topkapi Dagger*, the crowns, the 'Wise-woman' house and children charms, the Nativity pieces. Those were the designs that had been percolating the longest. Herb took Diana's sketches, making them more specific yet, indicating which gemstones would be set where, what size stones to order. He frowned at the sketches of Dinky. The dog was whimsical, to say the least. This job was going to be more fun than he had ever imagined any job could be! And they were fronting the money, taking most of the risk. Although, he was determining, then and there, to be successful for his sake, his family's sake, and theirs also.

At one o'clock, they broke, refilling their plates with warmer food, going back to brainstorming. Their shyness forgotten, they were really melding into a team. Samuel had opened his lap top, miraculously inputting the designs, making them so they rotated for a perspective on all planes.

With Diana's sketches turning from flat to 3-D, Mallory brought out photographs. Carlton laughed. Looked like he was going to have job security. They had enough ideas jumping to work him into his eighties! That was without his own ideas, forming in his mind for many, many years.

The girl's pictures were cute. There was a close-up of a pansy, evidently a new hybrid. Herb had noticed them in the early-spring flower beds. Delicate orange. Mallory wanted a lapel pin in orange stones. Padparadscha sapphires and Madeira Citrines, with bright lemon quartz stem and leaf, interchangeable to wear as an Omega slide. It would be beautiful. Merc pulled a picture from deeper in the stack. It was a proud "duck" family; the bright Drake leading his little household, the drab female with the little ducklings in a row.

Merc liked 'bikes', of course. But he was a lover of anything motorized or mechanized. Anything with working parts captivated him. He wasn't bad with old clocks and watches. He began drawing the 'duck' family, showing how the proud papa could be made to strut, one of the wings flapping, almost imperceptibly, and the duckling on the end swinging its little tail feathers.

Diana forgot about all his weird tattoos. If he could mechanize the jewelry-!

Excited, she began to remind them about Carl Faberge, the last Imperial jeweler to the Russian Romanov dynasty just before the Communist revolution swept them from power to their illegal executions.

Carlton's gaze met hers. He was very familiar with Faberge! He couldn't believe he was finally in an arena where he could be supplied with gold and gems to create masterpieces that could last a very long time. The jewelry chess pieces he created would far outwear the clothing line they were designed to coordinate with.

Diana just shrugged. "So be it!"

They all spent the afternoon engrossed. Herb was making piece by piece illustrations of the pieces that would make the sparrow. He liked Mallory's plan for making exquisite, expensive pieces, but also making more reasonable knock-offs of their own designs. The little sparrow would become available in eighteen karat yellow gold with pavéd Chocolate,

Champagne, and gray Diamonds; yellow and orange Sapphires for the little beak. Replicas would be available in sterling with Smoky Quartz, and Citrines.

Merc dissected the 'duck family' into pieces that would be moveable.

Herb loved the softly orange pansy, but he drew a diagram for the lovely purple and yellow blossoms, too, illustrating it glowing with deep and pale Amethysts, and yellow Sapphires. It was gorgeous. Diana drew a white dress with a pansy print border to wear with the yellow silk jacket she was wearing. Carlton admitted it would look cute with the pin shimmering from the lapel.

The creativity was interrupted by Diana's phone. Daniel! Time had really gotten away!

"Hi, Honey," she answered apologetically. "We didn't realize how late it is." As she answered, she was realizing she couldn't get back to Tulsa in time for church.

"Where are you?" Daniel questioned. "We're at Mallory's office! Marge said you were meeting somewhere else. I brought Jeremiah to Dallas, too. I called Pastor to tell him we're out of town. Thought maybe we could tag along with Mallie and Kerry at their church tonight."

Diana's expression registered relief. People at Honey Grove Baptist in Tulsa would find out soon enough about Cassandra's being gone. She realized that she and Daniel were neither one ready to start fielding questions about the situation.

"Sit tight in Mallory's office! We'll knot up this meeting and see you in a few minutes. Love you! Good thing you called when you did"

Hanging up, she explained their plan to Mallory, who nodded agreement.

Samuel spoke up, "Do you mind if dad and I come to your church, too? We don't have time to get back to Hope, either."

"Well, don't leave me out," Herb added indignantly. "I'm trying to learn more about Jesus too, you know."

They all crowded into one of the large SUV's for the ride to Mallory's office, then phoned Daniel to meet them, instead, at a restaurant.

Mallory's phone vibrated, and she checked caller ID. Lana Anderson! Her former pastor's wife never called her. Her first thought was a quick panic that something was wrong with David. Then, she knew it wasn't that. If something happened, Pastor would call. Lana would be too much of a basket case! She didn't answer, knowing that word must have reached the

Andersons about Cassandra. She didn't want to talk about it with anyone! But certainly not with Diana and Alexandra right beside her.

Even as their large party settled in at a table, Mrs. Anderson continued texting and phoning. Finally, Mallie turned it off.

"Who's trying to call you?" Daniel questioned curiously. As her guardian, he trusted her, but checking never hurt.

"Mrs. Anderson," she admitted. "She never calls me, and she isn't a gossip, but I figure she's heard some of the story about Cassandra and wonders what I know". Even as she responded, it made it sound like Mrs. Anderson was a gossip.

Daniel nodded miserably. "Even if you're not a gossip, this one's probably hard to pass up."

Mallory laughed in spite of herself. "Well you guys are so perfect, and rich, and have it so together. I guess people like to hope you don't really. It isn't very nice, but I guess it's really the way people can be. The Andersons are good parents; Mrs. Anderson's a good mom. She probably thinks she would have known how to handle Cassandra."

"I wonder how they could have heard anything already," Diana interjected. "She probably wants to talk to you about something entirely different."

Alexandra's eyes filled with tears. "Mom, I called Janni about it," she confessed. "I'm sorry. I shouldn't have talked about our family stuff."

Daniel started to respond sternly, but Diana caught his eye.

"She promised she wouldn't say anything to anybody! I shouldn't have trusted her," Alexandra's voice was more heart-broken than ever.

"It's okay that you talked to your friend, Alexandra." Diana's voice was always sweet, so caressing when she spoke her children's names. "She probably didn't break your confidence. John and Lana could have heard about it from any number of other sources. We don't know for sure what Lana wants to talk about, anyway. Give your friend the benefit of the doubt. I don't mind your talking to your friends, either. God gives us friends to help us through life's ups and downs. Daddy and I have been praying for the Lord to give you a good friend. We know you have a few friends in our church that are okay, but we really like Janni and all the Andersons."

Mallie was amazed. The Faulkners were wise parents. They didn't just get mad and scream at Alexandra for talking, but counseled her wisely on the value of friendship. At that moment the Lord gave Mallory peace about

Cassandra. They were as together as they seemed, and God and her daddy had brought them into her life.

At church, Kerry greeted Mallory and her visitors, taking them all to introduce to Pastor and Mrs. Ellis. The service was good. Alexandra went to the junior high department and Jeremiah to *Master's Club*. Kerry could hardly stand it that Cassandra wasn't with them. After the service, he pulled Daniel aside.

"Look, Kerry, I told you yesterday that I don't want to talk to anyone about it yet." Daniel's voice sounded more tired than it did defensive.

"Have you talked to her since she got there?" Kerry was usually too intimidated by the guy to push him, but Carmine's concerns had eaten him up for the past twenty-four hours. He just wanted to know how the phone calls and e-mails were working out.

Daniel's gaze met his, agonized. "No, we haven't talked to her. I called the number; it rang endlessly. E-mails wouldn't send to the address."

"So, basically, she's been abducted."

Kerry's blunt summation brought tears to the other man's eyes.

"That's drastic, Larson. Don't make any waves." Daniel strode away to catch up to his family.

When Mallory invited the Faulkners to spend the night, they agreed readily. Cassandra's absence shouted at them: from her empty place at their table, and from her deserted bedroom-suite. Mallory's home would be a respite from the acute memories in their own home. And, for some reason, they drew strength from Mallory.

Finally alone in her suite, Mallory phoned Lana Anderson back. If Lana knew anything about Cassandra, she didn't mention it. She was excited about everything the Lord had done for her. The beautiful new home being built, the new cars, her husband's expanded ministry. And Pastor Anderson had surprised her with a full length mink coat!

Mallory didn't rest well. She had a lot on her mind. For one thing, she wasn't tearing it up with her schoolwork. Getting the contract with Herb was gratifying, and the previous day with the jewelry designs had been awesome. The violin lesson had been interesting, but Cassandra's departure had overshadowed that. Her wrist still hurt, even immobilized, and she figured she should start praying for it to get better. Maybe her assumption was wrong that 'time would heal all wounds', or at least the doctor could. She should have prayed when she first hurt it.

Her talk with Lana had been strange, too. One good thing about talking to her was that she couldn't keep quiet about David, so Mallory received all the updates. She was glad to find out whatever she could, but she was actually trying not to think about him all the time. Seemed he was suddenly interested in violin, but he didn't have an injured wrist. She slept fitfully and was up early. Janice joined her for the early morning laps in the pool. She was wearing a cover-up, having her devotions on the terrace, when her houseguests joined her.

All wearing the same things from the day before, Diana without make-up, Daniel all stubbly.

Mallory moved her Bible and notebook to make room for them at the table. "I have lots to learn about being a hostess! You fixed a suite for me with everything I might need for a week. I'm sorry I haven't thought of doing that for you all."

She was genuinely ashamed of herself.

"Well, we don't have to move in with you. We love for you to come to Tulsa, and with the lesson every week, we thought it would be easier for you to spend the night occasionally if you didn't have to keep a bag packed." Diana smiled as she spoke! She was gorgeous, even without her make-up. Her hair was pulled back into a cute ponytail.

Mallory nodded. "It might be nice, though, if it worked both ways. I still have plenty of guest room, even if you kind of make that area your own. I'd love it!" She felt shy, insisting.

Diana hesitated, then laughed suddenly. "Okay, then, you're stuck with us. Do you mind if I call my shopper to get some of our stuff delivered today?"

"I would be delighted beyond words." Mallory was drinking her usual white coffee. Maria refilled her mug as breakfast appeared.

Diana was on the phone to one of her assistants, giving directions to purchase duplicates of the products they used at home, and to bring various clothing items from their Tulsa mansion.

Taking a mug of steaming coffee with him, Daniel went back inside to call his dad. It was a call he was dreading. He hadn't gone into the GeoHy office for the past two days, and he hadn't spoken with his father, as to the reason for his absence. Not that he really worked for his dad. His dad had nearly been in retirement from the firm until his conversion earlier in the spring. Daniel was dreading telling his father about their decision regarding Cassandra.

Daniel Jeremiah Faulkner, Jr, answered his cell. "Wondered when I was going to hear from you," he began.

I know, Dad," Daniel responded. "I should have called you Tuesday. Things really came to a head with Cassandra Monday night. I mean, I know she's just little…" His voice trailed off miserably.

"Little, but smart as a whip! Not just with her instrument, although that's amazing. But at reading people! Conning them to get her way. Most grown-ups haven't learned to manipulate situations and people like that little girl. She must have gotten that from you. Diana's nice."

Relieved, Daniel laughed. From the time Diana had come from Africa with him to be his wife, his mom and dad hadn't liked her. Well, she had upset their applecart. The established and respected Geological company was suddenly topsy-turvy as the heir-apparent received Christ, then turned against the atheistic slant to become a Creationist. Getting his dad mocked by the 'academic' crowd hadn't set too well. Amazingly, though, the company grew and prospered more with the new viewpoint. With American oil companies suffering hit after hit, some companies had suffered terrible losses, many going under. GeoHy was presently in the best shape it had ever been in. Hearing his dad tell him Diana was nice, was gratifying to him.

His dad was continuing on, "Mom and I are just kind of curious about the details. I mean, I guess we're hurt that you didn't even tell us you were negotiating with the great symphony orchestras of the world."

"Well, Dad, we weren't really negotiating with anyone. Diana and I talked about the way things were going, and we've prayed a lot." Tears reflected in his voice once more. "The only way to get Cass's attention was to confiscate her violin, but then we felt like that was cruel and unusual punishment." His voice reflected their anguish as parents.

"Well, you know, all the answers are in one incredible, slim Volume." His dad's voice was teasing, but Daniel wasn't sure what he meant. He knew he was quoting Mallory's words, wondering how his dad saw the interview.

"You mean we should have just spanked more?"

"No, no. That's not what I mean at all. I mean it's all harder than it looks; it's always clearer what other people should do, than what we should do with our own problems. The Bible is the Answer Book. Well, what happened when you prayed? How did my granddaughter end up in Israel?"

"Well, like I said, Monday night turned into the worst nightmare, yet. Mallory was spending the night, but Cassie didn't even care what Mallory thought. When we finally got her in bed, we talked and prayed until late.

We've known that we needed to find another teacher to take Cassandra farther. You know, she started playing, almost before she could talk. So, she had her own vocabulary, her own language about everything. Then, she'd ask Diana, or me, or *the Maestro* questions about her made up stuff, then fall apart that we couldn't answer her questions. Well, in Tulsa, *the Maestro's* the best there is, so we've thought about Diana's moving someplace else with Cass part of the time, because we want to develop our children's gifts and abilities. We figured we could all be together on week-ends. But, then, it didn't seem fair for Al and Jer to be deprived of their mom; they need her, too. And Diana has her design business. Which, she's willing to sacrifice all that, for the kids." Daniel was pouring out his story to his dad's sympathetic ear like he hadn't done for years. Well, his dad's salvation had broken down the wall between them, for one thing. He continued. "Evidently the scenario was traumatic for Cassandra, too. She was praying for some *violin people* to come for her. She got up Tuesday morning, wanted Diana to dress her all up in her dress she wore for Easter Sunday. Dad, it was awful. Sometimes, she wouldn't eat or drink. We've wondered if her being so gifted was making her crazy. Don't tell anyone this, Dad. Don't tell all of it to mom. Well, Tuesday morning I made waffles, and she really packed the food away. Then she wanted to get saved if that would make her prayer get answered about people coming for her. So, she asked Jesus into her heart—"

'That's wonderful!" Jerry broke in.

"I hope it is, Dad. Again, she was figuring an angle, even with God, to get her way. She finished breakfast, then just sat in the security room, focused on the monitor of the front gate. Before noon, this lady from Israel showed up, knowing everything about us. Not sure who talked to her. Or if it was just the Lord." Sobs broke forth. "And Cassandra couldn't wait to go with her! To get away from us."

"Easy, Son. She's driven by her talent! That's not a bad thing. Don't take it more personally than it is. I haven't told you this. I'm not sure why." Now his dad was weeping. "You and Diana are the greatest! And your kids. No one could make two people prouder than your mom and I are of all of you. I feel strangely that Cassandra is exactly where she needs to be."

Daniel was relieved beyond words. Evidently the Lord was answering the many dimensions of their impassioned plea. Daniel knew everyone wouldn't understand or agree with their decision, but it was a real load off of him to have his father's understanding.

"Thanks, Dad. You don't know how much you've encouraged me. We're in Dallas at Mallory's for a couple of days. See you by Sunday."

"Yeah, Son, take care. Hope we see you at church Sunday; we missed you last night."

"Missed you, too. We went to Mallie and Kerry's church. Al went in the junior high department, if you can believe it. She still likes Tommy Haynes. All this is scary to me."

"Yeah, it should be. Makes you realize you need the Lord. Not sure how I felt so confident I could make it without Him all those years. Go eat breakfast, Son."

Daniel returned to the breakfast out on the terrace, loading his plate eagerly. Diana came up behind him, clasping him around his waist. "Where did you disappear to? "she inquired, her lilting voice laughter-filled.

He turned to face her, hugging her to him. "Talking to my dad. He's so much different since he got saved. He and mom are proud of us. They're really proud of Cassandra and her talent. They think she'll be okay, and that she's where she'll be the happiest. He said not to take it personally that she was so eager to leave home." It was still hard for him to say it without crying.

❧ ❦

Herb Carlton was busy making phone calls. He knew countless people who were frustrated workmen like himself. People doing whatever jobs they could nail down to earn a salary to support themselves and their families. As stymied and frustrated as many of them were, they weren't eager to leap into the unknown with his new company. He didn't blame them. He had practically missed out, gripped by fear and indecision. He guessed he would have to learn a lesson from Mallory. He sent each of them applications for his new corporation. With handling such valuable supplies, their backgrounds would really need to check out. He promised not to jeopardize their current positions with his inquiries, trying to coax some of the talented craftsmen and women he knew, into starting part-time, working around their permanent jobs. He knew they would love what he was doing if he could get them started.

He didn't know anyone with secretarial skills. Except for Suzanne Bransom, of course. Since he didn't want to fight Erik or Roger for her, he figured he should try to think of someone else. Mallory was right, a good secretary from the get-go was going to be a necessity. Good people were going to be hard to find, and he said so to Merc and Samuel.

"Grandpa, we should pray for a secretary, and for the Lord to lead us to all the right workers. That's what Pastor told me and mom. It works." Samuel's voice was so different for the past few weeks.

Herb didn't know; his disbelief etched on every feature.

Unabashed, Samuel bowed his head and asked the Lord to send *Carlton Jewelers* a secretary.

One thing the CEO's had in common was their knowledge that they couldn't run their companies single-handedly. Good, loyal people were an extremely valuable commodity.

And that was what had brought Lilly Cowan from Israel to Tulsa, Oklahoma!

Chapter 12: WICKEDNESS

Ephesians 5:12 For we wrestle not against flesh and blood, but against principalities, against powers, against the rulers of the darkness of this world, against spiritual wickedness in high places.

Erik Bransom continued to pursue all of the cases that came across his desk, his new-found faith refiring him to fight wickedness on every front that presented itself, both as an FBI agent, but also as a Christian man. And, he was learning to leave the results to the people whose responsibility they were. He couldn't follow every prosecutor to make sure they performed according to his expectations. If they made plea bargains he hated, or lost cases he thought they should have won, if culprits got off on paper errors, he needed to continue doing the best he could do.

He admired Col. Ahmir, his Turkish counterpart. In some ways, he envied the guy his power and authority. But when he thought about it, he basically preferred the American justice system even with its faults and loopholes. Sighing, he worried about the problem that had sent him to John Anderson's study in April: the concern that the fiber of America's character seemed to be deteriorating rapidly!

He was seated at the kitchen table of their small apartment. He had started a pot roast, to be ready when Suzanne came in from work. Wednesday afternoon, they would share a delicious, if hasty, meal; before heading up to Murfreesboro for church. He checked on the concoction; carrots and potatoes, tender and appealingly brown. Smelled good. He removed it from the oven to slide in a pan of crescent dinner rolls. Not as fancy as the Faulkners' gourmet cooking, but not bad. He tore lettuce up for a salad and poured iced tea.

Suzanne arrived, turning her cheek for an affectionate peck, before she took the range over to make brown gravy from the roast's drippings.

"Smells good. I'm hungry. Thanks for having all this ready. How was your day? Have you heard from anybody?"

"My day was great. Guess Collins and Summers are still an item. She told him that Cassandra Faulkner's been sent to Israel to join the orchestra there. He called me up about it. Wanted to know my opinion, and I told him it's none of his or my business. Thing is, he thinks the woman convinced Daniel and Diana to sign a bogus contract of some kind. Collins thinks the child's basically been abducted, but Daniel's telling everyone not to get stirred up and make waves. I like Daniel and Diana, but I'd like to know if a crime's been committed."

Suzanne stared at him in shocked silence, having a really hard time processing the unbelievable information. She couldn't think of anything to say, and he had kind of answered any questions she might have come up with. She started to speak, then just closed her mouth, basically speechless.

"Gravy's ready." She placed the food into serving dishes, arranging it on the small kitchen table as Erik shoved some of his files out of the way.

He took her hand, "Well, let's pray." He bowed, thanking the Lord for the food, asking Him to bless the church service and whatever was going on with Cassandra.

They were both kind of quiet while they ate. Erik dished some ice cream and poured coffee, then, as he sat down for the dessert, his phone rang. His caller ID told him it was the youngest of his three daughters.

He couldn't decide whether to jump and run guiltily from the table, or talk to his child in Suzanne's hearing. He had never told her about his girls, or his previous marriage.

Shooting her an apologetic glance, he answered, "Hi Charity, what can I do for you?"

She was crying. He never knew what to say to women when they cried. Hearing his distressed child was no exception. He was immediately filled with alarm. He still wanted to dash for the breezeway, out of Suzanne's hearing. He should have talked to her about his past before this.

His anguished gaze met her wide, blue eyes.

She reached for his phone. "Hi Charity. My name's Suzanne. You need to stop crying a little, and tell us what's wrong."

The pitiful voice didn't demand to get her dad back, but tearfully poured her story out to Suzanne.

Finally, Suzanne responded reassuringly. "I know it's upsetting to you, but lots of babies get chronic ear infections and need to have tubes put in."

Erik reached for his phone back. He didn't even know his little girl had a baby. He didn't know if she was married or not. Now, he did leave the table.

"Okay, Charity, why are you calling me? I never got a birth announcement, or anything, to let me know I'm a grandpa. What, you need money now? So you can make a phone call?"

"Well, when have you ever called me?" she shot back.

"Your mom told me to leave you all alone. I've sent y'all all my money since we broke up. I've hardly kept anything for myself. Enough for an apartment and a little drinking money. Which, I don't need the drinking money any more since I quit drinking."

He paused; he should tell her his whole testimony, but he figured she'd laugh.

"Well, okay, sorry I bothered you."

"W-w-w-wait! Don't hang up! I'm sorry, Honey, can we start this over? Tell me what you need."

He talked to her in the living room as Suzanne cleaned the kitchen, then freshened her make-up. She picked both of their Bibles from beneath the stacks of files on the table, motioning that they needed to head toward church.

He was relieved. She didn't seem mad. He hoped she wouldn't be.

Charity and her husband, Terry, were both working jobs, trying hard to take care of their responsibilities. The baby was costing more than they anticipated.

Bransom refrained from saying, "You ain't seen nothin' yet," listening sympathetically, glad she was married, anyway.

"Okay, so what's the bottom line?" he questioned, dreading the answer.

Her little voice was filled with worry and tears, "Five hundred dollars. That will take care of the rest of her deductible. I'm sorry, Daddy. Our credit cards are over the limits, and we don't know what else to do."

His spirit soared. To her, five hundred was practically as huge as five million! It would have been a bomb dropped on him just a few months earlier, too.

He glanced over at his beautiful new wife. They were about to head up 278 toward church, but she was indicating a place where they could stop and wire money. He pulled in, hopping nimbly from the Jaguar.

"Okay, Honey, I'm wiring the money now. Keep in touch if you can, without making your mom mad. I love you."

"Thank-you, Daddy." She didn't repeat the "I love you, too." thing.

Back in the car, he faced Suzanne defensively, but then, he was at a loss for words. Talk wasn't his strong point, at best. "Guess I should have told you," he mumbled.

She reached over and patted his hand on the steering wheel. "Why? I didn't ask. It's not like you lied to me, or anything. I figured you had probably been married before. You can tell me as much as you want. I'm interested, but really, it's in the past. How old's Charity? You didn't know she was married?"

He was adding and subtracting mentally, trying to remember when his youngest daughter's birthday was. "She must be, maybe, twenty-two. Nah, If there was a wedding, I wasn't invited. Guess I have a son-in-law named Terry Hanson, and a granddaughter named Maribeth. Didn't think to ask for a picture."

Suzanne picked his phone up from the console cup-holder and sent a text to the last call received, "We want 2 c a pic of Maribeth."

Within a couple of minutes, his phone received the image, taken on the spot, of a smiling baby in a bouncy-chair.

Tears rushed to his eyes! Cutest kid he'd seen since Charity was little. Suzanne texted back the appropriate compliments, thanking Charity for sending it.

The Faith Baptist crowd was gathering, and there was a congenial buzz. David waved and headed toward them. Suzanne hugged him, and Erik slapped him on the back before they headed to a pew. The big mirror was gone from the back wall, and there was plenty of evidence that the remodeling project was getting underway.

"What's new?" Erik asked the teen when they were seated. David knew about Cassandra, and he wondered what the FBI agent knew, but his dad had sworn him to silence.

"I probably don't know anything that all your eyes and ears haven't reported to you about already," David replied amicably. "Mr. Haynes has my college career lined up for me, as soon as I convince my dad it's what I should do."

Erik grinned. "Your dad isn't your enemy, y'know, Cowboy. If it's what you should do, he won't be against it. He should be proud of you if you get yourself ready to do any honest job. That's the main thing. You think he'll be disappointed if you don't turn into a preacher?"

"I'm not sure. He's always so busy, it's hard to catch up with him for serious conversations."

"Well, I'll call him and make an appointment with him for you. He can probably work you in." The agent's droll expression reminded the teenager that lots of losers made dumb excuses. Without a doubt, the seasoned agent had heard them all.

David laughed. Erik was right. It wasn't his dad's fault that they hadn't had the conversation. "Ya got me!" he admitted.

Lana paused on her way to the piano to ask the FBI agent if John could have a word with him after the service. He agreed, but then he was nervous, wondering if his pastor was upset that he hadn't mentioned his first marriage to any of them. No wonder he made David nervous. He really felt like the Bible Study was directed right at him. Following the invitation, he accompanied John to his small study.

He hadn't been into the tiny area since the afternoon in April when he got saved.

"What's on your mind, Pastor?" He sank into the folding chair across from the desk.

"Monday night, Lana and I went out to see how our new house is progressing. We were wandering all over, checking everything out. Just as I was helping Lana back into the car, I realized someone was trespassing, watching us. Maybe I'm paranoid, but I'm pretty sure of it. I didn't think my family was going to need security people like the Faulkners have, but I don't want them exposed to danger."

"Monday night!" Bransom was trying not to explode. "And you decided to casually mention it if I showed up for church in a couple of days? You should have called me right then. Trespassing's against the law. If it was just a transient, you don't want him moving into your new house before you do. It's probably some connection with your former sheriff, so you shouldn't call the locals. I'll have agents out there right away, but if someone left any evidence, it's had a couple of days to degrade. You probably do need private security, at least as long as the Maloviches are out there. If we could get them in prison to stay, you could reassess the threat. You see anything again, don't wait." He was already making the call, ordering agents to the building site. "You need to come out there with me, show me where you were, where you thought you saw somebody!" He was moving toward the door.

Apologetically, he asked Suzanne if she minded going home with Lana while he and pastor went to meet other agents at the site of the new home. He would have felt bad about stranding her, even if he hadn't just received the call from his daughter. He had been planning to use the trip home to make sure his new wife was okay. Now, he hoped she wouldn't be mad about that, and about spending half the night at the Anderson's while he spent the usual crazy hours his job always seemed to require.

Before they could reach the site, the heavens opened. Lightning flashed, then thunder shook them. Well, so much for that. He phoned his agents to cancel the investigation. There probably wouldn't have been anything to glean, anyway. Instead, he requested some surveillance on the Anderson family. Usually local enforcement took care of things like that, but with the disarray in the Pike County sheriff's office, Bransom didn't trust any of the locals. He called Ivan Summers to ask what the ABI could do to help safeguard the pastor and his family. Ivan promised to do what he could, which probably wouldn't be much.

"John, you're going to have to start carrying. Wouldn't hurt for your wife and Tammi to learn to handle a pistol, either. Post 'No Trespassing' signs along your property lines. Signs won't keep the bad guys out, but it may protect you better legally, if you have to shoot someone."

John Anderson nodded thoughtfully. If his family's safety was up to him, he'd handle it! They were his responsibility before God. He could tell that Erik was sad, though, to admit law enforcement was lagging behind on being able to provide the public with safety. Everyone's carrying their own weapons out of fear of everyone else who was armed, bordered more and more on the total anarchy the agent was trying to hold back.

The pastor decided he should research handgun licenses and their increasing numbers in the past few years. He was an ardent NRA member, but the anti-gun lobby had a point. Point or not: they were losing! The increasing lawlessness would make a powerful sermon illustration.

Chapter 13: *WAITING*

Mallory headed down her driveway just as Aunt Linda drove up. She flagged her down. Her aunt was a houseguest, but Mallory hadn't seen her much. She hopped out of her car, approaching her aunt.

"Are you busy right now?" Mallie questioned. "You have time to go for a coffee with me?"

"Yeah, sure." Linda's voice was uneasy, but Mallie pretended not to notice. Pulling her car back into the garage, she rejoined her aunt, and they headed back down the drive.

"What's up with you?" Mallory opened, breaking the silence. "Are you rested up from the trips yet? I wouldn't have dragged you along to Israel if I'd known you and Mr. Carlton were cooling down your relationship. Sorry about that. I must have made it awkward for you. What happened? Can you tell me? I mean, it's probably none of my business."

Linda pulled into a parking space. When they were seated with their beverages, she responded.

"I'm not sure what happened." She was trying not to cry. "I guess I'm just not very good at playing this game. I never was."

Mallory sat perplexed. "What game are you talking about?"

"You know," Linda's voice was bitter. "The dating game. Personal relationships! It's all so hard. You scolded me for hiding in books, but it wasn't half-bad."

"Well, then, get another library job, and live the second half of your life the way you did the first half. Get a couple more cats and go for it. What happened with Mr. Carlton? It isn't a game, anyway! How you treat people! It's just the Golden Rule! Even if people don't respond back the way they should, God still blesses you for trying to treat people right."

121

Linda surveyed her niece, amazed. Absolutely gorgeous, her hazel eyes, steady and honest. How could a seventeen year old girl be so put together?

"I don't know what happened. When we got back from Turkey, I stayed here so I wouldn't be quite so far away from him. You know! If he wanted to pursue anything."

"Yeah, go on." Mallory took a sip. She had lots to do, and she and her aunt weren't really on the same page.

"He asked if he could call me sometime, so I said, 'Yes, sometime, but maybe we should back away'."

Mallie choked on her coffee. "Well, that must have hurt his feelings. You didn't act like you wanted to back away. Why did you say that?"

"Well, you know, it never hurts to play it cool."

Mallory nodded mutely. She kind of understood. She guessed she had sometimes tried the same thing with David. Some of the time, it had put them at cross purposes.

"Well, did you mean it when you said that? Were you really wanting him to back off?"

Linda burst into tears. "No! I just thought it was kind of what you're supposed to say. I didn't want him to think I'm desperate."

"Well, Aunt Linda, you aren't desperate. You have lots to offer in a relationship. Even without a man, you're totally able to fend for yourself. Admitting you're in love does make you vulnerable, but I don't think Mr. Carlton's playing any games or wanting to hurt you. He doesn't seem to be the lady-killer type."

Linda laughed through the tears. "So, I did say he could call me sometime, and he hasn't called at all."

"Well, you're not a couple of kids. Maybe he doesn't want to play games, wants to be serious with someone nice that's just honest, straightforward, and easy to read. Have you considered asking Jesus into your heart. You really need Him more than you need romance."

"Well, I guess I've thought about it. The main thing Herb and I had in common, though, was holding out against you Christians. I've probably overstayed my welcome as your houseguest. Maybe I'll look for an apartment."

Mallie laughed. "Don't think you've done that. I've hardly known you were around. You can use the pool and be a little more in evidence. The Faulkners are staying for a couple of days, too. Herb has agreed to be the master jeweler for Diana's and my jewelry designs. He needs a secretary. Are you a secretary? I know you're a librarian."

Linda shrugged. "I took the same office courses in high school as your mom. I can file, answer phones, make coffee. Of course, I had to be familiar with office equipment at the library."

Mallie nodded. Her aunt had been careful not to be pinned down about the Lord. They finished their coffees, making small talk.

Finally, Mallory asked, "Aunt Linda, can you get free for about an hour Friday morning to do me a favor?"

⊰ ⊱

Herb and Merc had been working long hours, first making a prototype of the duck family, working on the individual pieces and the methods for connecting them together for the desired effect. Herb marveled at his son's calm after several failed attempts. People had nicknamed him 'Merc' due to his mercurial disposition. From mild to maniac in under sixty seconds. Now, he just continued to work intently, figuring he had gotten closer with each try. Finally, success! The payoff for staying at it! Now they could create the piece, first in silver, for practice, before working it in gold.

Herb had the stones assembled. He was using coated green Topaz for the Drake's head, less precious stones, but still lovely. The babies would be pavé of the brightest yellow Citrines he could find. Champagne and Smoky Quartz were the main stones for the mother. The gems were tiny, one millimeter, for the most part. The work was painstaking, but the two men loved it.

Herb's phone jangled on the workbench, causing him to jerk, launching one of the tiny stones across the room. Wouldn't be easy to find the miniscule gem. He grabbed the cell. Lilly, again.

"Mrs. Cowan. I guess you know I'm working as a jeweler again."

"Yes, Herbert! It's about time! Tell me where my rock is!"

Herb knew she meant Mallory's pink diamond. "Your rock? I'm not sure which rock you mean."

"Oh, Herbert, don't play coy with me! I'm not amused. Nice facility you have there! All the gold and silver being delivered. All the polished stones. Why are you a traitor to use that inferior stuff, Darling?"

Herb knew she meant the colored gemstones, as opposed to Diamonds. Lilly was about Diamonds, more than she was about jewelry. She certainly had no use for any of the other gemstones. She had already blasted Mallory

123

for competing against her own Diamond mine by favoring other gems as well. Herb understood Lilly's frame of reference, of course. His dream had always been to work with Gold and Diamonds.

"So many safes there! A thief's worst nightmare. You have to hand it to Miss O'Shaughnessy for being savvy."

"Yeah." Lilly was making him nervous. Her knowledge was uncanny. He felt like she knew the contents of all the safes, and knew that the pink, uncut diamond wasn't in any of them. He figured she must also have already been made aware of their top-secret sketches and projects.

"You haven't answered my question about the Diamond!" Herb grinned to himself. Evidently she was done with the 'pleasantries'. "Well, Mrs. Cowan, if I knew the answer, I'm not sure why you think I should divulge information like that to you."

"Be very careful, Herbert!" Claws in her strident tone nearly raked his ear off! He knew she was ruthless, but her change from cajoling to menacing still shook him.

"Like you said, Lilly, Darling! Miss O'Shaughnessy is very savvy! I don't know where it is! I haven't seen it since you have! Why don't you let the Faulkners talk to their daughter?"

"Nice speaking with you again, Herbert, Darling!" Her voice dripped venom, and she clicked off.

⚔ ⚔

David was busy. After an early morning flying lesson, he met his dad and Roger Sanders at the Hope Country Club for a golf game. He wanted a chance to be with his dad to talk about his career plan, but when he mentioned golf, his dad immediately called Roger. Way to get a free game. Sighing, David wished his dad could get out of the 'poor-preacher' mode.

The game was fun; he lost, of course, but this game was better than his previous attempts, so he hoped he was on his way to becoming a decent golfer. He needed to return to the camp property to shower and change before heading to a home-cooked meal with his family.

Ready to head out again, he had a few extra minutes. Always before, extra minutes meant a nap! Now, rather than catching a few *z*'s, he picked up his violin. Unexplainably, he loved it. He took the time to go through the pages of exercises. He liked his personable teacher; he was eager for the next lesson.

He headed his truck toward Murfreesboro, turning on the radio to catch the news and sports. Boo! Rangers lost. He pushed in a CD, turning the music up to enfold him. A piano arrangement played by one of Mallory's favorites. The arrangement was powerful, "How Big is God?", transitioning into 'How Great Thou Art"! David punched the button to replay the selection. Mallory had worked and worked to learn the arrangement, been planning it for an offertory when her next turn came! Then, before she could present it, she was overwhelmed by her father's sudden death! Well, sudden, to her. Evidently, Patrick had been aware he didn't have long. David had been hit hard, too, by the loss. Since second grade, Mr. O'Shaughnessy had practically been a second dad to him! He didn't know how to deal with his own grief, let alone help Mallory deal with hers! Now, he listened to the selection for a third time, praying for her wrist to heal properly. He wanted to be a talented family like the Faulkners! With himself and Mallory singing, playing violins, the piano. He couldn't stop worrying about Cassandra! His little sister, Melody, was nearly the same age.

Turning his music down, he speed-dialed Shay's number, drumming on the steering wheel impatiently, waiting for an answer. It was going to the 'record your message' routine when Shay called him back.

"David! What's up?" Shay's voice sounded upbeat. "Everything going okay out there in the Wild West?

"Guess so. The west only gets wild when you Bostonian-types show up. Otherwise, it's peace, tranquility, and boredom."

Shay laughed. "Not what I'm hearing. You think it was Oscar and Otto stalking your mom and dad the other night?"

David was alarmed. First he had heard about it.

"I just played a round of golf with my dad, and he didn't say a word about anything like that. What do you know, Shay?"

"That's about it. Where did you golf? I didn't know you were an enthusiast."

"Hope Country Club, with Roger. He didn't say anything about Emma, though."

"Did he say anything about me?" Shay's voice was anxious.

"Just that he bought a new shotgun to chase you off with!" David never could resist teasing.

"That's okay, Anderson!" Shay got mad as fast as Mallory did. "See if I tell you what I know!" He cut off.

Laughing, David didn't call back. If Shay really knew anything new and interesting about Mallory, he wouldn't be able to resist telling. He listened to his song through once more before Shay called back.

"Make it quick! I'm almost to the house, and my mom's cooking awaits.

"Well, this isn't anything funny. You ready for some new worries?"

"Shay, cut the suspense garbage."

"Well, Mallory killed some people in Iran, and the Iranian government wants our government to send her there to face charges!"

The truck nearly left the road! David struggled to get it back under control.

"That's not funny, Shay!"

"Yeah, Dude, I'm not trying to be funny. Well, no one here will send her, of course. But you know how the Iranians are! They'll try her in absentia, and issue a fatwa. They have operatives all over the world to hit enemies of their state!"

"Shay, I'm home. I'll catch ya later." He broke the connection as he reached the town limits. He slowed his truck, turning into the church parking lot. Inside the empty building, he knelt to pray. He was grateful the remodeling crew had already packed it up for the day so he could enjoy a few minutes of solitude.

That story was crazy! Mallory? Killing people? He didn't think so! His face clouded. All because he had failed to report to Erik, his concerns about that blue car!

Lana glanced at her firstborn in alarm as he walked in dazedly through the back door of the parsonage. His big brown eyes stood out starkly from a pallid, agonized face.

"David, sit down, Honey. Are you sick?"

"No Ma'am. I just can't get used to all this crazy stuff! Someone stalking you and dad around! Have you heard anything about Mallory killing a bunch of people?"

She removed garlic-toast from under the broiler and poured spaghetti sauce into a serving bowl.

"Go wash your hands," she ordered. "Supper's ready"

"I just got out of the shower."

Her look stopped him. "Yes, Ma'am," he sighed before complying with the command.

Once they were seated with the blessing said, Lana asked her son what he meant about stalkers and Mallory. Evidently, it was just starting to sink in with her.

John's glance squelched the topic. A lot of information the little kids didn't need to worry about. He changed the subject, conversing happily, mentioning they might be able to visit *Disney World* later in the year, when Florida's summer relented slightly. Their eyes all sparkled at the prospect. Even Jeff and Tammi acted excited.

"Are you coming too, David?" Jeff questioned anxiously. He had reached an age when his big brother was his hero.

" I hope, so, Jeff! Sounds really cool. When Dad nails down a date, I'll start arranging with Brad for him to be available when I'll be gone." He was trying to accomplish a great deal, but Patrick had planned for their entire family to vacation together. It would be a lot of fun.

David helped clear the table and start the dishwasher. That was when he divulged Shay's information to his mother in greater detail. Sometimes, it was easy to panic his mom, but she sat down at the empty kitchen table, meeting his agonized gaze.

"I know you get really worried about everything! You always have! You're a really caring kind of a guy. Guess that's what mixed you up with that crazy girl up in Dierks. Don't forget, David, God's still on the throne! Dad talked to Erik Bransom about the trespasser, so the Feds and ABI are both kind of watching out for us. We're having security follow us for awhile, too. At least as long as Melville and his brother are on the run. All of us are getting pistols and learning how to handle them. Your dad did buy me a mink coat."

She was trying not to cry. "He's worried that my owning a fur, will have eco-terrorists after me."

It was too much! Iranian terrorists after Mallie, Eco-terrorists after his mom! The world really was crazy! Usually he didn't pray for the Lord to come back. He wanted to live more of his life on good ole terra firma! Suddenly, the *Rapture* sounded pretty appealing to him.

His career choice conversation with his dad was almost an anti-climax. Evidently, Agent Bransom had helped clear the way a little bit. More than likely, the Lord did it.

His dad just put his arm around him and told him he was proud of him.

⫚ ⫛

Friday morning at eleven o'clock, twenty of Mallory's friends and associates entered twenty different banks, from the banking giants to the smallest, locally owned establishments. Each person used his DiaMo credit card to rent a safety deposit box. With paperwork completed, each one went through the motions of stowing a valuable item.

Hearing about it from her office in Tel Aviv sent Lilly Cowan into a rage. She would be able to check the contents of each box, but it would take until Monday or Tuesday. She hated that. "Savvy, indeed!" She surveyed the exteriors of the institutions in question, the DiaMo members entering, caught on security. All dutifully provided to her! Trying to read each face that appeared on video, she tried to pinpoint which bank housed the rosy-hearted diamond. None of the honest, transparent faces looked nervous enough. The diamond was still someplace else. But, she would have the boxes all checked, just to be certain.

****

Returning from the banking business to Mallory's, the Faulkners took up residence poolside. The slides and play park were fun for the kids. When Diana went inside to play Mallory's piano, Daniel sat weeping. Their agreement was to weep privately and rejoice publicly. So far, they had managed it. With his wife out of earshot, he punched the phone number once again. Interminable, uninterrupted ringing. He had allowed himself to count a hundred rings, before. Now, after twenty-five, he gave up. He sat praying that his little daughter was safe and happy.

His cell vibrated. His pastor. He didn't want to talk to him right now. Maybe he had found out, and was calling to bawl him out. He dropped his head into his hands, ignoring it.

It disconnected, before beginning to ring again. Reluctantly, he answered.

If his pastor had heard anything about Cassandra, he didn't mention it in the phone conversation. He just wanted to say the board had okayed him to invite the Faulkners to present a concert on Sunday.

Thoughts flooded his mind. How could they without Cassandra? Why now? His family had been members at *Honey Grove* for more than eight years. Diana was finally church pianist, but often it seemed that the entire membership barely tolerated them. They tried to be loyal and faithful, knowing they served the Lord. It was the best church in the area, but they had really never felt included.

He told his pastor he would find Diana, and they would talk about whether they could be ready in time for Sunday.

Finding her wasn't hard. She was pouring her heart out through the piano music, so he headed to the music room. He figured she'd be upset he had left his post as lifeguard. Returning poolside, he called her cell.

He could tell she was crying. When he told her about the invitation to perform, her first words echoed his first thought. "How can we, without Cassandra?"

She joined him in the pool enclosure. They had to do it! The Lord would sustain them with His mighty grace. It didn't seem possible, but if He opened doors, they would go through. Now, every time someone mentioned the Lord's opening doors, they remembered the hotel meeting room in Istanbul. They smiled at each other through their tears.

Mallory, laptop set up in the library, was busy with her course work. To her amazement, she was loving the independent study. In Chemistry, she was studying chemical bonding, outer covalent shells, and all that. Which sounded dull, until you could see exactly what the text was trying to explain.

Some of the colored stones Herb Carlton ordered were Corundum. Mallory was amazed to notice the gems had a Chemistry-looking name. The gorgeous Rubies, and all the various colors of Sapphires were Aluminum and Oxygen. Even remembering her amazement caused a lilting giggle to erupt. She had always heard about $NaCl$, common table salt, a compound of Sodium (poison in itself) and Chlorine (the same). When they bonded together, they formed the chemical compound that helped flavor many foods. Not a poison, although Nurse Diana preached against it.

Now, she considered the Aluminum pot that was always one of her mom's favorites. Mallory had taken it outside once, to play with. (She could still remember the spanking.) And Oxygen, the colorless, odorless gas necessary for all human and animal life. God used those two basic atoms, to bring little gems into being, usually where they would never even be seen by anyone but Him. Tears filled her eyes. That was so neat!

Diana appeared with her laptop under her arm, asking to join her.

"Please do," Mallie responded. "Can you work on your designs from here?"

"I suppose I could, but I thought I needed to get busy and get some trips lined up."

One of Daniel's secretaries usually made travel arrangements, but Diana needed the diversion. They couldn't really take a trip right now; they hadn't been back from Turkey for a month, yet. Travel to Israel wasn't working out, either. She guessed Carmine Henderson had foreseen that.

"What kind of trips?" Mallie responded.

"Well, Aspen in November and the big gem show in NYC in December. Actually, this should all have been reserved before this."

Mallory was shocked. In rural Arkansas, they always took one day at a time. Realizing flights and hotels got booked so far in advance was amazing to her.

They both continued working, pretty much in silence. Diana interrupted to consult about who Mallie thought should attend the gem show. It was a DiaMo Corporation trip, with the corporation picking up the tab.

Mallory laughed, "Well, me of course. And I hope I can see the *Statue of Liberty* this time. Then you and Daniel, and the kids. Wow, Xavier will be born by then! That's too cool! Will you have a nanny, or someone to help entertain the kids? Then Herb, and Merc, and Aunt Linda. Maybe a couple more jewelers, yet to be identified."

Diana laughed. Mallory was fun, and nice, to think of including the entire Faulkner family, and an extra staff member or two. Of course, their normal security would accompany them on both trips.

Daniel, finally shaved and cleaned up, seemed a little less sad. He came looking for them, just as they both shut down their systems.

"Let's go out for some dinner. What are y'all hungry for?"

"Seafood along the Aegean on the bay at Assos," Diana responded quickly

He laughed. "How about Macaroni Grill in landlocked, hot Dallas?"

Chapter 14: WATCHFULNESS

The Faulkners reluctantly returned home, but at least they were somewhat buoyed up by the prospect of performing at their church. Sometimes, it seemed the nicer they were to everyone, the more resented they were.

Entering their music room to figure out what songs to put together, was unnerving. Daniel would perform the violin solos which had been Cassandra's. Diana preferred the Cello. On the mission field in Africa, her mother had taught her piano and trained her in voice. Diana didn't begin learning 'Strings' until she married Daniel. He was already great, and she didn't feel like she ever caught up. She felt that if her tones on the Cello were less melodious than they should be, at least maybe they didn't sound like fingernails on a chalk board!

Cassandra's gift on the violin was definitely inherited from her dad. Alexandra and Jeremiah were both good, increasing their proficiency by increments. Gifted enough, but it required work.

They figured they couldn't pull off "Great Is Jehovah the Lord". Maybe in a year or so, when Cassandra came back. Or when Mallie became proficient. They were sure she had the ability. So much hinged upon her wrist's healing correctly!

One song that had spoken to them powerfully since Cassandra's departure, was, "You Can Have a Song in Your Heart". They ran through it with Diana's singing a solo on the first verse, the kids singing a duet on the second, all of them singing four-part harmony on the chorus. Sounded good, but it was short. It seemed that songs were usually either too short, or too long. They decided Daniel should play the entire piece as a violin solo between the two vocal stanzas. It was powerful, with his pulling way back on the timing, allowing the instrument to swell with its full pathos, before returning to regular, upbeat timing as the kids came in.

That one was new for them, so they spent a good deal of time polishing it up. Then, they ran through several others they were more familiar with, just making the adjustments for Cassandra's absence.

※ ※

Mallie met Callie for lunch at the Galleria. They hadn't talked or gotten together since the trip. They hugged, then began eagerly catching up on all the news. Callie and Shannon had cooled off. By mutual agreement. Mallory knew her cousin lived in the same apartment complex where her mom and Erik lived in Hope. Erik continued to keep an eye on him; he seemed to be doing okay, but wasn't interested in going to church with them, or hanging out much. Mallie couldn't tell if Callie was sad about the cooled romance, or not.

Finally, Callie leaned across the table, making eye contact.

"Are you ever going to tell me about David Anderson, or not?"

Mallory met her gaze steadily, then broke into a smile. "Is he cute, or what?"

"Is he ever! Sorry I asked you about him. I could tell that was a faux pas!"

"Speak to me in Arkansas! I don't understand French!" Mallie responded. They giggled, but the conversation didn't return to David.

When Mallie asked Callie if she were planning to be in church in the morning, she shrugged, trying to avoid the issue.

Mallory simply passed over it. "I know I should go to our church tomorrow, but I really want to go to Tulsa in the morning and hear the Faulkners perform." She hadn't told Callie about Cassandra, but figured Carmine must have.

Callie's face brightened. "Oh, that sounds like fun. I've seen them on the Faith Baptist web site a lot."

"Hey, why don't you spend the night, and we can both go in the morning?" Mallory's voice was excited. She wanted to be faithful to her own church, but she was trying to get Callie warmed back up. Maybe she could be an encouragement to the Faulkners, too.

They shopped around, each making a few purchases. Then, before returning to Mallory's they stopped by the jewelry plant. Herb, Merc, and Samuel, just getting ready to lock everything down, took a few minutes to show Mallory their progress. She was impressed. Herb knew Callie from the trip, but Mallory introduced her friend to the other two.

The designs were coming together. Mallie had thought her picture of the duck family was the cutest thing when she snapped it. She was amazed when 'Motorcycle Merc' took to it the way he did. She watched as Herb pushed a pin against a recessed switch to activate the motion. The little family seemed to come to life!

"Little tiny battery will run it as long as a watch battery runs a watch; then it's replaceable."

"Yeah, plus you'd want to turn it off when you aren't wearing it, to keep it from waddling off." Samuel's amused voice.

"Well, we didn't want to hold you up when you were on your way out the door." Mallory was moving back toward the exit. "Have you found a secretary yet, though? I mean I know it's hard to find someone good when you can't advertise to the general public. You said, you know more jewelers than you do office-types. This may be a loaded question, but would you consider my Aunt Linda, as kind of a temp? I hate for your time to be taken up with the paperwork."

Herb didn't seem upset by the proposal. "That might be very helpful."

⊣ ⊢

Back at home, Mallory and Callie swam, but tennis was as off limits for the injured wrist as everything else. They were enjoying huge gourmet burgers out by the pool when Aunt Linda asked to join them.

Callie explained she was spending the night so she could accompany Mallory to Tulsa for the Faulkner concert.

"Oh, that sounds like fun!" Linda's voice sounded wistful.

"Well, the 'concert' is really just presenting the special music in a church service," Mallory explained. Her aunt was welcomed to accompany them, but she had continued to turn down Mallory's invitations to attend church with her.

"Yeah, I know. But the Faulkners are all so cute, and they're really good. I was really mad at Diana for talking to Herb on the jet to Turkey. No one ever paid any attention to me before. She probably had non-stop boyfriends from the time she learned to walk. Daniel Faulkner has to be the most handsome man I've ever seen in my life!"

Mallory was a little shocked but kept her composure. "Diana was talking to Herb because he seemed like he might be the answer to our

133

prayers for getting the jewelry going. She was right about that! He's a master craftsman! I figured he'd be pretty good, but he's fabulous. Merc's the real surprise, to me, though. Aunt Linda, I asked Herb if you could be his secretary, at least temporarily. He seemed relieved. He's too talented as a jeweler to do secretarial work, and you're too good at handling people and organizing, to be thinking about retiring. If you can start Monday, I can probably borrow a techie-type to come set up a system for the Carlton Corporation. His name's Sam Whitmore. He can teach you the system then, too. He's a little weird. A Trekki-type, but he's good at what he does."

Linda listened to her niece's sales pitch. Carlton Corporation! It would put her around Herb again. Maybe she could undo the damage to the friendship. And, to be on the ground-floor of a corporate start-up! A system, set up with her helping architect it. Keeping the inventory, doing payroll, billing!

"Well, since I can't start until Monday, maybe I should go to church with you in Tulsa in the morning. That is, if you girls don't mind."

"Not at all! The more the merrier!" Mallory proclaimed. "If you're serious about starting Monday, I'll call Daniel now to see if he can get Sam okayed for being here in Dallas on Monday!"

She placed the call, and Daniel phoned Sam right away. It would probably take up Sam's Saturday night to track down the components he would need. Nevertheless, Sam jumped at the project. He loved setting up systems, but he was also a little overly enthusiastic about Mallory.

Daniel had already warned the guy, explaining that his behavior bordered on harassment. Daniel didn't plan to let anyone in the corporate world hassle the ladies.

⊰ ⊱

Sam Whitmore went to work right away, finding the basic equipment for setting up a corporate system. Hoping he wouldn't be considered harassing Mallory, he gave her a call. Trying to sound as professional as possible, not calling her *Tater Tot,* he asked her if there were any operating system she preferred.

After apologizing for taking up his Saturday night, she put him in contact with her aunt. Armed with the information he needed, he made the purchases. Back at his apartment, he surfed channels. Like Saturday night was anything special. He wasn't surprised Mallory didn't like him. He didn't have a date life.

He was up on quite a bit of the corporate big-wig's personal lives. Carlton had liked Suzanne O'Shaughnessy when he first saw her. Then Erik Bransom married her quick, shutting Carlton out! But, then, Suzanne had a sister, Linda, also good-looking. So, Carlton was back in luck. Morosely, he wished Mallory had a sister. He knew Mallory liked Pastor Anderson's kid. He guessed the closest Mallory had to sisters were Faulkner's two little girls. Cute! But really little! And if Faulkner didn't like Sam's attention to Mallory~

Clicking off the TV, he considered the others. Emma Sanders liked Shay, but she was too young, anyway. Tammi Anderson was cute, but she and the attorney were waiting on each other while she grew up! Sighing, he started a computer game. Finally, he went to bed humming an oldie, "One Is the Loneliest Number".

⊰ ⊱

Daniel Faulkner and his family arrived at church early to set up and do a sound check. The pastor, also there ahead of time, demanded that Daniel accompany him to his office.

It was Daniel's first experience dealing with anyone's judgment about his baby. His pastor sliced up the rest of his heart! The part that wasn't already in ribbons!

The guy ranted crazily, claiming they had sold Cassandra, and they were being investigated, and they were going to jail! And, you shouldn't use your kids just so you can wear Sable! He finished by saying he wanted them to go ahead and perform since the mini-concert had been promoted to the members. He basically told Daniel that after that, they could hit the road!

Without a word in his own defense, he nodded mutely. He found Diana brewing coffee in their 'Singles' Sunday School room. He knew he couldn't pretend nothing was wrong, and get it past her. Her nursing instincts always picked up on pallor, high blood pressure, increased heart-rate, dilated pupils. She did notice, but he had looked like that pretty much since Cassandra's departure. She felt like she must look even more haggard than he did.

Since she didn't ask what Pastor said, he didn't tell her. They made it through the class. Must have only been by the Lord's grace. Later in the afternoon, he wouldn't remember anything about the Sunday School hour.

Somehow, Mallory, Callie, and Linda Campbell materialized by church time, sitting on the front row. That was such a huge boost, that again, it was hard not to cry. After a few opening comments, a congregational song, and a prayer, the pastor turned the service over.

Diana moved from the piano to the Cello, Alexandra to the keyboard. Jeremiah positioned his violin while Daniel adjusted the microphones. Then Daniel's violin was tucked beneath his chin. He nodded at Al, and she began the introduction as the others joined in.

Mallory watched them with pride. Daniel was wearing the brown suit he had worn to her little country church in Murfreesboro the week before becoming her legal guardian. Again, with the pale blue. Aunt Linda was right about his being handsome. Diana was wearing the blue linen maternity outfit with the matching London Topaz and Diamond jewelry. Her hair was down. She looked beautiful. You couldn't really tell her heart was broken, but Mallory knew it was. Alexandra was in soft pink, and Jeremiah wore tan slacks with a little navy blazer. His collar was open; evidently having escaped a necktie!

Tears sprang into Mallory's eyes and heart with the first powerful note! "You Can Have a Song in Your Heart". She had heard it before, although, not often for as pretty as it was. Diana's voice was beautiful. Mallory had heard her practice vocal exercises! Perfect pitch! Perfect placement! She sang the first stanza as a solo. The stanza was short, and they all sang the chorus together, beautiful blend! Then Daniel turned, bending down into the microphone with his violin. With some rippling grace notes, he was performing a solo. He was good: as if he and the instrument were one! Tears coursed down his face, soaking his chin rest. The strings resonated. as he slowed the tempo, expression pouring out with a poignancy that was astounding.

"Do not let your worries make the teardrops start."

But teardrops were already starting down Mallory's face; she dabbed with a linen handkerchief. She knew Callie and her aunt were crying, too. She figured the entire auditorium-full of people were weeping together. Part of her sorrow was still for her own loss. Although she could tell she was healing. Now, she really hurt for her guardians and their family! And for Cassandra! What on earth must she be going through with Lilly?

⚔ ⚕

The service was okay at Faith Baptist. Everything seemed to have relapsed into mediocrity, the hallmark of John Anderson's ministry. His entire family was there, including David. A great relief after his son's sporadic attendance and rebellion of the previous months. Tammi was settled down, too. Still, after the Spirit of Revival in April and May, the seeming summer doldrums weighed on the pastor's spirit. He guessed he couldn't expect to keep seeing such results, even on Wednesday nights! It was a great run while it lasted. Of course, much of it had been a result of Patrick O'Shaughnessy's death, and the turmoil of attempts on Mallory's life to prevent her inheriting. One attempt that had nearly robbed them of Tammi! Erik Bransom had received the Lord. Then Ivan Summers, Janice Collins, Delia and Shay O'Shaughnessy, Lawrence Freeman. Suzanne had either gotten saved or decided to 'get real' for the Lord. Brad and Janet were in and out.

He sighed. He sometimes thought his colleague in Hope reaped more fruit of his labor than he did. Erik and Suzanne had stuck, so far, but they just evened up the loss of Patrick and Mallory. As usual, it made him question his ability to write, to have a readership, a following. When Patrick's endowments established him, could he even keep it going? He was quiet during the family lunch, barely touching the fried catfish and okra that graced his plate. Usually his favorites.

Lana noticed. So did David and Jeff. It left more for them. They cleaned up everything, between the two of them, before making a heavy inroad with a tall, chocolate cake. They nearly drank a gallon of milk as Lana sat at the table with them. They could be a comedy duo, and she was the president of their fan club.

In his small, home study, John went through his sermon notes for the evening service. He hadn't been pleased with the outline before, now it seemed really anemic. He rose and paced. He couldn't think of anyone who could come fill his pulpit on such short notice. He had tried to convince David to preach before, but he hadn't even wanted to give his Valedictory address at high school graduation. He figured the Faulkners couldn't come on such short notice~ He pulled out his phone. He could at least check.

No answers from the Faulkners at any of their numbers! John Anderson thought that was strange!

꣑ ꣑

When their mini-concert ended, The Faulkner family took seats near the back of the auditorium. Usually, those places were the hard ones to get, but the special concert seemed to have drawn the crowd forward. Under the pretense of taking sermon notes, as was his normal habit, Daniel Faulkner was writing out a plan!

His pastor's words to him before the service wounded and angered him: more than that, they terrified him! He was grateful for the unintended warning.

With the final 'Amen', he was on his feet, ordering Diana to keep the kids close and stick with him as he strode toward the back of the auditorium. He knew well-wishers would be grabbing at them to compliment the music. It was crucial he get his family out ahead of the crush.

Still, Diana was moving the wrong way, trying to retrieve the instruments.

"Di!" His tone startled her into compliance. She grabbed both kids, and they hustled to the back!

Darrell Hopkins pulled the SUV up to the building to pick up Mallory and her friends as they exited with Janice and one of Callie's bodyguards. Daniel hustled his family into it, leaving Darrell sputtering in confusion. "Give me your pistol, Darrell. There's another one out in the other SUV. Give me your extra clips, too. You got any cash? Get Mallory back to Dallas!"

Perplexed, the other man complied. Daniel jumped behind the wheel and pulled into line with other cars headed out to restaurants.

He made his way to Wal-Mart as quickly as possible, trying not to speed, not to call attention to himself.

"Go to a fast food drive thru! Get lots of burgers, even more fries. Use your credit card. Try not to use your phone, unless I call. Don't answer any calls but mine. Come back in an hour, and pick me up right over by that driveway." He indicated a spot where he could climb back in, and they could leave the parking lot without getting tied up in the parking-lot traffic. He sprinted toward the store!

꣑ ꣑

Mallory obeyed Darrell's orders. Confused and alarmed, she couldn't figure why the Faulkners acted as they did. She was going to offer to buy a nice lunch for everyone. She was hungry, but Darrell was taking the other man's order literally. They drove directly to the helipad and lifted south toward Dallas. No lunch for a while. Mallory was hungry! But she was even more alarmed! She called Diana's cell. There was no answer, and her dread deepened. How could things get any crazier?

᛫ ᛥ ᛥ

Daniel Faulkner stood in line for what seemed like an eternity for the ATM machine inside the retail giant. At last, his turn. He didn't do this very often, but the read-out was easy to follow. Taking out the maximum allowed, he grabbed a basket, racing towards the sporting goods department. More guns would require paperwork. He grabbed a bow and some arrows; a couple of mean-looking knives; a couple of sling shots; a couple of rods, and reels, and fishing lures; sleeping bags; flashlights and batteries. He threw camouflage cover-alls, just an armful, from what he hoped would fit Jeremiah, to his own tall frame. Boots, waders, socks, binoculars, tennis shoes in myriads of sizes, hats and caps. Some thermal underwear on a markdown table caught his eye. He grabbed a compass and GPS device. Whatever they didn't need, they could donate later. With an eye on his high-end watch, he tore through the crowded store as fast as he could. In the grocery department, he swept canned goods into the piled-high basket. He groaned when he saw check-out. Nothing to do but wait as patiently and unobtrusively as possible. He used his credit card! This excursion and Diana's fast food would be the last credit card activity for no-telling how long.

Credit cards used in Tulsa, their home-town!

Checked out at last, he was heading toward the door, only to be called back. The credit card company needed some verification. He tried not to act nervous, trying to remember Diana's mother's maiden name. Miraculously, it came to him! Shish! What a question!

Fighting tears of terror, he forced the resisting cart across speed bumps and between cars where it barely cleared. Panic nearly overwhelmed him when Diana wasn't in the spot, waiting. Looking around desperately, he spotted the SUV down farther, at the next parking lot entrance. She was in the right place; he wasn't. He headed to meet her, and she caught sight of him.

All four of them desperately unloaded the cart, stashing the purchases wherever they could fit them in. With Daniel at the wheel, they entered

44 West to merge into 412, rolling toward Arkansas and the mountains there.

Since a portion of the route was Oklahoma toll road, and they had hijacked Mallory's Texas vehicle, Daniel was aware they would be forced to stop at toll booths. Worried, they pulled into a rest area, where they all slid into cover-alls, socks, and hats. Back on the road, Daniel laughed. "Honey, maybe you should take your jewelry off. It doesn't really go with the new outfit, anyway. As she did so, he removed his own watch.

At Siloam Springs, they filled the vehicle up, using some of the precious cash, used the restroom, and headed into the National Forest.

Alexandra and Jeremiah exchanged glances over the sleeping bags which separated them. It was getting pretty late on Sunday afternoon. Their parents always stopped for church, even when they were on the road. Of course, they knew something was going on; they didn't know what.

Diana still didn't know for sure. She was pretty sure they were starting a camping trip! Without the luxury of the RV! Not Daniel's favorite thing, either. She probably liked camping better than he did. She figured they must have suddenly become fugitives, but couldn't imagine why.

⚓ ⚓

John continued trying to contact the Faulkner family. He was past curious to worried. Their phones were turned off. Louisa, at their home, said she hadn't seen them since early morning. He prayed for them again. Maybe Erik would know something when he arrived for church in a little while. He finished the cake! Without milk! And headed back over to the church.

⚓ ⚓

Mallory kept trying to call too. Finally, she gave up, grabbing a very late lunch before heading to church for choir practice. Diana hadn't released her to use her singing voice, yet, but Mallory knew she could begin learning the choir arrangements by attending and listening. When the practice ended, she found a seat in the auditorium. To her surprise, Callie joined her. Max came over right away, eager to tell Callie everyone had missed her. Callie had developed a crush on the youth department president earlier in the year. She still thought he was cute, but after a brief conversation, she kind of got rid of him, eager to learn what had transpired with the Faulkners.

Kerry Larson showed up right at service time, leaving immediately, before Mallory could catch up to him. So much for friendly Kerry! Probably better for her with David and Tammi, anyway. She figured he must know something about Daniel and Diana, and he didn't want to divulge the information to her. More puzzled than ever, she returned home.

She probably did sleep some, but she was wide awake early. If reading her Bible calmed her heart, she couldn't really tell it for sure. She prayed through her journal, anyway, before Janice and another member of security joined her for the drive to the office.

-ﺍ ﺍ-

Sunday morning, local police, Oklahoma Bureau of Investigation agents, and people from Child Protective Services arrived at the secured gate at the Faulkners', flashing an impressive array of badges. Security opened the gate, but not the house. Law enforcement personnel were there, evidently, to take Alexandra and Jeremiah away, and question Daniel and Diana about the disappearance of their youngest child. The Faulkner staff explained that the family had left several hours previously, to practice some special music before their Sunday School class. Without a search warrant for the estate, the convoy headed toward the church.

This could look sticky! Rousting out church folk on Sunday morning. They were on a mission, though! To find out what really happened to little Cassandra Faulkner and rescue her siblings from the same pitiful fate!

Arriving at the church facility, they found a few stragglers wandering to their cars. Even the pastor was gone for the afternoon. Putting out an APB on the GeoHy SUV, they abandoned the search, figuring the family would be apprehended quickly.

-ﺍ ﺍ-

Erik Bransom heard the rumblings and accusations. Knowing the Faulkners as well as he did, he didn't believe any of the crazy rumors that were flying. He figured none of it was true, but rumors were dangerous. Any reporter who thought it would make a story could hound law-enforcement to delve into it. Any number of people in law enforcement could see the opportunity for a career-maker. A moment of fame! He didn't like it. The media really seemed to enjoy nailing the rich, the popular. Erik was aware that people abandoned their kids all the time, to far worse scenario's than

Cassandra's pursuing music in Israel, and no one ever knew or cared. But a chance to give Christianity a black eye! Or catch some news ratings. He was already nervous before his pastor informed him the Faulkners had dropped from the grid.

⊣ ⊨

From Siloam Springs, Arkansas, Daniel continued eastward on 412 as it narrowed, snaking into the *Ozark Mountains*. He didn't have a clue where he was going. (Using Geological maps, he had assisted law enforcement in rescuing some hostages hidden in caves farther to the south. That was a few months previously.) It was hard to believe he was now on the run! He briefly considered turning around. Surely if they turned themselves in and cooperated, everything would untangle itself. But he didn't want Diana arrested, even briefly. He was certain his attorneys could get them out on bond quickly. He couldn't imagine his beautiful wife in a mug shot, posted on-line. The thing that was driving them both, though, was the dread of losing Al and Jer. Surrendering Cass to her career was tough enough. His other two children's entering Oklahoma foster care was too much of a nightmare to even contemplate. And, authorities would remove the baby, too, as soon after his birth as possible.

He turned south onto a small state road, one of many that penetrated into the forest. The canopy of green made it seem like they were losing daylight faster than they were. Before they were aware of it, they were on top of a *Forestry Service* kiosk. Hiking wasn't free. Relieved, they realized it was closed for the night. The little rusted iron gate was closed, barring access. Backing up several yards, they went 'off-road', blazing their own little path around the small structure and gate. The ground was dry, and dust kicked up. At least no muddy ruts. Placing the vehicle in park, Daniel obliterated the tire tracks of their little detour. About five miles in, they came upon a huddle of neglected buildings. Evidently road maintenance vehicles were housed here at one time. Everything looked totally deserted and undisturbed. Too good to be true. Too easy for any hiker, biker, transient, to simply move in. If someone wasn't in residence, it was because Rangers kept an eye on the place to prevent that's happening.

"Okay. Let's be noisy." he instructed. "We're just a family looking for a creek to fish. Saw this gravel parking lot, and thought there might be creek access."

Everyone tumbled out of the crowded vehicle, glad to release some of their energy, and stretch. The kids had no trouble with being noisy. Checking the pistol's safety, Daniel slid it into his pocket, going around to the hatch, making a scene removing the fishing gear. A tackle box might make their story more plausible; he hadn't thought of everything.

It took a while to case the area. Their racket hadn't brought anyone out into the open. After easing into the various buildings, they were fairly certain they were alone. Still, Daniel pulled himself up into one of the trees, binoculars dangling from their strap. Pretty good vantage point. No sign of anyone for miles. Of course, after dark, all kinds of residents might return. There were a few piles of trash in some of the corners, but none of the buildings gave any indication of any permanent or semi-permanent residents. No signs of large animals, either. It might be a pretty good spot to spend their first night on the run.

"Okay, Honey, I'm going back up the tree. You pull the car around into this big garage-building. Jeremiah, you take a couple of branches and smooth the gravel back."

With fishing equipment stashed back inside, they all followed orders.

With a final sweep of the glasses, Daniel rejoined them. One of the large wooden doors was missing. They were totally exposed to anyone's coming up from the back. He scanned the wilderness at the rear of the property, concerned. Lots of cover. Someone out there could have been watching them the entire time.

He pulled the vehicle forward, backing it in. If an interloper should appear suddenly, he'd be on foot; maybe horseback. Daniel was ready to roar away in the powerful vehicle if necessary. He allowed his strained nerves to relax slightly. He smiled at his family for the first time in hours. "Okay, whispers! We're all staying in the car, for awhile, anyway. With the hamburgers that are left, we're going to eat the meat and cheese out of them. That's what'll spoil fast without refrigeration. We're saving the buns and French fries; they'll still be okay tomorrow. I'm not sure how long we might need to make our supplies last. It isn't going to be like we're used to."

His kids nodded soberly.

⇥ ⇤

The group at Hal's lodge, eating dinner together after church, was somber. Erik was especially filled with dread. At least he received word Mallory was back in Dallas at her own church. Then, secure within her home. Faulkner had kept her out of it. Actually, kept anyone from accepting culpability with him. Bransom prided himself on not being a crier. But, Faulkner was too nice a guy to have to go through what he was going through.

Usually, the agent felt like justice in America was such a sure thing, that no innocent person had anything to fear! Wrong! He wasn't for child abuse! But his dad had worn out his backside a few times when he was growing up. Now, parents had a lot to fear for disciplining their children at all. He sighed. That was the reason there were fewer and fewer disciplined people in America. If people didn't learn restraint as children, they were unlikely to get it later.

Faulkner was on the run with his family, and in America, now, there really was no place to hide. They'd be apprehended! In worse trouble for attempting to flee. If they didn't shoot anyone or manage to get themselves shot!

He knew everyone at the table was as concerned as he was. Besides the danger the Faulkner family faced as fugitives, Bransom was concerned that the Malovich brothers continued to hide within the cover of Arkansas forests. The cute family seemed like they would be at the mercy of anything that stalked around up there.

⚔ ⚔

Daniel read his Bible in the fading light. Usually, if they missed a church service, he would conduct one for his family. Singing, bringing a devotion, taking prayer requests. Now he just sought the Lord for himself. He hoped they were in a safe spot. Sunday night was slow in the wilderness; people returned to their homes in the cities to prepare for another work week. Tomorrow, they would have to forge their way farther in, maybe leave the vehicle behind. If they did that, there was no way they could carry all their gear and the heavy, canned foodstuffs. He praised the Lord for safety for the moment, anyway.

The sun had dropped beyond the horizon. They needed to work out their strategy for the night. Taking the headlights off automatic, he turned the vehicle on, easing it over, concealing it more behind the crooked, remaining garage-door. He needed to devise a way to open the car doors without bringing on the interior lights. Rummaging through the car's compartments, they found a few tools and a roll of electrical tape. Perfect! They taped it over the lights, and it was pretty effective.

One of the buildings housed a little bathroom, but with no water hooked up, it was useless. Daniel reconned a spot, and they took turns before bedding down in the vehicle.

Daniel didn't fall asleep. If his pastor's information was correct, people would already be searching for them. He figured they must have left a trail that practically glowed in the dark. What did he know about the capabilities of the government to keep track of every American at all times, wherever they went? He knew conspiracy theorists whose stories made his skin crawl. He figured he and his family were only minutes away from ferociously snarling dogs and an entire posse, intent on ripping their kids from their possession.

He quoted a verse to himself:

Psalm 56:3 What time I am afraid, I will trust in thee.

This was really his first chance to think. How far was he willing to go, to keep his family together? He wasn't sure he could kill anyone. His prayer was that things wouldn't go that far. What had he set in motion? He hoped Mallory was home safely.

He eased the door open, sliding noiselessly from the Captain's chair. Standing behind the shelter of the door, he gazed at the forested hill rising steeply from the edge of the property several hundred yards away. Bright, silvery moonlight bathed the area. The silence and magnificence of the scene engulfed him.

He gazed into the heavens. Stars sparkled brightly. "I'm afraid, Lord," he whispered. "I'm the most terrified I've ever been; even more scared than I was when I was so sick! I'm not sure why I ran! Maybe I wasn't trusting You! I don't know what to do!"

Tears poured down his face, but he tried to mute the sobs. Sound would carry through the silent night. Fingering the pistol in the deep over-all pocket, he walked the area again, before going back to check on his sleeping family. And he missed Cassandra! Pulling out his wallet, he gazed long moments at the most recent photo of his family. Photos Diana always insisted on! That he hated ! Not the pictures, just the ordeal of getting them done. Now, as he kissed the photo in the moonlight, he was grateful for what he had!

Circling around again, he took more notice of the junk; either stuff being stored here, or just left. Several cans of paint captured his attention. Carrying one of them from the deep shadows, he read the label: Gun Metal Gray. He smiled to himself. "Mallory, hope you don't mind if we paint your car."

He paced for a couple more hours, then loading a gallon of paint into the already-crowded space, he eased the vehicle from its protection onto the deserted road. No lights, just easing forward into the wilderness, under the cover of darkness!

Chapter 15: WEAPONS

II Corinthians 10:4 (For the weapons of our warfare are not carnal, but mighty through God to the pulling down of strong holds.)

Eric Bransom's voice was raspy. Never the most pleasant voice, then ten years of smoking-damage on top of that. Still, he sang as he drove the few blocks to his office.

His pastor felt like his sermon of the previous evening was a bomb, but to Erik, everything about the Bible was so new, that every sermon ministered to him. He had labored for forty years under the impression, that he could pretty well win any battle out there! As long as he had his badge, his gun, and his wits!

Now, he finally could see that the devil and wickedness were realities; that there was spiritual wickedness in high places. There were adversaries you couldn't just shoot, or even lock up. Everything made more sense from the broader perspective of his new Faith. Enlightenment really did come from every new verse of Scripture. His martial-arts training, somewhat ensconced in Eastern Religion, often referenced *enlightenment* and a *third eye* as something mystical and elusive. Now the agent could see that, 'when you read the Bible, the light slaps ya right between your two God-given eyeballs! And you don't need a *third eye*, whatever that is! Just need ta open the two eyes ya have, and your heart to the Savior!'

Pulling his agency car into his reserved space, he readied his key to unlock the office door.

When the lock didn't turn with its usual ease, he knew there was no sense in trying it again! He was done as a Federal agent. Glancing back toward the parked cars, he was aware of Jed Dawson's watching him; Jed's superior sitting in the driver's seat. Erik placed his weapon and badge on the ground, approaching their parked car carefully. Evidently they were afraid he might shoot them.

Both men stepped from the car, keeping their weapons concealed from any casual bystanders. There didn't seem to be any. Dawson unlocked the new lock easily with the new key, and all three men stepped inside the office. Jed frisked Bransom, checking for a second weapon, removing the big knife he always carried in his pocket.

"Have a seat, Bransom!"

Erik complied. Unsure why this was happening now, he sat, waiting for one or the other, or both men, to unload on him.

Finally Dawson exploded with "Antoine Martine! That name ring a bell with you? Thought we brought you to D.C. a couple of months ago to tell you to let some things drop!"

Bransom, genuinely perplexed more than angry, waited for elaboration He had been told not to pursue the investigation about Mallory's abducted employees, and the fact that 'whoever it was' had actually been targeting Mallory, either to take as a hostage or murder. He hadn't known Antoine Martine, the Federal Judge, was involved somehow, either in the crimes, or in halting the investigation. He couldn't figure out what they were saying to him, let alone how to respond. He was trying to process information, that, to him, didn't connect together. But if it did-

"Come on, Bransom!" Don Harris entered the conversation with some expletives. "You've been a rebel, but you're not stupid. Don't play dumb, now!" More of the unnecessary language.

"Maybe I am stupid and dumb. I'm not playing. And, it's true, I've gone off-road a few times, and been disciplined. I'm not trying to get my job back. Pretty sure I've been investigated and found guilty for all this to be necessary." He gazed around, before meeting Jed's gaze once more. Suddenly, it occurred to him he might be under arrest. Maybe he had done something, or they thought he had done something, not just to lose his job over, but to put him in prison. They hadn't read him his rights. They would have to, even though he knew Miranda forwards and backwards.

"Okay you, blankety-blank. Maybe you'd like to explain that little jaunt up to Dierks a couple of weeks ago!" More obscenity from Harris.

"Well, okay." Bransom was embarrassed, but what more could they do to him? He began the narrative with his seeing the picture from Melville's computer file, of David Anderson. Of its effect on Patrick O'Shaughnessy; then months later, on Daniel Faulkner, and on Mallory. He admitted, on him, too. If David were in a relationship with anyone else, they all planned to protect Mallory's heart. The picture suggested some type of bond between Sylvia and David. Erik had driven up there to check it out. He shouldn't have. It was the kind of thing Melville had spent his pitiful life doing.

He paused, red-faced. "I know, it looks bad. I didn't even check on my own little girls when I should have. Guess they all managed to get pretty decent guys without my background checks. I shouldn't have gone up there to run down a loose-moraled beautician. None of my business. That's why I went alone without telling anyone. Didn't know checking to see if David's truck was up there, would bring the Maloviches tearing out of the woods with their war wagon. I never heard of the Federal Judge, Antoine Martine, until after that incident. That's when I learned she was Sylvia's mother. I never heard her name in connection to the abductions of the DiaMo employees, or in getting the investigation dropped, until now."

"Okay, you still haven't heard of the connection!" Harris' voice.

"Yeah, whatever. Sounds like some kind of Orwell's <u>1984</u> *Double-speak*. Bransom's voice was tinged with amusement. "We <u>have</u> made it into the twenty-first century, by the way, Harry."

Harris hated being called 'Harry', but he was such a clown with his secret-agent persona, that the guys under him made fun of him. Harris seemed to believe that his order, about Bransom's not knowing what he knew, would somehow, erase his memory.

"Maybe you should hypnotize me or something, and tell me I don't know. If it's lost in my subconscious~ you know."

Dawson thought Bransom's remarks were pretty funny. Strangely, he believed the agent's story. Well, they had never had a problem with Bransom's telling the truth. Whenever he did things out of bounds, then was called on the carpet, he usually admitted, with plenty of attitude, that, yes, he had done such and such, and he would probably do the same thing in the same circumstances.

Dawson thought better to back-pedal a little, than to lose a good agent to a misunderstanding. And, he guessed that there could be misunderstandings! It had seemed like Bransom defied orders, after giving his word. He stayed on the edge sometimes, but he was good.

"So, you're telling us that you drove up to Dierks, strictly for some private snooping," Dawson clarified.

"I did," Bransom admitted. "Used the system here in the office to do the facial recognition of the picture, then to run the girl's address."

Dawson figured those actions might be against policy, but were pretty harmless compared to the liberties agents took within the system everyday.

"Show me the picture."

Bransom produced it immediately. Dawson took several minutes to study it. The pastor's kid was feet away from the girl in the photo. No passionate hugging, or anything. Could be read a thousand different ways. He guessed that was part of Oscar Melville's MO, that had caused him to be investigated in the first place. Drive around the county, snooping on anyone that was guilty of anything, or could be made to look guilty. Abusing his office! Abusing the right to own a camera!

The girl in question was Sylvia. Strange coincidence that Erik promised to give up on a case, and a private matter launched him into the scenario that could have been disastrous! No wonder the seasoned agent went in without any back up. No reason for him to think that checking on David Anderson would create an incident to escalate so fast.

Evidently, Harris was arriving at the same conclusion. Bransom was a hard-head, but he was a man of his word.

"Well, you shouldn't abuse privileges," Harris lectured lamely.

"You know, Don, he doesn't! He told you, he never even used the resources available to him, to spy on his ex-wife and kids. I don't know many guys that haven't done, at least that much."

"Just cuz he doesn't care about them," Harris responded.

Dawson shook his head, disagreeing. Erik cared about his family; you had to know him.

⊣ ⊢

In her office, Mallory tried to concentrate on the corporate business that mounted quickly if she didn't stay on it. She needed to talk to Kerry Larson about a few of the documents. He had been really helpful, at first. His seeming to avoid her at church the previous evening troubled her. If she made an appointment, she wanted to talk about pressing business concerns, and not the Faulkners.

Her cell phone jingled. Lilly Cowan! Yikes! She wasn't ready to talk to Lilly. Diana had made her promise to be nice to the woman. Now, she wasn't sure she could be.

"Lord, please help me," she pled as she accepted the call.

"Good morning, Lilly!" She strove for a normal tone. "At least it's morning here. I can't remember what time it is there. If, you're in Israel, I mean."

Lilly ignored the awkward attempt at humor and pleasantries.

"What is wrong with you, you crazy girl?" Lilly had a way of coming to her point!

Trying to remain calm and poised, Mallie laughed. "I'm not sure what's wrong with me, but I have a feeling you're getting ready to tell me."

"Mallory O'Shaughnessy, you are so stupid! Stupid! STUPID!" Lilly's voice increased in venom and volume.

"Well, I guess that explains what's wrong with me, then. Nice talking to you, Lilly." She disconnected.

Not surprisingly, Lilly called right back.

She ignored it, arguing with the absent Diana. "I tried to be nice to her. I didn't say one word about Cassandra! Just trying to act normal like she didn't swoop in here like a bird of prey, and fly away with a little girl in her talons. I'm trying to be nice, and she calls me to tell me I'm crazy and stupid! She's a fine one to talk."

Diana's voice insisted, anyway. Maybe it was the Holy Spirit. Besides that, the phone wouldn't stop.

"Hello, Mrs. Cowan, how may I serve you today?" Her voice had more of an edge on it than it did the first time.

"You need to take a hard look at what you are doing. I thought you were interested in the Diamond business. But, you have chosen to be a traitor. The Diamond cartel was ready to make you their so-called 'poster-girl'. A spokeswoman for the Diamond Industry. But you are so stupid."

"You're starting to repeat yourself, Lilly. I take it you're upset that I see beauty in other gemstones, than just Diamonds?"

"Don't ever say, 'Just Diamonds' to Lilly Cowan!" Her voice was filled with tragic melodrama.

"Okay, let me write myself a note. 'Don't ever say *Just Diamonds* to Lilly Cowan!' Okay, got it down, Lilly, you won't hear the expression from these lips again. Was that all you wanted?"

"You are trying to dismiss me? You rude girl! When it is all I want, I will end the call!"

Mallory grinned to herself.

"Are you still there, Mallory?" Lilly demanded when the girl didn't respond.

"Until you end the call!"

"Unh! You are so insolent! And you are very proud and have no respect! You think because you found that stone after forty minutes of searching, that you can do that any time. You are unbelievably presumptuous! After this, you might search for forty years and never find a comparable stone!"

Mallory didn't respond. Evidently, Lilly had never visited Pike County, Arkansas. She continued to listen without responding. Finally, Lilly ended the call! But not before Mallory was pretty sure she had heard Cassandra Faulkner screaming!

Trying to concentrate on paperwork, she forged ahead. If she couldn't sort it all out for herself, she could deal with what she did understand. Maybe she could put off the inevitability of meeting with her attorney. Whittling the mountain down one page at a time, she was feeling some sense of accomplishment. There was quite a stack to send over to Kerry's attention, but much of it, she felt, was dispatched with quite satisfactorily.

She sent one of the girls down to the mezzanine café to bring lunch to her desk. She ate in her office while she worked on schoolwork. The English Lit. wasn't as entertaining as American Lit. from her junior year. At least after the initial weirdness of *Beowulf*, it had gotten a little easier to follow. After reading two selections, she answered the discussion questions, forwarding the answers to Mr. Haynes' office.

His response was, "Do you know where the Faulkners are?"

She didn't. They weren't answering her calls, either. Maybe they wanted to be left alone. Already, she was telling herself Cassandra wasn't really in the background of Lilly's conversation. She didn't reply to the e-mail. She read a chapter in her Chemistry text. H-m-m, it wasn't all as interesting as combining Aluminum and Oxygen to make Corundum (Ruby and Sapphire) crystals. Something about valence electrons.

She tried the Calculus, too. Maybe she could call Callie to help her get going on some of it. Overall, she felt like there were some accomplishments to show for the day. Now, she was trying to figure out what to do about the next day. She thought she was supposed to see the orthopedist for a follow-up about her wrist, then be at Daniel and Diana's for her violin lesson with *the Maestro*. Well, the Faulkners weren't answering her calls, but if the plan changed, they would probably let her know. Before leaving her office, she lined up transportation and security for going to Tulsa, then sent a secretary to Kerry's office with the stack of papers she didn't know how to deal with.

Once home, she phoned Callie, who didn't seem really glad to hear from her. Her friend seemed to be pretty moody, but she did get Mallie going on a set of Calc problems.

"Okay, Lord, thank You that she helped me, anyway." She finished the next assignment the same way, sending it.

She requested a delicious crabmeat salad from her kitchen, carrying it pool-side, in spite of the heat. Pushing a glider back and forth gently with one toe, she sat immersed in thought. Dinky wanted to play, but when she asked him if it would be okay not to, he sank contentedly next to her.

It was really strange, not hearing anything from Diana. The Faulkners had switched their vehicle for hers, and disappeared! No one seemed to know where or why. Mallory assumed it was because of Cassandra. They probably needed a getaway.

-꼭 ꒢-

Lilly Cowan was having one of the best days of her life! That wasn't saying much. In spite of her power and position, she was a miserable woman. And, it wasn't a good day, in terms of locating the pink, heart diamond.

But she was feeling a certain jubilant glee, that Diana Faulkner was being forced into hiding with the accusations being made against her in regards to Cassandra. She hated Diana Faulkner! Not that Diana had ever done anything to her. But, she was beautiful, happy, and seemed to lead a charmed life. Lilly had already disliked her before showing up at the Faulkner's estate in Tulsa. But then, Diana looked gorgeous just sitting at home wearing silk and emeralds, like she was on her way to a state dinner, or something. Lilly had fumed inwardly, ever since. She couldn't see why Diana didn't just hang out in jeans like all the other American women she was aware of.

Now she hated that law enforcement wasn't pursuing the family like she thought they should. Evidently, Oklahoma law enforcement were rabid about the hunt, but the Faulkners had crossed a state line. Oklahoma people couldn't invade the jurisdiction of another state. The Arkansas governor didn't think the Faulkners were criminal, or in Arkansas, so ABI wasn't searching. The Feds weren't convinced any crime had been committed, or that the Faulkners had crossed a state line fleeing with the two oldest children. Lilly was in a tizzy of rage, while still ecstatic, that at least her beautiful nemesis was having a tough time.

Now, the rumor mill was claiming the Faulkners had inadvertently killed Cassandra, then made up the story about sending her to Israel. Police were looking for a body. Which, Lilly was thinking, if the little girl didn't shut up soon, she would gladly provide!

She sighed. She couldn't really. That was angering to her, too. So much hype about the gifted little girl. So, seeing an opportunity to beat out everyone else, Lilly had made the first grab, only to find that the little girl was a long way from being ready for the concert stage.

Even her call to Mallory wasn't as effective as she had thought it would be. The girl should have buckled to the pressure to push only Diamonds. She shouldn't really be pursuing the jewelry business, anyway. Why weren't Diamonds enough? "Because of Diana Faulkner and her hold over the susceptible girl," Lilly answered herself.

She planned to use every weapon at her disposal to triumph over Diana Faulkner! She spent the remainder of the day listening to the reports she could access, about the Faulkner family movements, and where Mallory's valuable uncut diamond lay hidden.

Chapter 16: *WANDERERS*

Daniel Faulkner deeply regretted not having become more of a survivalist. Even now, he figured the red SUV they were in must be visible from space! Without any photo enhancement. But if they cut limbs from trees to somehow affix for camouflage, trackers could follow the fresh wounds on the trees.

As a geologist, he always avoided as much field work as possible. For one thing, since he had picked up a nearly fatal disease drilling for water in Africa; Diana worried. Well, so did he. Every time his head ached or he got a fever, he panicked. He was a city boy, enjoying all the comforts of home! With a capital *C,* Comfort!

His eyes were tired. Wearing his contacts for twenty-four hours wasn't something he did very often. At Wal Mart, toiletry articles had never occurred to him: soap, deodorant, toothbrushes, toothpaste, floss, contact cases and solution, insect repellent! He could go on and on. Neither he nor Diana had their glasses with them, so if they removed their contacts~

As he angled east and south, the rising sun glared into his tired eyes. If he could just close them. Diana, sleeping with her captain's chair tilted back, stirred around. Adjusting the seatback upright, she looked over at him.

"I never knew we were moving," she smiled. "Did something happen?"

"No, everything was quiet. Haven't seen a sign of anyone. Honey, do you think~?"

"No, we have to keep going! How did you know all this was brewing?"

For the first time, he shared their pastor's remarks. She took it in silently, her blue eyes wide. They couldn't turn back! She switched on the radio, tuning for a newscast. Nothing about them, at least. They paused where a barely discernable path angled away.

She nodded. "Let's try it. I at least need a bathroom break."

He eased the vehicle from the pavement, traversing some stony spots carefully. The jouncing awakened the kids.

"Dad, I'll go back and brush over where you turned," Jeremiah offered. He was already moving as he spoke.

Pistol in hand, Daniel surveyed the area while his family stretched. They needed to move quickly from the open area where they were. He loped quickly across a grassy meadow to a tree line, hoping the trees meant there was a creek.

It did. The area was beautiful, seemingly pristine! To his right, the water flowed across open ground, but to his left, a bluff rose above the swirling water. Along the creek, there appeared to be just enough room to maneuver the vehicle into hiding beneath rocky ledges. Maybe they wouldn't have to abandon the car and their provisions. Well, for one thing, if the car were found, it would be a sure sign that they were here somewhere.

Rejoining his family, he told them he thought he had discovered a pretty good hiding place. The kids were a little too jubilant, and their parents hushed them quickly. Silence, total silence, was the order of the day.

Bouncing and jouncing across the meadow, he angled toward the bluff and the sheltered area. Eager to get out of the open, but not wanting to tear up the undercarriage, they finally made it.

Alexandra hopped out, banging the car door! And getting dirty looks from three people! "I forgot," she whispered. No one would forget again!

Binoculars dangling from his neck, Daniel climbed the rock face. Dense forest covered the top, practically to the edge of the precipice. Didn't seem to be easily accessible; he was relieved. Across the creek, another narrow expanse of flower-carpeted meadow, backed by more, heavy, dark-green forest. Thousands of acres out here. He hoped he had kind of found his own. His spirit lifted slightly, and he thanked the Lord.

He clambered his way back down, to see his wife and kids trying to fish the stream. Getting his Bible, he lowered himself to the ground, his back supported by boulders.

With one more warning to the kids to fish quietly, Diana dropped down beside him.

Drinking a cup of coffee!

"Where'd you get that?"

Laughing silently, she put her finger to her lips to shush him, then handed it to him.

"The styrofoam cup was left by Mallory or her guests yesterday morning. I washed it out with creek-water. You bought the coffee singles at Wal Mart. I built kind of a buried oven that doesn't produce much smoke. Some of the tribes used them in Africa."

He stared at her in amazement. "And you already rubbed your sticks together to make fire for it?" His amazed whispers were barely audible.

She laughed noiselessly. "You give me too much credit! We used the cigarette lighter from the car."

Still, not a bad trick! For a woman who didn't like to camp, she seemed pretty savvy.

The kids actually caught fish. Diana cleaned each as they came out of the water, burying the meat in her little cooker.

As a nurse, she wasn't bothered by fish guts. Even the two kids were getting biology-dissecting lessons from the deal.

Midmorning, he climbed the rock face again, scanning around three hundred sixty degrees. He couldn't see the smoke, and he knew where to look. When he came down, Diana was bringing water from the creek, washing off a stone surface for a makeshift table. No linens! No plates. Somehow, she hacked into a large can of ranch-style beans. Then, using the sharp lid as a makeshift spatula, she moved the fish to the "table", and poured the can of warm beans on top of the fish. Her plan was for the seasoned beans to impart seasoning to the fish, in the absence of salt. They used a combination of fingers and improvised utensils, and the food tasted good.

A sock and more water scrubbed down the eating surface for next time.

Reminding the kids to continue the silence, Daniel pried the paint can open with his knife- blade, stirring the aged paint with a heavy-duty stick. They improvised paintbrushes from leafy branches. Stepping into the door frame of the SUV, Daniel could reach across the roof. Pouring a puddle of the thick paint, he lifted Jer onto the roof to daub it around! A far cry from a custom paint job, but most of the red was disappearing. Then Diana came up with the idea of sprinkling sand and gravel in the sticky goo. Brilliant! They crumbled leaves into it, too. Poor Mallory, if she ever saw their handiwork!

They were actually having a blast! Lilly would have been disappointed, except she didn't know! They had even managed to give her spies the slip!

The custom, camouflage finish continued to progress onto the wide hood of the car, and down the door panels. Amazingly, when they viewed it from the creek, it nearly did disappear against the rocky outcrop. Except for the windows. Taking one of the extra camo-overalls, they cut them apart to devise car window sized curtains, smearing them with the remaining paint and sprinkling sand. When the paint dried some, they would hang the coverings by rolling the windows up to secure them in place.

Hand in hand, they all headed upstream to see what lay ahead. Every turn in the creek revealed fresh wonders. The area was incredibly beautiful. Neither like the mountains of Colorado, nor where they had traveled in Turkey. Just its own unique place!

About a forty-five minute hike farther up, they discovered a site which seemed even more ideal than their present setup. Daniel wanted to recon well beyond it, though. It would be ironic to relocate here, only to find they were five minutes from a busy campground and swarms of people. The scenes continued to kaleidoscope from one wonder to another, but there was no hint of civilization. Not even any trash! Quite incredible.

They figured Monday was a low traffic day for *National Forests* and public campgrounds. They hoped the weekend wouldn't bring myriads of tourists. They had no idea how long they might be in hiding.

The walking wasn't strenuous. They had gained some altitude, but nothing steep. Daniel didn't want to tax Diana. He prayed they would be back in their home, with all charges dropped, long before Xavier's due date.

"Okay, let's sit down and rest a few minutes. Then we'll bring our campsite up into here, where there are cliffs on either side of the creek."

His family nodded agreement.

Diana indicated they were all getting too much sun, insisting they all wear their hats. It was better camouflage, anyway. When they got back to the car, she wanted the kids to wear socks on their hands, or stay totally in the shade. She knew they thought she was being exceptionally nurse-Nancy, but they didn't have any antibiotics if anyone got an infection. There wasn't even a first aid kit. She planned to require first aid kits in all GeoHy and DiaMo transportation when she got back.

They made the hike back, being wary. There didn't seem to be anyone around, but the car full of supplies would be a magnet for any other fugitives from justice. Or even to harmless backpackers.

They eased carefully around the final curve where the vehicle was hidden. Gun gripped tightly, Daniel led his family's advance. Jerking the driver's door open, he aimed the pistol around the interior. Then he shooed everyone in through his door to save having four car doors' closing.

He turned the key, and the engine roared in the stillness.

"Honey, take the binoculars, and keep making sure no one's watching us."

They eased forward, going until the shoreline became too narrow, then easing into the stream bed, finally crossing a wide, shallow area, before rolling along the opposite bank. The stream narrowed, flowing more wildly. The bank narrowed to impassable where the cliffs above them nearly met. Perfect place! Or so they hoped!

They sat, gazing around. Shadows chased the brilliant sunlight away.

"Should we get out?" Diana whispered, at last.

Smiling at her, he nodded. "Yeah, then I'm gonna back up and turn her around. Just in case we need to bug out fast."

Her smile flashed in response. She wouldn't have thought of that!

The response to the kids' being hungry, was the buns and fries from the previous day. They chomped them hungrily without complaint.

Diana went to work on a new cooker, and the kids once more cast their hooks into the creek. Daniel listened to the five o'clock news. Still nothing like "Be On the Look Out" for this pack of criminals! Maybe his stampede was silly. Watching his kids fishing and playing along the creek, he knew it was better to be safe than sorry.

Diana had lined her little thing with tinder, so he pushed the lighter in. His contribution to the efforts. When it popped out, he joined her, and she started water heating.

Their car was still gooey, so it had picked up even more dust and junk in the course of the move. He secured the window coverings on the exposed side. It was amazing, actually. He trained the field glasses around again. However clever the Lord was helping them be, they still needed His protection.

Jeremiah caught another fish, and Daniel joined the fun. They quickly caught enough for another good meal, but Diana ordered them to keep fishing. They could cook up as many as they could catch, in case they weren't biting later.

She was right, the more they could live off the land, the longer their canned goods would last. The kids had found salt and pepper and ketchup in the bottom of the burger bags, so Diana seasoned the fish slightly, hoarding the remaining packets for later.

Before darkness descended completely, Alexandra and Jeremiah stuck more of the electrical tape over the remaining lights. The expensive car featured lighted running boards and other luxury features Daniel wished he knew how to disconnect. Every time they opened the hatch or one of the doors, lights came on. Even though they were covered with tape, they were still taking down the battery. Running the engine to recharge the battery used fuel, another commodity they needed to use very carefully. Daniel figured any approach to civilization for supplies would result in their getting nailed.

With darkness, they turned it in. Diana and the three kids nestled into their sleeping bags in the truck. Daniel bedded down on the hard ground between the rock face and the vehicle, figuring if anyone or anything approached, he could hear better.

The next thing he knew, sunlight was washing across him. He sat up stiffly, amazed. With no sleep at all the previous night, he must have been exhausted. Diana was moving around, but the kids were still sleeping. Smiling, she served him a cup of coffee with some fish and saltine crackers. He was still hungry, but they needed to conserve. He wondered suddenly if Diana had been eating. It would be like her to try to get by on too little, so the kids could have plenty. That would be dangerous for both her and the baby. He made a mental note to keep a watchful eye on her food consumption.

"You doing okay?" He reached for his Bible as he asked.

"I am," She responded thoughtfully. "It's so hard to get used to Cassandra's being gone. Every time I glanced toward the creek yesterday, to make sure the kids weren't drowning, I panicked every time, not counting three heads above water."

His gaze met hers, "Me, too." The tears flowed once more.

She dropped a line back into the water. More coffee, weaker this time to make the bags last.

Several deer appeared, posing regally, ears and nostrils twitching. Evidently they were making up their minds about their new neighbors.

Daniel and Diana watched, entranced. The graceful animals were magnificent! !And, it was nice to know that dinner on hooves came this way each morning. Practice with the bow and arrow would fill up some of the time, too. He would hate to wound one, and have nothing to show for it. He didn't want to chase a wounded stag all over creation, hoping it would eventually fall! Where he could drag it back ten miles! If, he didn't get lost!

He was thinking maybe deer hunting wasn't such a good idea! Maybe this ordeal would soon be over! With a good outcome!

The kids slept quite a while longer, evidently worn out from the previous day's adventure. Everyone was sunburned, so Diana was even more strongly encouraging lounging in the shade. Rinsing the same styrofoam cup, she mixed a hot chocolate packet, encouraging the two kids to share the cup and the beverage, also splitting a can of Mandarin oranges between them.

Each empty can was washed as meticulously as possible, then rinsed with boiling water, and Diana had used a small amount of the cooled water, combined with a salt packet to soak their contacts in. Resting their eyes, they nodded off, rousing to keep an eye on the kids, to scan the field glasses around, to take sips of water.

The splashing murmur of the creek, combined with the songs of birds created a symphony of relaxation.

Diana roused to tell Alexandra something wasn't nice, and Daniel looked around to figure out what she meant. Evidently, the kids were arguing in sign language. His eyes drifted closed again. Might not be such a bad experience, after all!

⚔ ⚔

The Faulkner family was enjoying relative calm because the search for them had evaporated.

Oklahoma authorities issued an APB on the GeoHy SUV by early Sunday afternoon, and law enforcement watched for it to head eastward into Arkansas. It only went a short distance, taking Mallory, her aunt, and Callie to the helipad. The chopper lifted away toward Dallas, and the SUV disappeared into a parking structure, to be returned to the Faulkner's estate later.

By the time the vehicle was discovered, several flights had lifted off, one immediately after Mallory's, headed to Dallas to rendezvous with a private flight to New York City. Investigators came to the conclusion that the family they sought had been able to leave the U.S. The search ceased while everyone concentrated their efforts on locating Cassandra. Rumors swirled crazily about what might have happened to the little girl.

The reinstated Bransom followed the scenario with interest. If the Faulkners were outside the U.S., they hadn't contacted anyone. When the FBI office was empty, the agent combed over the Geological maps that had been extremely useful before. But Daniel probably wouldn't try to hide his family someplace that Erik was familiar with.

The only thing Erik knew for sure, was that Mallory was sick with worry about them.

Chapter 17: WEIGHTS

Mallory tried to stay focused on her faith and running her race. Every day she asked the Lord to let her hear from Daniel and Diana; day after day, she suffered doubt and disappointment. She continued moving forward, regardless.

With the investigation stalling regarding the diamonds missing from the safety deposit box, she hired a PI. Kerry and Darrell were still worried. She figured Daniel was too, unless he was busy worrying about more pressing things.

Her wrist was improving, and she was singing again. With not knowing where Daniel and Diana were, she postponed the scheduled shareholder meeting. Tammi was disappointed. Mallory shook her head in amazement. The point of the meetings wasn't so Tammi could get to see Kerry. She forged ahead with schoolwork, DiaMo, the designs, her music, and church involvement.

In early July, she flew to Boston to tour the historical sites there, and in Washington D.C. with Shay. Erik promised he would call her with any news about the Faulkners. She didn't speak with Lilly too often, although Lilly talked to Herb and William Jacobson quite a bit. Even with all the trouble Cassandra's absence was causing for the Faulkners, neither Lilly, nor the Israeli government had made a statement as to Cassie's whereabouts. Mallie thought that was strange.

She loved Boston; she was actually born there. And she loved her grandmother's stately home where her dad had lived and grown up. It made her identify more than ever with his frame of reference, and it made her miss him more, again.

The Boston/New York game on the fourth of July surpassed anything she had ever dreamed about; she felt Boston won it just for her. She and Shay ate their way through the chowder houses and gallons of Boston-baked-beans. Shay was so much fun. Of course, Delia was, too, but since she was busy with her business interests and not interested in the tours she had taken many times before, the two teens, with their ever-present security, really enjoyed the bonding time.

Shay was worried about the Faulkner's; the search for his father's body was wearing on his nerves, too. Sitting at a table at the Boston zoo, licking ice cream cones, Mallie confided, "When we were poor, I always thought money would solve everything. My dad left me rich in money, but I have more on my mind than I ever did before."

Shay nodded. "Well, without our parents, we've had to grow up. Grown ups have more worries than kids do. But you're right, that money not only doesn't solve everything, but it also creates its own set of problems."

Mallie's eyes sparkled. "Yeah, poor us!"

Shay laughed. "You got saved when you were young, so this may not be as dramatic for you as it is for me. But having the Lord in my life, and in Delia's, makes all the difference in the world. I mean, Grandmother was so religious, but instead of getting peace, it made her more fearful. She is really a new person! So am I, and there are still plenty of concerns, but I'm just so settled in so many areas now."

"Like on Emma?" Mallory teased.

Shay blushed. "Maybe so. David told me Roger got a new shotgun to chase me off with. Do you think that's true?"

Mallory laughed. "No, that sounds more like David than Roger."

In D.C. they toured the Capitol Building, The Supreme Court, The Pentagon, The FBI headquarters, The Bureau of Engraving and Printing, the National Archives, and many of the museums of the Smithsonian. All fascinating, but hard to absorb, after awhile. Exhausted, after day three of touring, they sought refuge at a popular seafood restaurant on the Potomac. Wishing they could watch the sun set there, they moved along. Wednesday evening, they sought a church recommended by Pastor Anderson.

Trent Morrison and his family, members there, were in the foyer; he and Shay recognized one another.

"So, you're Mallory O'Shaughnessy!" His greeting was infused with warmth and humor.

"And I finally get to meet Trent Morrison," she responded! "Thank-you for helping look for the DiaMo employees!" Her smile sparkled through tears.

He invited her and Shay to sit with his family, introducing his wife, Sonia, and children that ranged from junior high to starting second grade. Two boys and two girls. After the service, they all went for coffees together.

The Morrisons were interested in the entire situation regarding Cassandra. Usually, curious, gossipy-types annoyed Mallory, but Trent Morrison had placed his life and career on the line to comb the Arkansas forests for the hostages the FBI had been ordered to give up on. They were a nice Christian family like the Faulkners, trying to rear Godly children by Biblical principles. Mallory thought they were genuinely concerned people, and opened up to a degree that surprised her.

They listened with hearts full of compassion, weeping as Mallory shared as much as she could.

The Morrisons changed the subject from Cassandra, to the trip to Turkey; and Shay and Mallie took turns sharing the highs and lows of the journey.

"So, seriously, you ended up in Iran?" Sonia's voice was awed.

"Yes, Ma'am, I guess I did," Mallie admitted. "But I don't even have a stamp in my passport to show for it!"

They all laughed at her doleful humor, but it was a scary story.

Their kids all bonded with the O'Shaughnessy teens, too, so the evening was enjoyable. The hour was late when they all hugged good-bye. The Morrisons invited Shay and Mallie back to D.C. any time, and they invited the Morrisons to Boston, and Dallas, respectively.

"Do you mind if we pray before we part?" Trent questioned. Hardly waiting for an answer, he bowed, entreating the Lord for the situation with the Faulkners, and for America. It was emotion-charged!

⊰ ⊱

Bob Porter grumbled as the camper once more rumbled through the *National Forests* of northern Arkansas. Morrison had convinced him to join another crazy venture! This time, their sleuthing was dual-purposed! To see if Daniel and Diana had holed up with their two oldest kids in the woods, and if the Maloviches, Oscar, and Otto, were still hiding in the same area!

"Maybe they buried the little girl's body out here." Porter's attempt at humor! Or something! Morrison didn't think it was funny! What he couldn't figure, was why the Israelis wouldn't speak, one way, or the other.

He pushed his shades back, digging at his tired eyes, thinking it wasn't really that strange. The Israelis were as felicitous of their allies, as it served them to be. The little girl was no big deal to them, either way. They gave Lilly Cowan of the Diamond Council, plenty of leeway. She could probably step over lots of boundaries without anyone's saying too much to her. Morrison wondered if he could raise enough of an outcry from American Christians and conservatives, to pressure them into a response. That nation didn't have enough friends in the world arena to alienate America too much. They would deal with Lilly, if it were in their national interests to do so.

"Get ya a shovel, and dig up the whole northeast corner of the state," he finally responded to the other Forestry agent "You'll find a fortune in diamonds before you find a fingernail of Cassandra Faulkner."

"Don't think we're allowed to diamond prospect on Federal lands. I'll mention to the higher-ups that you suggested it."

"Knock yourself out, Bob." He pulled into a space at a nearly-deserted campground. "Last guy to catch a fish, has to clean and cook 'em."

"Cool, I can out-angle you any day of the week, Morrison!"

⊰ ⊱

David was worried sick about Mallory. He prayed every day for her safety, but Shay's comment about Mallory's killing people in Iran, and her being under a death threat, terrified him. Even if they didn't kill her, but just kidnapped her again to marry off to someone- It just seemed like there was a bigger concentration of middle-easterners along the Eastern seaboard than there were in rural Arkansas.

He sighed. She didn't live in rural Arkansas any more, but in Dallas. As much of a melting-pot as any major American city. And even in rural Arkansas, he guessed, the Malovich guys were ready to rumble out to get her with that sinister looking- whatever!

Arriving at Phil Perkins', he grabbed his music and violin from the seat beside him. He liked Perkins and the violin lessons, a lot.

Phil's wife, Risa, greeted him at the door. David hadn't met her before, but he liked her, before he even made it through the storm door. She had a wide, fantastic smile, long hair, drawn back quite severely. Her clothing and jewelry were unique-looking, somewhat Bohemian. She was an artist. Phil had proudly showed David her paintings and sculptures which graced the otherwise typical modular home.

"Please come in, David," she invited. She had an accent, or a slight speech impediment, maybe a regional dialect. It blended for an amazing persona! Usually not aware of whether people did or did not possess a great deal of 'presence', David felt pleasantly bowled over by her.

"I got here a little early, I guess." His apology sounded lame.

"Yes, Phil warned me you might. It's actually refreshing to us to meet an 'Eager beaver'. Please have a seat at the table. Would you like some cake?"

"Oh, no thank-you, ma'am," he suddenly felt bashful.

"Coffee?"

"Nothing, thanks."

She cut herself a large, wedge-shaped piece of carrot cake, iced thickly with creamed cheese frosting, covered densely in nuts; and filled her mug with coffee, before joining him in the tiny breakfast nook.

"Phil ran a couple of errands. He hoped to be back before you came. Tell me about yourself. Did you change your mind about cake? How about, maybe, some milk? I just sat down, but help yourself, if you change your mind. Just make yourself at home here."

By the end of fifteen minutes when Phil bounded up the steps, Risa was totally up on the teen's life history.

His lesson was great. The price didn't seem steep any more. After practicing every assignment, he had advanced forward several more selections.

The instructor laughed. "I'm glad you're eager to learn, but I don't want you doing that again. Do you want to play every piece badly? Or fewer pieces beautifully? Scratching them out doesn't constitute playing a violin. Play the first piece for me again."

David complied. Then Phil took his instrument from him, playing the selection.

"Can you hear the difference?"

Fighting humiliated tears, he nodded his response.

"Okay, that's good. I'm telling you the truth, David, some people really can't hear the difference, or don't care about the difference. I can tell you've practiced. I have known people to come week after week, paying their good money for lessons, never taking their instruments from the case between times. Then they get mad that I didn't teach them to be proficient violinists. When you practice, concentrate, not just on the right notes and timing, but on the quality of the sound."

"Yes, Sir." David was disappointed. He guessed he had hoped to 'wow' the teacher.

Perkins laughed. "Who you in a race with, young man? Your girlfriend? You have an aptitude for this: for music in general, strings in particular. Forget about everything else, and concentrate on the music!"

David met the violinist's gaze and spoke softly. "Yes, Sir. I'm sorry, Sir."

⚎ ⚎

John Anderson and Kerry Larson met at the acreage for sale south of Murfreesbo. After waiting, hoping Daniel Faulkner would reappear to help with the decision, they were forging ahead without him. Kerry wasn't over the shock regarding Cassandra before the entire incident exploded into charges against the Faulkner family, and their subsequent disappearance. Everyone worried about them. Even though they were intelligent business people, even brilliant; no one would have staked much on their ability to evade arrest and fend for themselves.

The twenty-plus acres were a good buy. Arkansas real estate prices hadn't escalated as high as many places, but this land wasn't cheap. They were looking it over because Mallory favored it.

A hot, summer day, with high humidity, they waited, visiting, in John's roomy vehicle. Brad and David were on the way.

Tension between the two men was high. John figured he might really like Kerry, except for the situation with Tammi. Still, they had engaged in some small talk. Kerry knew that the pastor was assembling security for his family. It made him worry more about Tammi.

John Anderson still preferred the land next door to the church. Low-lying, a good portion of it was subject to flooding. And, diamonds seemed to accumulate there.

Before the discovery, it would have been a lot cheaper. Patrick O'Shaughnessy's will provided amply for his vision for the ministry's expansion, but the million and a half for the prime acreage was a huge chunk.

"Yeah, Dad," David had argued. "It's cheaper to build something small on stilts. You need to get a bigger vision. I know you don't want to waste 'The Lord's money'. You must tell us that twenty times a day. But, read again about the Tabernacle, and Solomon's Temple."

"David, I know that, but in the New Testament, more emphasis was placed on the individual people as the dwelling places of the Holy Spirit. Grandiose buildings are the hallmark of Catholicism and some of the other denominations."

"Well, yes; Sir, you're right," his son agreed. "But still, the land in town allows no expansion room. We don't need to waste money on elaborate stuff that's useless. Still, everything needs to look really sharp.

Brad liked the site. Large, relatively level, highway frontage. Easy access to utilities! It was really the only choice available. DiaMo owned the plot next door to Faith Baptist, anyway.

⊰ ⊱

Erik's tennis shoes beat against the pavement as he spurted into the last two blocks of his morning run. Always concerned that he was losing the battle for greatness in America, he felt like his cause was sustaining another blow.

Someone in Tulsa had decided to vandalize the Faulkner's property. Must have used forty cans of spray paint! Totally sad, while at the same time slightly humorous, the would-be artist sprayed:

"Diana Faulkner is a murderous! She murders little animals for her coats. Now it was easy for her also to murder her children. Where are they, Murderous? You deserve to die. How many animals are in your coats, Murderous? How much pain and suffering! Why do you say you r a christian? Thou shalt not kill! Murderous! Murderous! Murderous!"

Hardly brilliant! Criminals usually weren't. Bransom knew he wasn't exactly a genius, himself, but he knew the difference between the adjective, 'murderous', and the noun, 'murderess'. Of course with all the Faulkner's security cameras, catching the guy was easy. What made Erik mad was that the suspect was charged with vandalism in the little suburban court, fined, and released.

Bransom considered the act 'Eco-terrorism', falling under FBI jurisdiction, and subject to serious consequences.

Sprinting up to the apartment door, he halted, panting, to towel off. Suzanne was ready for work, reading her Bible with a cup of coffee in front of her. She looked beautiful.

"Any word from anybody?" He meant about the Faulkners, specifically.

"No, Mallory called to chat a few minutes about her trip back east. Guess she's feeling kind of let down, after the fun, and really worried about Daniel and Diana."

He nodded agreement before hitting the shower.

Marcus Jorgenson! Erik planned to keep an eye on him! Animal Rights activists had the right to free speech. They didn't have any right to damage property and try to force their opinions down the craw of everybody else. Glumly, he hoped this guy didn't tie to the Malovich boys, Sylvia Brown, or the Federal judge. Seemed to him like every time he tried to unravel anything, the same group was smack in the middle!

Also, strangely, he worried about the granddaughter he had never met. He still gazed at her picture on his phone, actually had placed it into his computer. Charity got the money; he wondered if the tubes were in yet.

As if reading his mind, his cell vibrated. Caller ID indicated that it was Christine, his ex-wife. Last person in the world that he wanted to talk to,- ever! And, he was pretty sure Suzanne hadn't left for work yet.

"What do you need, Chris?" His voice was terse and nervous. The only reason he could think of for her call to him now, was that she knew he possessed some money.

"Charity said you remarried. Is that true?"

Suzanne entered the bedroom to grab her handbag from the bed. She blew him a kiss, good-bye, and headed out.

Weak-kneed, he sank onto the bed. "Yeah. Why are you calling me? I asked you what you need. I have a busy day."

"Thanks for sending Charity the money for the surgery. The baby's doing lots better already."

"Okay, well, here's the thing, Chris, Charity can call and thank me, or I don't need any thanks. I don't want you calling me. If the girls need anything, they can let me know."

"Well, you probably wonder why I didn't have enough money to help them. You send us a lot."

"No, I didn't wonder. Look, you've done a good job. With the girls, the money, paying a house off. I know life takes plenty. Did the girls all finish college? They probably turned out better than if I stayed. For right now, I plan to keep sending you most of my government salary; like I've been doing. You still teach, don't ya? But leave me alone, please." He ended the call, hoping she wouldn't call back reaming him out for cutting her off.

She didn't call back, but he felt shaky for the rest of the morning. He couldn't figure out why she cared if he remarried. Unable to concentrate, he called Suzanne to make a lunch date.

"You want to just meet me here and eat in the cafeteria?" Her voice was cute and bright.

"No, not really. I want to go someplace where I can talk to you in private. I should have already told you a bunch of stuff."

"Okay, you want me to come now? Roger actually has some guests arriving later he wants me to take on a tour around the facility. That way, you can get it off your mind. How about McDonalds in five or ten minutes?"

"Yeah, love ya, Baby."

She was already seated in a booth with a couple of diet drinks by the time he arrived.

"Who called you this morning?" she asked first thing as he slid in across from her.

"Christine, my uh-uh former, uh-ex-" He couldn't get it to come out.

Her blue eyes were filling with tears. He couldn't stand crying. "Well, why did she call you? Did she need something? You can talk to me, Erik."

"Well," he took a deep breath. "We couldn't get along. I thought I tried, but it seemed like everything I did made her mad. She didn't like my being an agent, but she never said anything about it while we were dating. I always wanted to be an agent, more than anything." He knew everything was coming out in a jumble. "Charity was still a baby when we decided to call it quits. I always sent them all as much money as I could. Federal jobs aren't real high paying, but I just barely kept what I needed to scrape by on. Basically, my job was my life. My rewards came more from accomplishing good, than by the amount on a paycheck. Christine's a school teacher, and with the two salaries, she did a good job, raising the girls and getting them through college. I mostly send money so she'll leave me alone. That woman can get me madder than anyone I've ever dealt with. I've always been afraid I'd kill her and end up in prison with all the guys I've sent there." He paused, meeting her gaze. "I probably should have explained before now, where my salary's been going."

"So, why did she call?"

"Well, to tell me thank you for helping Charity and her baby. Guess if she follows the news, she figures I have more money now, marrying a wealthy widow. I don't know, Suze. I told her not to call me again, but I told her I'll keep sending what I have been."

Suzanne's smile lit up his heart. "That's probably what she was worried about. With the girls grown, out of college, and married, that you might cut her off. But you know, if she took care of all that responsibility as a single mom, I think she's earned something."

"I do, too, but I wasn't sure you'd think so."

"Oh, I do. I couldn't take care of Mallory by myself for three months, and she was seventeen."

"Hey, don't be too hard on yourself. I'm sure happy the way the Lord has worked things out for us." He kissed her hand and walked her out to her car.

His spirit was soaring as he slid into his government car. Terror over explaining things from his past had weighed heavily on him for the past couple of months. He reminded himself of Daniel Faulkner's sermon on FEAR!: False Evidence Appearing Real. As he thanked the Lord for helping Suzanne be so understanding, he felt another burden roll from his shoulders. Somewhere, the Faulkners were all doing fine!

⤙ ⤚

Kerry Larson returned to his Dallas law office with the real estate contract in his hand. Pastor had agreed to purchase the plot, but David had haggled the price down by nearly a quarter of a million dollars. The attorney thought regretfully that it was too bad Patrick wasn't there to see it. A skin-flint and saver, himself, the negotiation probably would have increased David's stature with the guy, at least a little.

Passing Sarah at reception, he gave her a friendly nod. "What's new, Sarah?"

"I guess the first of the lawsuits against Mallory. The papers are on your desk.

Kind of expecting it, but still feeling like he had received a sucker-punch, he moved mechanically toward his office. Never any way to guess who was claiming what, when it came to 'going for the gold'; someone else's gold! He had figured one or two of Mallory's abducted employees might try such a thing. But no one had resigned. Usually people didn't sue the people they still worked for. His law career hadn't been long! He was only twenty-six, but he had already experienced enough of human nature to feel like nothing could shock him. This did, though!

Two of the sons of Merrill Adams were suing Mallory for "wrongful death" in their father's recent demise. They were using statements made by Suzanne O'Shaughnessy and Hal Thompson, "That Mallory O'Shaughnessy knew there was a wasp nest in the tractor on her property, knew that their swarming could be lethal, that they were a public menace; and yet, she took no action to eradicate them!"

Kerry read it again, in consternation and amazement! Then, he placed a call to Suzanne.

Suzanne remembered showing up for work at the lodge on the Saturday morning in question, upset about the financial situation barreling down on her. Telling Hal about Mallory's seeming to emerge from her grief slightly, she had given him a detailed recounting of Mallory's tractor's having a wasp nest in it again!

"Well, Suzanne, try to remember who was in the restaurant that morning to hear you," Kerry probed.

"No one. It was really slow. Janet and the kids brought Mallory in for a coke, later in the morning. Then, that was the first time I ever saw Daniel and Diana. Is there anything new about them, by the way?"

"Not that I've heard. So, you told Hal about the wasps. Did you ever talk to anyone else about them?"

"Well, not that I remember. Well, everyone talked about the way God used the wasps to save Tammi, just as Merrill Adams was ready to pull the trigger. Ivan Summers and the ABI guys witnessed all that. Why are you asking me all this?"

"Just got curious," he replied. That was the truth. He wondered if Hal was an inadvertent player or a conspirator to help get some of Mallory's money. Money could do really strange things to people.

He called Mallory.

She related the story, but even as she did so, the stress and grief of that morning nearly overwhelmed her. That day had started an entire week of drama and terror she was trying to forget.

"Why are they suing me, and not my mom?" she questioned. It made sense, Suzanne, as the adult, would have been the responsible person for dangerous issues with her property. The answer was obviously because Suzanne didn't have nearly the amount of money Mallory had. You don't sue who's responsible! You sue who has money!

Mallory continued. "I wanted to exterminate the nest, so I could get my Bible back, but we didn't have money for even a can of wasp spray. Then, when I found all the hundred dollar bills, and went to the hardware store, I didn't even think of that! I put up a "No Trespassing" sign and a "Beware of the Dog" one. Guess I should have posted, "Beware of the Wasps.""

Kerry laughed. "Who would have ever thought that a hired killer, who trespasses on someone's property trying to kill them, could even attempt anything like this in America's courts? It's crazy! These guys are claiming what they're saying, based on statements made by your mother and Hal Thompson. They may call them as witnesses. You never know what a jury might decide."

"So, what are you telling me, Kerry? You think they can win?"

"Well, they won't win what they're going for; they may come away with something. You might want to consider settling out of court."

The shocked silence told him volumes. "Think about it," he encouraged.

Chapter 18: WILDERNESS

Days turned into weeks for Daniel, Diana, Alexandra, and Jeremiah. The kids, played, fished, and explored within view of the campsite, all practicing use of the sling shots, and the archery equipment. It was actually an amazing time of rest and rediscovery of one another.

Alexandra and Jeremiah both missed their little sister by now, and they all talked freely about her, discussing the decision, its reasons, and the ramifications. No one could have dreamed that it would have brought them to this place.

The stream continued to narrow from the levels of the early summer, and some of the afternoons were sticky and hot. A splash in the creek served as air conditioning and bath- times. With a heavy beard growth, Daniel resembled a mountain man. Some days the fish were less plentiful, but they also managed to hunt a couple of ducks with the slingshot. After a scary incident with a wild boar, he ended up in the oven, too, providing a couple of great meals.

And lots of time, just to all read their Bibles: together, sharing with one another, then privately, each having private prayer times, too!

Always, they remained vigilant! Considering the wonder, that, without their having a clue which way to go, the Lord seemed to have led them to a hidden spot where He continued to sustain them.

They talked a lot about Mallory and David, all the events leading to their guardianship of the girl.

Diana knew there was a folder belonging to Mallory in one of the seat pockets of the car. Now, they barely used the vehicle, at all, saving the battery and gasoline that were left, but she asked Daniel if she could open a door and grab the file.

Bored and curious, himself, he gave permission. Grabbing the folder, she rejoined him. With the coffee used up, they occasionally shared tea. Diana brewed the beverage, returning with a carefully hoarded cookie for each of them. Might as well make a tea party of snooping in Mallie's stuff!

It was a design idea, that, evidently, Mallory hadn't had opportunity to share with her, using a Scripture reference as a starting point.

Revelation 21:24 And the nations of them which are saved shall walk in the light of it: and the kings of the earth do bring their glory and honour into it.

Verse 26 reemphasized the point.

And they shall bring the glory and honour of the nations into it.

The verses fell within the beautiful description of the New Jerusalem. Perfect dimensions, built from or adorned with, all manner of beautiful and exquisite gems!

Puzzled, they both studied the verses. Not having particularly noticed them before, nor having ever heard sermons explaining them, their gazes met. The verses, enigmatic and mysterious, captivated them, as evidently, they had Mallory.

The rest of the file was pictures Mallory had snapped, and postcards from Turkey. *The Spoonmaker's Diamond, the Topkapi Dagger,* the bejeweled bottles, the diamond-studded coat of mail. There were handwritten notes to herself to research Carl Faberge, and the *British Crown Jewels,* on display in the *Tower of London.*

"What do those verses mean, Honey?" Daniel's voice, filled with incredulity!

Breathlessly, Diana answered. "They must mean what they sound like they mean. It's incredible, though." Her gazed traveled from the verses, to the pictures, to Mallory's scrawled notations.

Her voice was hushed, not just because of being in hiding, but because of the awe of the discovery! God is the Creator! He has created us in His image. That's why we try to create things! To leave something behind. The verses seem to indicate that some of the World's beautiful treasures might be on display in the Heavenly City! With Jesus being the Light of it, I'm not sure how soon I would want to go visit a museum. What does it mean to you?"

His brow furrowed. "I don't know. Most of the Bible is careful to tell us we 'can't take it with us'. It sounds like history must have produced some monarchs that were saved. Like we know about King David, and Solomon, some of the other kings of Israel and Judah. Probably some other monarchs in history knew the Lord. Didn't you tell me that you felt like the last Tsar of Russia and his wife sounded like they knew the Lord? Based on the correspondence between them? 'The glory and honour of the nations' does sound like it could mean national treasures and art objects. That seems to be Mallory's take, like these beautiful objects, already surviving through centuries, might be preserved forever in Heaven, the New Jerusalem."

Her laugh rippled softly. Like we save our kids artistic attempts on the refrigerator, maybe God plans to preserve some of mankind's attempts to create. I don't know, but it's interesting to think about. Maybe Queen Elizabeth's beautiful, golden carriage will roll up and down the streets of gold. I'm not sure how all of these different items might unify into one design theme. Maybe it can make for quite a number of individual themes. I love the *Topkapi Dagger!* Smaller scale replicas of it would be gorgeous with my other emerald jewelry and the emerald colored suit. It's maternity, so I may not be wearing it much more."

"Yeah, you may be wearing camouflage cover-alls forever. It sure seems like it. I'm ready to go home. Let's pray."

The kids appeared, Alexandra with a triumphant smile on her face. She held up a rabbit taken down with her slingshot.

"Way to go, Al!" Daniel mouthed the praise.

"I'll skin and clean it," he offered, proud of himself for his new wilderness lore. Placing the pieces into one of the empty cans, he added a can of green beans and potatoes. Let it all cook together for a few hours! It would be great!

They sat another evening, with the food devoured, watching the sun disappear into a dazzling orange spectacle, before night came, and the stars sparkled against the canopy of the heavens. They prayed together, before rolling into sleeping bags bunched side by side between car and cliff.

Daniel planned to head home, first thing in the morning.

⊣ ⊢

Mallory stayed busy. After Lilly's taunting challenge to her, she wanted to go home to Murfreesboro to pick up a more fabulous find than the previous one. Finally realizing a free day wasn't going to simply materialize, she decided on purpose to take a day. This time she was going armed to the battle! (At least, she wasn't going to be wearing pastel, leather heels!) Arranging with Janet the evening before, she announced an early departure: she could have her devotions in the car. "Not one of the choppers," she decided: "they were too much of an announcement that she was there!"

****

Following the dangerous episode in Dierks, Erik Bransom determined to find a lower profile vehicle. The idea which presented itself was the little used car Mallory had purchased in April. He and Suzanne had parked it at their apartment complex. He was trying to think who of his quarry would be familiar with it. Ryland O'Shaughnessy. Bransom was still certain he was dead, in spite of the fact that his body hadn't yet been located. And Oscar Melville (Malovich). That cinched it; he couldn't use it. It was a cute little car, though: too bad to just let it set up. He scrunched himself into the driver's seat. Even with the seat pushed all the way back, he felt like he was wearing a straightjacket. He fired it up anyway; he should take it for a spin around town and get it opened up on the freeway. His phone rang. Charity!

Accelerating up the entrance ramp, he answered. She probably needed money again.

"Hello, Daddy!"

It was strange to him how her voice could still affect him so. "Yeah, how are you this morning? You got the tubes in the baby's ears okay?"

"Yes, Sir. Thank you, Daddy. She's so much better already."

An awkward silence descended between them. Bransom didn't consider himself a conversationalist. "How's Terry doing?" he finally managed.

"He's okay." Her voice sounded brighter. "You need to meet him sometime."

"Yeah, yeah, that'd be nice." He hated to add, "Since I didn't walk you down the aisle at your wedding and meet him then."

"Mom didn't think you were too into weddings." Like Charity had read his mind.

"Well, even guys that don't like weddings, usually show up for their kids'. I figure I helped pay for it. It doesn't matter though, now. I just hope you got a good guy, and you're happy."

Silence again.

Tears wanted to come, as he realized she must not be.

"Where do you guys live? You still in Joplin? You didn't assure me you're happy. Is he not a good guy?"

"He's okay; everything's just so hard!" Her little voice nearly yanked his heartstrings out by the handfuls. "Terry finally finished his bachelor's degree in Chemistry, but the job market's been tough. Even chemists with advanced degrees have been reentering the job market. Finally, Sanders Corporation hired him at entry level. Now we have some benefits, and I think things are going to be looking up. Can I meet with you?"

"Sanders Corporation? Right here in town? Where are you?"

"I just dropped Terry at work a little while ago. I thought I might go push Maribeth around the mall in her stroller."

Bransom usually thought he had a pretty sharp, analytical mind, but for some reason, it was refusing to process her information.

"Meet where? How about McDonalds in fifteen minutes." He exited the freeway, circling back toward town, and called Suzanne.

"Just warning you I'm meeting a woman at McDonalds. My daughter. Not sure why she didn't tell me she lived right here the other day, before we paid to wire money. She said her husband, Terry, works right there for Sanders."

"Terry, Terry; doesn't sound familiar. Did he just start? Oh, yeah, yeah, yeah. Terrance Hanson. Wow, that's~ ! Wow, strange!"

"What do you mean, he's strange?" Bransom's worried growl!

Suzanne laughed. "No, he isn't strange. Just strange that I interviewed him and hired him, and didn't know he's related to us, to you, -uh- to us. I guess I should tell Roger. The guy's transcript looked good; Roger approved him, but I don't want Roger to think I'm hiring family without even making him aware of it. Let me know how the meeting with Charity goes.

His phone was vibrating before his call ended. "Daniel Faulkner" read out on the caller ID.

"Bransom! Who's this?" H was seized in terror's grip, that the Faulkners were in trouble, and someone had found their phone.

"Morning, Erik. This is Daniel. Can we turn ourselves in to you? We were planning to come in today, but the engine won't turn over. I guess we ran the battery down, in spite of our efforts not to."

"You shouldn't have turned your phone on. Where are you?"

"Someplace southeast of Siloam Springs, by a creek sheltered by bluffs. Are we in trouble?"

"Well, I don't know. Did you guys kill Cassandra?"

"Kill her! Is she~?" Faulkner couldn't get the rest of the question out. Tears sprang to his eyes. He couldn't meet Diana's gaze, but knew she had tensed beside him.

"No, no! Sorry! Didn't mean for that to come out that way! Did you send her to Israel? We can't figure out what's going on. I'd like to meet with you. Turn your phone back off for now. Can you call me back in two hours? Will y'all be alright 'til then? You hurt or starved?"

"We're doing okay. Call you back at eleven."

With the cell turned back off, they settled back under the shade of the bluff. The morning was hot, already.

They had made every effort to keep their locale pristine, carefully saving every can for use as water containers, dishes, and cookware. The rest of the trash was ready for them to haul out with them.

Daniel's Bible lay open on his lap, but Diana was playing with the kids in the sand and gravel, where the water had retreated.

Do you think there are diamonds here?" Alexandra questioned Diana.

"I don't know. Why don't you go ask your Mr. Geologist-Father?"

Daniel laughed at his daughter's excitement at the idea. "I don't know," he responded. "When Mr. O'Shaughnessy hired us, he concentrated our search from the diamond crater, southward. This is farther north, but there's no proof that Arkansas diamonds are limited to the area where they've been found. If you do find some here, this might be Federal land. I'm not sure if we're in the National Forest, or not. Wouldn't hurt for you to search while we wait 'til time to call Mr. Bransom back." He was pretty sure they wouldn't find any, but it might keep them occupied. The kids had continued to use sign language. He almost hated to leave from here, and have to listen to them fight again!

"Let's stop in Hope for more coffee," Mallie suggested as she closed her Bible and journal. "Go through McDonald's drive thru. I'm eager to get home and dig around."

Her little car, well one like hers, anyway, caught her attention as they pulled into the busy drive-in. Her thoughts flashed back to the afternoon with David, when he helped her shop for it! She spotted Erik climbing out, as he caught sight of her vehicle. He flagged them down. He couldn't see Mallory through the tinted windows; the vehicle was new, still showing dealer's tags. He knew it was Mallory's vehicle because it proclaimed DiaMo proudly from door panels on both sides.

He ripped into Janice Collins for the advertisements. "Get that sanded off. You might as well paint bulls-eyes, as DiaMo! It's not like Mallory deals with the public and needs this kind of advertising, anyway!"

He knew he sounded grouchy. He couldn't figure out why no one had any sense! He thought Collins did! Now, he wondered.

And his heart was troubled. Christine really had placed a barrier between him and his girls. Finally, one of them was reaching out to him. Within the fifteen minute gap before meeting her, the Faulkner family and Mallory's security concerns had crowded in. He was desperate to talk to Daniel Faulkner, and always glad to see Mallory. But Charity had been squeezed out of his life forever! He was putting her first this time!

Janice hustled Mallory inside, sending one of the other security people to improvise a way to make the logos disappear.

Erik followed them in, looking around for anyone he thought might be Charity. No one in the playground. Maribeth was probably too small for that anyway. Then he saw her; struggling to get in the door with the baby, and evidently, everything they both owned! He grabbed the door, and Charity dissolved into his arms.

Mallory helped with some of the baby paraphernalia, getting the mountains of stuff situated at a table.

"Hello, my name's Mallory," she introduced herself.

"Mallory, this is my youngest daughter, Charity." Erik found his voice, completing the introduction.

"Oh, and who's this?" she was already grabbing for Maribeth. "Nice to meet you, Charity. Do you live around here? Wow, your baby's adorable! Well, Janice and I are going to have some coffee. We'll let you guys visit."

"Hold on, Mallory, what are you guys even doing here?" Bransom's curiosity.

"Heading on a diamond-hunt. Lilly told me I'm arrogant to think I can just go find nice stones any time. I still think I can. I always could."

Charity was taking her in, amazed

Erik didn't like the plan. Glad to have heard from Faulkner. The guy needed to get back to civilization and clip Mallie's wings.

"You still haven't heard anything at all about Daniel and Diana?" she checked. She figured she was driving everyone crazy, when they didn't know anything either.

"Keep your phone handy. I'll call you this afternoon."

"Okay. Nice meetin' ya, Charity." Her *Yukon* was back with big magnetized signs from some real estate agency covering the DiaMo signs. She and Janice hurried out, and the vehicle headed up 278.

Her spirit soared. Erik knew something about the Faulkners, but he was trying to visit with his daughter and grandbaby. It wasn't anything bad, or he would have been sad, and he would have called her.

They reached her small home-town. Faith Baptist, on the lot adjacent to the DiaMO plot, was abuzz! With power saws and other tools. Wow, the remodeling was progressing! Brad's truck was there, but David's wasn't. Pastor's wasn't there, either. It would probably be hard for him to study with all the racket going on. She wondered if his office would be bigger and nicer.

The noonday heat felt pretty intense as she hopped from the air-conditioned vehicle. The creek was way low! That was good. Studying the sandy bed where the water had retreated, she decided to pray. "Well, Lord, maybe Lilly was right about my being insolent and haughty. I can't find anything unless You allow me to; I need your help."

She pulled a rake, a shovel, a trowel, and a sifting screen from the back, then sprayed insect repellent. Ticks could be a real problem. Remembering Erik's words, she placed her phone beside her on a polyurethane gardening pad. Focusing on a large stone, not really a boulder, but large enough to affect the water's downward course, she raked leaves and debris from the areas behind it. Then, using the shovel, she pushed it deeply into the sand, dropping the shovelful into the screen. Then she swished it in the creek to rinse off the larger gravel and wash away anything small enough to filter through the screen. Smacking it upside down to empty it, she eyed the stones that were left. No diamonds. She repeated the process.

She had scanned the area before beginning. Just to see if anyone was snooping around. No silhouettes in the trees, but Lilly always possessed an uncanny knowledge of all that went on in this opposite side of the world!

Sipping a bottle of water, she surveyed her chosen area. It was an amazing thing to her that diamonds had been discovered in every state of the Continental US, but one. She had heard that on reasonably good authority, now she wondered which state had yet to find one.

One Geological explanation for the wealth of diamonds in countries south of the equator was connected to glacial movement. The explanation was, that in the previous ice-age, glaciers had been more abundant in the northern hemisphere. When they advanced, they milled out the stone, leaving thicker layers of top soil. The southern hemisphere, with less glacial activity, was covered with little to no top-soil. She smiled. Deep top soil made it possible to produce abundant crops! Nice for people who like to eat. She wasn't sure how much validity the story carried. Or when an 'ice age' actually started and ended. Creationists believed the earth to be approximately six thousand years old; that an ice age would have been connected with all the cataclysmic upheavals related to the world-wide flood.

Recently reading about Lake Kelsey, Colorado, she was aware of diamond discoveries up there, near the border with Wyoming. It was interesting to think about miners in the eighteen hundreds, panning those creeks for gold. She wondered how many diamonds flung aside in their frantic search for the golden shine at the bottoms of their pans.

"Are you getting tired yet?" Janice questioned. She was pretty sure she was supposed to keep vigil rather than grabbing any of the mining gear. She hoped so.

Mallory laughed. "Actually, no. I always had so much fun playing all over the place around here. Always with David. Often with Tammi, too, and just other bunches of kids. My dad always told us we weren't finding diamonds." She continued scraping lightly with the trowel. Snakes were always a possibility, and she didn't want any nasty reptilian surprises. She was dying to hear from Erik about Daniel and Diana.

That reminded her of Cassandra! which reminded her of Lilly and her taunting voice!

"Time to quit messing around and find a stone to make Lilly eat her words."

Since there hadn't been any good rains for several weeks, the little eroded rivulets that often revealed diamonds were not in evidence. She directed her attention to gravel in a wide bend of the dried up area. Another shovelful, another swish in the water, another screen full of gravel smacked upside down. Her eyes glittered! So did the stone, right in the center of the material. This one was nice! Not pink. But colorless. The quality looked good, without any damaged parts. She guessed maybe twenty-five carats. Not the *Kohinoor*, but strictly nice! Placing it into a gem jar, she continued searching. It wasn't easy to get here anymore; she might as well keep looking, while she was here. She was waiting to hear from Erik anyway.

Using the trowel, she scraped at more of the gravel where the diamond had just come out. Unsure of what was there, she rinsed another screen. Several little brown ones and a yellow. Definitely a diamond concentration. She was intent, forgetting the heat, placing trowels of the gravel into the screen, rinsing, swirling, emptying upside-down, scanning the washed stones. More of the white-white ones. One was larger than the first, having a really great-looking end to it.

⚏ ⚎

When Daniel turned his phone off, he allowed his gaze to meet his wife's. "Erik said to turn the phone back off and try him back in a couple of hours. I guess no one's too worried about us. I thought he was saying that Cass was dead, asking if we killed her. But evidently that's just how crazy all the speculation's gotten."

His expression was troubled, confusion in his eyes.

"Maybe we should dig back in, if they think anything like that. We still have some supplies, and lots of cash." Her voice didn't sound convinced.

"Well, I'm calling back like he told us to. Maybe they got a fix on the phone, and they're closing in on us now, although I doubt that. Anyway, I'm not fighting or resisting anyone, unless it seems like immediate, physical danger."

Locking gazes, she nodded agreement.

Still, they were pretty amazed that gossip and suppositions about Cassandra had reached such an extreme.

⚏ ⚎

Charity visited with Erik until Maribeth grew fussy; then, he helped her out to the car. When he asked if she needed any more money, she told him that wasn't why she called. Standing at her car door, he finally gathered his courage to tell her about the Lord.

Tears filled her eyes. "I know. I heard about you. When Maribeth was in the hospital getting the tubes in her ears, we met Nell. She was one of the nurse aids. She couldn't talk to us about the Lord then, but she and Merc came to our house Saturday morning. Terry and I both prayed that prayer. I guess the Lord was really what was missing in our lives. We really do love each other, but we both thought marriage partners were supposed to fill up all the empty spots. We were both disillusioned with each other and our marriage because our ideas about romance weren't realistic.

The baby was fussing more, so he sent her home, inviting her to call any time.

-≒ ╞-

Daniel turned on his phone, calling back right on time. He began again to describe their campsite, then remembered the GPS device from the Wal-Mart excursion. He gave the coordinates, then once again asked if they were going to be arrested, forfeiting Al and Jer to CPS.

Bransom was still perplexed by the entire situation. Law enforcement had found the contract, signed by Daniel and Diana. Oddly, there was no place for Lilly Cowan's signature. He wished she had signed something they could track down. Too wily to get herself pinned down, evidently.

While Daniel spoke with Bransom, a biker roared up the creek, seemingly from nowhere. Before Daniel could grasp the pistol in his pocket, the biker dismounted, approaching cautiously, showing himself unarmed.

"Merc!" Diana's joyous voice as she recognized the intruder. "How on earth did you find us?"

"Well, I know this area fairly well, biked up around here for years. When your cell came up a couple of hours ago, I got a fix. Been finding my way back up in here since. You found a really nice spot, looks like. We've never been here before. No trash; not many people find it, evidently."

Releasing a gas can from its mounting on the bike, he moved toward the vehicle.

"Remind me never to let you guys do any painting on my stuff," he laughed as he viewed the new custom-finish. Hope your battery isn't clear dead. Pretty hard to jump off from a bike battery if it is."

"Let's pray." Diana's suggestion.

Actually, killing the couple of hours digging in the gravel had yielded rewards! As Merc and Daniel dealt with the mechanical issues, Diana and the kids resecreted their treasure. They could research the coordinates to find out who owned the land,! And the mining rights! Very interesting!

The engine fired up with the first attempt, and they began rolling forward. Merc led the way out, down a state road, 23, and they all cried when they passed through a tiny town named 'Cass'. Continuing along the same road, they crossed Interstate 40, then continued southward, leaving the Ozarks, entering the Ouachitas. They snacked on some of the last of the crackers as they continued to follow little-used roads. They were still trying to stay hidden, but those were the only routes there were.

Bransom didn't think they should return to Oklahoma yet, so he reserved cabins for them at Daisy State Park. About seven o'clock, they rolled in, to be greeted by Erik, Suzanne, and an emotional Mallory!

Several agents and Mallory's security hurried them to the privacy of one of the cabins. Everyone got a good laugh at the 'paint job' on the DiaMo car; Mallory thought Daniel and Diana, in their camouflage, were even funnier. Daniel's hair and beard were kind of long and extremely scruffy. When Diana and Alexandra removed their camo-hats, their hair was cropped short, and Diana's color had grown out completely, leaving it her natural, soft brown.

They all hugged for the longest! Then, with everyone suddenly hungry, Bransom sent a couple of agents to the restaurant to bring back plenty of food. Everyone ate, trying to catch up on details. At ten, they all watched the news. Eric's phone rang, and he stepped outside.

-¤ ¤-

Trent Morrison and Bob Porter gave up on their searches for both the Faulkners and the Maloviches. Word was, that Faulkner had fled to Europe with his family, although Morrsion couldn't fathom that. Even with the wealthy-set's ability to charter private jets, exiting the U.S. covertly wasn't that easy. Morrison didn't think they had left the country. He didn't know where they were.

His efforts to raise a strong outcry and get a statement from the Israelis hadn't gathered much momentum. People were always so engrossed in their own problems. Finally, the Lord helped him think of a contact who might be helpful.

As an employee of the *US Forestry Service*, his organization was overseen by the *Department of Agriculture*. With many hits to farming and agriculture within the US, the *Department* didn't get the respect

Morrison thought it should. Laugh at agriculture and farming now! When food supplies got short, as he felt they were going to, America would be sorry she had fled the farms for the cities. Fossil fuels being exhausted was spurring bio-fuels, but using corn, sugar cane, whatever, to synthesize fuel, was reducing food available for human consumption. He admired Israel for being a world leader in agriculture. Truly seeking out methods to make the deserts bloom, they had pioneered 'drip-irrigation' and many other innovations. He had once met an Israeli who was pretty high up in government, at an Ag conference Trent hadn't worked on establishing rapport with the guy, but his options were limited. He placed a call to the parallel agency in Israel, asking for Simon when a heavily accented voice answered.

It took several minutes to track him down, but at last he reached the guy he was looking for.

"Hello, Simon, this is Trent Morrison with the *Department of Agriculture* in the US."

A pleasant laugh rolled from the middle east. "Glad to hear your department hasn't been phased out yet. Are there still two of you on the payroll?"

Morrison laughed. It was funny, albeit in a sad way. "Yeah, I'm trying to get the Israeli lobby on my side."

"Glad you know who has influence with your government." Simon was enjoying himself. He remembered the personable American.

After a few more jokes and the pleasantries of inquiring about families, Simon suggested Trent get to the point.

"Well, Simon, I called you because you're the only person in the Israeli government I've ever even met. I need a favor."

"Well, my friend, you are in very bad luck, then. I am pretty far down in the hierarchy. And, why should I do you a favor, if I could?"

Usually the low-keyed Trent would have given up, backing from the awkward situation as gracefully as possible. But this was the only shot he could think of. Praying silently, he pressed ahead.

"Man, you got that right. We don't know each other. We exchanged business cards once. I didn't pursue any kind of friendship. I appreciate your even taking my call. I'm, gonna let ya go, but can you tell me anything at all about a Lilly Cowan, involved in the Diamond Council?"

"Not from here. Good-bye, Morrison."

Defeated, Trent slid his phone back into his pocket. He was sitting in his office, trying to think of something else! Anything else, when his phone vibrated.

International number. "Trent Morrison." he answered.

"Why did you ask about that person?"

"Well, I'm not trying to create any problems, but I think she brought a little girl, a violinist, to Israel from here in the U.S. I'm not sure Ms. Cowan's guilty of fraud, but it seems the little girl's family received the impression they would be allowed access to communication with her. It's hard to go into all the details since I know you're busy. It would help the Faulkners a lot, if the Israeli government or Lilly would verify to our government that Cassandra is there, and that she's okay."

Simon was aware of bits and pieces of the information, and he didn't like Lilly Cowan. But, she was powerful; and crossing her required extreme caution.

"I can't make promises. I can talk to some people familiar with everything. Why is your government determined not to let parents train their children?"

"Ya got me. Well, people get crazier and crazier here. More families breaking down, so there are more 'boyfriends' or whatever, trying to deal with kids that aren't their own. So, child abuse is a real problem in our society. I can't deny that. Really tragic stories of what children suffer, even if they aren't abused to death. But a lot of them die. That makes their defenders over-zealous, at times. It's scary for me to deal with my kids in the proper way, for fear I might lose them to the authorities."

"Glad I'm an Israeli." Simon's smug tone.

He had a point, Israeli family values were much stronger, with a real love and respect for children, as well as the extended family.

"I will work on a meeting. May take a couple of hours. People were not overly pleased with Ms. Cowan's method for getting the little girl. Now that it isn't working out at all, they may deal with her. Call you back at this number?"

"Yeah, yeah, thanks. You're right, you didn't owe me any favors. If you can help with this situation, I will be forever in your debt."

Simon wasn't surprised at the words! He heard words like that all the time. The surprise to him was the sincerity in the guy's voice.

Trent was encouraged. A couple of hours! He figured a couple of weeks, if the guy had thought he could accomplish anything at all! He headed onto the beltway for home.

❧ ❧

Mallory got the worst scolding from Diana! She was so glad to see her, but then, Diana was upset about Mallory's abusing her wrist searching for diamonds. Diana pointed out, that, not only was Mallie going to lose the mobility in the joint, but she had been out there, because she allowed Lilly to gig her!

Tears stung Mallie's eyes as she tried to keep from crying. Diana was right about her wrist. What amazed the girl the most, was Diana's determination to remain such a steadfast Christian toward Lilly. From Mallie's first encounter with the *Diamond Council* executive, she and Diana had coveted to pray for the woman's salvation. That was before either of them had any idea that Lilly was even aware of Cassandra. Lilly's treatment of the Faulkners was reprehensible, but with her lilting laugh, Diana simply confirmed her faith that God was using Cassandra and the entire incident, to remove the scales regarding Himself, from the Israeli woman's eyes.

Awed, Mallory bid the Faulkner's good-night. She was planning to spend the night with her mom and Erik in one of the cabins and return to Dallas in the morning.

Erik came in, finished with his phone conversation.

"They should have stayed where they were a while longer. They still had quite a bit of non-perishable food, and they were turning into really good hunters and fishermen. Dawson didn't order me to arrest them. He's sending extra surveillance to make sure they don't slip away in the night. In the morning, we have to take them in to talk to them. Somebody'll be along to take the kids." He swatted at a tear.

Mallie sank into a kitchen chair, stunned, trying to think what she could do. She wondered if she could get any kind of temporary custody of Alexandra and Jeremiah. Maybe she could sneak out, warn them, and they could still slip away into the woods.

"Let's pray," Erik's voice, hopeless, wasn't sure it would do any good. It was the only legal recourse. He was sworn to uphold the law.

Before they could assemble into a little huddle, Bransom's phone rang again. Trent Morrison!

Listening to the other federal employee, the anguish on Erik's face turned to wonder; then a broad smile broke free. "Man, Morrison, that's the best news I've ever gotten! We owe you a big steak! Well, more than that! Man, that's unreal! Guess I need to call Dawson back."

"He probably already knows. Their Prime Minister called the President. Lilly's statement in Israel claimed, 'The Faulkners certainly aren't guilty of abusing, or even disciplining their children'. Evidently the *'Diamond-witch'* has met her match in Cassandra!"

When the conversation ended, Erik sagged into a deep recliner and sobbed!

In her little bedroom in the cabin, Mallory knelt next to the bed. She was tired, and her wrist hurt. Thinking about the Faulkner's sojourn in the wilderness reminded her of her own close call! A close call, which suddenly occurred to her, might also be connected to Lilly Cowan. Now, she wondered if the guys in the strange, blue car in Dogubayazit were operating on their own, or for some smuggling ring, or at the behest of Lilly; so Lilly could 'have her be rescued', putting her in Lilly's debt!. Far-fetched! But then, life often was.

Climbing between the covers, she sang softly, "My Lord Knows the Way Through the Wilderness". Then she was asleep!

Chapter 19: WAR

Dallas summer continued with relentless heat, making Mallory grateful for the air-conditioned life she enjoyed. She wondered how people survived before.

Her school work was as relentless as the heat, very challenging, but it was all fascinating. She loved the Chemistry course, which had, at first, plunged her into despair. Like the valence electrons and chemical bonding. One of the things Erik's chemist son-in-law pointed out when he guest lectured a Sunday School class at Faith Baptist, was the built-in tendencies of everything in the natural world to stabilize. You could combine some elements, get a big bang, then stability would reign again. He spoke from:

Colossians 1:17 And he is before all things, and by him all things consist.

The meaning being, "In Him, all thing are held together." Terry also referenced what Scripture said about God's having placed boundaries for the ocean waves. Sometimes, cataclysmic events could trigger a tsunami, causing waves to surge in higher and farther than normal. But after the event, the shoreline would return to the usual tide-levels. Everything remained under God's careful control until the time when He would cease to hold atoms in their stable structures, creating an ongoing chemical reaction to melt this heaven and earth; (atmosphere and planet?) Mallie was glad Pastor Anderson had given the newly-saved academic the opportunity to teach the class. Terry was a great illustration of 'secular' knowledge revealing an even more awesome glimpse of Who God Is!

What her dad had wanted her to grasp much sooner! That there is no such thing as 'secular' knowledge! Secular Misinformation, possibly! But all true knowledge revealed the Divine! And it dovetailed perfectly with Scripture.

She sat gazing at her monitor, tears sparkling on her eyelashes. She always asked the Lord to reveal Himself more whenever she opened her Bible. And of course, He always did. But, to her, schoolwork had always capsulated in her mind as something separate.

As amazed and humbled as she felt by the revelation dawning, she still closed down the Faith Baptist page. Just so happened David was in a lot of the video, too!

⚐ ⚑

The Faulkners continued to spend a good deal of time in Dallas reacclimating to civilization. Diana, surprisingly, was in no rush to reach the salons for color, cut, and nails. She didn't have much interest in working on any clothing designs, and had even turned down Mallory's invitation to accompany her to check on the jewelry production. For one thing, Mallie knew they missed Cassandra more than ever. Diana reassured her that she wasn't depressed, but just regrouping spiritually.

They were establishing a new routine, wherein, they all traveled to Tulsa on Tuesdays for the soup-making and violin lessons. Although Mallory's wrist had rebounded to where it was before her diamond search, *the Maestro* still wasn't allowing her to touch her instrument. She was frustrated, knowing David was ahead of her. She couldn't figure out why he was pursuing violin, anyway! Just because she was, and he had to win! He was so annoying!

Then on Wednesday mornings they would all return to Dallas, attending Calvary on Wednesday evening with Mallory and Kerry.

Finally, Daniel returned to Honey Grove Baptist to retrieve their instruments left behind in the rush earlier in the summer. Not surprisingly, they weren't still at the front of the auditorium. He made his way to the office complex; it was time to face his pastor, anyway. Clean-shaven now, Faulkner knew he looked gaunter from his experience, and older. Shaking hands with his pastor was one of the hardest things he had done in a long time. Diana always told him he needed to be more forgiving and 'other-cheek-turning' with people. Her Christian discipline always amazed him. Being as civil as possible, he loaded his instruments and beat a retreat.

-≒ ⊨-

When Mallie remembered to tell Daniel and Diana about the Adams' lawsuit against her, they were hardly surprised. Their experience with their own personal wealth, was that, 'if you had anything, somebody would be after it'!

They agreed, "It was crazy". When she told them Kerry was for settling out of court, they agreed. That was the reason she paid Kerry the retainer she paid him.

But it baffled her. Merrill Adams trespassed on her property twice! Going past her warning signs like they weren't there. When he made it off the first time, he should have quit while he was ahead. But instead, he returned! Passing the signposts again! That was when the nest of wasps stung him to death! When he was there, trying to murder her! But then, Tammi Anderson got off the bus at her house, and Adams nearly killed her instead. Even if Adams had been successful in eliminating Mallory and her mom, her Uncle Ryland wouldn't have inherited everything. There were laws against that!

She decided to call her mom and Erik. Telling the entire incident to her mother caused Suzanne to remember complaining to Hal that morning, about the wasps repeatedly trying to claim Mallie's old tractor. Now, she wondered how Adams' two sons got their information. Just by coming into the lodge and chatting Hal up, evidently. She took her phone to Erik so Mallie could tell him the story.

On his way to his office, his eyes glittered with the challenge! Adams had kids? Trying to shyster Mallie out of some money? And Larson was saying to pay? He didn't think so!

Once at the office, he started to call Larson. Thinking better of it, he stopped the call, accessing the morgue records from Adam's autopsy report, instead. No 'next of kin' seemed to have been located. If Adams had sons, they didn't care enough about their father to claim his remains and give him a burial. Now, suddenly, they were grief-stricken over his 'wrongful death'? What's wrong with that picture? That might be an interesting point to make before a jury. Erik was hoping the two men's only appearances before juries would result from criminal charges he planned to file! Not in their civil suit against Mallory!

He was still sitting there contemplating the seeming dead-end, when his phone vibrated. Caller ID told him it was Shannon O'Shaughnessy. "Thanks, Lord," he chortled as he answered the call.

"Hey, O'Shaughnessy, what can I do for you?' he answered. "Where ya been keepin' yourself?"

"Just been hanging out inside my apartment, mostly. I'm just calling to thank you that the *Treasury Department* didn't seize the money my uncle left me. I know you helped a lot with that."

"Well, Shannon, that's pretty much a miracle. I'm pretty sure the *Treasury Department* doesn't hold its breath whenever I speak. Larson and the Faulkners and Mallory were all in there pitchin' for ya, too. But to win out with the *U.S. Treasury*, when money's at stake! There's no explanation for that, but God!"

"Oh yes, Sir. I'm a believer. I was as good as dead when I started saying, 'Hail, Mary's' "

"Yeah. Hey, Shannon, can I buy you a steak for lunch to celebrate?"

"I'm not going out much."

Erik had just figured that out. The kid was terrified! Otto Malovich had been on the brink of executing him when FBI agents and Boston SWAT had burst into a warehouse, rescuing him in a way usually only seen on TV! Now, if Shannon had money, too! Suddenly, the agent was aware he hadn't done the young man a favor by getting him released from jail. He either needed to get him into protective custody or put him where there was already security in place. Of course, if the Maloviches wanted Shannon dead, Bransom needed to keep him way separated from Mallory. Having both Shannon and Mallory together would create a target the criminals wouldn't be able to resist! He continued.

"Yeah, probably pretty smart. How ya gettin' groceries and stuff ya need? I'm gonna come pick ya up for that steak! Then I'm gonna protect ya somehow, if it's only by throwin' ya back in the slammer for now."

Shannon agreed, and within fifteen minutes, he was seated across the table from the agent.

Steaks ordered, Bransom leaned across the space, lowering his voice as much as possible.

"What do you know about Merrill Adams?"

Shannon sighed. "I really told you everything in interrogation. I was terrified of the guy, even before his face got blown apart. Of course, then the disfigurement was horrible! But he was more sinister-acting than ever, after that, too!"

"He have any next of kin?"

"I guess. Isn't that who's suing Mallory?"

"You know about that already?" Bransom was surprised. Since he had just heard about it, he had assumed it was news.

Shannon laughed for the first time, beginning to feel safer and relaxed. "Yes, Sir. Since I've been scared to go out, all I've been doing is talking on the phone and e-mailing. Shay talks to me quite a bit. He told me some goons are after Mallory's money. I never knew anything about Adams or his family. Our mom tried to keep us out of it. Guess you know she died for her efforts. Shay really beats himself up over mom's death. Can I show you a picture of our mom?"

"Looks like she was a beautiful lady, Shannon. I'm sorry for your loss. You staying in touch with Callie?"

"Mom was beautiful. Of course, I loved my dad, too. I kind of believed him when he swore he had nothing to do with Mom's 'accident'. Shay's convinced he did it!"

"Well, no use you boys fightin' about that now. State of Massachusetts did an in-depth investigation, and nothin' pointed to your dad. You know he was no saint, but there's no proof he harmed your mother. Just sad now, you two fellas without her. What about Callie?"

Shannon laughed again. "You writin' a gossip column, Agent? My days are numbered. No use being around Callie and exposing her to extra danger!"

Erik attempted once again, to talk to Shannon about his need for salvation, but Shannon assured him he was a better Catholic, now; and as soon as Oscar and Otto were in jail, he could be more faithful to attend Mass.

Steak lunches devoured, Bransom turned Shannon over to a detail charged with the responsibility of getting him some protection.

꿍 ꜟ

After another week in Dallas, Daniel and Diana decided it was time for them to resume their normal life. All four of them and Mallory left early on a Tuesday morning, so Diana could visit her doctor before time to prepare a soup dinner and have lessons. Mallory saw the sonogram and heard the little heartbeat! It was the most amazing thing! After the lessons, *the Maestro* lingered, finally being able to discuss Cassandra without emotional breakdowns on both parts. The world-class violinist knew people internationally in all the realms of classical music, but 'mum' was the word about Cassandra! If anyone out there had any knowledge of the little girl, they weren't talking!

Alexandra and Jeremiah went to bed; Daniel stayed in the music room long after *the Maestro's* departure, playing piece after beautiful piece. Mallory could still hear the music floating up to the design studio.

Diana's musical laughter was nearly back to normal as she confessed to Mallory that they had snooped through her file in the SUV. She explained that they were getting pretty bored, lonely, and worried about her, explaining how hard they tried, to save the remaining battery power.

"Tell me the whole story," Mallie prompted.

"Maybe when you tell me what happened to you after you got kidnapped in Turkey" Diana countered.

At an impasse, they both laughed. Tired, they discussed the *Topkapi Dagger*. Diana was suddenly interested in the jewelry designs already in production, eager to talk to Herb about the newest theme.

"Well, we should get some rest, but I want to talk to you about those gray pictures you took that morning on the Bosporus when it was stormy!"

"What about them?" Mallory thought she had merely managed to capture the gloom, failing to portray the atmosphere of the awesome morning.

"They are absolutely amazing. Made me really sorry I got you such a cheap camera. I just looked out that morning, thought, 'it's stormy', and never took my cameras out. I've been wanting to redecorate our bedroom suite, but none of my pictures seemed to lend themselves to any inspiration. This is so beautiful! The rainwater cascading down the glass softens the scene even more. Then, the soft yellow car lights floating in the sky!"

Opening her large sketch book, she showed Mallory her adaptation for interior design. Gray marble areas gave way to silvery carpet, punctuated occasionally with pale-yellow, subtly-patterned, Persian rugs. Walls were treated with silvery gray, softly-textured silk, woven with the subtle mural of the hazy bridge, the yellow headlights glowing softly through the foggy gloom. The bed was covered by silver, quilted silk, heaped with matching cushions and pillows, interspersed with a few pastel yellow ones. Silver draperies blended softly with the wall-coverings, tied back with yellow, silk ropes.

"That is elegant beyond words!" Mallory couldn't help thinking about growing up with her little *Pooh Bear* bedroom. Sometimes the quantum leap was hard for her to grasp.

"I love it, and so does Daniel. Of course, he isn't hard to please. I love the faint outlines of the famous, landmark mosques, but with Islam spreading like wildfire in the U.S., Daniel didn't want mosques in our bedroom."

"Guess I can see his point. The *Aga Sofia* was a church first, then a mosque; now it's a museum."

"Yeah, and it looks exotic and amazing in your pictures. With the minarets, it still looks like a mosque. I'm ready to go to bed, I think. You look tired, too, Mallory."

Emotional strains from Daniel's violin were still wafting up to them. He had switched from classical to hymns. "Ho, everyone who is thirsty in spirit."

"G'night, Mallory, he spoke to them as they passed. "Honey, I'll be up in a little bit." He spoke as he stowed his instrument gently in its case, and moved to his office, closing the door softly.

He had plenty on his mind. Bransom had told him about the graffiti, although the damage had been repaired. Bransom was wanting to keep track of the nut who seemed to think it was a logical step from buying a coat to killing your kids. Faulkner became more aware, every day, of a class war in the U.S. The press would get a copy of his water bill, making a big deal of how big his grounds were, and how he was using more water than 'was right'! When there was rationing, he abode by it, too. He was a giver, not only tithing and habitually adding extra offerings for church and missionary projects, but trying to be a generous, caring employer. God kept blessing him for it. That was a Scriptural principle, but there was just a resentment he sensed very often. His lush property supported a wealth of trees, but evidently the 'tree-huggers' weren't impressed with his feeble attempts to restore the 'lungs of the planet'. People usually preferred to find fault, than to recognize the positives.

His screen saver showed their family portrait, and he paid special attention to it. So often, he didn't really take note; just taking things for granted. All three kids had already changed a lot since the sitting before the Holidays. Al looked like a cross between him and Diana, Jeremiah was Daniel made over, and Cass looked like Diana! Beautiful family! He had so much to be thankful for. He opened his picture file, clicking to start a slide show. The first one started with their wedding. He gazed into Diana's beautiful, blue eyes, remembering the first time he ever looked into them.

After finishing his Bachelors and Masters degrees in five years, he toured Europe for six months. Prior to his salvation, being a spoiled, rich kid, it had been a wild time. His dad decided it was time for him to settle down, so he brought him home to Tulsa and GeoHy, before sending him to central Africa in search of water deep under the desert sand. Within twenty-four hours of his arrival, he was practically dead of some raging infection. Terrified and in agony, he was transported by truck to the nearest medical facility of any type, three hours away. He could still remember the hemorrhaging, the hallucinations, the coming to his senses long enough to be terrified of dying. The clinic wasn't much, stale and stuffy, staffed mostly by Africans who spoke very little English.

When he finally opened his eyes to focus on anything, Diana sat there, her beautiful eyes filled with compassion. He honestly thought he was in the process of dying, and that she was an angel sent to ease him across. He laughed. That was when his idea of angels was based on Medieval paintings instead of the Bible.

Maybe he thought she was an angel, too, because she kept talking to him about Jesus. Then, she would disappear, and he would think she was just another hallucination, albeit, a much nicer one than most of them were. He shuddered at the memory of the illness. Whether she was real or not, he was in love.

His parents arrived, aggrieved at being asked to offset some of the expenses to the under- funded clinic, thinking Diana was using their son's illness to extort money from them. She prayed over him, and nursed him back to health. When he was strong enough to fly home, she accompanied him. Her mom and dad hadn't forgiven them yet.

His beautiful, beautiful Diana! He loved her then, and he loved her still, planning to love her forever! She was an easy person to love! And he adored his kids. The losses due to miscarriages made him have a greater appreciation for the three carried to term. And the fact that they were into the third trimester with Xavier was a victory, too. He tried not to miss Cassandra, but just to be grateful for her, her life, her gift, her special place in his heart that physical distance couldn't lessen.

Diana's Sable coat was finally ready. He had ordered it a year ago, but with the steep price tag, the furrier kept waiting for enough pelts to exactly match, to complete the luxurious, full-length garment. Impatient for the gift, Daniel had finally suggested that someone dye some pelts to match. Oh, my, No! Dyed was bad! Really, really bad!

He hadn't told her about the graffiti, for several reasons! The main one's being it would ruin the surprise he had planned for her for so long! Now, he wondered if she would be surprised at all.

He loved showering her with surprises! Although shopping could be a pain. Telling salespeople he needed something special for his wife, usually brought a lot of wisecrack comments about his needing something to get him 'out of the doghouse'. His efforts to explain Diana's loveliness and worth, usually just brought more of the same! It was true, what the Bible said, loosely paraphrased, he would look it up later. But "to the pure all things are pure, and to the wicked, everything is wicked". People often had such jaded minds that they refused to believe he was different; Diana was different; their marital relationship was different.

Sadly, many of the Christian men he knew razzed him about giving gifts to Diana that made them look bad. He just loved her. Having her at his side made him successful, made him want to excel, made him want her proud of him. He was proud of her, and of his children that she worked on constantly, keeping them looking sharp and acting polite and intelligent.

He gave up trying to martial his thoughts away from Cass. Cassandra seemed to have been born knowing how to win. Daniel felt all children were 'strong-willed children'. Before Al was born, he had heard the expression, "As the twig is bent, so grows the tree." So, he and Diana's plan was to nurture the pliable little saplings into a love for the Lord and respect for parents and authority. What a shocker! Al wasn't born pliable, at all, but with a definite willful nature that wanted its own way! All the time! The twigs came into the world, already bent the wrong direction by an innate, sinful nature. Redirecting them required discipline and perseverance, breaking the self-will to reset it the right way, submissive to Authority: parents, teachers, and to God. Jer presented his own challenges to their parenting, but he and Diana kept the upper hand there, too.

Then came Cassandra! From the beginning, she was a real Daddy's girl, which, he had kind of liked. Now she seemed like a convicted felon, who likes a weak link in the fence, not for itself, but for the perceived benefit of freedom. She shone her smiles on him because she could manipulate her way around him, showing her temperamental side to Diana, who met her head on, creating a few major rows. That was before they ever placed a violin into the chubby, little, out-stretched hands. Her gift and love for the violin mirrored his, and they were soul-mates! As long as she got what she wanted! Which, more and more, was being allowed to play her instrument without interference! He sighed. The turning point really came after the Easter night concert at Faith Baptist in Arkansas. The congregation responded well to the entire family, but they were especially wowed by the little five year old who could set the violin on fire! She loved the applause, the spotlight, the compliments! The monster was full-grown, overnight! Then, after performing in Istanbul, using the violin purchased by Carlton, Cassandra refused to return to real life.

He sat, watching the slideshow through again, tears flowing freely. Weeping, he poured out his soul in prayer, once more. That Cass had sincerely been saved, that she would miraculously grow in grace, that she would be able to learn whatever had been causing her such vexation, that her life would be useful to the Lord! That was their goal for all of their children.

As he closed his computer, he felt defeated, lonely for his little girl thousands of miles from home. He wondered if she were homesick; he hoped she was too happy to be. But even though he felt defeated; by the newscasters, the jewelry sales people, the animal rights advocates, and resentful Christians, he quoted one of his favorite verses:

> *II Corinthians 2:14 Now thanks be unto God, which always causeth us to triumph in Christ, and maketh manifest the savor of his knowledge by us in every place.*

His lone voice, spreading the savor of the knowledge of God? It seemed like the vulgar salesmen weren't listening to his voice at all, as he protested. But he was winning! He was making a difference! He couldn't always see it, just had to accept it by faith, because the Bible states it as a fact!

⊰ ⊱

Lilly Cowan was fighting several fronts, too. Cassandra Faulkner! The girl reminded her of a short story by a famous American author, O'Henry, *The Ransom of Red Chief*! She couldn't remember all the particulars about the story, except a couple of bad guys kidnapped a rich man's kid to hold for ransom. The surprise ending was that the outlaws received the ransom money, with instructions to keep the bratty kid. She sometimes felt like the Faulkners had somehow wittingly set her up, to get her to come take Cassandra off their hands. Still far to stubborn to relent, Lilly held on determinedly.

Mallory O'Shaughnessy was proving to be an equal challenge! The girl seemed aware of the fact that she owed Lilly a debt; that was what was keeping her within Lilly's grasp, at all.

Herb Carlton swore he didn't know the location of the rosy-pink 'heart' diamond, and also claimed not to know whether the girl found any diamonds worth keeping on her recent foray. Lilly's minions were still attempting to learn the contents of the twenty safety deposit boxes. In addition to that trick, ten of Mallory's friends were in the process of each installing another safe in their homes. Lilly thought it was all smoke screen, but it took time and man-power to be certain! The most recent trick had the woman in a fury; several of the inner circle of DiaMo, burying something in their flower beds, like they were old-time pirates, or something!

That trick worried Lilly the most! Surely, the girl wouldn't be idiotic enough to place it into the ground! She would never find it again! It would be lost for all time!

Lilly knew that diamonds, with their slick surfaces, and comparative density, exhibit a tendency to bury themselves.

Then, a very striking blow, when an American, Trent Morrison, manipulated Simon Cohen to take measures against her. They would both pay! As soon as she could figure out a way! And she was working on it! Hard!

Now the Faulkners were back in their lavish estate! Neither one saw a minute in jail. Evidently, their family all camped out together, enjoying a lark, to return home to extravagant gifts like a full-length, Sable coat! Lilly didn't mind the fur trade; she was for it! But she couldn't stand for the handsome Daniel Faulkner to adore Diana so much! Lilly wasn't pretty, and her limp resulting from an equestrienne fall from when she was ten, made her very self-conscious. In spite of lacking the "charms' helpful to a woman's success, Lilly had been very successful, rising to a very coveted position. She had a ruthless drive that pushed her ever onward. But her personal life was a disaster. That fact had bothered her from time to time. But now, seeing Diana Faulkner's happy, charmed life, just proved to her that some people could have it all! Professional success, personal success, happiness! If she couldn't have it, neither should they! Maybe that was why she continued to put up with Cassandra!

⊰ ⊱

Mallory had a particularly tough day on her daddy's birthday. She woke up crying, had a few dry moments during the course of the day, before crying herself to sleep at bedtime. Even so, she realized two or three weeks had passed since the last time she had cried for him. She really was improving.

And, with the Faulkner's return to normalcy, a shareholders' meeting was being scheduled. At *Niagara Falls*! Mallory could hardly believe it. Six months earlier, she had stood on her sagging front porch in Murfreesboro, Arkansas, quoting the first stanza of *Renascence*, by Edna St. Vincent Millay.

> *"All I could see from where I stood,*
> *Was three long islands, and a wood."*

She had hardly been anywhere exciting in her entire seventeen years. Now, since May, she had traveled across the U.S., departing from New York City, to tour Turkey, west to east. Then to Israel! Boston, actually going to *Fenway* for a *Sox* game, the sites in D.C. Now, *Niagara Falls*, part of which were in Canada! Then skiing in Aspen in November and the NYC gem show in December!

Standing on the terrace adjoining her suite, she gazed out at her pool surrounded by brilliant flower beds, she laughingly quoted the final stanza.

> *"The world stands out on either side,*
> *No wider than the soul is wide.*
> *And he whose soul is flat, the sky*
> *Will cave in on him, by and by."*

Chapter 20: WEDDING

In mid-August, everyone convened in Niagara Falls, Canada, checking into a luxury hotel, where their tower suites overlooked the dazzling rainbows and mists of the falls.

David hadn't seen Mallory since early June when they had ended up 'by chance', having lunch together in Tulsa. Standing by a pillar, where she hadn't noticed him, he watched her, amazed, as she checked the group in through the concierge check-in. She looked amazing! A softly-draping, pale-orange dress flattered her with both color and style. High heeled pumps and handbag matched the delicate color exactly. As he approached her, he could see her jewelry sparkled in the same exquisite hue, little pansies with interwoven stems and leaves of shimmering lemon quartz. Closer up, he could see little lime flecks crocheted into her dress.

Shy around her, but wanting her attention, too, he spoke suddenly. "Hey, Erin!"

She jumped; so did he! "David! Hi! I didn't see you there. How's the camp coming?"

He looked really handsome! Wearing tan slacks with a blue oxford shirt and navy blazer, no tie; he looked sharp, business-casual! Dark hair, cut shorter, it was tousled up, but with a semi-part on the right side. His skin was bronzed, a contrast with his dazzling smile. And he was tall. Mallie was five-eight, without the heels, and she still had to look up to meet his intense brown eyes.

"The camp's great. We've had a few days of mini-camps, so that means we've started making contacts with some area kids. The stables are nearly finished. The main building should be 'in the dry' by November when it gets really rainy. They're working hard toward that end, at any rate! The architects are studying the plait sites for the ministry headquarters. Looks like your jewelry designs are becoming a reality. That's beautiful. You just took a picture of a flower in a flower bed, and Carlton did that?"

"Yeah. And when I first tried to talk to Mr. Carlton on the way to Turkey, he told me Erik just invited him because we had empty seats. That kind of made me annoyed, because no one was even being friendly to him. You couldn't even tell he was Erik's guest. So, I'm wondering, 'Why's he even along? Duh, Mallory! The Lord was answering our prayers!"

David laughed. It was an amazing story!

"Here's your room key." She held it out to him, showing long tapered fingers, with perfect nails polished to match her outfit. "A couple of coaches are coming for everyone at one, to take us to the *Falls*. See ya later."

She was gone, leaving a hint of fragrance. He watched her ascend in the glass elevator before finding a house phone to track Shay down.

Shay and Shannon met him in the hotel restaurant, since the three of them were always hungry. All devouring hefty burgers, they caught up on the latest news.

Shannon and Shay had seen the *Falls* numerous times, since the famous attraction wasn't that far from Boston. They were telling David that the *Basketball Hall of Fame*, in Springfield, MA. would be an interesting side-trip. David was pretty overwhelmed, just getting to see the famous *Falls*, but Shay and Shannon were badgering him to ask Mallie about the extra jaunt.

"Hey, you guys ask her! You're her long-lost cousins! Where's Cooperstown from here? Now, the *Baseball Hall of Fame*! That, she'd go for!"

"Oh, yeah," Shay chortled. "You got that right!"

She pulled out a chair to join them. "Go for what? You three look like a dangerous mix."

"*Baseball Hall of Fame!*" Shannon was the brave one.

Her gaze traveled from face to face, tears filling her eyes. "Daddy and I were always going to go there. Well, we should still look into it. Work it out, Shay."

⚜ ⚜

The Faulkners arrived, causing their usual stir, even in the high-end hotel. Diana's hair was still shorter, but was highlighted blond once more. Her outfit, the palest wash of pink, back-dropped jewelry of '*Bleeding Hearts*, carved from Rhodonite, showing a definite Faberge-influence. Strings of pavéd diamonds laced the flowers together, sparkling from white gold. Her nails were the palest, pastel pink, but the most amazing thing was her radiant personality.

Daniel, the constant *Ken Doll* at her side, projected in a tan, tweed, silk, sports jacket, and medium brown slacks. White French cuffs, diamond cuff links, silk tie striped in browns and tans, always, new-looking shoes!

Alexandra and Jeremiah, dressed to perfection also, stood like martinets beside their parents during the expedited check-in.

⚓ ⚓

At the *Falls*, Mallory stood mesmerized, listening to the rush of the water, gazing into the hypnotic, swirling depths. Wow! The place was nearly as powerful as *The Place of the Skull* had been in Israel. Everything new and exciting made her miss her dad; things she would have loved to share with him! Still, he had made all this possible for her, and she knew he would want her to be happily enjoying everything. As she gazed into the powerful eddies, a miracle took place. The guilt and burden and grief rolled away from her, and she knew without a doubt, they wouldn't return. Her spirit was free!

⚓ ⚓

At eight, everyone reassembled in a spacious meeting room, high above the falls. Formal dress required, not that anyone minded. The men, in custom-made tuxedos, the ladies in long pastel gowns, competing with the rainbows beyond the plate glass, created a soft hum of conversation and activity. Mallory, in fitted yellow, taffeta and Canary Diamonds, moved graciously among her guests. She was trying not to notice how handsome David looked in formal attire.

Appetizers allured from silver chafing dishes. Daniel helped himself, joining Erik, Roger, John, Kerry, and Tom. Erik was confiding to the men of the group some of the recent intel from Col. Ahmir, in Turkey. A secondary explosive in the device had failed to detonate! The reason they were all alive! There were enough explosives to incinerate both coaches and their contents. No proof the Maloviches were involved! An extreme group, active in Turkey, though outlawed, claimed responsibility. None of the men believed that. Ahmir also told them that the medic, first on the scene, was amazed to learn Sammy was already back to normal. They also discussed some other security incidents: someone's trespassing on the Andersons' new home site, and the graffiti incident at the Faulkner's estate. They continued to assess and upgrade security measures.

Callie and Donovan Cline arrived, almost in sync with Mallory's grandparents, Meg and Martin Campbell. Last to arrive were Merc and Nell with their four sons. The group continued to move around, forming one conversational group, then kaleidoscoping into different, colorful patterns. Herb, in white tuxedo, and Linda, in a sparkling, white, bridal gown, took their places at the center of the head table, decorated lavishly with white lilies and roses. Merc, Nell, and their sons flanked Herb. Linda's parents, Suzanne and Erik, and Mallory sat next to Linda. The group was settling eagerly into ornate chairs at the lovely place-settings.

John Anderson asked the blessing, then an army of servers advanced swiftly, placing a salad at each spot. Prime rib and baked potatoes followed salads, then plates were cleared as Herb and Linda mounted the dais to stand facing John Anderson. Diana played the 'Wedding March', Suzanne stood by Linda as Matron of Honor, and Merc next to Herb, as Best Man. Daniel and Diana sang 'The Hawaiian Wedding Song', followed by the vows of a Christian wedding ceremony. A kiss, cutting of the cake, a thrown bouquet, and the bride and groom were gone. Mallory retired to her room, not waiting for cake. Getting her aunt married off had not been an easy job! She brewed the little pot of coffee, sitting down to log onto her laptop.

There were several projects she needed to complete for her various courses, but her attitude toward her courses had changed radically in the past several months. School work and learning were now a way of life. When she announced her major in Geology, everyone who knew her asked her if she were sure she didn't mean 'Gemology', with an *m* added. Laughing, she assured them she knew the difference. Geology led you to the gems; Gemology taught you what to do with the gems once you found them. She was pretty interested in pursuing both!

She created rough outlines for both projects. One fit; the other seemed to require too many main points. The topic must need to be narrowed down more. Another twenty minutes, and that one was more under control, too. That would help her to limit her research, too, to what was necessary.

That finished, she gave her *Power-Point* presentation for the morning stockholders' meeting, a quick brush-up.

Erik called her, asking her about some of the fan mail. She thought she was pretty smart to put Marge in charge of it, but Erik wanted to look at it, at least occasionally, to make sure no one really dangerous had her in their sites.

Then Diana phoned her, inviting her back down to the lobby, where some of them were having coffees. Sounded fun, so she quickly wiggled back into her enchanting dress.

Arriving in the lobby, she joined the Faulkners, Andersons, Sanders, Haynes, Kerry, and Delia; placing her order for a latte. A couple of hotel guests tried to join them, making fun of the tuxes.

"Hey, hey, Waiter, could you bring me another drink?" He was addressing Daniel, who simply responded he would gladly buy him a coffee to help sober him up.

They kept on, becoming more and more belligerent about the corporate group's being dressed up.

Erik suggested the intruders move along or return to their rooms. He didn't display his badge. Noisy drunks in a Canadian hotel weren't within his jurisdiction.

"Hey, hey, hey! Look at me: I'm really a prince! Come dance with me, Cinderella!" One of them tried to present Diana with a courtly bow, falling clumsily onto her.

Her security stepped in, since the hotel's hadn't made a move. The rest of the group's private security formed a wall, cutting their employers off from the annoying drunks. The revelers, not increased in wisdom by being 'under the influence', continued mouthing off, spewing obscenities and threats. Mostly, they seemed to be ticked off by the 'formal dress'.

Private security ushered their charges into one of the empty lobby restaurants, before complaining to the hotel management. The night manager suggested the formally attired contingency all go change and come back down, trying to "blend in more."

No one in the Christian group was trying to make trouble, but, 'blending-in' wasn't what they were all about, either. They thought they had a right to express themselves with their clothing. Maybe not in Canada! They had the distinct impression that the U.S. wasn't that different. You could wear Goth, vulgarity, lots of stuff. But just dress up? Everyone wanted to know why. They acted miffed that you did it without their permission. The message was loud and clear. "Fit in!"

"Oh, there was a wedding? Well, okay, but go get 'comfortable' now that it's over. Or, better yet, just have a dressed down, blue-jeans wedding."

Diana got tired of the line. "I just want to be comfortable." But even if everyone around her really did want to be 'comfortable', what right did they have to insist she 'be comfortable' according to their standard of 'what's comfortable' and what isn't? Her beautiful designs were constructed with the appropriate amount of 'ease' built into the fit, so that they moved comfortably with the body's motion. To Diana, most people's 'being comfortable' smacked loudly of 'being sloppy', which, if that was what other people wanted, that was their business. She never said a word to anyone, "Why are you dressed so plain, sloppy, and conformed?" She figured that was their business. She got tired of having well-intentioned people trying to get her to be more like them.

She thought her position was Scriptural, or at least, not un-Scriptural. The priestly garments were made beautifully, with great attention to detail. Esther slid into 'royal apparel' when she coveted the favor of the king. Joseph cleaned up and dressed up before entering the court of Pharaoh. Often God referred to Himself as coming, clothed in Honor and Majesty, or appareled for Glory and Virtue. She translated that to mean that women should dress virtuously, yes! Definitely! But Gloriously, also! Her blue eyes danced! When the servant met Rebekah, to take as a bride for Isaac, he gave her jewels of silver, and jewels of gold, and raiment! Diana adored the beautiful language of Psalm forty-five, about Ivory Palaces, fragrances, and dressing in garments of fine gold.

Conversely, she knew Lucifer clothed himself with all the beautiful gemstones before pride caused his fall. All of their blessings could lead to pride and backsliding, but she could think of some pretty prideful poor people, too. She laughed. Not that she was judging! Well, maybe she was a little.

In her prayer journal, she prayed daily for the Fruit of the Spirit, one of which was Meekness.

"Honey, did that guy hurt you?" Daniel's concerned voice brought her out of her reverie.

Her gaze met his, "No, I'm fine. I'm actually glad the kids got to see an example of the effects of alcohol. We warn them a lot, but it kind of rolls off. It's scary that everyone's so used to drunks, that they just excuse their behavior. 'Oh, they're just drunk. It's your fault they attacked you. You shouldn't look nice'."

Erik Bransom, overhearing the conversation, realized sadly, that she was right. America was in trouble. Like if some crazy driver committed a moving violation, could have caused a wreck, but beep the horn, and you're the one that 'deserves' to be shot! Crazy rationale permeating all strata of American society. "Crazy rationale!" he laughed at his own oxymoron. Between many Americans' being under the influence of drugs, alcohol, or both, and having their reason clouded by media and entertainment's mores,~ Well, it was frightening to think about. Like the guy who vandalized the Faulkner's property! To him, using animal skins was the height of immorality, selfishness, and wickedness! Damaging other people's property was no big deal! They deserved it! And the country was frighteningly full of people who would agree. The guy also thought having a fur coat was worse than if Diana had killed Cassandra. When did everything get so crazy? Well, when did animals get rights? He didn't remember hearing about that amendment to the Constitution's being ratified! Oh! That's right! It hadn't been! Just the Power of the Press again, and all their racket! Give them a week, they could probably brain wash most of the unthinking public into anything! Scary!

He reentered the conversation with those cheery thoughts put into words.

"You know, Erik, you're exactly right." John Anderson spoke slowly and thoughtfully "The Bible teaches that when the Antichrist seizes power, as millions of Christians disappear in the Rapture, that God will send 'strong delusion' so people will believe his lie. Seems like the stage is set for that, already. I mean, my kids have watched *One Hundred, and One Dalmatians*, a thousand times, although I'm not too fond of any of Hollywood's productions. I mean, I watch movies on TV, and on video, with the *Curse-free TV* video player. It's entertaining, and hard to preach against. But, think about Cruella De Ville. Of course, she really is a bad character, but that movie makes kids think that Lana and Diana are the same, because they have furs. I was just watching a police program where a young man had committed a crime. His wealthy mama, (wearing a fur), was a real 'dragon-woman', determined to keep her son from paying his debt to society. None of the nice roles present ladies in furs. I'm afraid it's a portrayal that all wealthy people are wicked, not having earned what they have. Everyone loves the idea of *Robin Hood*. Socialism has pervaded our thinking, and it's fueled by the media and entertainment industries. Which is odd, because many of the entertainment moguls are multi-millionaires, even billionaires Of course they all splatter their charitable contributions all over the grocery-check-out magazines." John had captured the conversation, everyone listening in agreement.

"Well, it's kind of the same thing with diamonds. Like a class-war against the status symbols of the wealthy. Now, furs are on the taboo list, and with the big 'Conflict Diamond' controversy, you nearly have to wear your diamond's 'origin certificate' whenever your diamonds are likely to garner attention." Daniel Faulkner paused to smile at Diana. "Yes, people commit atrocities on one another, because of diamonds, or anything with any value at all. People fought and warred before diamonds were discovered, and they'll still fight over something else when diamonds are exhausted. Diana and I agree that it's okay to own status symbols. Like Judah, in the Old Testament; one of the twelve Patriarchs, he was well off. Remember he left his signet ring and walking stick with Tamar for a pledge? They were pretty cool things, distinguishable as Judah's. Of course, when he attempted to redeem the items, his friend couldn't find Tamar or the incriminating possessions. We think it's a lesson about being careful where you go. Losing things is an inevitability. I mean, I've lost a watch on the golf course. But Diana knew I was golfing. If you're somewhere you're not supposed to be, your cool stuff can catch you."

"That's why people need the Lord," Diana inserted as she nodded agreement with her husband's words. "If you understand your Bible, there were always distinct social and economic classes. Of course, Judas Iscariot pretended to care about poor people, and Jesus stated that we would always have poor people among us, and whenever we want, we can do things for them. But what? Just hand out lumps of cash? It's easy to see how that works, by studying most lottery winners. People need Salvation and the wisdom that comes from knowing God. In Proverbs, it says, it's better to get wisdom than rubies, and understanding than fine gold. If we have wisdom and understanding, we can earn the riches, and have a chance of hanging onto them. If there are just riches without wisdom and understanding, we quickly lose the wealth to foolish spending and con artists. Like the old saying goes, 'A fool and his money are soon parted'."

Delia loved the stimulating conversation and being around her new friends. Maybe the oldest in years of anyone there, but younger in heart than ever, she ordered more coffees for every one in the group, and a plate of assorted desserts, slipping her credit card to the bar tender, or whatever he was. She wanted this corner of the world to see that Christians could have more fun than anyone, without morning-after embarrassment, and a hangover.

And she didn't want the *Cinderella* night to end! She loved elegance, but aside from her fine linen business, it had become almost non-existent for her. People just didn't bother any more. The sixties and the hippie movement changed America's values and culture to such an extent, that the word 'Revolution' was really an apt description of what had happened.

Tammi had never worn a formal before, either, and she couldn't believe the Princess feel it gave her. The palest aquamarine, her dress was a dream; fitted bodice joined by self-fabric piping to a long bouffant skirt which swished gracefully with her every movement. The jewel neckline was complimented with a beautiful dog-collar necklace. A large Aquamarine, the focal point, was surrounded by small pearls, centered in multiple strands of pearls. Dangles of Pearls and Aquamarines danced in the ambient light with each tilt of her chin. A wrist corsage from her daddy completed her look. She hadn't said much, just listening interestedly to the adults who surrounded her, and oh-so aware of Kerry!

Mallory was quiet, too. David, Shay, and Shannon weren't in the group, so she couldn't help wondering where they were, and what they were up to. And, she had caught Tom and Joyce exchange startled looks when Pastor had mentioned Lana's fur. Although they had apologized to her for their conversation about it, evidently their feelings were still the same.

"What's new with my law suit?" she asked Kerry when a lull came in the conversation

He shook his head. "Still wangling with the other attorneys. Offered ten thousand to each, which, they should accept. They still want the quarter million!"

"Yeah, don't we all? I don't see how they even want to admit they were related to the guy!" Mallory's eyes flashed.

"Who's suing?" It was the first Pastor Anderson had heard of it, and he couldn't believe it was the sons of the killer who had nearly murdered Tammi in cold blood! His face drained of color, just remembering.

"Well, you just keep stalling them along, Larson," Erik's wry voice inserted itself. "I'm planning a nice surprise for those two boys that has nothing to do with a quarter of a million dollars!" His voice was even more of a growl than usual.

Mallory and Tammi excused themselves to the ladies' room, and Janice accompanied them, watchful.

"Isn't this fun?" Mallie exclaimed when they were both reapplying lipstick before a long, spotless mirror. "Remember all our talk about getting out of Murfreesboro and seeing the world? Now we've been to Turkey, and we're at Niagara Falls. And I've already seen Boston and the *Red Sox* play?"

"Yeah," Tammi agreed. "You always told me to keep trusting the Lord and He could turn things around fast, like He did for Joseph! I didn't believe you, though. I thought it would just go on forever, the same-o, same-o! And you always loved the Bible story of Rebekah, in her little home town, with no cool bridegrooms in sight! But Rebekah just kept being sweet, even offering to water some guy's camels for him."

"Yeah, and he paid her for it with really valuable jewelry, which would have been nice, if the story ended there. But those were only 'tokens for good'. The best was yet to come, with a prince of a husband, twin boys, and a place in God's plan!"

"Mallie, do you think Kerry will keep waiting for me?" Tears sparkled in Tammi's dark eyes. "I tried to talk to Mr. Haynes about rushing up graduating, like you and David. He didn't laugh, but I thought he wanted to. Then, he just told me it wouldn't work. Then, Daddy was mad at me for even asking ."

"Well, I think Kerry'll wait, if he's really the one the Lord has for you. You didn't ever work very hard at your grades. Now, you should just be serious about academics, more than rushing through. And, I haven't graduated early. I'm still working on my senior year. I'm working on some college work concurrently, because it's all interesting, and I want at least a double major. And, I'm still going in the teen department at church, because Daddy never wanted me to try to get ahead of where I should be. Don't let Mr. Larson cause you to miss out on being a teenager; it's what you are."

Tammi's hands flew up. "You always preach!" She was partly annoyed, and partly amused.

"Yeah, you just complimented me on some of my other best sermons. Being a preacher's kid, you should know better that to get me started."

When they returned to the group, everyone was saying goodnight. It had been fun, but the shareholder meeting was scheduled for nine.

Erik and Daniel personally checked out Mallory's room, assuring her they would both leave their cell phones on, too. Checking that all was secure, they told her good-night.

She lay awake a long time, staring at the detail of the ceiling in her suite. Whether it was the coffee or David, causing sleep to flee, she wasn't sure. She wondered curiously about her aunt and Herb. Both had been single a long time; she wondered if the adjustment would be hard for them. She couldn't figure out where the guys had gone. She slid her feet into curly slippers and paced. She probably should calm down and read her Bible.

They couldn't be up to too much, with security following them everywhere they went, could they? She was really managing to get worked up, letting her imagination run away with her, when her cell vibrated.

Shay's phone! "Mallory!" she answered coldly.

"Are you in a bad mood?" The voice didn't sound like Shay's.

"Shannon?" she questioned, unsure.

"Yeah, did we interrupt something? We've been up here in David's room, and I started asking lots of questions about stuff. So, we've been talking and studying the Bible. I got saved, and Shay thought you'd be real happy about it."

"I am real happy about it, Shannon! That's the greatest news I could ever hear! Wondered where you guys disappeared to."

"Yeah, Grandmother just stopped to tell us we missed a fun party in the lobby, but if we had known about that, things might not have developed the same way, so I'd end up saved. Were you mad we weren't down there? Oh, I get it! David, my man, I think you may be in trouble with my cousin!"

Mallie was humiliated as she heard Shannon start to rib David. The last thing she needed! She could hear David's response.

"I think your cousin stays mad at me; you got any clues on how to get on her good side, and stay there?"

"Hey, Shannon, happy for your decision! You think you'll go to church at Faith with my mom and Agent Bransom? Or in Hope where the Sanders go?" She was trying to save the conversation.

"Oh, well, I'm still a Catholic! Ha ha! Just kiddin'! got ya, didn't I?!"

She laughed too. He really had hooked her. "You guys are crazy. See ya in the morning."

Chapter 21: WINNING

Not having slept very well, Mallory was in the hotel conference room before eight, already dressed, having eaten a bit, and finished her devotions. Everything was set up according to specifications. Amused, she checked the door, remembering their May meeting. This looked like they should have quite a bit of privacy. Her brow furrowed at obvious breaches they must have in their security. How did Lilly Cowan know everything they were all doing, almost before they did?

No mystery as to how Lilly had been aware of Cassandra and her talent! Cass had burst into the limelight Easter night when she performed at Faith! Then again, in the hotel lobby in Turkey! For anyone interested in the DiaMo/GeoHy group, following them through their church web sites wasn't hard. She gazed around curiously, wondering if any listening devices were secreted somewhere in this room.

Walking quickly to the front desk, she requested a manager, and was ushered immediately into a spacious office, where the operations manager rose courteously, extending a hand across the broad desktop, beginning an immediate apology for the previous evening's incident with the offensive revelers.

Mallie's smile flashed. "Oh, thank you. I'm not here to complain. I have a question about our conference room. It looks perfect, but our business is pretty confidential. We seem to have several outsiders who are more interested in our business than we are."

"Ah, Corporate Espionage! Always a problem. It may be some of your own people. Even if you pay them well, there's always the possibility that business rivals will offer them more in exchange for privileged information."

"Yes, Ma'am," Mallory agreed politely. "But, do you have any equipment to check for listening devices? And also, if your wait staff could just make food and beverages available on side tables, I would like to be able to close the doors during sessions so people aren't coming and going while we discuss things we feel are sensitive."

Nodding agreement, she pressed the intercom to speak with the hotel's head of security. When he realized Mallory was in the office, he began with the same apology, mentioning he had already scheduled a meeting with his staff to address their response to the previous evening's incident.

"We'll discuss that later," the manager's clipped voice. "Miss O'Shaughnessy wants to know if we have equipment for an electronics sweep. If we don't, we need to get on top of that, right away, throughout the entire chain. We want industries to hold corporate meetings with us."

"Yes, Ma'am, on my way."

Damon Hodges met Mallory in the conference room. Bald, with a droll, round face, he knew his stuff. Mallory figured ex-military and law-enforcement. He talked like all the other Canadians. On his cell, he commandeered a crew to reset the meeting in a another room. While they did that, he called his superior who oversaw all the security for every property in the chain. They needed to be able to guarantee privacy to all their guests.

The food manager appeared, too, arranging for food and beverages to be self-serve, eliminating hotel employees from overhearing privileged information.

Everything was in place in the switch-over by the time the group gathered at nine. Standing at the entrance, Mallory smiled a greeting to everyone. She was hoping she had upset Lilly's applecart!

She looked gorgeous! Wearing a chocolate brown jacket dress with matching wedge-heeled, peek-a-boo toed shoes, she looked no-nonsense business. On her lapel, she wore a Faberge-inspired pin: a dandelion puff of spun gold and platinum, sprouting from a carved, rock-crystal vase. It was cute, looking like it would blow away with a 'puff'. Herb Carlton was absolutely amazing! The piece of 'rock crystal' was from Arkansas, too!

The meeting began with a prayer by the pastor, and his calling the meeting to order. Then he presented the first report of the day, showing the acquisition of the twenty acres, the remodeling of the Faith Baptist property, the arrival of some of the recording studio equipment, the publications, the journal articles, and the Anderson's new home, nearing completion.

When he paused to ask if there was any new business relating to the reports, Mallory had a question. A trespasser on the property had occasioned the Anderson family members' getting personal security. No one had been caught on the site again, but Mallie was suddenly concerned for the nearly-finished home. What if someone tried to burn or vandalize it?"

Daniel stood, thanking John, addressing his questions to Erik. Another serious chink in the armor. Mallie's property, the Faulkner estate, Delia's Boston mansion, were all walled, with cameras and security measures in place. The Anderson's luxurious new home was pretty exposed and unprotected up to this point. They took a break, and Brad called the architect to look into what would be necessary to enclose the home with walls and gates, late in the process. That call was followed by one to his brother-in-law to get dogs on the property ASAP. **No Trespassing** signs were already up, he gave orders for stationing **Beware of Dog** signs at intervals, too.

Hotel staff replenished the buffet tables and beverages, but the doors were left opened, both to the mezzanine, and the kitchen. Another prayer, and the Faulkners began presenting a mini-concert. Beginning with, *You Can Have a Song in Your Heart*, they performed it exactly as they had at their church, earlier in the summer. Extremely moving, but the hotel staff made a point of closing the doors. The next song was one Mallie hadn't heard them perform before, 'Satisfied', the chorus joyfully proclaiming, 'Hallelujah! I have found Him!" One more, 'Ho, Every One Who Is Thirsty', a solo by Diana, accompanied by strings, ended with the promise, "While you are seeking Me, I will be found"! The notes died away, and John gave a devotional.

The meeting broke for lunch in the hotel restaurant. The group actually enjoyed interacting with other guests, most of the time, if they weren't drunk! Daniel and Diana nearly always received compliments on what a cute family they were, how well-behaved the kids were. Mallie knew all of that made them really miss Cassandra. Her mind traveled back to the April, Saturday morning, when she had first seen them. She was still as blown away by them now, as she was then. More so! Because by now, she knew what caring, joyful, compassionate Christians they were.

Diana was wearing the yellow suit again, with the pale and deep purple Amethysts and yellow Sapphire 'Pansy' jewelry. People who had been reluctant to jump on the creativity wagon with Herb, initially, were now eager artisans to create in the precious materials they had once only dreamed of. Mallory missed her head-jeweler and her aunt, hoping they were having a great honeymoon.

An imposing looking older couple, sitting a couple of tables away, couldn't resist starting a conversation with Diana, about how impressed they were with her family, but also with the entire group.

"I hope you don't mind if I ask, but where are you finding such beautiful clothing? I think all the nice stores are closing, and every place else only sells blue jeans."

Diana laughed. "I was hoping you'd ask. Actually, I'm a designer. Here's my business card. I won't put a hard sell on you when you're eating your lunch. Thank you for the compliment. This is Mallory O'Shaughnessy. She owns a diamond mine, and we're partners in jewelry designs, too. Actually, everything we do is Biblically based. God is the ultimate Creator and Designer. We love some of the artwork from history, too. Like, Mallory's pin is influenced by~"

"Carl Faberge," the newcomer finished. "Miss O'Shaughnessy, I've read some articles about you. Are you really only seventeen? You look so elegant! Our granddaughter's seventeen. Well, we kind of despair about her."

"Well, clothes and jewelry aren't the answer to that. The way kids present themselves is just a symptom, of being unmoored, spiritually. Jesus has made the difference in my life! And Diana's designs come in second. Actually, my grandmother and cousin have made some beautiful clothing designs for me, too. Here are their cards; we all promote one another. Diana designs a lot with silk, my grandmother is a linen fanatic, and my cousin Shay, designs in wool and Alpaca! And since we were in Turkey in the spring, he has gotten interested in Angora."

"Thank you so much. You can be sure you'll be hearing from me, and from my friends, too. My husband and I noticed you all last night, in the formal attire: it looked like all of you were enjoying yourselves. We occasionally have taken cruises where people dress formally for dinner, but that seems to be slipping into the past, too."

She seemed sad.

"Yes, but we all get tired of having "them" dictate to us!" Diana's joyous move smoothly back into the conversation. "You and your friends who still like elegant occasions can create your own. It's funny, though, if you do, you'll get lots of off-the-wall remarks. It amazes me how people can't mind their own business. If I wear a fur, people always have something to say. They don't think the day's cold enough, or something!"

"Yes, that's right. The wind-chill can be zero, and people still say things like that." The newcomer added whole-hearted agreement. "Last fall, we traveled to New York City. The weather was unseasonably mild, but I carried my fur with me since the hotel maids always try it on if I leave it in the room. It would have raised less of an alarm if I had been carrying a bomb!"

Diana laughed again. "Do you have a card?" she questioned. "I mean, I won't call you to push our designs if I don't hear from you.

Her husband presented their business card; he was a Florida Real Estate developer. Floyd Boggs; his wife, Myrna.

With lunch completed, the group assembled for afternoon sessions. Reports came from Delia, Shay, and Diana, respectively. It was all informative! The designs for the coming seasons were exquisite. Some of the projects were still on paper, although fully detailed and glossy! Others hung on racks, manifested in beautiful fabrics, accessorized with rich, supple leathers and dazzling jewelry. It was all so cute! The *Chessmen* line brought oohs and ahs. Mallory had been so reticent in suggesting it. Of course the idea might not have been much without Diana's amazing talent and abilities! And her hive of workers, whoever and wherever they were. The *Sparrows* and *Of More Value* line, already having reached market, was bringing in a deluge of orders.

Dinner was an extravagant affair, revolving high above the spectacular falls! Small-town Mallory hoped she would never 'get used to it', but that everything would always hold the same wonder for her. Her eyes shone luminously as she took in the awesome panorama spreading beyond them. The food was superb with outstanding service. With the meal complete, many of them walked back to the falls, watching the water tumble endlessly to the whirling eddies below. Mallory was amazed that the 'water cycle' was able to supply endless millions of gallons of water to the wonder, which never ran dry, nor even seemed to diminish.

Back in the lobby café for coffees again later, their joviality burst forth with its usual gusto. None of them lived problem-free lives, but every one of them exhibited a genuine *joie de vivre*, due to their salvation and walk with the Lord!

Mallory's enchanted laughter! Everything was so much fun! Whether she was home, watching a game with Dinky, or in luxurious hotels with her friends and associates, she loved her life. She loved the DiaMo demands, and she loved her studies! Even as she laughed and joked with everyone, revelation was overtaking her regarding another assigned project. Another paper for chemistry, once again about a chemical compound would be due in a few weeks Already having read tons of data on water, and having hands full of note cards she hadn't referenced, she was excited about writing a paper on water as a solvent. That would be narrowed down more, as she advanced through the project. It was fascinating to her how atoms, dissolved in water, combined with each other, to crystallize as gemstones!

At eight thirty the next morning, the group exited the hotel, past the readied meeting room, to convene in a park pavilion three blocks away. The morning was lovely, the picnic breakfast-fare spread sumptuously; they could hear the rush of the falls, experiencing the sparkling rainbows and mists.

⊰ ⊱

Ready for bed in Israel, Lilly was furious! So far, all her snooping had accomplished, was to get her in on a Gospel meeting! The last thing she wanted from the annoying Americans! She was furious! And she was nervous!

Her government had paid for Mallory and her entourage's visit to Israel, where Lilly had been the liaison person, to convince the American not to discount her diamond prices. Lilly knew the Turkish merchants were ready to present an enticing offer! One Mallory had promised to turn down! That was before Lilly had grabbed Cassandra. Now the Diamond Council was nervous that the girl would change her mind! What Lilly needed was the inside scoop about the plans for the diamonds. Hearing the success of Diana's business just made her churn more with hatred for the other woman. The group's move to the park, away from listening devices, put a wrinkle in her plans. Plus the gorgeous picnic atmosphere seemed extraordinary to the miserable eavesdropper. It seemed as if everything she did to harm the group, turned into blessings for them! None of them even seemed to miss Cassandra, and now Lilly had the responsibility and expense of her 'acquisition', as an added burden.

⊰ ⊱

Daniel began with a devotional, reading three verses.

James 4:1-3 From whence come wars and fightings among you? come they not hence, even of your lusts that war in your members?

Ye lust, and have not: ye kill, and desire to have, and cannot obtain: ye fight and war, yet ye have not, because ye ask not.

Ye ask, and receive not, because ye ask amiss, that ye may consume it upon your lusts.

After a prayer, he continued. "Well, with God's blessing on our lives, people do envy us. It is our responsibility to give Him the glory, and try to witness, explaining that God's love and provision for us, can be theirs, too. Of course, Satan doesn't want that glorious truth to dawn in their hearts! Everyone should get saved and start asking the Lord for everything they want. We should ask Him for the things we need, true! But also for our wants! God's Nature is kind and giving. If something will be less than His best for us, He holds veto power! How kind, though, that He usually grants to us so vastly. Of course, everyone here has a work ethic, too. If we aren't careful, we feel pretty self-sufficient, like we earned everything ourselves, and we're entitled to all of it. That's wrong, too. I mean, I know y'all know that. But, I always need to be reminded, so I figured I should remind everyone. For this reason, there's an undercurrent in our country, that is becoming more dangerous every day. We know God is for equity and equality, but not for Socialistic thought. He isn't against our accumulation of wealth, or against our having nice things to show for our productivity. We are not supposed to 'make haste to get rich', by stealing, cheating, gambling, killing! But by honest endeavors that in themselves, benefit mankind. We should then tithe and share, but the Bible teaches that the more we share, the more God heaps back on us.

Diana reported yesterday, on her upcoming lines and earnings projections. What she didn't say, is how much she gives away!"

He smiled at her as his eyes teared up. "She keeps trying to give her expensive clothes to people. She loves to put things together for Mallory, and Mallory keeps trying to buy some of it! The truth is, when she gives it away, orders pour in! Her staff can hardly meet demand right now! Then, she gave a sweater to Delia, and now she gets orders from Boston all the time! Conversely, when Diana wears Delia's designs, people ask about them, and Delia gets sales.

And y'all have received really nice jewelry gifts from Mallory and DiaMo! Let me tell you something! Patrick worked hard to put everything in place, and Mallie works hard to keep it going. And, she gives. She always tithed on her babysitting money, when it was just a dab.

So, we share, but people resent our having anything to share with! And they don't like who we give to, and what we still have.

A philanthropist gave several million dollars to a university athletic department, and the story made the newspaper. Instead of people saying, 'How kind and generous.' most of them blasted him. 'Oh, there are so many more worthy causes than that!' Probably the only people who truly approved of the gift were the people involved with the university who benefited from the gift."

He paused, and the group laughed. Most of them could relate.

"There are always causes. I hate to see sick and crippled, or starving children. I know many charitable organizations are seeking cures for diseases. We know, though, that disease will never be eradicated, and death will reign in mortal bodies until the 'Curse' is lifted. Most benefactors try to save or help physical lives, while we seek to make eternal differences.

Anyway, I want to stress that the Devil would love to destroy our group, because we are accomplishing great things for the Kingdom. Let's don't fight and war among ourselves, but just share our hopes and dreams with Jesus!"

He prayed again and called the business meeting to order before giving Mallie the floor.

She took her place at the microphone as material was being distributed. Laughing, she thanked her guardian and confidante for the devotional, confessing how envious she was about David and Tammi and their equine acquisitions.

And she really was. She didn't want a horse, now, to copy them! And riding would be an unnecessary exposure to danger for her, while the Maloviches were still at large! Yep! She was jealous!

Her report was astounding! The Faulkner's campsite, within the boundaries of the National Forest, did reveal diamonds in the sands of the creek bed. The family had <u>not</u> removed any gems from the Federal land. The good news was, that the precious gems originated farther north than any of them were aware of. Claims were being staked along waterways, south of the *National Forest* So far, all stones were very nice!

The meeting closed with a report on the jewelry designs and sales. Floyd and Myrna Boggs had already acquired the Dandelion brooch, and were eagerly awaiting the first catalog featuring more jewelry. The group voted to form a limited partnership with the Florida couple to represent their various ventures to friends and customers in Florida.

Mallory reported on the situation with the Turkish contingency, where DiaMo had entered a contract. Since discounting prices was an impossibility, she had contrived another incentive for the foreign business: a joint-advertising campaign, with Mallory as the spokesperson, promoting the gems as *American*, and therefore, 'conflict-free'. (Well, so to speak)!

The afternoon was free for shopping, resting, or taking the side trip to *The Baseball Hall of Fame*. Then dinner at eight, formal attire requested.

Cooperstown wasn't necessarily close to anyplace, but after a chopper ride through upper New York State, they arrived in the charming town. Viewing Baseball's Greatest's exhibits fairly quickly, they grabbed a lunch before heading back.

Showering quickly, Mallory slipped into the formal and jewelry she had worn in Israel, wishing she hadn't sent the pictures to everyone in the e-mail. The gown was stunning, and she quickly joined everyone else as they assembled over aperitifs. Delia spoke animatedly with the Boggs. Evidently, they knew quite a few of the same people. Mrs. Boggs used Delia's Irish linen all the time, and she felt like she was practically conversing with a celebrity. Delia introduced Shay, and the new couple were as impressed with him as they were with Mallory. Herb and Linda, after a couple of days honeymooning, had resurfaced, and Herb was thrilled to learn one of his jewelry pieces had already been snapped up. It was a gorgeous evening of refinement and grace. David was handsome in his tux! All jokes aside, he didn't look like a penguin at all. Mallory wished the 'ball' didn't ever have to come to an end! However- everyone was scheduled for early departures in the morning!

Chapter 22: WARRANTS

Erik Bransom slammed into the cell where Steven Barton awaited trial for his April attempt to rob Suzanne. After agents checked Barton's trail of rap sheets across the country, they added charges of attempted kidnapping and attempted murder. The criminal, wanted for various armed robberies throughout the Midwest, was hopefully, at the end of his crime career. Herb was willing to testify, as was Suzanne, if necessary. Bransom was hoping and praying it wouldn't be necessary. The suspect was being sent, first, to St Louis, to face charges there, for a string of pawn shop robberies. Usually targeting guns and weapons, when he saw Suzanne leave the Western Arkansas Pawn Shop with Mallie's fabulous ring, he figured she and the ring would be an easy target. It scared Erik worse, the more he found out about the felon.

"You better hope you get a long stretch in Missouri, Barton! Whichever way, I'm pretty sure you'll never know another free day! Why don't you talk to me about your gun business? Seems like it was a pretty sweet operation you had going! We haven't found most of the weapons you stole. Figure you filed the numbers: you ship overseas?"

Barton glared belligerently. International arms dealing was a federal offense. He knew the agent was drooling to charge him federally.

"Talk to my lawyer!"

Bransom leered into his face, "I'm talkin' to you, Hotshot! You ever hear the name, Merrill Adams? You know anything about him and his two boys grievin' over their papa's death? You ever sell any guns to any of them?"

Erik was watching the criminal closely as he threw out his bait. Sure enough, a moment of panic before the insolence returned.

Gloating, the Federal agent turned to leave. "See ya if ya ever get back from Missouri. I'll tell all your partners in crime ya said 'Hello'!"

Erik's expression was grim as he returned to his agency vehicle. Shaking that tree had been productive. Barton evidently didn't want his name mentioned in relation to Adams! He had blanched white as snow at Bransom's parting gig!

Back in his office, Erik set up a crosscheck between Barton's known associates and Adam's. Might take awhile, but he planned to find the link. Evidently, there was one.

In one way, he was totally amazed anyone could have the audacity to sue Mallory over the wasps' stinging Adams to death. It was an amazing thing that anything so stupid could actually tie up the court's time, and a jury's! But, it had brought the two boys out of the woodwork. Bransom couldn't help believing Adam's two boys were probably following in their daddy's footsteps. It had been an interesting thing to look into their pitiful, sordid, little lives. They definitely needed money from Mallie's estate! Jus cuz they needed it, was no reason they should be entitled to it. Erik would never have thought of delving into the family life of the dead hit man. But, now that they had so stupidly shone the spotlight on themselves-. He was grinning ear to ear before the computer spit him out a list. The broad grin somehow, broadened further. And to think, he always used to cuss computers!

The Faulkners, home from the corporate meeting by Saturday afternoon, spent their Sunday in their usual routine, having established an awkward truce with their pastor. Still no word from or about Cassandra. They continued to cry in their prayer closets, smiling bravely in public. With their daughter's sixth birthday nearing, they were assembling and wrapping a vast array of special gifts. It was hard; not knowing if she was still trying to be too grown up for toys. They continued to search out things they hoped would bring her delight. They planned to ship at least ten days early, to be sure the gifts wouldn't be late.

As Daniel picked up his briefcase to head for his office on Monday morning, security notified them of a problem at the front gates. An officer of the court had arrived to serve papers. After being escorted into the kitchen, the authority presented the documents. Orders to both Daniel and Diana to appear before a judge at ten o'clock, bringing Alexandra and Jeremiah, as well as the 'contract' relating to Cassandra.

"Okay, thanks. We'll be there," Daniel assured. "In two and a half hours! We'll be there early. Do we need our attorney?"

≈≈

Nearly the same scenario in Dallas as Mallory's vehicle emerged through her automatic gates. Her papers ordered her to appear before a judge in Pike County, Arkansas at one o'clock. Still a scramble to ready one of the choppers and a crew without advance notice. She didn't even think to invite Kerry along! Or to notify her guardian!

≈≈

Clint Hammond blanched as his secretary informed him Daniel Faulkner was on the line for him, filling him in briefly on the issue. "Don't try to run again," he advised quickly, as he picked up.

"Yeah. I don't think that's an option at all, at this point," Faulkner agreed. "Think law enforcement has a pretty close eye on us. At least they didn't arrest us!"

"Yeah, that's at least a good thing. Fax me your notice to appear. That tells me more details and where the hearing will be. I'll meet you at nine-thirty. You always do, but dress sharp."

≈≈

Judge John M. Holliman entered the small court room where Mallory sat waiting. At the bailiff's order, she rose respectfully.

"Miss O'Shaughnessy, you may approach the bench." The judge leaned forward, gazing down at her over the tops of reading glasses

She moved forward, meeting his steady gaze.

"You're here without your attorney and your dog?" His smile and tone were friendly, and the teenager relaxed slightly.

"Yes, Your Honor. This summons was kind of sudden. I never even thought of calling Kerry. Am I going to need him?"

"I'm surprised you didn't let him go after the way he set you up before. He was working in your late father's best interests, more than in yours."

225

Mallory didn't respond. Doing her daddy's wishes was in her best interests, even when it wasn't exactly what she wanted.

"Do you remember this court reserved the privilege of checking on your welfare and progress periodically?"

"Uh, no, Sir, not exactly. Everything's still kind of a blur to me. But, I don't mind telling you how I'm doing. Do you need my academic records? Are you concerned about the Faulkners? Do you need the corporate books to prove that Daniel, as CFO, isn't fleecing me?"

Judge Holliman nearly smiled. The young woman was pretty perceptive.

The bailiff will swear you in, then your remarks will all go on record.

〜※〜

Lilly Cowan was as nearly ecstatic as possible! Always in physical pain, and emotionally more crippled than her physical malady, that was saying a lot! Finally, authorities were dealing with the Faulkner family. Lilly's triumph, though delayed by Simon's meddling, hadn't been snatched from her completely! She couldn't wait to see Diana Faulkner in an orange jumpsuit, being led away in chains. She smirked wickedly as she ground out a cigarette. One of her minions was providing her with a live feed from outside the court building in downtown Tulsa. An 'anonymous' tip, leaked to Carole Lee Whitfield in Little Rock had brought her and her crew to Tulsa to 'scoop' the story with a local sister-station affiliate. Why Lilly wanted to give the Faulkners, who were associates to the diamond industry, such a black eye, defied reason. But she did! With all her being, she wanted Diana Faulkner destroyed! The diamond industry had survived worse scandals. This kind of stuff kept it interesting, anyway.

〜※〜

Trent Morrison and a small group of field agents were taking turns with Bob Porter and his men, searching the northwestern corner of Arkansas for evidence of gang activity within the National Forest. Morrison was amazed. Porter, so reluctant to be drawn in, initially, was now nearly on a personal crusade. Various agencies working together, had accumulated quite a bit of evidence from the large vehicle impounded in Boston and the trash picked up at the Pike campground. Now, they all wanted to locate the remaining vehicle, and to apprehend the criminal element that had escaped their clutches that day in Dierks. He smiled when word came from Bransom. The pawn shop thief, and his illegal weapons sales were somehow connected. And Adam's two dumb sons were pulling a noose around their own necks, and those of their father's cohorts. You could almost always count on greed!

"Thanks, Lord," he whispered!

-≒ ≓-

Alexandra Faulkner was terrified! Upon arrival at the courts building, she was pulled aside to be questioned by some child advocate experts. Her daddy had tried to reassure her that everything was going to be okay. "Just tell the truth." She didn't want to tell the truth. She wanted to swear her parents had never laid a hand on her! That they didn't believe in spanking. She didn't want to end up going home with people she didn't know! Tears poured down her cheeks. She wished Cassandra would have just behaved! And she was worried about her little brother. Surely, he was more scared than she was.

"I want my brother," she begged.

"Okay, Alexandra, don't be afraid. My name's Lynne. I help children all the time, out of sad circumstances. Jeremiah's talking to one of my co-workers. We're just supposed to talk to you about what's going on with you. If you go into foster care, we may be able to place you with your brother. How would that be?"

Alexandra stopped crying, staring at the woman in disbelief. That was a STUPID question!

"It would be terrible" she answered, suddenly controlled and icy. Alexandra could be snotty when she chose to be! And, when her mom and dad weren't around!

"Go ahead and ask what you like. My parents don't ever mistreat us! They try to teach us what's right so we don't turn into a bunch of heathen criminals. They didn't sell our little sister, or kill her! We all love her, and miss her. She's going to come out of this, not only a great concert violinist, but a great person! My mom and dad are great Christians and great parents. You can find great character references for them, if you want the truth!"

-≒ ≓-

Clint Hammond sought for his client's family at the designated meeting spot, but they were nowhere to be seen. His first anguished thought was that they had seen an opportunity to flee again, and had taken it. Dread flooded over him. Their earlier 'vacation' hadn't landed them in legal trouble because they hadn't been served. And amazingly, the Israelis provided a statement at the last minute. This was a totally 'different ball of wax', whatever that meant.

Before he could locate Daniel, Carole Lee Whitfield located him. Jabbing her mic into his lip, she demanded to know if his clients had once more, defied the authorities, and fled the country with their children!

Mystified, he met the strident woman's gaze! He couldn't figure out how the press hounds were on top of this, already. He planned to make sure it was no one in his office! He knew it wouldn't have been Daniel! He decided to try to use the woman to his own and the Faulkner's advantage. She obviously wanted the Faulkners guilty of all charges, before any were even filed, and with disregard to whether there was any evidence.

He smiled his most cooperative and conspiratorial smile, waiting to answer until a few other mics and cameras joined hers. He wanted to make sure his words got to the world. Some stations might choose not to air his statement, but the ratings for any of this would be irresistible somewhere.

"I'm Clint Hammond, and I represent the Faulkner family in most of their legal matters!" He smiled again, posing as if he were enjoying the media attention "Usually, corporate-related matters, as the Faulkner family is well-respected in the Tulsa, corporate world. As you know, Daniel Faulkner is a third generation geologist; his grandfather was on the ground-floor of making Tulsa into the 'Oil Capital of the World'. There isn't a finer business man in Tulsa than Daniel Faulkner, or a finer family man. He's a fair employer, and a fairly large employer, in the Tulsa area. He is representative of what corporate America should be."

He was trying to create a philibuster, yacking himself, to stave off her barrage of questions. The anchorwoman was too rude, or too savvy, and broke in irritably, demanding again whether his clients had disappeared.

"He was advised not to," Hammond responded, again being as theatrical as possible "Why is it not obvious to people that he must be a good man and love his family, to take the drastic action he has taken? Do you not think it's alarming that good American families are being attacked this way?"

The reporter sneered. "Tell us the truth about Cassandra. Maybe we can be more understanding! Is it true Mrs. Faulkner came out of the deal with a full-length Sable coat?"

"I think the press has been told as much about Cassandra, and her choosing to further her career in Israel, as anyone knows. I have a copy of the contract the Faulkers signed. There were no terms for any type of remuneration for either Cassandra, or her parents. The wording was extremely vague! And I think, misleading, if not downright fraudulent! It would be like Daniel to purchase a coat for his wife. He's a loving husband, as well as a good father. They are well able to afford their lifestyle without selling their children!"

He attempted to dismiss himself with a curt nod, but she wasn't giving him an escape. Anything he said, she could refute, and he was giving her ratings.

"Cassandra is five years old!" Carole Lee's voice was charged with sarcasm. "And you are telling us that 'she decided to travel to Israel, by herself, to further her violin studies ?"

"Yeah, I think that's basically what I said. Wow, you're quick. You seem to have a fairly good grasp for what people say." This time, she didn't try to stop him, but began her own diatribe and opinions again, still trying to string together the totally unrelated issues of Cassandra and the coat.

⊰ ⊱

Jeremiah Faulkner wasn't as scared as his sister was worried he would be. Some guy named James was trying to ask all kinds of questions. Jeremiah tried to strike a bargain. "Can I ask you a question for every answer I give you?"

Seemed harmless, so James agreed to play the game. These battered children could be hard to get through to, so this cute, open, little boy was a pleasant change.

"What happened to your little sister?" he opened.

"She went to Israel to play her violin in their symphony." The body language was relaxed, meaning the child believed he was telling the truth. "James, if you die today, are you one hundred percent sure you'll go to Heaven?" Jeremiah, boldly asking his return volley.

The guy laughed uneasily. "Ha, Good one, Jer! Guess ya got me. Did your parent's repeated beatings of Cassandra cause her to want to leave home?"

"Whoa, it's still my turn. You didn't answer me," Jeremiah had folded his arms across the front of his little navy blazer, leaning back into his chair with a frown. "If you die today~"

"Okay, Jer. Enough of your games. I ask questions; you answer. You're wasting my time here."

"Well, Ja, I'm sorry you feel that way. I thought this was your job. You're actually wasting my time, too. This is one of my last days to swim and play before our tutor comes back." Brown eyes flashed from the face that was a smaller, smoother, version of his father's.

"Look, Buddy, just tell me about the beatings! It doesn't matter, you're on your way into foster care, anyway. If you just tell me what I need to hear, I'll see what I can do to keep you and your sister together."

The kid didn't flinch! He sat motionless, eyeing the advocate.

"Okay, James, here's the deal. You should be trying to find out the truth, not get me to say what you want me to. Don't call me Jer! My dad calls me that. And, he calls me, Buddy, sometimes. I'm not your buddy, and you're not mine. I'm trying to tell you how you can go to Heaven for sure, by asking Jesus into your heart. You can't send me or my sister anyplace, unless Jesus has someplace he needs us. Like, He needs my sister in Israel."

Prodded to wrath, James turned furiously on the child. "You have no idea who you're trying to mess with. I have authority to send you where ever I please. Your miserable little life is in my hands!"

The door opened and Clint Hammond stared incredulously at the scenario.

"You trying to intimidate my client?" Jeremiah was the first member of the Faulkner family the attorney had managed to locate. "Get his sister for me, too. You ready to deal with a lawsuit? Maybe you should take a class or two about being compassionate and comforting to children."

⊰ ⊱

John Holliman asked question after question of the girl who had appeared before him, everything being meticulously recorded by the court reporter. Some of it was friendly and genuine concern about the girl and her completion of her academics. He was impressed, not just by her grades, but by her genuine interest in acquiring knowledge and learning. He received a travel tutorial on the wonders of Turkey, Boston, Israel, Niagara Falls, and the Baseball Hall of Fame. Her father had evidently turned her into an avid sports fan, as well as a corporate CEO. She was fun to talk baseball with. She was a charmer. Relaxed and open, she was creating a character reference for her guardian that would be difficult to refute. When he tried to coax information from her regarding how she had been able to free herself from her Middle-Eastern captors, he hit a wall. He hit the same wall trying to learn about the Faulkners and their dealings with Cassandra. Amazing. She wasn't trying to hide anything. It was just none of his business. Or of the courts.

He could have cited her in contempt, except that she graciously declined to answer, carefully polite and respectful. He chose to let it go.

"You know, when you turn eighteen in November, this court considers you an adult. What are you planning on doing then?"

She laughed, a pleasing, joyful laugh. "Probably have a birthday party and keep doing what I'm doing. There won't be any alcohol. I feel the Bible is against it strongly. It's basically what destroyed my dad's body. He quit drinking when I was born, but at the last, 'it (alcohol) still bit him like a serpent, and stung him like an adder.' She was referencing a verse from Proverbs.

"Well, you're entitled to your opinion. It's easy though, to try to push your opinions on others." It was a mild rebuke.

"I hope so," Mallory was still respectful, and thoughtful. "Since we all have to share the same roads. How many DUI's does this court deal with each year? How many of those offenses hurt people and damage property? It seems like lots of people with rabid opinions can spew them all they want to, even if human lives aren't at stake. They are trying to force everyone in the world to comply with their little causes. And I say 'I'm against alcoholic beverages, when they cause loss of lives of thousands of innocent people', and you caution me against my stance."

"Well, what you're saying isn't very popular. If you're talking about the 'animal' thing, that's kind of in vogue right now. You know, a lot of Hollywood people pushing it." The judge was smiling like a benevolent Santa Claus

"Well, we should be more worried about right and wrong, than about what's 'in vogue' or the popular movements. I'm sorry. We've probably digressed a lot. When I turn eighteen, I still want the Faulkners to be involved in my life and decisions. I'm amazed the way my dad found them and got them involved with my life."

"Yes, It does seem amazing. What about the young man who spoke up that day?"

Mallory was flustered for the first time. "What about him, Your Honor? The Faulkners are real nice about him, too. I think they let me see him far more than my father would have liked. My dad really liked David, but then David had a rebellion thing going on; he burned my dad's trust."

"What about your trust?" The question was searching.

"Well, my trust is in the Lord. I still really like David, although I try to put him out of mind. My dad was definitely right about our being too young to be serious. If he's the Lord's will for me, everything will be okay."

Judge Holliman nodded. He needed to choose his words carefully. "Well, you have really pretty hair; be careful where you go for haircuts. You are free to go, Miss O'Shaughnessy. In six months, call and schedule an appointment to report back to this court."

He pounded the gavel, and the bailiff escorted her out into the bright, hot, afternoon sunlight.

⚎ ⚏

By two o'clock, the judge had surveyed everything the Child Protective Services had been able to muster. It was nothing. The judge thought the tapes of the interviews with the children could nearly appear on *Funniest Home Videos,* if the shows were still being made. Neither child seemed to have a crushed or broken spirit. They were respectful and well-behaved. Kind of a nice change from many of the surly youth he encountered. The CPS asked to be allowed to show up at the Faulkner mansion at any time for surprise inspections. The judge denied the request unequivocally. He thought the family had done nothing to cause them to forfeit their Constitutional Right to Privacy. Sometimes these agencies lost their perspective, growing power hungry. He was ready for a vacation. He wondered curiously where he might be able to hole up with his family next to a fishing stream for five or six weeks.

⚎ ⚏

Erik Bransom visited with Suzanne over a steak at McKenna's. Still in a small apartment, seemingly without time to find property to begin building a house, the steakhouse was a nice luxury. He listened to her recounting of her day, fascinated still by her voice, her laugh, her personality. Every day, he loved her more. Well-intentioned friends had tried to slow his fast romance, quoting the old adage, 'Marry in haste; repent at leisure'. So far, he hadn't felt one pang of regret. Well, Suzanne was part of the wonderful Salvation package. His getting saved had placed him under the 'honey-bucket' of God's goodness. He tried to explain his sudden blessedness, but people wouldn't really give him a chance. Their minds were made up. They thought the 'religion' part was crazy, and he was having a 'lucky' streak, and besides, he had married money.

Finishing her narrative, she asked about his work. Right now, everything he was learning was sensitive. It was exciting, but he was barely divulging any of it! Except to feed to Summers. The ABI was still very interested in the whole tangled mess Bransom was supposed to leave alone. He expressed his concern again, about the problems with obtaining convictions against identical twins. After studying what pictures he had of the two, he couldn't find any distinguishing characteristics.

Suzanne nodded sympathy. "Well, evidently, one of them can't see to drive! Or they don't care about flower beds."

Erik laughed. He wasn't sure any of his suspects had ever had any particular concern for flowers. They were all the 'less sensitive type', who would run over their grandmas in the commission of a crime. Flower beds would have been real low on their lists of what to be careful of. Even as he laughed, he paused in mid-guffaw. Maybe one of the Maloviches did have a vision problem, and one didn't. Might be one angle for differentiating between the two. He should look into every possibility that presented itself.

"Might be something to that," he admitted, growing serious. "You mind if we go back to the office from here? You got your camera with you? You still got the pictures from Turkey on it?"

⊣ ⊢

Jed Dawson, Bransom's FBI superior, was in Dallas, enjoying a steak dinner with Kerry Larson. He was trying to 'tip-toe through the tulips' or among land mines, or something! He was picking his way carefully. Trying to pursue justice without wrecking his career was turning into a tricky thing. Bransom had used an expression that had stuck, about '... being wise as a serpent, and harmless as a dove'. Dawson didn't know it was from the Bible, but it seemed like good advice.

Arnold and Barnett Adams, who went by Arnie and Barney, suing Mallory O'Shaughnessy's estate, were being strung along by her attorney.

Whatever out-of-court settlement was agreed upon, would be paid to the two. That's why Larson didn't want to agree to anything but the barest minimum for baiting the hooks to lure the two into the sting. But, the two balky boys were greedy, thinking since Mallory had a lot, she should pay a lot! To them! Go figure!

So, the settlement had to be legit! Putting up the girl's money.

"Offer twenty-five thou, each. If this drags out to go to court, they may figure things out and disappear. Mallory's better off losing fifty grand than ending up dead. Make the offer, Larson, so we can grab the loons. Warrants are ready. We have proof that they at least helped their daddy obtain sniper rifles. Makes them accessories to lots of hits and the attempts on Mallory, even if they never pulled any triggers. Then, we think they'll roll on plenty of other associates. They have lots of information."

The server came to fill their iced teas.

"Mallory's the hold up. She's as feisty as her dad was! Maybe worse! Well, I don't blame her for feeling like they shouldn't even have a shot at such extortion. It isn't right! She's young enough and idealistic enough to think everything should be 'fair' and 'right'."

Dawson nodded sadly. He had once treasured the same notions.

"Talk her into it anyway. Tell her a jury might give them a million! That isn't outside the realm of the crazy possibilities. Get her to agree tonight!"

Kerry was frustrated. "If she agrees, the Adams want half a million. Why do you think they'll settle for a tenth of that?"

"Tell them it's fifty thousand right now, or probably nothing while you delay it indefinitely through the courts and a trial date. You're the fast talker, here, Counselor. They're pretty desperate. Tell them a 'bird in the hand is worth two in the bush'. Get them and Mallory together at the table."

⚖ ⚖

Erik transferred Suzanne's pictures of Pamukkale to his computer, enlarging them section by section.

"Suze, will you text or e-mail everyone in the group to get their pictures and videos of this site to me, as quick as they can?"

"Yeah, sure." She went to work on the request immediately, without asking why.

Erik gazed lingeringly at each image. He had made a mistake in leaving all of the investigating of the Turkish crimes in the hands of Col. Ahmir! Not that Ahmir wasn't good. The Turk sent new information along as quickly as possible. The Turkish were going overboard to cooperate, wanting to solve their own criminal cases at the same time.

None of Suzanne's shots captured Mallory, or any signs of the felt hat and binoculars. Mildly disappointed, he asked her some more questions while he waited for some of the other images to arrive. Not everyone would be able to comply with the request immediately.

"Did you notice anything out of the ordinary that day? I was paying attention to you; didn't notice Mallory get up there by herself. Then, when she got scared and tumbled down the mountain, I just griped her out. Still never dawned on me something big was up, until David started telling me off. By then, everyone was on the coaches, and we were on the road. I need to call David."

"Evenin', Bransom," David answered. "I just got Suzanne's text. Guess you're trying to put together what happened up there that afternoon?"

"Yeah, that's right, Cowboy. Try to remember everything you can, and write me up a statement of all you observed, as well as impressions about the events of that day."

"Will do, Agent. What happened to that Turkish guy they arrested? His scaring Mallory, causing her to fall, could have killed her. He should face attempted murder charges, and she should sue for the injury to her wrist. Lucky for him that's all she hurt!"

The teen's impassioned speech brought a grin to the agent's face. Not bad ideas! Not bad at all!

᛫ ᛭

Kerry must have caught Mallory in a particularly good mood; she acquiesced immediately to the agreement she had rejected previously. He set up a tentative time for the next afternoon for the meeting, letting Dawson know.

He was feeling relieved about that when he received Suzanne's text for him to submit his Pamukkale pictures to Erik as quickly as possible. Not sure why, but hoping it was for something good, he was working on it when Erik called.

"Hey, you don't give much response time," he laughed as he answered.

"Yeah, not trying to rush ya, Larson, but hurry!" Followed by a laugh. "I am trying to put together a picture of where Mallory was, where the 'hat' was, when she got scared and fell! Then, I called David, because I think he saw more of what was going down, than anybody. He pointed out that it's just a miracle she didn't kill herself falling, when she noticed what she thought was Melville, coming to choke her again! That's what she thought was happening! Of course, Ahmir hasn't released that guy. People don't get out of trouble over there as easy as they do here. I called Ahmir, at David's bright suggestion, to see if Ahmir can get charges to stick of 'attempted murder' since a fall from where Mallory was, could have killed her."

Kerry was listening. He thought it was a stretch. At least it would be, here, in the U.S.

"Something else David has been wondering about. Can Mallory file a civil suit in Turkey for that guy's actions causing her wrist injury."

"I'll look into it," Kerry agreed, catching on quickly. "I'm sure the guy has no money. The whole thing may scare him into giving Ahmir more information. Although, the Turkish authorities probably already 'coaxed' more out of him than he ever knew."

⚐ ⚑

Lilly, enraged by the Faulkner's return to their elegant home, still as a family unit, vented her frustration on everyone around her.

⚐ ⚑

Merrill Adam's two sons, with a sleazy-acting attorney, agreed to the twenty-five thousand, apiece, signing documents agreeing not to make any further claims against Mallory O'Shaughnessy and her estate, as related to the 'wrongful death' of their beloved father. Sneering at her and Kerry Larson, they exited the court auxiliary building, to be arrested for 'accessory to murder'. The particular incident happened in Concord, Massachusetts, where they would stand trial separately, first. If for any reason, they managed to be acquitted of those charges, they were guilty of many other similar crimes.

Bail refused, both men seemed very willing to incriminate each other, and their friends, in an effort to negotiate any kind of break for themselves.

Chapter 23: WISHES

Acts 27:29 Then fearing lest we should have fallen upon rocks, they cast four anchors out of the stern, and wished for the day.

Over Labor Day, the Anderson family moved into their new home. It was beautiful, totally furnished with lovely new furniture and accessories. Mallory heard about it with great satisfaction. That had been an important goal for her daddy.

The parsonage was emptied of the Anderson's belongings, refurbished and nicely appointed for a prophet's chamber or for missionaries on furlough. The church board retained the oversight of it. It probably looked better than it had, new.

"They probably won't allow any missionaries with rowdy kids into it." The Pastor confessed the thought, not placing the bitterness into words. None of that mattered now; they had God on their side. He walked away whistling, 'If God be for us, who can stand against us'!?

The ministry building was under construction, and the main building at the camp was really taking shape. Renovations of the church were going more slowly, due to the need to have a meeting place ready for each service. Slow, but advancing.

In Dallas, the summer heat continued unabated, and Mallory stayed busy with her company and academics. She still loved the Geology, but she hadn't forgotten her original plan for attending Bible College. She asked Mr. Haynes to add a course, New Testament Survey.

On September twelfth, David turned eighteen. Most of the group celebrated at Hal's Lodge in Murfreesboro, with everyone presenting gifts to show the specialness of the occasion. Mallory gave him a funny card, a new ball glove, and an evening at the Ball Park in Arlington, to watch the Rangers play. With the baseball season's winding down, nearing the play-offs, he would need to utilize the gift quickly.

"You better not come back without catching a 'home run'," were her instructions.

His other gifts included a new saddle and some other gifts related to *El Capitan*.

His parents paid for six months of his violin lessons with Phil. It was a fun night of genuine caring, laced with plenty of good-natured teasing. When the party ended he returned home with his family; he really loved the expansive new house, the pool, and the exercise equipment. Not that the construction projects weren't a work-out! He contributed a lot to the heavy work, although the projects were requiring quite a bit of time on the phone and at the desk. And, he was taking an entire semester of college courses. Discovering that Mallory had added a course in Bible, he followed suit, wishing he could think of something before she did.

Tammi, in her junior year at Murfreesboro High, was studying more than she ever had, determined to bring her grades way up. Occasionally, Mr. Haynes would okay David to join her for lunch in the school cafeteria. She was actually making a few non-church friends, managing to influence them positively, inviting them to church and activities.

And, of course, the beautiful new home was working like a magnet to help all of the Anderson kids make friends. Kids seemed to love the friendly atmosphere of the shimmering pool, the game room full of games, the giant flat-screens, the trampoline, and the over-flowing refrigerator. The home and the pastor's family extended gracious friendship that the little parsonage was never able to provide.

Finding help with the cleaning and maintenance hadn't required Diana's gifts in that department. A widow, Mary Hayfield, who had been a member at Faith for several years, had approached Lana before the home was even completed, to ask for the job of overseeing the house and the kids. She was now a resident of the apartment created for that purpose, and she was amazingly gifted at running everything from the pool maintenance, to laundry for the large family, to cleaning, and shopping for groceries. She hired high school kids, as well as other people from the community she was aware of who needed some extra income, and were willing to work for it. She was truly an 'iron fist in a velvet glove'. Actually a miracle! The way God worked it all for good, for Mary, for the Andersons, and for the others who were able to supplement their incomes, was absolutely incredible!

⊰ ⊱

On the legal scene, Kerry Larson, in conjunction with a Turkish lawyer, pursued a civil suit relating to Mallory's fall at Pamukkale. They didn't expect to win any remuneration, but the small-time wrongdoer suddenly sprouted deep pockets, offering to settle out of court, for quite an exorbitant sum. After agreeing to the settlement, Ahmir's associates attempted to trace the source of the money. Evidently some slush-fund set up for that purpose, he couldn't positively link the pay-off to any of the gangs they suspected of involvement. A dead end as far as nailing Oscar and Otto, but it did cover Mallory's orthopedist visits.

And her wrist was better! Over all, a good thing, except that Daniel and Diana were now pretty firmly insisting that she practice the piano, and learn violin. She was busier than ever.

She wondered if they were trying to keep her so busy she couldn't even think about David. If that was the case, it wasn't working. She still missed her dad, although, since her 'experience' at Niagara Falls, the overwhelming grief had eased. She missed Cassandra, too. It was a burden that just lodged in her heart, never quite letting up. Every day, she prayed earnestly for the Lord to bring her home.

In spite of that, she had managed to normalize her relationship with Lilly Cowan. Like it or not, they needed one another. They probably talked once a week.

Herb's business was growing, causing Diana's and hers to go forward at the same time. Although, Lilly, was still a passionate "Diamond" enthusiast, she finally admitted that the colored stones were beautiful, too. Herb and his expanding number of employees formed many of the pieces, painstakingly working the metals by hand. There were different methods they used, depending upon the desired end-results. They also often used 'findings', jewelry components they ordered, that simply required stones to be set in them with a little finishing

The changes in Erik's disposition had brought his other two daughters to re-establish a relationship. Although, they were older than Mallory, she really liked them. So did her mom, which was a really neat thing, too.

Mallie reevaluated her prayer journal. The Lord had given her lots of friends, so she reorganized to be more effective praying for them. There were lots of exciting answers, but quite a few people still hadn't made their decisions for Christ. She moved their names to the front page. Carmine Henderson, Donovan Cline, Lilly Cowan. She wasn't really sure about her Aunt Linda. She also added Col. Ahmir, Bob Porter, and Jed Dawson. She was praying for salvation, too, for the bad guys: Oscar and Otto, and Arnie and Barney Adams.

The Faulkner family held a special place in her heart! So did the Andersons! And David! So she had sections for them and their needs.

Growing suddenly curious, she went to the Faith Baptist web site. She tried not to overdo using this avenue of information. She really was still interested in what was happening in the church where she had gotten saved and been a member for ten years. But mostly, she hoped for glimpses of David! Her search was more than rewarded. His first violin solo, "Wedding Music"! It was a pretty song, and he did a really good job on it. Someone Mallory didn't know accompanied him at the piano. Pastor thanked him, calling him, Phil. Ah! David's violin teacher. She hummed the melody for the rest of the day, still seeing David in her mind's eye, as she fell asleep.

In Tulsa, the Faulkners still tried to reach Cassandra, trying extra-hard on her birthday, so they could sing to her and ask if she liked any of her gifts. To no avail! Their tracking numbers, followed eagerly, indicated delivery. That was all they could find out.

Still trusting the Lord, and presenting a brave face to friends and enemies alike, they awaited delivery of their baby.

"You think he'll take Cass's place?" Daniel questioned despondently of Diana.

"Not possible!" Her smiling-through-tears response. "You know how newborns are. They demand time and attention. So, he will fill up more of our time, and our thoughts."

Her visits to the doctor were weekly now, and the baby had dropped, in good position, if nothing changed. He was pretty active, and they both delighted in his vigorous kicks, punches, or whatever they were!

The nursery suite was ready for him! All done in *Winnie the Pooh*, much to Mallory's chagrin. With the new addition to their family, and the conversion of their guest suite to a special space for Mallory, they were cramped. *Cramped* being a relative term. Cassandra's little suite was a shrine! No way they could take that space back. Surely, she would be home soon! They were building on, and after Xavier's birth, Diana was planning the transformation of the master suite to the new theme, the rainy mural of the Bosporus Bridge.

Sam Whitmore loved working for the GeoHy/DiaMo corporations. His former career with the Treasury Department made him extra appreciative of the private sector, especially the nicest people of the private sector. With his intricate knowledge of their systems, he continued to be impressed. They were all even more honest and generous than they seemed. Which still continued to strike him as odd, since his impression was that Christians should be destitute. He finally asked Faulkner, "How can you say you're a hundred per cent sure you're going to heaven, when the Bible says it's impossible for rich men to get there?"

Whitmore could be a smart aleck, but that wasn't his tone, so Daniel took a minute to consider his words and answer the question carefully. Even as he was considering, he was realizing that Whitmore wasn't even on any of their radars to pray for!

"Sit down, Sam," he indicated one of the chairs across from his desk. "Actually, the Bible's sayings get tossed around until they are pretty inaccurate renditions of what it actually states. I think you're talking about the words of Jesus in:

Mark 10:25 It is easier for a camel to go through an eye of a needle, than for a rich man to enter into the kingdom of God!

But then, Jesus continues on in the same passage, what all that means. That it's hard for a rich man, who <u>trusts in his riches</u> to enter into the kingdom. It takes humility to admit you are powerless to redeem your own soul. Most of the time, rich people aren't willing to humble themselves. Some scholars interpret 'the eye of the needle' to represent smaller doors in the city walls, where there could be entrance and exit when the massive main gates were closed up. A camel could get through, but it had to be unloaded completely and go through the low clearance on its knees. A pretty good picture of coming to Jesus. Then in verse 27b, Jesus clarifies His teachings even more:

With men it is impossible, but not with God: for with God all things are possible.

Believe me, Sam, I didn't come to the Lord as a self-sufficient rich kid. I came to Him as a terrified, dying man!"

The computer geek sat eyeing Faulkner through thick glasses, which magnified his tears into the proverbial 'crocodile tears'. He didn't know

241

the story of Daniel's past illnesses: he didn't need to know. Sam Whitmore knew that was what he was! A terrified, dying man! Oh, he hadn't been diagnosed with anything imminently fatal. He just knew you couldn't make it out of life, alive!

He received Christ, leaving the office with a burden rolled away! And another happy tidbit! Diana Faulkner had several younger sisters!

❧ ❧

Cassandra Faulkner paused on her return from school. The day was hot and sunny! They all had been! She hated Lilly's oppressive flat, well she hated Lilly, too. Now they had finally arrived at an understanding, of sorts. Do it Lilly's way! For ten weeks, she barely left the enclosure of her room, let alone getting out of the flat. But then, school started, much to Lilly's relief. Cassandra hated school too, but for the glorious solitary walk to and from, she was in heaven. She had discovered a little litter of kittens, all really cute. Each day, she hoarded small bits from her own paltry food supply to lure the little fellas out so she could play with them. She loved the kitties, too, because they spoke English. She never knew she 'spoke English' until she got here and couldn't understand what anyone was saying. She was surrounded with Hebrew.

Although she had tried to resist learning letters and numbers at home, she had absorbed a great deal. Now, whatever she had learned was useless.

Today, she had received a whipping from the schoolmaster. Determined to speak the only language she knew, today, she had finally capitulated, speaking a string of Hebrew words Lilly always used. Evidently, not the kind of Hebrew little school girls were allowed to say. She didn't know what any of it meant. But she got in trouble, as usual, which meant no supper when Lilly read the note. She played longer than usual with the kitties before scampering 'home'.

❧ ❧

John Anderson was in his small office at the church, trying to work on sermons, articles, and books. The construction noise and dust were worsened by the opened windows, but for some reason, the work had affected the ancient air conditioning system. He wasn't into a new routine enough to accomplish much from his home office. Too much temptation to hit the pool, the games, or even the refrigerator. His tall frame had gained twenty pounds since the restrictions on the grocery budget had let up. His head was starting to ache, between the heat, the racket, and the allergens, but he was getting some work done. Glancing at the clock on his computer screen, he decided to give it another thirty minutes before breaking for the day.

"Pastor Anderson!" A voice at his doorway startled him.

His heart gave a lurch! The girl from the picture with David! Bransom had learned that her name was Sylvia Brown. Anderson felt trapped, knowing her presence here wasn't a good thing.

"Miss Brown, how may I help you?" The courtesy was forced.

"I came to tell you a few things about your son! Some things I'm sure you aren't aware of!"

The pastor had an expensive feature on his computer to pick up his voice as he dictated his writing, a faster way than keyboarding. He eased up the volume, also switching on the cam. He needed to protect himself from whatever this girl had on her mind.

"My son; I have two."

"Don't try to play games with me! David made me some promises! He told me he didn't like Mallory O'Shaughnessy any more, and he loved me! Now, of course, he's trying to crawl back into her good graces since she has all that money!"

John shrugged. "So, why are you here now, telling me this? If David could change his mind about 'liking' Mallory, maybe he's changed it again about 'liking' you. That's not an unusual thing with teenagers. Maybe you should let it go."

"Well, do you not care that your son only likes a girl for her money?! I would think as a pastor, you would have more ideals than that! I'm here to tell you, I'm marrying your son! What do you think about me as a member of your family?"

He shook his head, bemused. "Well, if you are God's will for my son, I'll welcome you with opened arms."

Suddenly she was across the small space, trying to sit on his lap, trying to force her lips against his.

He jumped to his feet, causing her to tumble ingloriously to the floor. "I wasn't finished," he spoke again from the doorway. "If you are God's will for my son, I'll welcome you with opened arms, but don't get your sheets and towels monogrammed yet."

She had regained her feet, almost like a cat, to snarl her parting remark. "If I can't have him, no one will!"

Shaken, he placed a call to Erik Bransom.

⚔ ⚔

Monique Celine Prescott cleared passport control at DFW International Airport. Blue eyes, fair skin, and blond hair attracted attention; she was slightly aware of it, but it was a normal response to her. When a guy next to her on the flight from Paris tried to become overly friendly, she tried to witness to him, and he pretended to sleep for most of the remainder of the flight. Now, grasping her carry-on, she made a beeline for the exit, to fall into her sister's arms.

Laughing, she stood back, tears in her eyes, viewing her sibling for the first time in over eleven years. "Are you sure your doctor gave you permission to come this far from home? I could have connected on to Tulsa. Just because I've delivered babies before, doesn't mean I want to deliver yours, here!"

Diana laughed. "I'm almost that ready! I can't believe you're really here! You remember Daniel, and of course, Alexandra's grown up a lot. And Jeremiah!" Crying harder, she admitted she wished Cassandra could be here to meet her aunt. "And this is Mallory O'Shaughnessy."

Monique's smile dazzled, as Daniel grasped her one piece of luggage, and she hugged, Alexandra, Jeremiah, and Mallory in turn.

"Wow, you travel light," Daniel observed, dropping the single, small bag into the hatch of the new Yukon.

"Nothing he ever accuses me of," Diana enjoined cryptically.

"I figured you'd be worried about a lot of luggage coming in from Africa. That's why I didn't bring anything with me, and why I laid over in Paris."

The nurse in Monique could relate to the nurse in her sister, and the concerns about Daniel.

"I scrubbed down with a strong disinfecting soap, went shopping for something cheap, scrubbed down again, and bought another new outfit. I messed up my passport, swabbing it with alcohol."

"Well, we try to trust the Lord about it," Diana's voice.

"I know! But that's no reason to take risks. No big deal! Now you'll have to help me get fixed up with a fabulous new wardrobe! Stuff Daddy will approve of, though!" Monique ended on an anxious note.

244

"She designs clothes the Lord approves of," Jeremiah spoke up. "Are we ever going to get to meet our Grandpa Prescott?"

They were all headed up highway one twenty-one from the airport, toward Mallory's.

"I don't know if they are ever planning to return to the States. Maybe when I return to Africa, you can accompany me for a visit." Her voice and inflections were like Diana's but more pronounced, kind of a British accent, with joy thrown in! Mallory was captivated.

Daniel's cell vibrated, John Anderson. "Hey, Pastor, how's everything in Arkansas?" Faulkner had liked Anderson from the beginning, but with his own pastor's recent coldness, he felt more of a bond to the Arkansas ministry than ever.

Anderson was trying to describe his confrontation with Sylvia Brown, but Daniel was trying to put a halt to it until he could address the situation out of Mallory's hearing.

They rode in awkward silence. Finally, Alexandra piped up, "Well, that was smooth! Now we all wonder what David did now!"

⊶ ⊷

Erik Bransom was mad! His pastor had called and hung up before saying anything. Erick had called back, alarmed. If the call was inadvertent, or John had changed his mind, he could answer now, and say so. It left Erik wondering if his throat was cut!

He called Lana, then David. They neither one knew where he was. Reminding himself not to swear, he headed his car toward Murfreesboro. Earlier, he had thought someone was running surveillance on him; now the same car was following him again. Double his worries for his pastor; he placed his weapon next to him on the passenger seat, speed-dialing Faulkner. No answer there, either! Something was definitely up.

⊶ ⊷

Arriving at Mallie's estate, Daniel headed into the library, closing the door! He couldn't get Anderson to answer his call. Dialing Bransom, he learned the agent was on his way up to Murfreesboro to check the situation out. All Faulkner could tell Erik was that Sylvia Brown showed up at Faith Baptist to say stuff about David. Faulkner hadn't been able to listen to the details or make any response because Mallory was in the car. Daniel explained that Mallory had heard enough of the fragmented conversation to make her worry and wonder.

Monique freshened up in the suite at Mallory's before succumbing to the snowy linen bed. When she awakened, everything was dark. The clock beside her said a little after three. This must be what they called jet lag. Still groggy, she pulled on a thick robe, peeking out cautiously as she cracked the door open.

A terrifying growl erupted in the darkness, followed by, "Dinky, hush up. It's safe for you to come out. He doesn't bite." A light flipped on.

"Mallory, you aren't asleep?" Monique's amazed tone.

"Actually, I couldn't sleep. Are you hungry? You kind of slept through dinner. Let's raid the kitchen!"

Monique was pretty sure Mallory had been crying. She knew Daniel was the girl's guardian because she had lost her father. She wasn't sure what to say, so she followed quietly to the kitchen, where they rummaged together, making peanut butter and jelly sandwiches. That was actually a first for the missionary's daughter, who liked the concoction, although it was difficult to dislodge from the roof of her mouth. The tumbler-full of milk helped. They were visiting, despite the difference in their ages and backgrounds when Diana joined them.

"Hey, don't leave me out!" She was fixing a sandwich, pouring herself a glass of milk. "Wow, you were tired! I tried waking you up to go out to dinner," her arm around her sister's shoulder. "I can't wait to catch up."

"Well, I'm going back to bed, so you guys can visit," Mallie felt awkward.

"No, don't go. Have you been crying about David, and that 'mysterious' phone conversation?" Diana was actually blocking the kitchen door.

"I try not to. I'm just trying to focus on other things and trust the Lord about him. Sometimes, it gets hard." She dissolved into tears. "I think I kind of know what was going on. I think Judge Holliman was warning me to stay away from Sylvia and letting her cut my hair. But I haven't seen her since the morning she came to church with David. She called me yesterday to tell me they still love each other, and she's marrying him. She told me, he told her, he 'didn't like me any more', but now he's acting like he does because of my money."

"She called you? Okay, we're getting you a new number. We need to get Monique a phone first thing, anyway." Diana was amazed at the stylist's nerve.

Mallory was wiping her nose and eyes, trying to stop crying. "Were you going to tell me what happened with Pastor? Daniel found out, didn't he?"

"Well, Sylvia showed up at the church, catching Pastor off-guard. I guess it's a good thing he has that computer app that takes dictation! It helped him be able to record her conversation, and his responses. He told her that 'if, she's God's will for David, he'll welcome her to his family with open arms, but not to get her sheets and towels monogrammed yet'." Diana omitted the part of the girl's trying to throw herself at John.

Mallie smiled bleakly. "Yeah, she was mad when she called me. It makes me more scared for David's safety than ever. You know what they say about a 'woman scorned'."

"Yeah, and for your safety, too. Erik's frustrated she has a Federal Judge for a mother!"

"Well, you need to find out what's been happening with your family." Mallory realized they weren't including Monique in the conversation, and Diana wasn't getting the updates about the Prescott family.

Monique's story was more dramatic, by far, than Mallie's little 'puppy love' with David. Mallory kept trying to tell herself that's what it was, because her dad had used the expression more and more in the weeks before his death.

But Monique! Diana called her Niqui, which Mallory teased her about, since Diana refused to call her children by shortened forms of their names! And Mallory thought that the name, 'Monique', was as beautiful as the girl bearing the name.

Monique was in love with one of the African Christians. She hadn't intended to fall in love with him. He had received the Lord just before turning twelve, radiating joy and growing in grace, spending as much time at the mission as possible. He suffered terrible persecution in his village, and even after years of begging God for his tribe's salvation, not one had yet capitulated. Over the years his friendship deepened with the missionary and his children; especially the one his own age!

Mallory thought sadly it sounded like her and David's bonding in second grade.

Ba-ta-ha-yay was his name! Diana could remember his radiant little face, a really loving and special guy, even as a child. Niqui would have married him in an instant, but the tribe would have ostracized and persecuted him more than ever. He made the painful decision to marry the woman in the tribe his father had promised in childhood. Maybe if he were obedient and faithful, his father would see Jesus in him. He had married the unsaved woman! He was miserable; everyone seemingly more hardened against him and his Jesus than ever! When his wife had complications in childbirth, Niqui had responded, delivering the baby and keeping Ba-ta-ha-yay's wife stable. Tragically, the father-in-law had discerned the emotion that still tied Niqui to his daughter's husband!

Stirring the rage of the entire village against the Christian he claimed was a mockery to his daughter and the tribe, he started a manhunt to catch the fleeing Ba-ta-ha-yay and inflict tribal justice! It was awful!

Tears poured down Mallory's pallid face as she listened, barely able to believe such tragedy could really happen!

The Prescotts had spirited their daughter to the U.S. to save her life.

"Is the rest of your family in any danger?" Mallory didn't mean for the question to be stupid.

"Oh, yes," Diana's barely audible reply. "They always are! But this makes it worse!"

⇥ ⇤

Judge John Holliman, in his office, removed his glasses, rubbing his eyes. His eyes were tired; they usually were. But he was wiping tears.

After Mallory O'Shaughnessy's departure, he had requested as much paperwork as anyone could get their hands on that related to her. Of course, he was aware of the wickedness of human nature, so he wanted to check out the behavior of everyone who had access to the girl. To his surprise and relief, everything seemed better than above-board.

The Faulkner family! They definitely had money and privilege! Not nearly as much, though, as O'Shaughnessy had accumulated for his daughter. Holliman had heard that they were 'helping themselves' to the girl's fortune. Not the case at all. The arrangement O'Shaughnessy had worked out seemed to be mutually beneficial to everyone involved!

Same thing with Pastor John Anderson! O'Shaughnessy's gifts to him and his ministry were because the guy was a good guy! Which actually seemed to be the case. It would be in the Anderson family's best interests financially, for their son to marry the heiress. But, the pastor was as much in favor of slowing the relationship as everyone else. Pastor and Mrs. Anderson also wanted what was best for Mallory, even if that wasn't their son.

Bransom, same thing. Really crazy about the girl's mother, and concerned for the safety and well-being of Mallory.

He closed the file, and sat staring across the room. He was amazed how everything could interrelate and fit together so seamlessly for everyone involved. Rooting through the stack of files, he found the one he had glanced over earlier. The girl's lavish Dallas mansion!

Not quite completed, and sitting on the auction-block for several months, the builder was on the verge of losing it. Somehow, an acquaintance of the builder knew the Faulkners, who knew Patrick, who was seeking a beautiful home with tight security for his daughter. Tight-fisted Irishman, O'Shaughnessy fell in love with the locale, and Mallory was set up! And she loved everything! Well why not?

He turned off the lights, heading for home, still puzzled. How could everything work out so perfectly? Time and time again? Was there really a God, and did He really care enough about people who loved Him to work everything together for their good? He thought he could remember something like that from his few times in Sunday School as a child. He shrugged. Just lucky coincidence! Wished he should be so lucky!

Chapter 24: WOW

Mallory was late on Monday, arriving at her office. Marge met her gaze scornfully before gazing pointedly at a decorative wall clock. Attempting pleasant professionalism, Mallory instructed the receptionist to place a lunch order with the building café, to be delivered to her desk as quickly as possible. Hurrying to her spacious corner office, she sank behind her desk, surveying a stack of calls to return. Sorting them quickly, she sent a couple of the messages flying immediately into the trash.

A call from an executive with the chain that owned the Ritz-Carlton, where they had stayed in Istanbul earlier in the year. Puzzled, she returned the call. The executive was in a meeting, but his assistant explained that it had just come to their attention about the difficulty with the corporate meeting room. He was amazed that local management had acted annoyed by the group's expecting privacy for their corporate meeting. He was offering Mallory and DiaMo some refund, or a few free nights in the future.

It reminded Mallory of the opportunity to witness. Curious, she inquired if anyone from her corporate entourage had lodged a complaint about the situation. Assured that that wasn't the case, the executive assistant said the incident had just recently come to the attention of the corporate office. Mallory refused each proffer, simply asserting that everything had been wonderful! They had all been impressed with the comfort and level of service. They wouldn't hesitate to book the chain in the future. She disconnected, knowing that the Lord would bless her for not exacting anything extra from the company. The American executives expressed to her their perplexity that some of the foreign managers could set up a room without a door. Smiling, Mallie knew the Lord had arranged it, especially.

Her next call was to return Tad Crenshaw's! He might have interesting news! She pressed her speed dial to contact her mining foreman.

With the lingering hot summer and dry conditions, the Little Missouri was barely a trickle below the *Winding Stair Rapids*. With claims staked along that stretch of river, Tad had been overseeing what mining operations they were able to accomplish within the environmental guidelines: both state and federal. Actually, the limitations didn't chafe with Mallory as much as they did with many people. She loved the scenic beauty, wanting to see it preserved for the enjoyment of her kids and grandkids!

"Hi, Tad, this is Mallory. What news do you have for me?"

He laughed. "You aren't going to believe how God is serving the diamonds up to us out here! Big ones! Already cut, and set into rings!" He laughed again, waiting for her to 'get it'.

"You guys found the ring my dad gave my mom? It was still right there? I guess that cooks my dad's theory about the gulf."

The foreman laughed again. "Well, I'm not sure where your mom was when she tossed it. We're a couple of miles below the falls and the campground, so it's moved a ways. It was lodged pretty tight into a crevice. What do you think Bransom will have to say?"

"I wouldn't venture a guess. Listen, Tad, how many guys know about it? Lilly has eyes everywhere, I think. Who knows where the Maloviches are? You need to really watch your back."

Already having been a hostage early in the spring, due to the valuable gems, Tad responded, "Yes Ma'am, I'm at Starbucks near your house. Just dropped the ring into a safety deposit box. Wow! That was some rock!"

"Yeah, Tad. Thank you. Any diamonds along there that aren't in rings yet?"

"As a matter of fact, yeah. Being sure everyone is turning them over is a problem."

"Nothing new!"

⸙ ⸙

Suzanne was packing her attache case with some work to take home when her extension buzzed.

"Suzanne!" Her professionalism masked any annoyance she might have felt.

"Mom, you're never going to guess what!" Mallory's exuberance!

"You and David are engaged." It was the only thing she could think of that would make her daughter that elated.

"Oh, don't I wish! Next best thing, Mom!"

"Uh, Diana had her baby."

Mallory laughed, "Soon, I hope. Maybe then I can quit worrying. No, Tad just called me, and they found a big diamond in the river below the rapids!"

"Ah, a reminder of my idiocy. Just when people are about to let me live that down~"

"Well, Mom, it is gorgeous!"

"Yeah, Mallory, but I nearly got killed carrying yours on me. It scares Erik and me both, just thinking about it. Why don't you call the museum at the Park and ask if they would like to place it on display there with the *Strawn-Wagoner?*"

"Well, that's a good idea, Mom. You sure?"

"I'm positive."

Mallie disconnected, impressed. Her mom had basically thrown her dad's heart away with the ring. Mallie had barely forgiven her. At least now, her mom was being careful of Erik's heart. Tears filled her eyes as she called the visitor center at the state park.

Wow, Mallory had been certain the Lord would bless her for declining the proposal from the *Ritz*! But payback wasn't always this swift!

⚔ ⚔

Diana phoned to let her know they were all heading back up to Tulsa! To Mallory's relief! She worried about Diana's approaching due date, being so far from her doctor and hospital.

Mallory told her about the miners having found her mom's ring, then changed the subject to ask if she or Niqui had received any news from the rest of her family, still in Africa.

Diana simply left it at: 'no news'. She hated to weigh Mallory down with the real depth of her concern. No use spilling to Mallory! She couldn't do anything about it. Well, she could pray; she was a real prayer warrior.

"Actually, Mallory, I wanted to invite you to come up with us. We want you to be with us when Xavier's born, if you can work it out."

Tears sprang up in Mallory's eyes. "Well, yeah, sure, I'd love to. I'll go home and pack up for a few days and see y'all later."

Daniel's voice cut in. "We're on the toll way now. Just meet us in about ten minutes. See ya in a few."

"Yes, Sir," she was responding. It kind of sounded like an order, but the call was already disconnected. She jammed the remaining messages into her handbag, throwing some 'in box' documents into her attache. She wasn't sure how long she was going to be up in Tulsa. She wished her laptop was with her. Diana had told her all of her babies always came two weeks late!

"Janice, we're on our way to Tulsa to wait for a baby," she announced.

Nodding, Janice escorted her to the helipad, where they boarded quickly, before rising and angling northward toward Tulsa.

To Mallie's amazement and chagrin, Xavier seemed to have other ideas about when to arrive! Apparently, he didn't know or care about the precedent set by his sisters and brother.

Niqui had kept trying to tell Diana, all day, that she was within twenty-four hours! Diana's continued response, 'That would be too good to be true!'

The chopper crew was more nervous than Mallory was, so they pressed it to set down as near the hospital as possible, as quickly as possible.

Racing down hospital corridors, trying to keep pace with the gurney, Mallie caught sight of two different signs. One announced *CHAPEL*, another *Waiting Room*. She tried to break for one or the other, but they pulled her along until they were all in a spacious labor room.

"Have a seat, Mallie," Daniel offered. Just in time, too, because her knees buckled her into an oak rocking-chair. A curtain drew around Diana, and when it pulled back, she was in an inglorious hospital gown, and prepped for delivery. All vitals good! Diana's and the baby's! Exam showed nearly dilated.

A jolly obstetrician joined the nurse, and Xavier slipped free. Niqui watched, intrigued, as Daniel filmed the delivery of another son. Then Niqui took the camera, to film as the nurse handed 'Zave' to Daniel, and Daniel placed their new infant into Diana's eager arms. He was pink and beautiful. A quivering cry, peculiar to newborns, filled the room.

At eight: thirty-seven P.M., October ninth, weighing seven pounds and nine ounces, Xavier Michael Faulkner made his debut.

Mallory had been terrified, but the wonder of the little baby brought the color back to her cheeks. When she called her mom to make the announcement, Suzanne was happy for the safe delivery, but not happy about Mallory's witnessing the birth.

"Well, I can't stay totally naïve forever, Mom. It's really a very beautiful thing."

"Yes, it is. But your dad still wouldn't have liked you being in there."

Alexandra and Jeremiah, playing *Skipbo* had seemed pretty impervious to their surroundings, but now they were checking out the cute little new brother.

"Let me take a picture of everyone," Mallie offered. She got a cute one of the five Faulkners. It made her miss Cassandra, so she was certain it was worse for all of them.

"Okay, Mallie, you get into one!" Niqui's cute voice, insisting.

Then, Mallie was in the picture, but she wasn't.

Frowning, Daniel deleted it. He pushed Mallory in next to Diana, crunched with the other two kids. "Okay, you can smile, now. Try it again Niqui!"

This time, it was beautiful!

⚎ ⚎

The Arkansas governor called Mallory at eight the next morning. He and several higher-ups within state government had convened until late. The security for the *Strawn-Wagoner* diamond was the maximum they could afford. Regretfully-truly, truly, regretfully, they were declining her generous offer to exhibit Suzanne's ring at *The Crater of Diamonds State Park.* They suggested she offer it for display to the *Smithsonian.*

Barely finished with that conversation, her phone was buzzing again. Lilly!

"This is Mallory," she answered.

"You must list that ring with *Christie's!*"

Mallory grinned. Strange the way you never had to wonder what was on Lilly's mind.

Heading to breakfast, she sank back onto the edge of the bed, instead. Something like that hadn't even occurred to her.

You know, Lilly, I've heard of *Christies,* but I'm sorry to say I really don't know what it is, or what you are saying exactly, I should do."

Lilly was taken aback that Mallory seemed more respectful than usual.

"Well, it's a world-class auction house. That diamond ring, with its story, will bring a greater price by far, than its appraised value. Christie's lists it, and rich people bid on it. But, if you lend it to a museum, be certain

254

everything is in place legally, that it is being lent, and not donated. Please don't donate it!"

Mallory laughed. She had been quick to place the ring up for grabs. The book of Proverbs talked about people 'becoming poor who deal with a slack hand'. That meant, there needed to be a balance between being stingy, holding onto everything; and being slack, holding onto nothing.

"Wow, Lilly, I'm glad you called. Do you know an agent, or someone who can handle the deal, that's fairly trustworthy?"

"Well, I might be able to assist-"

"Okay, Lilly, whatever the usual commission is. Diana had her baby last night, if you want to let Cassandra know."

The conversation concluded, not surprisingly, with Lilly's being far more interested in becoming the middleman for the auction of Suzanne's ring, than in Cassandra and her baby brother's birth.

꾹 ꜩ

In the kitchen, Louisa directed breakfast. It was turning into an elaborate meal, but Mallory was the only one there. Before she could inquire, the kitchen door flung open, and Niqui and all five Faulkners entered. Diana and Xavier were home already, Diana looking more like she was returning from a salon, than from giving birth.

As the dishes were being cleared away, Daniel opened his Bible for a short devotion before the kids started their school day, and he went to the office. The phone rang, and he frowned as Louisa moved toward it. Usually just some crazy interruption by people claiming not to be telemarketers, who asked for you by first name, like they were acquaintances, but who were really telemarketers. Now, he was hoping it was that, and not devastating news about Diana's family.

Louisa handed Diana the phone, and she looked around the table, stricken, as she grasped it.

"Hello, this is Diana!"

Everyone could hear a man's voice on the other end, and Diana burst into tears, even as she tried to signal to them that everything was okay.

They could finally make out that it was Diana's father; somehow, they had all been able to smuggle themselves into Johannesburg, and they were aboard a flight to London, ready for take-off. He cut the conversation short.

"What happened?" Niqui's tormented voice. "Are they all okay?"

Diana had risen to place her arm around her sister. "They're all fine. They got word to get out, so they did. The mission's burned, but Daddy didn't really think they meant the family any real harm. Or they wouldn't have made it."

"It's all my fault." Niqui.

"Come on, Monique, God's still on the throne," Daniel reminded. He read some verses from the Psalms, and they all prayed.

"Come on, Baby, don't cry," Diana's gentle voice to her little sister. "They're all safe, and they're on the way here."

"But, they wanted to stay there forever, and I've ruined everything."

"No, Niqui, I think Daddy actually sounded relieved to be giving it up. Everything's going to be okay."

⚔ ⚔

Tom Haynes sat at his battered desk in his office at Murfreesboro High. Another school year was in full swing. After haggling and finagling since early in the spring, he had brought the School Board, the faculty, and the Student Council officers, into agreement about something different for Homecoming. Quite a triumph, and he was budgeting a little extra to make sure the evening would be a success. Maybe the kids would go for it from now on.

Instead of the traditional dance, he had put together a banquet, with elegant decorations, with some musical entertainment and a comedienne. David and Mallory were already honorary Homecoming King and Queen, with the rest of the court nominated by teachers and voted on by the student body. Joyce double-checked with the caterer; and everything seemed to be going smoothly.

Now, Tom was nervous. When he first mentioned it to Mallory in early September, she had declined. Not taking her 'no' for an answer, he had simply encouraged her 'to think about it'.

Now, he was realizing her 'no' had meant. 'no'. He called her back, telling her how important it was that she attend. This was their chance to prove to the whole town what a nice time kids could have without dancing. She just had to show up! And, she would be David's date. Hadn't it been her dream to be Homecoming Queen on David's arm?

"I'm really sorry, Mr. Haynes, that you still got everyone to agree to the change. I did tell you I couldn't come, when you first asked about it. I know, if my dad were alive, he wouldn't let me. The kids are still the same, the chaperones are still the same. Probably, Pastor would still prefer for David and Tammi not to attend. I know how hard you try, to be a good Christian in the situation you're in. Daddy always respected you a lot, and so do I. I can't come, though."

"Because of Faulkner?"

She wished she could blame him! He didn't know anything about it; at least not from her.

"No, Sir. Because my dad would have told me not to, and he would have said 'No' because it's someplace I have no business being."

When she hung up, she was pretty sure her principal wasn't 'respecting her' for her stance. He was pretty ticked off. Tears filled her eyes.

Her dream to be on David's arm for Homecoming? No! To be on David's arm for life, maybe! She wasn't interested in returning to Murfreesboro High for anything. She knew how all the girls would be dressed, what they would all chattering about, for 'after' the school-sponsored part ended! Drugs, drinking and sex! David should have refused it, too. But, he had to have the attention! Show up in a tux! Get a center page in the yearbook! Be the big shot!

The formal nights as a corporate officer in Niagara Falls, evidently, hadn't quenched his thirst. That had been a 'nice' occasion; there would be more. Maybe 'nice' still wasn't' what he was looking for.

Trying to shake it off, she went in search of Diana. With little Xavier, she and Monique were out on the patio, enjoying a perfect October day. Diana saw her.

"Come on out, Mallory. It's absolutely gorgeous out here!"

The girl complied, climbing into a hammock, stretching lazily. "It is perfect here! The breeze is actually a little invigorating."

"Maybe summer finally decided to relinquish," Diana agreed.

"Your Zinnias look good. I love all the colors they come in! My mom likes them, always had lots of them in the fall. I guess they're pretty easy to grow. Hers were always the biggest and best in the county, though."

Diana nodded agreement, focusing her attention on the beds Mallory was admiring. Strange, to be surrounded with beauty, and not see it. In her heart, she asked God to forgive her. She placed her newborn on top of Mallie in the hammock. Photographing her sister's delicate beauty, and her new baby, she had failed to take note of the flowers. She was blessed beyond measure. She snapped a candid of Mallory in the hammock with Xavier.

"Are you okay, Mallory?" She was alarmed. "What's wrong?"

Mallory laughed. "You are hard to get stuff past. Daniel's right about that. It isn't anything."

"Oh, that deal at the high school? Are you sure you don't want to go? At some point in time, you may regret skipping ahead."

Louisa appeared with tall glasses of tea. Mallory accepted a glass, gazing at it reflectively. Iced tea always made her think of Kerry Larson now. "I wonder what Kerry thinks about Tammi's going." She met Diana's wide, blue-eyed gaze. "I know my dad didn't want me to get ahead of where I should be in life. That's why I go to the teenage class and activities at my church. I am still a high school student, but sometimes I feel like I don't fit anywhere." She was trying not to cry. "My dad wouldn't budge about my going to school activities. You know, he always badgered Pastor and Lana to try to compete. We had 'dress-up' banquets at the church for the 'poor us' that couldn't have the real fun! But daddy was right. Most of the kids just use Homecoming and Prom as springboards to do more of what they want. They're all planning to push the tables out of the way, and dance anyway. Most of the sponsors, either don't care, or they act worse than the kids do. It's as hard for one of the sponsors to speak up as it is for the teens. I wonder what Tommy's doing."

Diana frowned; she wished Mallory hadn't brought Tommy up!

⇥ ⇤

David picked his tux up from the drycleaners, pulling the plastic and tissue away immediately, to make sure the cleaners hadn't ruined anything. His mom always said, that the more the cleaning was wrapped up, the more they were trying to cover up what they had ruined. Buttons still on, zipper still worked. He tried it on, just to be sure it wasn't shrunk.

He nodded to himself approvingly in the mirror. Hanging the garments back carefully, he remembered Mallory's ribbing him about being a Narcissist. The morning before Patrick's will, which had left her a very, very rich lady! Remembering countless of his dad's sermons on the evils of money, he prayed yet again, that Mallory's wealth wouldn't ruin her.

A couple of days, and he and his queen would reign at Murfreesboro High! He was excited! He called Suzanne to ask what color Erin's dress was, and if she wanted a corsage for her dress, her wrist, or her hair.

WEALTH: A Mallory O'Shaughnessy Novel

He caught Suzanne off-guard and confused. "Oh, Tom didn't tell you Mallie isn't going?" I mean, Mr. Haynes! She told him over six weeks ago. I'm sorry, David."

David disconnected the call as smoothly as he could manage. Mallie wasn't coming? He called Haynes, who confirmed the fact. Haynes was mad at her, and David was getting mad too. "Big shot! Always parading around with her nose in the air, even before inheriting millions! Erin go bragh!" Angry tears made him angrier than ever! He dashed them away! And he was idiot enough to think she'd marry him, at the end of five years! She wouldn't even be by his side for an evening? An evening of triumph, that they deserved?

Trying to calm down, he called Tammi to ask her if she knew Mallory planned to be a 'no-show'!

Tammi could tell when her brother was mad. "Calm down, David. Did you invite her?"

"Well, Mr. Haynes did! I thought it was all arranged. I called Suzanne, about ordering a corsage, and she informed me, or I would have probably showed up, looking really stupid, thinking I had a date!"

"Thanks a lot! I'm going without a date! Does that mean I'll look stupid?"

"No, everybody knows you have someone on the hook that beats out all the high school guys, by a long shot!"

"Well, Duh! They know the same thing about you! Mallie's pretty sure her dad still wouldn't have wanted her to go. You know how the majority of the kids are! But, you should call her and ask her to come with you. She might change her mind."

"I'm not allowed to call her! Did you forget?"

"Well, I haven't forgotten, as a matter of fact! You get so stubborn! Evidently, Mr. Haynes had everything set up with the Faulkners so you could be with Mallie for an evening. I'm sure they all figured you two would converse, which might be kind of nice for both of you! Why don't you call Daniel and ask him if you can call Mallory and invite her to be your date for Homecoming? It's nicer than the way you've just always assumed she'd be there! He'll probably like the formality that you ask him, and that you ask Mallory! David, are you listening to me? Trust me, I know."

He hung up, madder than ever! Call Faulkner? He didn't think so! Guy would probably really tell him off for even asking! Daniel Faulkner didn't have any business lording it over Erin, anyway!

He pressed a number. "Hey, Sylvia, how's it going?"

Cassandra was farther from Lilly's than she had ever been before. She had gotten into a maze of narrow streets, not sure she could find her way back. For the moment, she wasn't worried. Carrying her favorite kitten with her, she wandered on. Today was a holiday from school. She hoped Lilly didn't know! She hadn't told her! A whole day, just to be outside, and away from Lilly and her help! Hearing strains from a violin, she advanced quickly. A violinist, not really, really good, but okay, was playing on a street corner for the coins people threw his way. Wow! She wished she knew where Lilly had hidden her violin! She could use some money! Perplexed, she perched on a low stone wall to watch and listen.

Tears wanted to come, but she forced them back, resolutely. She was formulating a plan. Tonight, when Lilly was asleep, she would find her violin! She had tried to find it before; of course she had begged Lilly to give it back, even promising to be good. Now she wondered if Lilly had sold it! Lilly was mean!

While she sat there, a big group of people passed her, barely noticing the street urchin. A man was their leader, and he was teaching them all something. In English! Curious, she drew nearer, listening intently, following their gazes as they all stared at the same big building. She had noticed it earlier, because an oddly dressed man in a black deal, who had lots of gray hair and gray whiskers was standing beside it. She heard something about 'Jesus', and tried to get in even closer.

Hands grasped at her, thrusting her away roughly. "Watch out. Some of these little kids are pickpockets." It was the teacher. They all filed away, into the big building.

Fearing loss of her freedom, she scampered away to listen to the violinist some more. He played a couple of lively things, bringing her smile to the light as she clapped along. A few more coins came his way. Gathering them up, he moved toward a food stand to make a purchase.

With his purchase made, he stood, eating, conversing with the vendor.

Unable to resist any longer, Cassandra grabbed the instrument, playing exactly what she had just heard, only better. The vendor and the musician stared at the little girl in surprise, but made no move to stop her. She played on as coins clinked into the case at her feet. Most of the pieces she loved, she couldn't perform to her own satisfaction, so she continued playing simpler pieces. Someday, though! She would discover the elusive secrets.

She began to play 'Amazing Grace' just as the tour group exited from the *Church of the Holy Sepulcher.* All those people broke rank, moving to hear her, throwing lots of money!

Cassandra stopped playing, meeting the wondering gazes of a group of people who looked like mirror images of her. They passed by, reassembling with the bigger group. Puzzled, Cassandra played the favorite hymn again as the group disappeared on their tour.

Suddenly shy, she returned the instrument to its owner. "Can I have a few of the coins?" she questioned hesitantly.

She wasn't sure he understood English, but he scooped her little hands full of various coins. She wanted a bit of bread, but wasn't sure how to make the purchase, so she skipped away, hoping to be able to find her way back to Lilly's.

Chapter 25: WOE

Mallory and Diana threw their energies behind Americanizing Monique; showering her with clothes, accessories, and jewelry! She acted overwhelmed and delighted by everything. She loved the pools and plenteous amounts of food. But, her heart was broken!

That was before the hideous images of tribal vengeance on Ba ta ha yay began appearing on the internet. Mallory was aghast, having never seen anything like it. Even with all the talk about Martin Thomas's victims, Mallory had been shielded from the morbid details. Now she gazed on evil as she had never imagined, her heart breaking for Diana's delicate sister. No wonder clothes and shoes weren't cheering her up.

It made her more nervous about Sylvia's threats regarding David.

After arriving safely in London, the Prescotts called, stating they planned to 'take holiday' before coming to the States.

Xavier was darling, and in spite of Diana's determination not to 'spoil him', he hardly knew a second of inattention. When Diana put him down, Monique would grab him at the first hint of a whimper. Then Al and Jer played with him every second they got a chance. Daniel clung to his infant son desperately, from the time he came home in the afternoons, until bedtime.

Mallory, having dealt with all the documents she had brought with her, returned to Dallas, to check on everything there, bring some more work and her laptop so she could continue her academics.

The Maestro, either not knowing, or not caring, how many 'papers' she was already working on, assigned her to do research on Bach, and write a paper. At least, he was finally allowing her to actually play her violin. Harder than it looked, of course. She still wished she had never mentioned it!

On Friday, she insisted she needed to go home for the weekend. She knew Diana was worried about her and the Homecoming parade and game in Arkansas.

"Don't worry about me. I know I've made the right decision. Mom and Erik will tell me all about everything. The Andersons will all be at the game. Kerry's handling it; so can I."

Smiling, she hugged Diana and Niqui, kissing Xavier on his head. "See you Tuesday for lessons and soup." Ducking the whirling rotor, she boarded the chopper.

The air held a definite chill as she transferred to a golf cart for the run to her house. Felt like Homecoming and football season. Whistling, she checked the mail in the entry way, giving Dinky an affectionate rub. She was happy to be home. Requesting Pepperoni pizza, she sank into a recliner in the game room, turning the TV on automatically. Baseball was over, the Sox had had a decent season, but didn't even make the play-offs.

She frowned as Carole Lee Whitfield's face filled the screen on the Dallas station. One of the advantages of moving to Texas was being rid of the Little Rock anchor woman! What story could she have that would interest viewers outside of Arkansas?

A startled cry escaped Mallory's lips! Murfreesboro's Homecoming? No one cared about that little town! In Arkansas! Let alone in Texas! Her gaze fixed! David! His date, *Silver Beret*, looked a lot like Sylvia Brown, except she had her hair cut weird, dyed silver, and her make up was all silvery and sparkly. Her dress, what there was of it, was sequined with silver. Then, the camera panned quickly across the rest of the court. Tammi looked cute in fuchsia. Tommy Haynes was finally looking like a teenager instead of a little kid.

Carole Lee was mostly there because of David Anderson. She tried to get a story from him, or a statement, but suddenly the 'world's biggest ham', didn't have much to say. Sylvia seemed to be enjoying the attention, more than anyone.

Mallory's cell was ringing, but she disregarded it, her eyes riveted to the big screen. She knew who the calls were from. Everyone was seeing the spectacle David had decided to make of himself! This was probably showing in Tulsa! Her mom and Erik and the Andersons were all right there, witnessing the pitiful exhibition, live and in person! Finally, time for kick-off, although the anchor woman didn't seem interested in the small-town, high school, football game, at all! Mallie changed channels and fed her pizza to Dinky.

"Hi, Diana," her voice was a whisper. "I'm fine, but I don't really want to talk right now. See you Tuesday."

She didn't answer any of the other calls. They always got together about everything else. Diana could pass the word along, "That she was just fine!"

Finally, she made her way to bed, pulling her daddy's picture into her arms.

"Daddy, you were right about him! I've been worried he loves Sylvia! He doesn't love her! He only loves himself! He's using her, and she's crazy as a bedbug! You're right, Daddy, he doesn't care about me!"

She cried until she couldn't cry any more, as she hadn't cried since the days immediately after her daddy's death.

"Why did life have to hurt so bad?"

⚞ ⚟

Daniel Faulkner didn't know when he had ever been so mad! It took everything Diana had, to keep him from going straight to Murfreesboro to settle Mallory's score for her!

"You'll do something you'll regret, and you'll end up in jail! That won't help anything! If we need to go anywhere, it should be to Dallas, to be with Mallory. Why don't you call Erik or John?"

He didn't want to go to Dallas! He figured Mallie's heart was breaking, and was afraid if he saw her, the little restraint he had, would be gone. "How could anybody be so stupid? So unfeeling? So, so~?!" He raged around until he was exhausted, before he and Diana, both, finally fell into a troubled sleep.

⚞ ⚟

Tom Haynes, anguished, and drawn, left the police station at three in the morning. His banquet had turned into a fiasco, resulting in his being assaulted, and several of his students' being arrested. More bruised in spirit, than in body(which was saying something), he had refused medical treatment. He drove slowly around town, back past the now quiet school campus, past the church, around the site of the new John Anderson Ministries headquarters building under construction south of town. He drove down to Hope and back, out past the Diamond Park, crying, listening to his favorite gospel group. His cell rang, Joyce, asking him if he was okay. It was six; he was sorry she was awake so early on Saturday.

"Let's meet at Hal's for breakfast," she suggested.

"I think I just want to move away in the middle of the night." His voice was filled with bitter tears. "I'm sure not ready to face anyone at breakfast. Sorry, Hon! I know you enjoy that! Why don't you and Tommy go? Is he doing okay? If you go, though, be really careful about what you say to people. This is still kind of a powder keg."

When he thought nothing could be any worse, he received a furious call from a parent! Four of the kids had just been in a terrible wreck! One dead, one critical, two scraped up and scared! Dazed, he returned home. How could this happen?

⊰ ⊱

Suzanne went to her office at Sander's Corporation bright and early on Saturday morning. Actually, the first frost sparkled across the landscape, and fog hung in the low places, as she pulled into the empty parking lot. She liked the brisk weather, but her heart was heavy. Now instead of listening to Patrick rage around about David Anderson, she had listened to Erik, nearly all night, about the same thing! She was hurt, too, because she had still been trying to believe in David. Well, she had work to do. Unlocking the glass doors of the executive building, she hurried to her office, starting a pot of coffee.

While it brewed she moved around the building, watering the plants and cutting off leaves that didn't look pretty. Returning to her office, she poured a mug of coffee, opened her computer, and started on some correspondence.

A tap at her door startled her. David stood there, looking awful!

"What are you doing here? We're closed."

"I saw your car. Can I talk to you?"

"Not right now, David. If you need to talk, maybe you should find your dad."

The anguished boy crossed the threshold. "Please, Suzanne, I can explain everything."

"She said, 'not now'!" Erik's voice behind him made him jump. "Maybe you need to hit the trail, Cowboy, 'fore ya get yerself in trouble ya can't get out of!"

265

"Yes, Sir!" Erik was one of the people David was hoping not to face very soon! If ever! He sidled past him and made it to his truck as fast as he could without actually running.

⚞ ⚟

Mallory, awake early, read her Bible out in the brisk morning air, poolside! "My heart is fixed on Thee! My heart is fixed on Thee," she kept affirming desperately. Without cleaning up, she slipped into an old pair of warm-ups and went to work at her computer. "My heart is fixed upon Thee. Stay busy. Don't think!" a manicured nail smacked 'print', and her *Bach* paper was finished. Actually, an interesting glimpse back in time! Guess she wasn't the only one to have problems! Forcing herself to concentrate on several English Literature selections, she wiped her eyes and nose for the thousandth time. Then, the tears flowed even more copiously after her mom called to break the news to her about the accident involving her classmates.

Heavy, under-aged drinking was cited as the cause for the wreck, but the parents were trying to crucify Mr. Haynes about it. Mallory shook her head, bewildered. That wasn't fair. Mr. Haynes had the Highway Patrol come as often as they would, to show gruesome movies and warn all the kids about drinking. Trying to blame him for such a tragedy was a stretch!

At noon, she sipped some soup, but she wasn't hungry.

Good news! Her batting cage was installed, and ready to go! Finally! Just in time, too!

Smack! "Anderson's a line drive down the first base line! Whack-o! pop foul! Out past the center field fence. Home Run! Yea for Mallory!"

"Are you having fun?" It was Kerry. She had seen him come out, but she was trying to ignore him. Evidently he was the spy sent to make sure she hadn't strung herself up over David.

She was cold, in spite of all her physical exertion. "Care to take a couple of swings at him?" She offered the attorney a bat, her eyes shooting sparks.

"Why aren't you answering your phone?" Kerry's question.

"Because! I don't want to talk to anyone! I told my mom to text me when funeral plans are arranged for Kyle. Not sure I'll go, but I'll send flowers."

"Someone tried to shoot David."

266

"Wasn't me. I've been here all day! Trying to work voodoo on these balls. If he has a headache, that's me! Maybe it was *Silver Beret!* I kind of thought she was making threats when she called me one day.

Larson actually loved batting cages, thinking he should install one in his yard. He had plenty of room. He declined a turn, though. Mallory was quite the hitter! Left-handed! Evidently still taking it easy on her right wrist.

The fact someone was shooting at David was a concern to her; like terrifying! At the moment though, she didn't want Kerry to know she cared. She sure didn't want David to know, or Sylvia!

⚔ ⚔

John and Lana were in shock! Were they back to square one with David just when they were relaxing about their elder son's recommitment to the Lord?

In tears after the 'half-time coronation ceremony', Tammi had located her parents in the stands, begging to go home. Hearing some of the rumblings among the student body, she knew trouble was brewing. Finding the three youngest kids, they all departed before the game ended. Now, mid-morning Saturday, no one seemed to know where David was.

The pastor, with his Bible spread open on the kitchen counter, poured another mug of coffee. E-mails were updating him about the fiasco; the car wreck, the arrests, the assault on Haynes. It seemed that David wasn't involved in the brawl. Anderson wasn't sure when his son disappeared, where to, and if he was still with his date! His heart ached so hard he thought he might be sick.

"I thought he loved Mallory," Lana's voice inserted itself into his misery. She was starting a fresh pot of coffee brewing. "Why doesn't that girl leave him alone?"

He met her gaze. She didn't know about Sylvia's visit to him at the church office. He still wasn't planning to tell her. Faulkner and Bransom were both aware of it. Bransom's techs had taken the conversation and video into evidence, although the girl's tie-in to the 'out-of-bounds' investigation made the agent nervous.

"Well, not to defend David's behavior; it's pretty indefensible, but the devil is really fighting for him."

She nodded, mopping her reddened nose again.

267

꿪 ꙫ

Suzanne's being alone at Sander's headquarters on Saturday, hadn't struck Erik as a really good idea; but he figured it would probably be fine. He was mad at David for this whole latest shenanigan! But then to head straight to Suzanne? How was she supposed to help him with Mallory, if he was so dumb!? Then Suze was telling him to get lost, and he advanced toward her anyway!

After that, he sent Suzanne to Dallas against her and Mallory's wishes. He didn't care. He thought Mallie needed her mom. He was cruising northwestern Arkansas. Why not? Pretty country! He cased Dierks. His not seeing David's truck wasn't proof of anything. He couldn't tell if the girl was home, and David was gone; if they were still together someplace. His heart felt like lead. He wasn't even a golfer, but he pulled into a driving range anyway, just to hammer some balls. He was as proud of Mallory's hitting as he would have been if he had been her coach instead of Patrick.

Back in the agency vehicle, he swung through Kirby. When David moved from home before, he kept an apartment up here. For the past six months, David had been splitting his time between living at the camp, and his parent's home. The boy's truck wasn't in evidence here, either. The agent couldn't figure out why he was huntin' the kid. If he wanted to talk to him, he missed his chance earlier at Sander's. If he was really wanting to find him, the camp was the best bet, and the horse! Bransom figured that would be his escape if he pulled something this dumb. Thinking of Suzanne and the dimension of joy she brought him, he prayed for the Lord to help him not to do anything this dumb, to jeopardize what he had. Just that quick though, it could be easy to throw away what you have!

꿪 ꙫ

David saddled *El Capitan* as soon as he could get to the stable. The stable at the camp would soon be finished. He was glad, then reminded himself he didn't have any rights whatsoever, to board his horse on the camp property. He was probably done working for Mallory. He still kept trying to blame her, though, for his lapse in judgment. She should have just come to Homecoming like everyone wanted her to!

He wished he could have talked to Suzanne. He wanted to promise her nothing had happened with Sylvia. Bransom had run him off. He had thought the agent was kind of his friend.

He fed an apple to his horse, enjoying the nuzzle, and slipped one to *Star*, before swinging up into his new saddle. All the nice birthday gifts! Because he had been behaving better, trying to live for the Lord. Now he felt defeated and humiliated! Erin go bragh just should have been there. The fight wouldn't have happened, or the arrests, or the car accident. He took off at a gallop, still justifying his behavior, blaming everyone who had ever slighted him! Blaming everyone he could think of to blame. He slowed to a trot, then paused to allow *El Capitan* to drink from a shallow place along a stream.

The weather was chilly, and the foliage was a riot of color. He headed back to his truck for his jacket. The flash of a shiny object on the path caught his eye. He reigned up, sliding from the saddle as a shot split the air!

His first thought was of hunters. The camp was clearly marked off-limits to hunters, but hunters didn't always obey signs. He still took cover as another shell zinged past him. If this was a hunter, he must be the quarry!. Allowing himself to slide down a steep embankment, he summoned *El Capitan*.

Sheltered from the marksman on the ridge, he fished his pistol and cell phone from the saddle bags. He returned one shot. Let whoever it was know that he was armed, but save the rest of the ammo, in case whoever it was pursued. He didn't think that would happen. Seemed to be someone interested in sniping at him from a distance, more than someone who wanted to bring the fight to him. Still, there was a lot of open space for him to cover before he could get back to the stable and his truck. His anger dissolved into tears of fear.

⊣ ⊢

Mallory really was not happy to have her mom en route to her house. The crying and staying out most of the day in the chill were making her feel like she might be catching cold. She showered and dressed up, applying make up carefully over her tear-ravaged face. What an awful twenty-four hours! She wished she could suffer privately. She just wished she knew if David had ever kissed Sylvia. She was trying to keep the tears from starting up again, ruining her make up job, when Suzanne arrived.

"Mom, I wish you had stayed home. I don't think I'm going to be very good company!" Her voice caught in a sobbing wail. "Kerry said somebody was shooting at David. Were they really? Who all stayed for the banquet/dance? I knew the kids weren't really going along with Mr. Haynes. They were laughing about the whole thing all along."

Suzanne stood inside the door, surveying Mallie indecisively. She didn't have any more of a clue what to tell her now, than she did when Patrick died. She had really failed the 'Mom-test' then, running to Hope to ask Roger Sanders for her old job back.

"Okay, Mallie, let me get in the door. Have you eaten anything at all since you got back from Tulsa yesterday?"

Mallory nodded. "Pizza last night, and some soup for lunch today."

Suzanne frowned. "How much pizza? How much soup? Did you get any sleep?"

Mallory answered with a frustrated motion with her hands. "Not much, not much, not much! To pizza, soup, and sleep."

"Well, okay, I'm pretty mad at David, but not enough to lose my appetite."

Mallie nodded. "What sounds good, Mom. I'll try to eat something with you. I'm trying to trust the Lord and not be upset."

In a few minutes, they were eating salads, steaks, and fries in the sitting room of Mallory's suite.

Her mom's gossipy personality was taking over for the first time in months. Suzanne really was a transformed woman. But now, she was purposely entertaining her daughter with all the juicy tidbits about everybody in Murfreesboro.

First Mallory smiled, then was laughing with her mom, as they raked people over the coals.

"Okay, Mom, you've told me the scoop on everyone but the one I want to hear about."

Suzanne's blue eyes serious again, she met her daughter's anguished gaze. "I don't know, Honey. When Tammi came into the stands after half-time, telling her mom and dad trouble was coming, Erik and I left, too. You know, the Murfreesboro police always have a presence at the games. Erik didn't want us to be where trouble was brewing; didn't want to be there as a law officer, when stuff wasn't his jurisdiction. I thought David seemed kind of embarrassed. He should have been, but I don't know!" She shrugged. "We went home and went to bed. This morning, I was behind on some stuff at the office, so I was catching up, and David tried to talk to me. He saw my car, so he came in. I was there alone, and he startled me."

"You weren't afraid of David, were you, Mom?"

"No, but I should have locked myself in. So, when I thought I was by myself, and he tapped at the doorway, I nearly jumped out of my skin."

"Yeah, so what did he say, Mom?" Mallory thought her mom could have started with the fact that she had seen David just this morning.

"Well, Mallie, we were all so mad! Pastor's ready to kill him, and for a change, Lana's ready to help him!"

"What did he say, Mom?"

"He said he saw my car outside, and then he asked if he could talk to me."

"I just told him I didn't want to talk to him yet. He wanted to pursue it, but Erik saw him come in, and followed him, and told him to 'Hit the trail'."

Mallie nodded. "So, he got *El Capitan* and 'hit the trail', and that's when somebody shot at him? Kerry told me someone did, and I care, but I don't want anyone to know how much."

⚞ ⚟

Ivan Summers had a prisoner in an interrogation room at the Hope police department. His reflection showed numerous claw marks and scratches sustained during the arrest. It would have been easier to wrestle a bear.

"Wow, Summers, you nearly lost an eye there," was Bransom's cryptic comment. "Why'd ya call me? I've nearly lost my job over this a couple of times, already."

"Why'd ya come? No one has a gun to your head. Actually, this is a separate incident."

Bransom's wry laugh. "I've thought lots of this really was separate incidents, to find out it all ties into a central mess. Your girl's nothin' but trouble. Maybe you should get a rabies shot."

"Come on, Erik, don't leave yet, the party's just starting. Take a look at her I.D.!"

Hooked, Bransom took the Arkansas Drivers License, studying it closely. It was amazing! Had to be phony; the girl's name wasn't 'Sylvia Beret', and she wasn't twenty-one. With so many security measures incorporated into legitimate licenses, Bransom's guess was that someone in the transportation department must have helped with it. That was scary.

271

Still an Arkansas deal, though, Summers should be the one to deal with it.

Erik couldn't resist, though. He was still so mad at David, and at this girl for her part in hurting Mallory!

Eyes dancing, he slammed the door behind him as he and the ABI agent entered interrogation.

"I don't think you should be in here, Agent!" Her eyes shot darts.

Ignoring her comment, he looked at the license still in his hand, before meeting her hostile gaze mischievously.

"Wow. Yesterday, you were nineteen, now you're already twenty-one. Your hair's gone all gray. Remind me not to drink after you, you must have picked the wrong chalice."

She met his gaze scornfully. She didn't have a clue what he was talking about. She didn't care.

Summers thought the Fed's comments were hilariously funny. "Yeah, she chose poorly," he rejoined. They were both in stitches over whatever the joke was.

"She sure did." Bransom's smiling countenance was suddenly ferocious. "Attempted murder, smoking gun in hand. And drugs, too. More than enough for a party of one. Guess she was trying to earn a little pocket change. You need to throw the book at her. I can't! Yep, she chose poorly!"

He stormed back out, still holding the piece of plastic. "What kind of police department you running here with no fresh coffee?" he demanded of one of the detectives.

Someone sprang into action to remedy the situation.

"Save me a cup when it's brewed. I'm goin' for donuts."

In his car, he phoned to ask Suzanne how Mallie was doing.

"I'm just fine, Erik. Tell me what's going on, and I'll relay the updates to Mom. I'm tired of being the one getting second-hand information."

"Well, I still don't know where David is. Miss Brown's in jail. I'm trying to figure out how she has a really state of the art 'fake' license. There should be enough charges to hold her forever, except for her powerful connections that make no sense to me."

They talked for a few minutes, and he disconnected. Three dozen donuts in hand, he drove slowly back to the station. He was actually amazed Dawson wasn't already eating him out. Probably too busy changing locks out again.

In his mind, he was trying to make order from the chaos. He pulled some of the jumbled pieces from his memory.

The quashing of his investigation from nearly the beginning, evidence 'disappearing', buildings just 'poof-catching fire'!

Tears were filling his eyes as revelation dawned on him! Tears of relief. Maybe America wasn't in as much of a moral morass as he had thought. Like Suzanne had done a few times before, he had jumped to conclusions! Well, who hadn't? He thought the word from 'higher up' meant bribery, or some other miscarriage of justice. With his being ordered from the case, he had turned it over to the Lord,(Well maybe he had meddled a little since then) the Righteous Judge.

"Lord, thank You," he whispered. The whole Arkansas, Dallas, Boston, Turkey connection was part of some international crime syndicate. His digging out Melville had caused his agency to collide with some other agency, some other ongoing investigation, probably involving the safety of agents deep under cover. A good thing, overall, going down. Except that the powers-that-be had planned to sacrifice Mallory's employees on the altar of their on-going investigation. He knew someone wanted to lop off the 'head of the monster'. For that, he was glad. He still wanted the Maloviches, even if they were only the toes! And he was glad Morrison and Summers had persevered in their quest, saving the good men whose lives had been at stake.

For a police department nearly empty on a late Saturday afternoon, there were plenty of hands in the donut box. The sergeant in charge was pleasantly surprised. Usually Feds came in making their power plays, ordering the locals around like they were complete yokels, scarfing up their donuts.

Summers emerged, his abused face looking even worse, more swollen. His defeated expression was even sadder than the wounds.

"Had to cut her loose?" Bransom's sympathetic question.

"It makes no sense!" the anguish in the Arkansas agent's voice resonated deeply with Bransom.

"Yeah, it really does," Bransom's soft response. Still madder than mad at David Anderson, he called to give him a heads up that Sylvia was on the loose again, with her gun back in her possession.

Chapter 26: WORDS

October colors and bright blue sky were deceptive. A driving wind from the north was freezing! So much for an outdoors breakfast. By now, Mallory loved every space in her home, but the country part of her loved the outside and landscaping. Too cold, they changed their minds, quickly moving into the warmth, even turning on a fireplace. Actually, the first occasion for using the special feature.

"Mallory, this place is amazing!" Her mom's voice echoing her thoughts.

She hugged her mom. "Yeah, it really is You should stay here and go to church with me. I'm not sure the choppers can fly with so much wind. I don't want you trying it, anyway."

Suzanne nodded. Always questioning her own maternal skills, she was glad for an excuse to stay. She missed Erik, but he was right. She needed to be a mom to Mallory, whether she knew what to say and do, and even if Diana Faulkner seemed more natural at it.

Lingering in front of the cheery fire, enjoying another mug of coffee and cocoa, the reflective, bonding time just felt good. Mallory didn't eat much, simply requesting a fruit smoothie. At least the fruit contained nutrients. Probably as good or better than pizza, her daughter's usual diet preference. Suzanne wasn't even sure. Maybe she could check with Diana about a protein the staff could add to the smoothies.

Mallory dressed in an outfit from one of Diana's new fall lines. Various coordinate groupings often bore names. This line's inspiration- *Spice Market*, from the previous spring's trip to Turkey, and the amazing Istanbul Spice Market. The solid color separates bore names such as *Cinnamon, Sage, Paprika, Nutmeg, Ginger, Saffron, and Basil*. A bright print, featuring the market's zingy-colored displays, was featured in some of the lining fabrics, large silk twill scarves, screen printed sweaters, and blouses.

A soft, buttery-yellow, leather suit, in *Saffron*, was trimmed with rich, brown mink at the cuffs and collar. Since the weather wasn't that cold, Mallie removed the detachable fur. Better! The fur was definitely cute, though, giving an entirely different look for another time. A soft ivory turtleneck peeked from the jacket, and a large silk scarf, printed with the colorful spice array, looped gracefully. Her jewelry suite of citrine, smoky quartz, and hessonite garnets shimmered at wrist and ear lobes. Elegant!

Suzanne was ready to go. In one of her summer dresses.

Well, as far south as they were in the U.S. some of the fashion rules hardly applied. One day, the high might be in the thirties, and you wore boots. The next day or so, might be eighty! Bring on the sandals.

Still, her mom looked kind of funny. And her mom had just been talking about everyone else's fashion gaffs she had noticed at Homecoming.

"Mom, I have an Alpaca wrap from Shay. Here, put it around you. You need to find some winter clothes. They're even more fun than summer ones."

"Well, you're turning into a real 'clothes horse'. I always wanted a lot of nicer clothes than we could afford. Now, it doesn't matter that much."

Mallory shook her head. "Yeah, it does, Mom. Think about it as helping the image of the Sander's Corporation."

-≒ ≒-

David was at Phil and Risa's. Not to say that they weren't mad at him, too, but they were at least speaking. When he got the call about Sylvia's release, he was pretty shocked. He offered to find another place to stay, not wanting to place the Perkins in jeopardy.

"Nah, I'll go get our car out of the shed, and put your truck in. Maybe she won't expect you to be here," was Phil's response

Risa had made a delicious pot of chili. It tasted pretty good, especially since the weather was so brisk.

Phil and Risa both retired early after making up the sofa bed. After watching hours of college football, David finally fell asleep.

Risa was up early, frying bacon, baking biscuits. David grasped at this blanket, trying to make sure he was decent, groping for his jeans.

"Your clothes are in the dryer. That's why you get breakfast in bed. A one-time deal, so you better enjoy it." His hostess thrust a brightly colored

plate into his hands, heaped with biscuits and gravy and a side of bacon,
A huge tumbler of cold milk appeared, too. Before he finished with the
meal, his jeans reappeared. Risa mended a rip in his shirt, then ironed it
for him, before disappearing into the bedroom.

⇥ ⇤

Daniel and Diana showed up early for church, as usual. They were planning
to dedicate Xavier to the Lord, but they were always early. Daniel had
resigned his Sunday School class after his pastor's harsh words, and because
they had been going back and forth between Mallie's church in Dallas,
and here. Without the careful oversight by the Faulkners, the singles were
drifting away. After getting Al and Jer dispatched to their classes, they left
Zave in the nursery for the first time, before finding places in their adult
class.

Niqui showed up just a couple of minutes before time to start.

"I'll introduce you to some of the singles after church." Diana's whisper
to her sister, just as the class began.

⇥ ⇤

Kerry Larson was relieved to see Mallory and her mom enter the church
in time for Sunday School. He couldn't really tell if Mallie had a cold or
was still sniffling and crying about David. Herb and Linda showed up.
Since Herb was splitting his time between his Arkansas pawn shop and
the Dallas jewelry design studio, he often attended Calvary. Mallory was
relieved her mom could go to their class with them and not have to sit
alone. She hurried to her class. Callie was there; her attendance had become
sporadic at best, but Mallory was happy to see her

"Wow, your outfit is really elegant. You hardly fit in with the teens;
why don't we move up a class?"

"Well, let's stay in here for today," Mallie whispered back. "It's time
to start."

She spent part of the class thinking sadly, that she really didn't fit in
anywhere. Then, scolding herself for the self-pity, she thanked the Lord
for the friends and relatives she did fit with. They were a pretty incredible
group. She guessed she had lost sight of the facts, while spending the
week-end being sad that she didn't fit with the little knot of students at
Murfreesboro High.

She sang in the choir, then joined her mom, her aunt, and Herb for the sermon. It was really great. She definitely had a cold, but emotionally, she felt much better. Just something about being with good Christians, singing, and hearing the Bible preached! She invited Kerry to join them for lunch, and he accepted eagerly. Callie joined them, too, and it was just lots of fun. Calling Diana, Mallory apologized for not being more communicative, telling her friend excitedly how many compliments the outfit had garnered. That people were eager to accept business cards to be in touch about placing orders.

Daniel and Diana were both relieved that she was springing back. Reaffirming the Tuesday routine, they hung up.

Back at home, Mallory pulled a soft throw around her, snuggling into one of the recliners in the music room, where another fireplace burned cheerily beside her. She watched the Zinnia's out in her flower beds bobbing their heads madly in the stiff wind. She loved the lively riot of hues. She should take a picture, but she didn't feel like hopping up for her camera.

Suzanne fixed them both cups of hot tea, laced with honey, and joined her. "Your flowers are all still pretty." She seemed to have read Mallie's thoughts.

Mallie laughed. "I was just thinking the same thing. Take a picture with your phone, will you, Mom, and e-mail it to mine? I'm too lazy to go get my camera. I should be doing something, but it feels so good just to veg by the fire."

"You stay busy all the time. We aren't under the law any more about observing the Sabbath, but the Lord made the Sabbath for man, because He engineered our bodies, and He knows how we should care for them. Why don't you just take a nap, and give yourself a chance to get over your cold?"

Mallie napped until time to head to choir practice. Still stopped up, she returned to church anyway. It was just the beginning of cold and flu season. She prayed not to start an epidemic traceable to her.

❧ ❧

David went to church with the Perkins. It was a lot different than he was used to, but the sermon was good. Well, not as good as his dad's, but he did feel uplifted. He needed uplifting.

Back at the Perkins, he phoned Kerry Larson. "Hey, Larson, what's happenin' in Dallas?" His attempt at nonchalance made the attorney even more furious than he already was.

"Not sure. Why don't you subscribe to the Dallas Morning News? It probably gives the best overview."

"Yeah, I may do that. I would like the answer to a legal question."

"Well, hire an attorney. Or try an organization that gives free legal aid."

"Well, I just was wondering how someone could get arrested for shooting at me, and get turned right back onto the street with her gun still in hand."

"I don't know! Interesting question. Why don't you call her and ask her? You still got her number?"

Kerry pushed disconnect. Anderson wanted to act like a fool, mess with a crazy girl, hurt Mallory, he could figure stuff out for himself! Kerry was immediately concerned that since Sylvia had missed David, she might come after Mallory. He couldn't figure out how the kid could be such an idiot.

He placed a call to Faulkner. "Hope I'm not messing with your Sunday nap," he began as soon as Faulkner answered.

Daniel's pleasant laugh. "I was just debating whether to call you and risk waking you up. Mallory called Diana, seeming to be a lot more chipper. What's your take, since you actually saw her?"

"Well, I think it's a great thing Suzanne came. She thinks she isn't a good mom, because she didn't know how to comfort Mallory about Patrick, and she's at a loss for what to say about David! Guess we all are!"

"I could say plenty about him!!" Faulkner's voice from pleasant to ferocious in under sixty!

"But, she's a good mom," Kerry continued. "She hit town asking Mallie if she'd eaten. Fussing at her for staying out in the cold. Sometimes just the 'mom-thing nagging' can be reassuring. But, I didn't necessarily call you to brag on Suzanne's mothering skills. I called because David asked me how Sylvia Brown can be back on the streets with gun in hand. It made me more concerned than ever for Mallory's safety."

"You heard from David? Where was he? Pastor and Lana were hoping he'd be at church this morning, but he wasn't. They're real worried about him."

"I didn't even ask him where he was. I'm pretty mad at him.

"Well you're right about your threat assessment on Mallory. I'll give Hopkins a heads up, so he can gear up vigilance. I'll call John, too, let them know David's still kickin' around someplace. Are you still planning on going skiing the first of the month?"

"I am. I'm trying not to get too excited. I have lots cookin' on the legal burner, but Carmine's amazing. Jacobson's been glad he didn't pass on her like he was plannin' to. How's your church going? Any thaw with your pastor?"

"Not sure about that. We dedicated Zave this morning, and I think Pastor still has lots of questions about whether we are really trying to bring our children up in the 'nurture and admonition of the Lord'."

Larson tried to be sympathetic, although the same questions had plagued him since Cassandra's departure.

"Do you hear anything about Cassandra at all? You know, you and your attorney could get the State Department involved in getting the Israeli's to send her home."

Daniel changed the subject back to Mallory. "So you think our Survivor's going to survive this incident, too?"

Still puzzled by the other man's attitude about getting his daughter back, Kerry replied gruffly, "Maybe so, if we can keep Sylvia Brown from putting a slug in her!"

-≒ ≓-

David spent another night at Phil and Risa's. Since their church didn't meet on Sunday night, the evening with nothing going on kind of got on his nerves. He should have been driving toward Tulsa for a meeting with the architect. That was another problem eating at him. Feeling like he and Brad were doing a pretty great job at the camp, he was shocked not to pass an inspection. The wiring, according to the specs, was supposed to be really high grade. Considering the children and the remoteness from any fire departments, that was a good thing. Now, a state inspector was saying much of the building was below grade. Way below. David could only surmise it was the sub-contractors, lining their pockets with O'Shaughnessy money. Nothing new. But he couldn't figure out why Brad hadn't caught it. Which created a possibility he didn't want to think about. Surely Brad wasn't trying to skim extra from Mallory. He was making more now than he had ever made in his life, and he had gotten saved!

Even after Phil and Risa fixed his bed and left him to himself, he couldn't fall asleep.

Mel Mason's demand for David to show up, even claiming the possibility of 'Fraud' accusations, was enough to make sleep flee. He finally fell asleep, deciding not to show.

⊰ ⊱

By Monday morning, the wind from the south had caused the temperatures to warm. Mallory headed for work, surrounded by an extra security perimeter. A fact that fired her already smoldering fury with David Anderson. If he wanted to slip his own head into a noose, that was his business! His foolishness didn't have to expose her to even greater danger. Her cold was pretty miserable too!

Situated behind her desk, she quickly became engrossed in piles of paperwork, to be interrupted by a call from *Sullivan and Mason*! The first she was aware of any problems with the construction! Mason carried on as if the builders were acting on her orders to erect dangerous buildings.

Finally, she interrupted the tirade. "Okay, this is the first I've been aware that there's a problem. I am sorry. I will get to the bottom of stuff and be back with you before close of business today. Everyone leaves there at four? I haven't been on top of everything as much as I should have been, evidently. Let me be clear. David Anderson knows about this, and he simply failed to show up for his appointment? He didn't call anyone to cancel, or explain why he couldn't make it?"

Confirmation from the other end. She hung up, color flaring brightly to her cheeks. She fought tears. David's date life was his business! His tarnishing the O'Shaughnessy name with his shenanigans! That was her business! She punched his number.

⊰ ⊱

Heading toward Little Rock mid-morning Monday, David was alarmed by a call from Mallory's number. She would only call him if she were in danger. Dread sweeping through him, he prayed for her safety. Hopefully, Sylvia wasn't crazy enough to go after Mallory.

"David Anderson," he responded.

She ripped into him!

280

"I just got a call from the architect, David. Maybe you should let me know what's goin' on next time, so I don't get blind-sided! They said you knew about it! You had an appointment this morning! You didn't show, and you didn't call! I don't care who you date, but if you can't keep your head in the game, maybe you should resign. What? You tryin' to get fired so you can collect unemployment?"

She paused briefly, waiting for his response.

"Well, I just became aware there's a problem. I've been trying to figure out what the inspector's talkin' about."

"You knew about it last week! You haven't been to the site with the inspector, to see what he means, to get his opinion about who might be involved. Basically, you seem not to care. You managed to get your tux cleaned and make Homecoming. Evidently you've become trapped in an endless childhood. Get to the site, then get to Tulsa with some answers for Mel! Before four! And stop saying my money's ruining me! You don't know the first thing about me! I have a good name! When you represent me, you better have your head on straight!"

"Yes, Ma'am." Trying to keep resentment from showing. "I really have been going over it and over it in my mind. I hate to point the finger at Brad."

"Why? If he's cheating people and risking lives with substandard materials, everybody needs to know. You haven't even had the nerve to call and ask him for an explanation!

You're too scared of your friends and making sure everyone likes you!"

"Well, that might be part of it. I was actually afraid to confront him about it. People get killed for less; I didn't know what to do."

"Yeah, but you decided to put if off til after Homecoming. Your dad would have been the reasonable person to express your concerns to, but you didn't talk to him, because you didn't want him to find out about your plans to get with Sylvia again. I'm waiting for an apology and an assurance you'll take care of this!"

"I am sorry, Mallory, about lots of stuff. I will take care of things."

The phone went dead. He exited at the next interchange and placed a call to the state inspection agency. Getting the electrical guy, he explained who he was and which building project he was referencing. The guy was mad, and he really didn't seem to believe David wasn't involved with the scam. Brad Walters wasn't a new name to him; that was the only thing really helping David with the inspector. Promising to halt construction and remedy all the problems, he disconnected to call Brad. No answer! Brad was no longer a user of the cell service.

He raced back to check the stable. Brad's horse, the trailer, and all his tack were gone! At least *El Capitan* and *Star* were still in their stalls. David was annoyed. The double trailer was half his! Still a relief! Maybe Brad was just skipping, and there wouldn't be a confrontation. Brad was tough! David wasn't eager to tangle with him. Not that tangling with Mallie was any picnic! Of course she was right. The dig about his being 'trapped in an endless childhood' hurt. Well, served him right!

He phoned *Sullivan and Mason*, apologizing for the missed appointment, not trying to offer up any lame excuses. He promised Mel he was ordering a stop on the work at all three properties until they could assess the scope of the problem. Fear gripped him. Probably the slabs, nothing, was up to par. All the time lost! The expensive building materials ruined! More humiliated than ever, now he wished he had taken time to read his Bible. The last couple of weeks, his priorities had been pretty scrambled.

"Lord, I'm sorry," he whispered.

⚟ ⚞

Mallory called Roger Sanders. Not surprisingly, her mother answered.

"Hi, Mom, this is Mallory. Could you have Roger give me a call when he gets a chance? I'm not sure Brad's been such a great contractor. I just wanted to know if Roger ever had any problems with him or any of his buildings. Mum's the word, though, Mom"

Suzanne laughed. It did sound like an interesting tidbit. Mallory knew her weakness.

"I'll keep it to myself. Putting your call through."

"Hello, Mallory, what can I do for you?" Roger's professional, Type-A personality voice."

"Hello, Roger, I'm not sure how to start, since you suggested Brad as a contractor. I know he wasn't the contractor when he worked on the buildings at Sander's Corporation. Did you have any problems with sub-standard materials that didn't meet the drawing specs? I'm not sure about everything up to the point of the 'electrical' inspection, but we got an "F" on that. The architect is furious with me, and David, and everybody, thinking we don't care anything about the safety of kids at the camp."

The revelation alarmed the businessman. For one thing, he had advanced Brad, suggesting him as foreman for the various ministry projects. If Brad was crooked, Roger was sorry to have recommended him. It also made him question the standards of some of the Sander's Corporation complex. That could be bad!

"Wow, Mallory, we passed all of our inspections with flying colors. I'm really sorry I gave Brad a glowing reference, if he's been trying to skim from you. Have you talked to him?"

"Not yet. I told David to handle it. I'm not upset with you for your recommendation. I was eager to put him to work and give him a chance. Most of the people have panned out great. I guess it shouldn't be such a shock that a few disappoint. Thanks for taking my call."

Roger hung up. He was sorry for Mallory. Sounded like real setbacks for her building projects. Tons of time and money lost. He felt sorry for David, too. A lot of responsibility on a kid who didn't have a clue about what he was dong. He couldn't shake his uneasiness. Sander's Corporation was a chemical company. Plenty of highly volatile chemicals on the premises. His specs had been top-of-the-line too. His words 'passed with flying colors' troubled him. He paced. Any spark could blow his world apart! He couldn't take any chances! He pressed the intercom.

"Suzanne, find me some kind of independent building inspector!" Mallory's words had made him uneasy.

-⊰ ⊱-

Oscar and Otto Malovich seemingly had disappeared from the face of the Earth. Well, that was a lot of area. Sophisticated equipment wasn't revealing them anywhere in Arkansas. No sign of them in Western Turkey or Eastern Europe. Sylvia Brown's state-of-the-art fake driver's license worried Bransom. No telling what name the criminals were using now. They could be anywhere!

Ahmir's suggestion was that they were dead. Having failed in their various attempts to eliminate the people who could testify against them, they had actually compounded their problems. Ahmir thought the pressure put on Barton, his weapon sales to Adams and his sons, and the fear of which of them were incriminating the others, would have been enough to seal their fates. He reminded Erik that Shannon had been at the point of being executed for far less.

"Well, show me bodies, and I'll stop huntin' 'em," was the FBI man's response.

Ahmir, still basking in the glory of solving multiple crimes with the discovery of the smuggling route, felt his American colleague was being overly tenacious.

"You think this is more limited in scope than it is. Like if you drag the Charles River long enough, everything will unravel for you. The people you seek probably fed fish in the Mediterranean" Ahmir's deep laugh

"Yeah, you're probably right. Thanks for all the files on them. Can you try to dig up a couple more facts about them for me, though?"

"Who's paying for this, my friend?"

"The Turkish government. This is in your interest, too. Just find out if one of the boys was known to have any type of vision problems."

"That shouldn't be too difficult. It's recently that they become difficult to follow."

Erik laughed. "Good, let me know."

He hung up, gazing at his still opened Bible. His morning's reading actually had been in the book of Judges, about Gideon. God had used a surprising strategy to give victory to the Israelites. To make the opposing forces think they were surrounded with no escape. In the pandemonium and confusion, the soldiers all fought and killed one another.

Maybe the crime syndicate had purged out some of the members! Wasn't outside the realm of possibility.

Especially since, "With God, all thing are possible."

Chapter 27: WILES

Mallory spent a busy afternoon. Her first order of business was to apprehend the fleeing Brad Walters. Janet and the twins were not with him. Mallory wasn't sure if he was deserting them or if he planned to send for them later. He had grabbed his horse, evidently showing what was a priority with him. At least Sarah and Sammie wouldn't be in harm's way when the arrest went down.

Her next move was to order a body scanner. Used after every shift in Africa, she planned to use it occasionally, to help keep her miners honest. So much for trust!

Asking the Lord for guidance, she opened her Yellow Pages and pointed at a page of CPA listings. *Smith, & Sons*! Right! Closing her eyes, she pointed again, *Browning and Harper*! Sounded less suspect. She placed a call, setting up independent audits for all of her departments, from Marge and her petty cash to Herb and all the jewelry components.

Aware of her move almost immediately, Daniel and Diana gave her grudging credit. Pretty savvy move.

Lilly just wondered why the girl was as trustingly naïve as long as she was.

⚜ ⚜

More nervous than ever, Roger called Beth, confiding his concern, and asking her to be in prayer. Wishing he could enlist the prayers of his pastor, but not wanting to create a panic with the rumor mill, he decided against it. At three, he strode out to reception to greet the inspector Suzanne had located. Dean Bancroft, a tall, slim guy with salt and pepper hair, offered a firm handshake.

"Why am I here? Your secretary said the city passed the electrical inspections for all of your buildings. Your being a chemical company, they should have been pretty stringent."

"I hope everything's fine. I recommended a guy who was involved in my construction to be contractor for a friend. He has messed her buildings up, unbelievably. I guess I just need to know his dishonesty started with her, and he wasn't skimming here."

Deans' gaze took in the sharp-looking complex. "Which buildings are the most suspect, in your opinion? How deep do you want my snooping to go?"

"Deep as it needs to go."

The inspector met Sander's gaze sharply. "You have any idea what you're saying?"

Anguish in the businessman's face answered the question. "However much it costs to fix, if you find problems, won't be as devastating as having the whole place blow! The lives it could take, or ruin! For my bottom line! Bring help out if you need to. I'd like to know before the day's out, if possible."

As the inspection progressed, Bancroft and his sons were shocked! Not just a grade or two below specs, but barely commercial wiring in the two newest buildings. One was the Executive Office Suites. At least no chemicals were store or used in that edifice. He ordered power cut immediately, crashing the electronics system, including the phones. Gritting his teeth, Sanders thanked the Lord. Everything could be restored; he was pretty sure the system wouldn't lose all his data. Pretty sure.

Cutting the power to the largest, state of the art warehouse was far more of a nightmare. Careful humidity and/or temperature controls were an absolute necessity for maintaining the stability and quality of many of the reagents and inventory.

"Can you give us some time?" Roger's desperate plea. He wasn't sure where he could get any of the stock relocated, that would maintain the proper controls, anyway.

Dean met his gaze sympathetically. "Sorry. I'm telling you, Roger, this is bad. This wiring is so hot and over-loaded. I need to notify the fire department."

Roger nodded, going to his office to order evacuations of the entire facility. If the warehouse blew; glass, at least, would fly in the other buildings! Maybe the Fire Chief would have some suggestions for removing the chemicals. Stepping back out into the late autumn afternoon, he called his insurance agent. Tears wanted to come. It seemed like Brad was coming to the end of his damage, and Mallory's call had come, just in time to avert a disaster!

Passed with flying colors? Brad and the contractor over him must have paid some hefty bribes to the city inspectors. Roger planned to nail them, too. A failed inspection would have been far less costly than this was going to end up being. His family worked here, came out to see him. His friends worked for him. All placed in unnecessary jeopardy, so some already- well-paid guys could get 'just a little bit more'.

◄ ►

Leaving from her office late Monday afternoon, Mallory had planned to head home. Instead, she called Diana to ask her if she could come up there, extra-early for the Tuesday schedule.

"Absolutely, Mallory!" Diana's always reassuring voice. "You don't ever need to ask, or wait for a formal invitation. Guess you've had quite a day! Roger, too. Did you hear about that?"

"No, something bad about Brad?" Mallory wasn't ready for any more bad news. It usually came if you were ready for it or not. She was sad to hear about trouble for Roger's business. It sounded like he would take some heavy inventory losses. Several fire departments had helped eliminate the threat of some of the stuff's becoming unstable. The shells of the buildings were still okay, but the interiors would have plenty of damage from rerunning the wiring.

The city inspector insisted he didn't take any bribes. His excuse was that since Roger was important to Hope and the local economy, he had just assumed the city government wouldn't want any of the inspections at the Corporation to fail. If he had received money or gifts, it wasn't evident by now. Apparently he wasn't in the habit of passing inspections for cash. What a goof though! Inspections weren't made because of politics! They were made for Safety concerns. The Fire Chief was in a rage, and so was the insurance company!

David called Mallie back just before she boarded the chopper.

On her arrival, she told Diana she really wasn't hungry.

"Mallory, your mom told me she's not sure you eat, at all. You still sound pretty stopped up. At least drink some juice."

287

"Yeah, I probably should have canceled coming up here since I have a cold. At least I should have waited for tomorrow."

"We're already kind of sniffly, too. It's hard to keep from getting colds and passing them around. We could have been exposed seven to ten days ago, or maybe it was really the cold snap. I guess no one knows for sure, yet. We're glad you came early. Does a smoothie sound good?"

It didn't, but she didn't want to argue with Diana. She drank it, with the protein additive! It was kind of gaggy, and she obediently swallowed some pills to help her nose and achiness. They were all getting ready to watch a movie, some recent, new release that looked exciting. They had some state of the art deal that cut out bad scenes and unsavory language. It also seemed to remove parts central to the plot. Mallie wasn't sure. With the Benadryl, large comfortable chair, and little rest over the week end, she kept falling asleep, anyway.

She loved her own house, and most of the time she loved the solitude. Sometimes, though, it just felt good to be here.

Xavier was a little stopped up and fussy, but he was adorable. Mallie took him and changed him, since she hadn't been following the movie too much anyway. She was bringing him back out when Daniel received a call from his security at the gate. A few minutes later the house was overrun.

⚞ ⚟

After his conversation with Mallory, David called the Perkins to thank them again for their hospitality, and to confirm that Phil hadn't disowned him as a violin student.

"Well, Risa says, 'Don't push it again'. Phil laughed, but David figured they both shared the sentiment.

Disconnecting, he called his dad.

"David, where are you? I think you need to get home right now!"

His dad sounded mad, which was no big surprise. David was relieved to be told to come home. He had been afraid to try it. Of course, there was always the possibility his dad would pound him, and still throw him out!

"Yes, Sir. I'm just leaving Tulsa. I've been at the architects. It's quite a drive."

"Well, I hope you're getting the mess straightened out! Get some coffee! Stay awake!"

"Yes Sir, just filled up with gas, and got a huge cup. I should be home by two."

"Well, take your time. Don't get a ticket. Stop and sleep if you have to."

He hooked his phone to the port, turning up his music.

He probably shouldn't have said as much to Mallory as he did. But, his apology needed to be for more than the sloppy job on her building projects. He apologized for his attitude about the Homecoming fiasco, and for his inviting another girl, to 'get even'. Now, he couldn't figure out what had possessed him to make such an error in judgment. Maybe he <u>was</u>, 'trapped in an endless childhood'. She was cute; she could sure rip your hide off.

He thought of a Scripture verse:

I Corinthians 13:11 When I was a child, I spake as a child, I understood as a child, I thought as a child: but when I became a man, I put away childish things.

David Anderson grew up that night as he drove home to Murfreesboro, Arkansas.

⊱ ⊰

Mallory gazed in amazement at the crowd pushing their way through the Faulkner's front door. Diana stood frozen, tears cascading down her cheeks. Niqui seemed speechless, too. Daniel recovered himself first.

"Hey, y'all come on in. Wow, this is a surprise! A nice one! How was your vacation? Did you see much of Europe?"

Mallory stared, speechless, at a room full of Diana clones. And her male counterparts! Finally, one of them stepped toward her with a smile and an outstretched hand. "I'm Park. I know you're Mallory. I've seen you on the Faith Baptist web site, and in other pictures, too."

She shook his outstretched hand, dazed. Was he ever cute! They all were.

Finally, Diana, unfrozen, flung herself into her dad's arms, then her mom's. Niqui was the first of her family she had seen in over eleven years. This was quite the reunion.

"I need to find you all places to sleep~"

"No, you don't, Honey. Don't worry about anything. We're all checked into a nice hotel, and we've eaten. We just want to visit a little."

Preston Banks Prescott's voice was amazing. He was amazing! When he noticed Mallory and smiled and winked at her, it made the sun come out! And it was after nine o'clock at night! Wow, that's where Diana got it from!

Alexandra and Jeremiah became the center of attention as their grandparents, aunts, and uncles made over them, taking turns passing Xavier around, too. They created quite a crowd in the comfortable family room, but as they relaxed, they made their ways to the game room, the music room, checking out other areas of the house. Counting Niqui, Diana had nine brothers and sisters. Diana was the oldest, and the only 'rebel' to have left home!

Finally, Daniel steered the conversation to where his in-laws had spent their holiday. Smiling triumphantly, Preston presented a picture of Cassandra. "Israel," his laughter was genuine and relaxed.

"Where did you take this?" Diana had let out a cry of consternation! "She's filthy! That dress looks as if she hasn't had it off since the day she left!"

"Ah, now, Sis. She's just you made over. She was at the *Church of the Holy Sepulcher,* playing with a kitten. Looked just like you! She tried to work her way into our group; the guide thought she was a pickpocket, but Mother thought she heard the guide talking about Jesus, and came over. At any rate, by the time we emerged from the church, she had appropriated a street musician's violin, and was playing *Amazing Grace*! It was beautiful! Everyone in our group threw coins. I know it sounds odd, but she's where she needs to be. She's like you! A winner! Stubborn cuss, but a winner!"

"We miss her so much! We question our decision every day."

"Well, yeah, sure you do. But for now, she's just fine."

"Mama, what do you think?"

"I think she's beautiful. It was all I could do to keep from hugging her up. I wanted to stop and talk, but Father didn't think we should."

"So you made it into Israel with no trouble?"

"Indeed we did! Saw lots of spots I always dreamed of seeing; then we were invited to get out, and stay out!"

"Well, why?" Diana's voice, puzzled.

"Guess someone noticed all the family resemblance!"

⊰ ⊱

Donovan Cline picked up his extension quizzically. A 'colleague' he hadn't heard anything about in forever. Must need something! Cline didn't have many friends.

The other chemist was relating the professional gossip hot from the grapevine. A couple of buildings at Sander's Corporation, shut down for substandard wiring. "Sanders has this reputation for being such a 'straight arrow', and he's been bribing inspectors!" A smug smirk in the gossipy voice rankled with Cline. For one thing, the news alarmed him. His plant was up to code, when it was built. Now, he was realizing, codes had probably changed, and the buildings and wiring were getting old. Expressing that concern to his associate, he ended the call.

Roger checked his jingling cell phone, annoyed. Cline?! Busy and disheartened, he still took the call. Pretty much the last person he cared to talk to, ever!

"Hello, Donovan, what do you need?"

"Well, I guess I need to know what I can do to help out. If you can hire a refrigerated hauler, I have some warehouse space. May be able to salvage some of your stock. Then, when your warehouse is fixed, maybe you can house some of my stuff. I'm sure lots of my facility needs the wiring updated. What happened, to get your attention?"

"A call from Mallory, asking me about Brad Walters. It's really strange she called me. I don't think she was blaming me for setting Brad up with her. Anyway, it's amazing she called. This is pretty bad, but it's averting a total disaster."

"Yeah, maybe for me, too, and a bunch of us. We have insurance, but I'm sure if the insurance investigators could prove faulty wiring, it might be impossible to collect. Even if insurance replaced the buildings, there could be endless lawsuits, and it can't make up for hits to all your business revenue if you have to rebuild everything. Get Suzanne busy finding a truck; I'll start making some space."

"Thanks, Cline," but the phone had already disconnected.

Suzanne, evacuated from her office, accessed her iPhone yellow pages to begin inquiring about a truck. The first hauler wouldn't be available for eight days, but when she explained her problem, they referred a competitor. By ten that evening, eighty thousand dollars worth of chemicals were moving toward Dallas.

An exhausted Roger headed for home. Cline had a shift put together to unload the truck when it arrived at his company. Roger gladly offered to pay the extra hours and rent the space.

"Nah, your bad experience may be saving a bunch of us the same grief, and even worse. I'm glad to pay an extra shift. The warehouse hasn't been full, anyway."

⚔ ⚔

Diana's family stayed pretty late. A bunch of them had started playing Monopoly; finally Diana insisted Alexandra and Jeremiah go to bed. Their school would still be at the normal time in the morning. They left the game where it was, to finish another time. Relieved for the break, Mallory said her good nights to everyone. Parker Everest Prescott was winning, with a hotel on Boardwalk. He was really fun and funny. He spoke four languages, and he had embarked upon the task of teaching her French!

By the time she hit the sack, her cold was feeling better. Evidently the medicine she had taken earlier was helping.

"Where's Niqui?" she questioned curiously when she joined the Faulkners for breakfast.

"She preferred going to the hotel with her mom and dad," was Daniel's response. "That's lots of fun for them. Quite a group, huh?"

"Yes, Sir. It's amazing they saw Cassandra."

"Yeah, Diana's convinced she hasn't had a bath since she got there."

Mallie laughed. "Yeah, but I could get dirty so quick after my mom had me all cleaned up. I never looked like she bothered, most of the time. And I liked it just fine."

Diana reentered the open area of the kitchen to hear Mallory's comments.

"I wonder if Cassandra was picking pockets."

"Well, your mom didn't think so. We've been praying for Cassandra to grow as a Christian. Let's believe she wanted to hear what they were saying about Jesus. I saw that church, and I was blown away, thinking it was the spot where Jesus died, and was buried, and rose again. Kerry explained the whole *Via de la Rosa* thing is mostly a Catholic pilgrimage. Like one of the 'stations of the cross' is where 'Veronica wiped Jesus' face off with her veil'. That's not in the Bible at all. Then one of the other 'stations' is a handprint in the stone wall, where Jesus supposedly rested, as he was led to Calvary. But the guide said the Jerusalem of Jesus' day was actually buried by about twenty feet of rubble, from building over the ruins through the centuries. His handprint wouldn't have made an impression in solid stone, anyway, but of course, that's what they think is miraculous about it."

Jeremiah was suddenly crying, unexplainably.

"Hey, Buddy, what's wrong?" Daniel noticed it first.

"I don't know. I guess Cassandra was so naughty, and now she gets to be someplace cool."

Mallory laughed. "Well, Jeremiah, this place isn't too bad."

"Well I know that! But Cassie gets to be where Jesus was!"

"Well, if you really want to go to Israel, you should write it in your journal to remind you to pray about it. Israel was cool. We went to the *Wailing Wall,* where people come from all over the world to make special prayers. It made me realize Jesus is everywhere, and he always heard my prayers from Murfreesboro, Arkansas."

Diana was perplexed. She knew her father was in possession of vast sums of money. Still, he wouldn't choose to waste it staying endlessly in hotels. She wished her planned additions to her home were already in place.

Smiling suddenly, she reopened her prayer journal. Mallory was right. Pray over everything, and keep yourself reminded. She asked the Lord to provide a nice place for her parents and siblings to stay, until they decided what to do.

In the kitchen, she checked the thawing process of several chickens. A little chicken soup would taste delicious, Jewish penicillin for Mallory's cold, although seemingly, she was feeling better.

Then, an e-mail arrived from her parents that they had found a house! The on-line video revealed a stunning showplace. Evidently their plan was to resettle in Tulsa! Amazed, she wasn't sure if that was good or bad. Then, she decided it must be good. Her dad was convinced the Lord was in it!

Daniel, home early from the office, tied on his apron and began chopping onions and carrots into the refined chicken broth. Boning the chickens carefully, he returned the meat to a couple of huge, simmering pots. It was smelling heavenly. Diana mixed a couple of kinds of dough. One for home-made noodles, the other for biscuits. They always made lots, but Mallory thought they must be planning for all the Prescott's to join them. She was amazed at how eager she felt to see Park again.

She removed the Cannakale soup set from the cupboard over the counter. In Turkey, Mallory had stayed amazed by the quantity of dishes Diana considered to be a set. Now, delightedly, she could see why. A big part of loving hospitality. Big families! Lots of food!

The weather was cold again, and a freezing wind seemed to sweep *the Maestro* and the Prescotts through the door with one tremendous gust.

"Get in, so Diana can close the door. We don't have to heat up the outdoors!" Mr. Prescott's admonition to his family sounded so much like Mallory's daddy, that she had to remind herself he was in heaven. It made her like Mr. Prescott even better.

With the hearty meal finished and cleared away, everyone crowded into the music room.

Alexandra went first, playing her assigned and dutifully practiced pieces for the glaring teacher. He didn't mind the audience; that was just usually his countenance, unless you somehow managed to please his ear. Then Jeremiah, Mallory, Diana, and Daniel. Daniel didn't really still need lessons, in Mallory's opinion. Just a chance to show off how good he was, and how bad they were in comparison. As the novice, she felt totally humiliated. It made her really determined to head home early in the morning and be able to get in lots of practice before next week.

⚗ ⚗

Bransom heard about Brad and the substandard materials, sadly. People sure knew lots of ways to gouge each other. Clinics like the one that hadn't really helped Cline; baggage-handlers, hanging onto just one little suitcase; someone's incorporating slightly below-par wiring. Walters was in trouble, though. Well, he should be. Mallory, being extremely nice with her new wealth, trying to pull friends and neighbors up with her! Not a very nice way for Brad to repay her kindness.

With one ear, he was tuned in to Suzanne's phone conversation with Diana about Mallie's upcoming birthday; mostly he was checking his e-mails. Word from Summers! Walters was behind bars. Evidently pulling a horse trailer had slowed his flight! Idiot!

He gazed forlornly at his screen while Suze's voice laughed and talked around the edges of his awareness. Evidently, the Federal Judge, Antoine Martine, wasn't corrupt, but part of a bigger scheme by some agency! To nail, not just Oscar and Otto, but people much higher in an international crime syndicate. Her daughter, Sylvia Brown, Bransom thought was a loose cannon, jeopardizing whatever the sting was. But he wasn't totally sure about that.

The big problem was still the waning morality and honest character in America. More people, with no consciences figuring ways to 'steal identities', steal kids, steal anything! The *War on Terrorism*, a real threat, was diverting law enforcement manpower to that front, leaving doors wide open for all kinds of other scams and schemes. He guessed it was like Pastor Anderson kept saying: "Everything set up, waiting for the *Rapture of the Church* and the entrance of the *Antichrist.*"

Bransom was still hoping to bust some figurative 'chops' in the meantime.

An e-mail from Ahmir brought a throaty chuckle. Otto Malovich was missing an eye! To an injury, stemming from an accident at a boys' orphanage where the twins spent part of their boyhoods! Interesting! He shouldn't have laughed at Suzanne.

Chapter 28: WILLINGNESS

As October days flew by, Mallory was beginning to forgive David. At least, he wasn't party to the plan to bamboozle her. He was nearly as blindsided as she was, and his fear of confronting Brad wasn't just a popularity thing, but a real sense of danger. She was pretty sure her dad's plan had been to have Pastor more in charge of the building projects. Actually, David's only qualification for the expansive jobs, was that he had worked part time at a lumber yard. Brad's job was to have helped fill in the teen's knowledge, not take advantage of his inexperience and trust.

And, the damage wasn't as extensive as first feared. Tests on the slab revealed it to be inferior to the specs, but not likely to cause structural failure. The rewiring would cause delays and expense; all in all, not the catastrophe envisioned by both. The church remodel wasn't showing any problems, and the ministry headquarter building was still in the drawing stage.

The architect charged a two thousand dollar fee for the missed appointment: the CPA deducted that amount from David's check. He should have showed, or at the least have shown the courtesy to call!

Her jewelry designs were beautiful beyond words! A lavender-y Zinnia sparkled with Arkansas amethysts in sterling silver. Lilly hated the idea of incorporating Sterling Silver into jewelry, rather than gold. Especially with diamonds. Mallory didn't agree. She liked the lines being blurred slightly between fine jewelry and costume jewelry. No jeweler in his right mind would place an exquisite gem in anything less than fine gold or platinum. But Mallory could remember trying to get something kind of nice with her small amount of babysitting money. Just some little piece that claimed to be 'real' diamonds in her price range, was such a lift.

She wanted other girls like her to be able to do the same.

Actually, the teensy diamonds utilized to pavé some of the silver jewelry, would have at one time, been discarded. It was an amazing story, actually, how diamond cutters in India had impacted the entire diamond trade, by being willing to polish the tiny gems. Somebody saw value in the discards. Kind of the same thing that had changed the market's opinion of brown diamonds.

Aside from assigning someone to the Zinnia pin for her right away, Herb's employees were busy filling orders for the Nativity jewelry. That was really the main market Mallory was interested in; Christian Witness jewelry. Of course, lots of crosses were already on the market, and Crucifixes, although those were pretty Catholic. A few signs of the fish. She wanted elegant designs available, across a broad price spectrum! Most Christians didn't mind making quiet, yet powerful testimonies of their faith when it was possible. She thought it was sad that Christians were being asked not to wear 'crosses' in jewelry designs to their jobs. It seemed that obscene people were allowed 'free expression', and the ones with a message worthy of proclamation were being silenced.

⚎ ⚎

The Prescotts closed on a beautiful home in Suburban Tulsa, and Diana was ecstatic and busy helping get it furnished and turned into a showplace.

"Have your dad and mom always been rich?" Mallory questioned Diana innocently. She had checked the on-line listing for the beautiful home, and phoned her friend.

Diana's laugh. "Missionaries, by popular definition, to be any good, have to be dirt-poor! That seems to be the most cherished notion." She directed Mallory to check out several passages:

Mark 10:29 & 30 And Jesus answered and said, Verily I say unto you, There is no man that hath left house, or brethren, or sisters, or children, or lands, for my sake, and the gospel's,

But he shall receive an hundredfold now in this time, houses, and brethren, and sisters, and mothers, and children, and lands, with persecutions; and in the world to come eternal life.

"Those, and parallel passages in the other Gospels, either startle most Christians, or they don't like them. Sometimes their minds are made up about stereotypical Christianity, and they hate to let what the Scriptures actually say, upset their preconceptions!"

Diana's lilting voice continued on. "My grandparents went to Africa with the support raised that their mission board insisted on. When they arrived in Central Africa in 1960, there was a lot of chaos. Well, there's always chaos, especially in Africa. They moved into the interior, seemingly with as little as everyone around them. The tribes actually accepted them, helping them build the mission. But it was never anything fancy. The support money just accumulated in a bank in London. On the field, if we had drawn on the money for anything, some of the Tribal Lords would have smelled the money like sharks smell blood. If they had known we had anything, we would have been kidnapped for ransom or killed. What sounds familiar about that? But, it made us pray. I can remember one year, there was a pretty severe drought. No one had any food, including us. If we had left, we couldn't have gone back, so we just prayed for the Lord to meet the need for us and for the villagers. One of the most amazing stories, although there were lots of amazing stories. We heard a plane; we were kind of far removed from flight paths. Anyway, it was sputtering, and the pilot put it down in an emergency landing. It was a cargo plane for one of the big agricultural firms, filled with yams! I'm telling you, nothing ever tasted as good as those yams did! Anyway, all that support money for my parents and grandparents has accumulated for the best part of fifty years, compounding interest! In British Pound Sterling! I think they've earned what they have now, everything compounding back to them as they forsook comfort and family for the Gospel's sake."

Mallory was amazed. Diana was so cool, and she had the most awesome stories. No wonder Parker was so fascinating, too! Between their exotic experiences and their ability to 'spin yarns' about the events, they were spell-binding!

Diana was also putting together an eighteenth birthday party for Mallory. November first, a Tuesday night, Mallory would believe she was coming for the usual Tuesday night happenings. *The Maestro* wasn't happy with the plan. He was glad to come to the party, but felt strongly that the lessons should go forward, with or without the festivities.

Everyone was planning to come! Shay and Delia coming from Boston, all the Prescotts, Eric and Suzanne, with Erik's daughters and their families. Lilly regretfully declined, but everyone else was in. Diana's eyes sparkled with anticipation.

One thing troubled her, though. Park and Mallory! Daniel thought it was great! After the Homecoming debacle, he was still furious with David, relieved Mallory was seeing the light about him. Parker was a great guy! Diana simply saw her little brother getting set up to be hurt. If Mallory were on the rebound, it wasn't fair to use the first guy to come along.

"Come on, Honey. Mallory isn't a person who uses other people; you know that!" Daniel's not-so-convincing argument. "I don't understand what the deal is; surely you aren't such a romantic you think she has to end up with David, just because they were childhood sweethearts. Remember, Patrick wanted her to have a chance to meet some other great, Christian guys."

Diana's face set resolutely. "But not her brother." Usually one to pray and leave things in the Lord's hands, this had her upset. She wasn't sure if she should try to talk to Mallory about it, or to her brother. Not being able to wait until she could speak to either of them, she confided to her dad, as they supervised drapery installations at the house.

He hugged her. "Why you asking me? I've been mad at you for years for your choice, running off with Daniel! I just knew God was doing it all wrong for you. That you were rebelling against me, against Him! I should have kept my mouth shut and waited it out. I'm sorry, Honey. We can't keep people we love from hurt. It wouldn't be good for them, if we could. Dealing with hurt and disappointments is the only way we grow, as people, and as Christians. I wish Park would end up with Mallie, but I don't think it's going to happen."

"You don't?" She tried to keep the hopeful tone from showing.

"No, I think they have a real affinity for one another, but Park wants to get back to the mission field as quick as he can. Mallory feels like the Lord has planted her where she is! Africa's a long commute!"

"He wants to go back?" Her voice was filled with a new dread.

"Back to Africa~somewhere! He's trying to decide on one of the larger cities, reach urbanites: Europeans, Americans, the native population, and build a church. He needs a wife; like I said, I don't think it's going to be Mallory."

⌐ ¬

David was at a loss, trying to decide what to give Mallory for her birthday. He took a morning, walking the mall in Hope. Not exactly a Mecca for shoppers! He wasn't sure he could find time to shop in Dallas before the big day, or if he could come up with better ideas just because a mall was bigger!

On the way to his lesson, he was hoping Phil wouldn't bawl him out again, for the deal with Sylvia. Thinking about her caused him to check his surroundings uneasily. She was still loose, somewhere, with a gun.

Pulling up next to the Perkins' and pulling his violin from the seat beside him, inspiration seized him. "Thanks, Lord," he whispered.

The lesson was good. David possessed plenty of natural ability. Even with giftedness, discipline was a must!. That was what worried Phil. David liked the instrument now, as a new interest. He wasn't sure his student would stick when it required determination.

At the close of the session, David pulled out a wad of cash, sliding some bills loose importantly. Phil accepted payment for the lesson because he needed the money. He still wanted to rap the kid a good one on the noggin!

"Hey, Phil, I haven't been able to figure out what to give Mallie for her birthday, but just as I got here, I thought about getting her a better violin. She's using the one Cassandra didn't like. Can you give me some pointers on what to look for, to find her a nice one?"

"Sorry, Son. Guess I can't. See ya next week?"

Back in his truck, and out of sight of the house, David beat the steering wheel, frustrated with himself.

What was wrong with him, that he always tried so hard to impress everybody? Phil and Risa obviously didn't have much money, but they had befriended him, putting themselves in danger to help him. But, then, he was trying to grind his money in the man's face. Well, maybe just because he had never had much before! But, neither had Mallory, and he was pretty sure she was acting a lot classier! Then, his asking his teacher for some pointers to pick out a new violin! The answer was obvious. Try it out, and see how it sounds! He was just trying to let Phil know what a nice present he was going to come up with for Mallory. Trying to prove to everyone, now, how much he cared for her.

He stopped by the house to visit with his dad, explaining the deal with his violin teacher.

"I was just a jerk to him, Dad. What's wrong with me? I'm just needy for attention and respect."

"You want to feel important, be important," John was helping his son describe the feelings.

"Yeah," David agreed. "I think it's because you and mom kept having kids, so you couldn't really devote your attention to me. The babies were always the ones doing the 'cute things', and I was always the big, mean, bully brother. 'David, stop it!'."

John Anderson was so amazed he didn't know whether to laugh or get mad. The sad thing was that David was serious, watching earnestly for his dad's agreement with his perception. Having begun a game of pool, John figured this was a discussion that required eye contact and full attention. He suggested they move to his office.

David made a shot. "Oh no, I'm not getting on the wrong side of your desk again."

"Well, okay, I'm the one who's in trouble for not paying you enough attention, you can have the 'big chair'. Be on the 'right' side of the desk."

David hung the cue stick, moving swiftly behind the large desk in his dad's spacious home-office.

Sitting in the 'wrong' chair on the 'wrong' side of the desk didn't affect his dad's approach at all.

"I'm sorry, Son, if you've felt that way. You want to blame me for where you are, go ahead. I'm a man; I can take it! There was never anything wrong with your mother, and how she's cared for you, and how she's treated you. You know, she still thinks you can do no wrong! I think she taught you better manners than what you exhibited at the Perkins'. David, everyone wants to feel like the *Kingpin*! To be the *Kingpin*! If you remember, that's what the devil tried to tempt Jesus with! I don't think Jesus blamed Mary and Joseph! He just told the devil to get lost. He quoted Scripture! Your problems, if you really can't figure it out for yourself, come when you get out of the Word! Son, the self-worth you're looking for, can only be found in the Lord! When people dote on us, it makes us spoiled, hungry for more, demanding more! Don't interrupt! When you spend time with the Lord, He validates you as a person, comforts your wounds. When you lower yourself before Him, then He lifts you up. But when he does that, we need to be careful, still, not to be arrogant. All our attempts to elevate ourselves are futile. Are you sure you know the Lord?"

Tears hung in his son's dark, unfathomable eyes. It was several seconds before he could respond. "I know I'm saved, Dad! I don't think I know the Lord very well. I want, to, though."

A slight chuckle. "I believe you do, but there aren't any shortcuts! Go apologize to that man, and to your mother!"

"Yes, Sir! Glad I was in the 'big' chair; no tellin' how ya might have chewed me out, otherwise."

John sat, listening as footsteps died away and the door slammed. "Son, I haven't chewed you out, yet," he whispered into the solitude.

⊨ ⊨

Parker looked up from his computer, frowning, as the 'drapery' person invaded his space. The whirling drill sent stuff falling onto his keyboard.

"That pictures of Liberia?" The guy on the ladder questioned him past a mouthful of screws. Parker met the other man's curious gaze. "Surprised my sister didn't tell you not to put your screws in your mouth. She's a nurse; she's always nervous people are about to choke themselves to death."

He spit the metal into a huge paw so he could laugh. "She mentioned that, every room we been in. She's a nice lady, though. Why you looking at those images? You a Sociologist, or something?"

Another whir of the drill, more fallout. Park snapped his laptop shut. "You where you can take a break?"

"I'm self-employed. I can take a break whenever I want; why should I take one with Mr. Sociology-boy?"

"Because, I'm doing research, and you can be my subject!" Parker's mischievous response. "No, seriously, are you familiar with Africa? Do you have family there, still? My family's all missionaries, well have been. Some of them are here to stay. I want to go back, though. We've always been in rural areas. Now, I want to go to a city and start a work."

"Got family in Nigeria, I think. Things change on a daily basis. I got saved because of American missionaries that reached my aunt there. Then my aunt called my mother in Chicago, to share the Good News with her. Then all of us kids believed. One of my brothers pastors now, in Detroit."

"What's your name?"

"Go by Shank! What about you?"

"Parker! Nice to meet you, Shank.

They sat down together at the kitchen table with ice cream bars and cokes.

"Tell me you aren't really thinkin' 'bout Liberia! Maybe I shouldn't say so, but I don't think a pretty, blond-haired, blue-eyed white man like you, would last fifteen minutes there."

Parker sighed. "I'm afraid you're right. But, I can look at it, and let my heart break, and pray. I know I need to be 'wise as a serpent, and harmless as a dove.' I'm not sure the Lord needs any self-appointed martyrs."

The big man sitting across from him sat in wonder. This house was amazing! The custom drapery job was a real coup for him. He already admired Mrs. Faulkner, even if she had nagged him about using his mouth for a 'screw dispenser'. He wasn't sure why the kid eating ice cream with him was willing to turn his back on digs like this to return to Africa.

"Yeah, maybe you should put your 'martyr complex' on hold for awhile. Your sister's involved with some of those Arkansas diamonds. Everybody in Africa's nervous Americans are just after the natural resources. There'll be a perception that you're there for diamonds, posing as a missionary. Wouldn't be the first time that was actually the case."

Parker nodded thoughtfully. "I'm plannin' to settle north of the diamond-bearing regions. You make a good point, though. I know I'm young, too. I think I'd like to be on staff of an established church for awhile. I can do deaf, music, youth, outreach, teach English, teach in Bible Institutes. I know four languages and some of the tribal ones, as well. Where does your aunt go to church in Nigeria?"

⚔ ⚔

Mallory received lots of calls wishing her a happy birthday, but no one was mentioning getting together with her. Slightly suspicious, she was guessing the music lesson evening might also turn into a birthday party. She had no clue who might be there! She figured her mom and Erik, the Prescotts, maybe some of the Anderson's. She hadn't seen David since Niagara Falls, and she knew people were still livid with him for the situation with Sylvia. He probably wasn't even invited; probably wouldn't come if he were!

She kind of wished she and Parker were an item. She liked him, but there was no point in letting her feelings get out of hand. They were on different courses. He knew his destiny! She knew hers! They couldn't meet!

His success, even his life, in Africa, would depend on his being a million miles removed from an interest in Carbon chunks vomited upward by volcanoes. While, for mysterious reasons know only to God, she was immersed in them up to her eyeballs! Not that she was complaining! She couldn't help smiling to herself as she gazed into her closet! Something for a party she didn't know anything about.

A cute denim skirt, blinked magically into existence by Diana! The Lord had given her the cute style in April. It fit cute, and had some style features. But, then, blood spatter had ruined it when she smacked Oscar Melville with a rock, and then a board. Diana's staff had taken it apart to make a pattern and reproduce it for her.

She slipped an ivory, chunky-style turtleneck sweater on with it, pulling the *Spice Market* silk scarf through the belt loops, then pulled on tan riding boots, transferring her handbag contents into a *Hermes* tan, saddle-leather bag. Heavy gold bangle and hoop earrings. Cold morning! Her first chance to wear the Lynx jacket!

Tears filled her eyes as she checked her reflection in her mirrored dressing room. Never in her wildest, wildest flights of fancy, could she have imagined anything like this! Darrell had already taken her overnighter, her computer, and her office work to the golf cart for the ride to the helipad. Whistling 'Take Me Out to the Ballgame', she moved briskly to join him and Janice!

⊱ ⊰

David was talking to Shay; or trying to. Everybody was still incredibly aloof with him. He was trying to find out what he and Delia were giving Mallory for her birthday. He hoped she wasn't going to end up with ten violins, with his being the worst one of the bunch.

"Does it have anything to do with her music?" he questioned desperately.

"Look, Dude, take it easy. You do know that all Diana's family are moving to Tulsa now, right?"

"Yeah, my mom and dad have mentioned it. Something about one of Diana's sisters got 'em all run off?"

"Yeah, I guess, that's kind of a rough, condensed version. You knew one of Diana's little brothers asked Mallie to marry him?"

"Yeah, Shay, I knew that, and that Iranians are all trying to kill her, but they all want to marry her, too, and shove her into their harems. If I want headline news, Dude, I'll tune in to CNN. Just tell me if you know if anyone's giving her a violin."

"Not that I've heard about! Later!"

⊱ ⊰

Niqui and Parker were in downtown Tulsa. The air was freezing, which they weren't accustomed to, but it was a neat change. They lunched in the street level bistro of Daniel's office building. This was fun. They had started out to find Mallory a gift, now their arms were laden. Monique's personality and giggle would erupt, now, occasionally, through the pain of her loss.

"I'm treating," Park's insistent voice.

"You keep saying that, and I haven't argued. Am I supposed to offer?" her laughing response. "Are you hurt by Mallory's response to you? Do you think she's superficial to stay here with her diamonds instead of going to the mission field with you?"

"There's nothing superficial about Mallory. Daniel said she has this loser boyfriend, and I hate that! She deserves the best. She's right. She's diamonds, and I have to be as far removed from diamonds as possible. Di's curtain man showed up, annoying me to no end! Drilling and making noise, and showering sheetrock dust into my computer! But, he was my sign from God I was asking for! His aunt in Nigeria is talking to her pastor about my coming onto staff with him. I've already e-mailed back and forth with him. The church can't afford a budget for more staff, but when I told him I have support, he couldn't believe I'm really willing to work with him. And to think, I nearly told Shank to get out, and come back later. Anyway, he reminded me again to stay far removed from any perception of being interested in African diamonds.

"No way, Bro! That is a cool story! Do you think any of us will ever get married?"

He laughed. "We seem kind of hopeless. Maybe we should pray about it."

Her eyes filled with tears. "I don't know about you, but I have been."

"Yeah, for things to work out with Ba'ta. But they didn't. You need to keep from being bitter. I don't know how Di keeps from being bitter with that Lilly-woman! Wasn't Cassandra cute, though?"

"Of course! She looks just like me!" Monique was laughing more than she had in months.

"No, she looks like her Uncle Parker! She sure stared at all of us, didn't she?"

Their food arrived, and they ate in relative silence. Finally Parker remarked reflectively "The church where I'm going is a mix of Africans, Europeans, Asians, Americans. Maybe the Lord has my wife waiting for me there. Mama wants me to wait until after Christmas, but Niq, that's almost two months!"

She nodded. It was hard not to do what Mama wanted. And impossible not to do Daddy's bidding. "After Christmas! You can book the flights now, though."

He laughed. "You ready to head home?"

"No, I'm going up to Daniel's office. Diana said he has a tech guy that can work miracles. I'm going to see if Daniel can ask him to look at my laptop."

"That thing needs more than a miracle. Let's just go shop for a new one for you. A techie will laugh you clear out of the world if he sees that thing."

"It has all my files!"

"Yeah, pictures of Batahayay and his baby. It's a miracle your computer stopped that bullet for you. By the way, the woman and her family have rejected the baby. Rob Masters is trying to work out an adoption with a family in Atlanta. Mom and Dad didn't really want you to know. They don't want you trying to get him."

"If it's someone Rob knows, it must be a Christian family. I wouldn't want to try to take him. I wouldn't be able to provide anything Batahayay wanted for him. A black, Christian, American family! That's about the best chance there could be. Thank you for telling me. That makes me really happy!" She burst into tears!

"Excuse me, Miss," a voice at the table next to theirs. "I heard what you were saying. I'm Sam. Can I see your laptop?"

"I guess there's really no point-" She extended it toward his outstretched hands.

"Wow, this is pretty old. Did it work okay before the bullet hit it? I have one that's newer than this, that I don't use. I can get it for you. Maybe I can transfer some of your data. If you don't mind my taking it, I can get it back to you at the party tonight."

"Are you invited?" Niqui's cute voice.

"No, but maybe I can crash the gate to get your info back to you!"

⊰ ⊱

Diana lured Mallory into the design studio; easy enough to do. They could stay occupied for hours while all the guests arrived downstairs. She figured Mallory knew something was up, anyway, but it was fun to play along.

Mallory was gorgeous! Diana didn't mind 'business casual' when it was so positively stunning! "Don't turn your back on that handbag," she laughed.

"Thanks for the warning." A similar one was already stashed away for Diana for Christmas. But, it was good to know the gift would be a hit! They were placing finishing touches on Fall/Winter designs for next year. Diana's favorite of the upcoming lines was the one featuring the lovely emerald-set, jewel-encrusted *Topkapi Dagger*. Emerald green and ivory wool separates, accented with silk-printed pieces featuring the famous jeweled weapon, were turning out to be the most elegant designs yet. Mallory hadn't seen all the Spring/Summer line, although they had discussed everything often. It was cute, too. One item was a cute blue and white print dress patterned after the travertine shapes at Pamukkale. Smaller, and more uniform, it wasn't obvious what the inspiration had been. It was a gorgeous dress, though. Featured with either blue or white jacket, or matching print coat, the coordinates made for versatility. The drawings indicated pearl jewelry, or "Sky-blue" Topaz intermingled with Diamonds. Mallory loved the pearls with the blue jacket! But, it was all cute! Hard to pick!

⊰ ⊱

The elegant mansion, dressed for a party, was a sparkling, hospitable welcome from the increasing chill outside. Coffee and food aromas wafted through the space, and fires danced cheerily in nearly every room.

"Hey, girls, *Maestro's* here, and soup's on." Daniel's voice through the intercom.

Mallory shook her head. "Why are transmissions from the *Space Station* less scratchy than that?"

Diana laughed. It was the truth. Everyone who worked on their system made it worse.

Actually, Daniel's so-normal tone nearly convinced Mallory that things were as usual. Or, that if anything were up, it would be later.

She descended the stairs with Diana, to have a mob jump out from hiding, yelling, "Surprise!"

She jumped a mile, and tears sprang to her eyes!

"You mean we pulled it off?" Diana's amazed gaze meeting Daniel's.

Pretty much everybody was there! Food was heaped everywhere! Music room, dining room, kitchen, game room, poolside (indoors), den! A special birthday 'throne' decorated at the head of the long dining room table beckoned the guest of honor. With her plate heaped high, she moved toward her place. She wanted to talk to everyone. Her grandmother, her mom, Shay, Callie! Everyone looked great, and she wondered if she was too casual. The Lynx dressed her up more, but was a little hot inside. She loved the fireplaces and the hospitality and warmth the Faulkners and their home offered in such gracious abundance.

She liked her throne, but then couldn't resist the need to mingle. "Thank you for coming, Grandmother." She kissed her cheek. "How are y'all doing?"

Delia laughed. "Well, you know most of how we're doing, so I guess you mean specifically with getting involved with a good church. I've thought Catholic for so long; I mean ingrained all my life. Sometimes, I have to stop myself. Thank you for letting me keep Patrick's Bible. I love reading out of it. You can't imagine how dear it is to me. I like the church we go to, but I wish we could go to Faith. Patrick loved it and John Anderson so much."

"Yeah, me too. I'm liking Calvary better every time I go, but it still isn't the same," Mallory sympathized. "Did Shay already find Emma?"

"Hope so," Delia winked mischievously.

The party was a lot of fun. Most of the romantically interested people managed to congregate in the same area, except for David, hanging with his parents. Shay's announcement had kind of hit him like a thunderbolt! He didn't really even believe it, until his arrival at the party and his observation of an 'angel-boy' shadowing over Mallie.

"Who is that?" his dad finally whispered.

"One of Diana's brothers." Stating the obvious, kind of a dumb question!

With everyone full, but still nibbling, Daniel garnered everyone's attention for the gift time. A cake rolled in, lit with eighteen candles, studded with sugar diamonds. The Faulkner's string quartet backed up *the Maestro's* violin solo of "Happy Birthday', joined by four part harmony from the guests. Mallory laughed. "That was so high-brow, I'm not sure I'm at the right party! Thank you, everybody."

"Speech, speech," Shay demanded.

"That was my speech, Shay. Keeping it short so everyone can have some cake, and I can open my presents."

"And we appreciate that, Madam Chairwoman," Shannon joined in the fun.

A phone call from the front gate interrupted the festivities. "Niqui, did you tell Sam Whitmore to come here tonight? He could have brought your computer to the office to me, tomorrow." Daniel's perplexed voice.

"Well, he offered to come over. Can he come in?"

"Yeah, send him up." Daniel instructed security at the gate.

Diana greeted Sam at the door, inviting him to fill a plate and join the party. Evidently, Niqui must like him some.

Mallory opened a singing card from Delia and laughed delightedly at a little jingle about a "Princess" granddaughter. The gift, an itinerary for a mid-February trip to Hawaii! Delia laughed, "Just think, I'll have to miss the snow and cold in Boston to take you to Hawaii. In Dallas, you probably won't be as eager for a break in the tropics, but I figured a visit to the volcano would pique your interest."

"Wow, you got that right. How exciting ! I can't wait!" Volcanology was just one area of the field of Geology. Delia's gift resonated with her granddaughter.

Her gift from Daniel and Diana, and the kids was the *Bethlehem Star* DVD, an amazing telescope, and the Astronomy software Larson had used to arrive at his amazing conclusions about the mysterious occurrence in the heavens announcing the birth of the Savior.

Oh, I wanted this so much, and I've never gotten around to ordering any of it. Oh, this is amazing. Thank you so much." She dissolved into tears, melting into Diana's arms.

"What is it?" Parker was looking at the case of the DVD, intrigued.

"It's the most amazing thing. Maybe we can all watch it again in a little while." Mallory's smile at the guy made David's stomach squeeze. She wasn't wearing an engagement ring; maybe Parker's eighteenth birthday gift to her? She was still too young. He was in anguish.

Tammi handed her a couple of CD's of their favorite gospel singing group of guys, and they both screamed for awhile. He couldn't figure out what it was about singers that sent girls into hysterics. He caught Kerry's gaze, who evidently didn't mind the fact that Tammi was more ga-ga about singers she didn't even know, than she was about him.

Her mom and Erik were giving her some kind of fancy expandable awning, so she could have her devotions outside, even in cold and rain. They were installing an outside gas heater, too.

"Maybe you should just replace her tractor." David's cryptic suggestion.

"Oh, that thing was awesome. I miss it!" Mallie's expressive eyes alight.

"What tractor?" Parker was into knowing everything.

"It was a piece of rusting junk my dad bought to park on top of a diamond pipe. And it was so much fun. We played everything in it! It was a rocket, an airplane, a fort, a fairy castle, a train, an Indian tipi. We played in it for hours on end. Then, when I got older, it was just my quiet spot. I had my devotions there, and just dreamed my dreams."

"Well, it could be all those fun things," David interrupted. "Most of the time, she just wanted to play house."

Shannon, recently into books, presented a huge book of baseball stats, facts, and trivia. She could have probably written one comparable, but she loved it.

Mrs. Prescott presented a large, rectangular basket-trunk she had woven from some of the tall grasses in the Faulkner's landscaping. It was incredibly beautiful, perfect for a space in her home Diana had been unable to fill with something 'just right'. It was amazing!

Finally, she was pulling at a new violin case, opening the latches. The case and the bow were new; the instrument was not. Mallory drew the bow, already rosined, tentatively across the strings, playing a few bars of 'Jesus Loves Me' A mellowness she hadn't been able to produce brought a delighted giggle. "Wow, that's nice. Let's hear you play something." Her eyes sparkled as she challenged him the way she always had.

"Nah, not fallin' into that trap again. Can't wait for your first recital, though." He was glad she liked it. More gifts followed; nothing from Parker, though. Maybe she'd already received a gift from him. He was deep in discouraging thought when Daniel shoved a piece of cake at him.

"That violin sounds good. Where did you find it?"

"From a concert violinist going through tough times. He would have rathered sell me his soul. Can I talk to you?"

"Believe me, David, you don't want to talk to me! I would think I'm the last person you'd want to hear from!" Daniel was still as furious now as he had been the night of Homecoming.

"Not the last," David disagreed. "Maybe the third last, or the fourth."

"Yeah, Erik's first, then Suzanne, then Diana! How could you do that, and then think there's anything you can say?!"

Daniel moved along, offering cake and beverages to the other guests.

"Hey, Dave!" Shay was the only person in the world who called him that. "Challenge you to a game of pool!"

David rose resolutely, following Shay to the game room.

Parker was already playing! With a twin brother, or a clone, or something. They introduced themselves: Parker Everest and Alexander Grayson Prescott. Thankfully, they went by 'Park' and 'Gray' David thought it sounded like the Prescott's had put Diana in charge of naming her little brothers. Poor Guys!

"When we finish, one of you can play the winner," Gray's cheerio Britainish voice.

"Okay, when you finish what? Have you guys ever played pool?"

"Since we first got here."

Evidently having made up their own game, they were having fun. And they were hilarious to watch. They had amazing, effervescent personalities, just like Diana.

Mallie, Callie, Allie, and Emma couldn't resist the pool table antics, descending on the match with plenty of giggling and blushing.

"Who's winning? I'm looking for someone to take me on in a game of Chess."

David gazed at Callie, amazed. Evidently the two good-looking new guys were luring her from her shell. Park accepted the challenge before any of them could warn him.

"This should be good," Diana spoke up brightly from the doorway, placing Xavier into Mallory's hands outstretched for him.

Parker's gaze lingered on Mallory's attention to his baby nephew. Passing David for the Chess game, he lowered his voice conspiratorially. "If she ever wants you to play house with her again, maybe you should consider it."

Chapter 29: WARMTH

November in Dallas was fairly balmy, the weekly jaunts up to Tulsa were colder. Life was a whirl. Colors, patterns, seasons, painted amazing blurred images. Mallory wondered if this was the influence behind the *Impressionist Movement* in the art world

Park's attention was turned to Callie. They were evenly matched at the Chessboard, and they chattered at one another giddily in French and German, with some occasional English smattered in.

First flattered by his attention, then miffed at the loss of it, Mallie forged ahead. At least her friend still explained the mysterious Calculus to her enough that she was keeping up with her class. The jewelry business was receiving orders they were barely keeping up with, as more skilled workers were being drawn in to help meet the demand.

Mallory, enchanting in a jade wool suit, wore one of Herb's most Faberge-inspired creations, yet. An elegant brooch on her lapel featured a life-like sprig of Lilies-of-the Valley, executed in pearls and rose-cut diamonds on a golden stem with carved Neophrite leaves. Her clothing and jewelry usually garnered quite a few compliments wherever she went, giving her opportunities to meet people, offering her business card and those of her associates. She loved the daily demands, trying to earn the privilege of getting away for a ski trip, and the New York Gem show.

Nearly everyone converged on Aspen! Mallory's love affair with the Rockies was instantaneous and complete. Taking part of a morning, she traveled with Shay to visit an Alpaca ranch. Loving the cute, gentle animals, she was glad they weren't harmed by the annual shearing for their soft fleece.

The skiing was fun; she started in ski-school with mostly little kids, and by noon they were all buzzing around her, ready to increase their level of difficulty. She thought they were all pretty cute; but exhausted, she removed her skis to go in search of some hot food. Purchasing Frito pies and cokes for too much money, she and Janice found an empty table, both sinking gratefully onto the bench. Her mom and Erik joined them. Erik was teaching Suzanne to ski, but hunger had gotten the best of them, too.

The view was beautiful, and they liked the charm of the resort town. Some of the 'charm' seemed a little manufactured, but overall a pleasant place to stroll around and gaze at some of the wares offered by local artisans (or the Chinese).

Later in the afternoon, Mallory tried a more advanced slope. She felt out-of-control. David had skied one time before and gone straight up to 'Black'. She didn't know if he was that good, or if he just thought he was. The experience was fun, but she spent time helping with Zave so Diana could ski with Daniel. They were really nice to each other, and always got along. Mallory liked snuggling the little baby better than hitting the slopes, anyway.

⊰ ⊱

Almost immediately upon return from Aspen, Thanksgiving was on top of her. She planned her first big event in her own home. Not ready for tinsel and lights, she adorned the spaces of her home with cornucopias, spilling colorful squash, vegetables, and Larson Apples.

Her guest list included the Andersons; the Haynes; Erik and Suzanne, and his daughter's families; Kerry; Callie and Mr. Cline; Carmine; Aunt Linda and Herb; and Merc and Nell's family.

The day was definitely brisk; fireplaces glowed warmly as soft Gospel music enhanced the atmosphere. She loved Christmas, but decided her own Holiday tradition would commence on December first! Not that some of her shopping wasn't already done.

Beautiful china, silver, and crystal graced table linens provided by Delia. Tapers yielded dancing flames as each guest took his place at the laden table. Erik blessed the food as Mallory tried not to think about her first Thanksgiving without her dad.

The food was amazing! Huge turkey, ham, and the usual trimmings. Waldorf salad featuring the delicious apples, crunchy celery, and pecan halves, replacing the traditional walnuts.

Conversation and laughter lent a gracious hum to the affair. Lots of passing serving dishes around for seconds; some managing to stash away third helpings. Everything was good. America was truly a marvelously blessed nation. Flawless help cleared plates away, and Mallie rose from her spot, switching on big screens to bring football games to life. Kids began pulling out games, sorting through videos, dibsing turns at the pool table, practicing darts.

Mallie's suite was open, allowing her guests to check out the terrace where the gas heater and awning were installed, and where the telescope opened windows to heaven.

Tom Haynes loved the *Bethlehem Star* DVD, too, having tried to obtain permission to show it at Murfreesboro High School. Barely recovered from his recent fiasco, he didn't pursue showing the video when his first petition was rejected.

"You could invite some of the kids to your house," Mallie suggested. She was puzzled why Pastor Anderson wasn't eager to show it at church. Maybe the guy who made the discoveries was a Neo-evangelical, whatever that was.

Everyone seemed to want a long turn at the telescope. Mallory loved it. She was pretty sure she knew what to get some of the people on her Christmas list that she had considered 'tough to buy for'. Maybe not so tough, after all!

David was quiet, watching football; no booing and cheering with his usual gusto. He sampled all three pie selections: pumpkin, pecan, and apple, sipping coffee, sitting alone in the spacious den, while the others were either in the game room or jiggling for turns at the telescope. No one was warming up to him too much yet. He was sitting, soaking up the gracious ambience, when Mallory came through.

"Did you get any pie?"

He laughed. "Three pieces: I couldn't decide."

Her eyes met his. "Good, I can't decide either. Since you're the taste-tester, what's your official recommendation?"

"Thanksgiving! Better have at least one piece of pumpkin. It's what the pilgrims and the Indians would have wanted."

She laughed. "In that case, go get me a big piece with lots of whipped cream and a cup of coffee. Don't say it's for me."

"Be right back! Don't go anyplace!" Raiding the largest slice, he zoomed back. If she was talking to him, it didn't matter so much about everyone else. They talked and laughed softly while she nibbled at the pie. She was gorgeous: flawless, ivory skin; burnished, coppery hair; funny, happy personality; talented and smart. And Rich!

⇥ ⇤

The Faulkner home was also an island of delights. Not too surprisingly, Callie was missing Mallory's spread in favor of the Faulkner's and Prescott's. Turkey and Rack of lamb graced an elegantly appointed buffet table. Gourmet candied apples delighted eyes and taste buds, among the pies and pastries at the dessert table. Sweet cider splashed through a fountain.

Parker proposed to Callie, and although she was expecting it, the tears of wonder still overflowed. Their plan was to get the license on Monday, and then be married in the pastor's office at Honey Grove as quickly as possible. They were working on a visa so she could accompany him to the mission field after the first of the year.

Pretty much everyone thought it was a bad idea, but the young couple thought they had the mind of the Lord.

Surprisingly, Cline was for it. He signed permission for his under-aged daughter, and even Carmine, with her legal skills, was unable to negate it. She wasn't sure she was against it- maybe just a little more time!

⇥ ⇤

December brought out Christmas decorations, and Mallory's display along the walls and gates of her estate were themed to *Wise men still seek Him.* One side of the gates showed the traditional manger scene with Mary, Joseph, and Baby Jesus in the manger, surrounded by shepherds and animals, crowned with angels and the star. Wise Men on camels approached. The other side featured a church, a Bible, and modern-day seekers from each continent. Christmas music played softly, featuring the Faulkners singing *Wise Men Still Seek Him, Tell Me the Story of Jesus,* and other carols which magnified the advent of the Savior. In spite of security measures, the display suffered some degree of vandalism. Mallory didn't want it to be purposely offensive, but since Jesus was a 'stone of offense', plenty of people didn't like it.

She was busy with finding gifts for everyone. The popularity of the telescope with the men was a boon. Her attempts to acquire the DVD for everyone were frustrating. Backordered until mid-January. Still, she placed the order. The information was worth waiting for. She really did have a *Hermes* bag for Diana, but she also ordered a special piece of Jewelry from Herb and Merc. A smaller replica, swagged with gold and jewels, Faberge picture-frame, fashioned into a lapel brooch, holding the picture taken right after Zave's birth. Mallory loved being scrunched into the family. She wondered if there might be a way to insert Cassandra's face in with the rest of them. She didn't know if that would help Daniel and Diana's loss, or make it worse. Every day she prayed for Cass to come home! Or at least communicate.

⚜ ⚜

The crowd attending the gem show included Mallory, Herb, Linda, Merc, the Faulkners, and Niqui, accompanied by their private security. Staying at a Hilton in downtown Manhattan was a thrill. For the first day of the show, Mallory wore a soft, brick-red suit, fashioned in wool crepe with cute back-belt design, self-covered buttons, and bound buttonholes, so perfectly executed that they were actually part of the design. The Platinum and Gold dandelion puff and her nine-plus carat diamond ring added their élan!

She loved being at the *Gem Show!* It was better than being a kid in a candy store! Even better than being a kid in a candy store with lots of money! Cut and polished gems sparkled and flashed beneath lighting designed to enhance their appeal. Gorgeous! Gorgeous! Gorgeous! In every hue! From inexpensive amounts per carat, to hefty amounts! Cut in sizes from .5mm, to headlight sizes. Herbs first selections from one vendor brought Mallory's checkbook out.

"Whoa, whoa," Daniel's amazed voice halting her. "Use one of your credit cards."

"Well, can't the CPA get the records as well from the check?" Mallie's earnest question.

"Yeah, that's not the issue here. Your different credit cards have perks attached that can be really valuable. Airline miles, or cash back, or gift cards. Also some leverage for your satisfaction with your purchases. I know your dad blasted using credit, because of paying interest. But these cards get paid off before you owe any interest. Everything for you to gain, and nothing to lose, by your using them. Sadly, poor people support this system. But your not using it doesn't help them. Just the credit card companies."

She was amazed by the new revelation. She had actually started making more cash transactions, personally, and corporately. She was surprised to learn she was mistaken This was another way the rich got richer and the poor got poorer.

"You know, it's really like the words of Jesus in:

Matthew 25:29 For unto every one that hath shall be given, and he shall have abundance: but from him that hath not shall be taken away even that which he hath.

That same verse must be repeated at least eight or nine times in the different Gospels." Daniel's voice, explaining. "The amazing concept is that Christians are the 'Haves', and the unsaved are the 'Have-nots'. We should be as wise as possible about financial matters, not being slothful in business, like Paul admonishes in Romans. And all Christians are equal heirs to the goodness of God, but if they don't really believe that, they don't appropriate by faith."

Mallory was sure her jaw had dropped, gaping hideously. It was so different than the mind-set she was used to. It made sense, though; getting the airline miles. Maybe the Faulkners could go to Hawaii, too, to see the volcano. Daniel and his dad were both Geologists.

All the colors were beautiful. The gemstones exhibited many different qualities: hardness, light refraction, color saturation, cut; some relatively rare, some bountiful. Herb and Merc possessed great respect for some of the opaque gems, too, appreciative of the vast spectrum of designs, from their own rich imaginations, as well as the designs commissioned by Mallory's company. They ordered Rhodochrosite, Turquoise, Onyx, Mother of Pearl, Jade, Heliotrope, and varieties of agate slabs and cabochons.

Viewing the treasure trove through their eyes, she was amazed by the patterns and designs within the stones. Cut a cross-section, polish, mount, and wear! Cute! Cute! Beautiful!

Isaiah 40:28 b ...there is no searching of his understanding.

No intellect able to comprehend God and His infinite greatness! In color! In design! In everything!

She mentioned the vein she had discovered while trying to find her way back to the hotel in Dogubeyazit. Herb nodded, intrigued.

"Royal blue, flecked with gold! Very beautiful, especially in the finest qualities. Lapis Lazuli! Found in Afghanistan! Other places, too. We should also purchase some of that; maybe Malachite, too. She followed them to a vendor's stand featuring both materials. She loved the cut and worked pieces, but also loved seeing what the treasures looked like where they were discovered. 'In the matrix' was the expression used in the industry to describe one material embedded within another, as found naturally. Herb handed Mallory a large, bubbly-surfaced rock, a dull green. That was Malachite; Copper in the lovely stone caused it to be the swirly colors of green. Often, the lovely material was smelted for the expensive Copper ore. Too bad! Was Mallory's opinion.

A trip to FAO Schwartz to shop for the kids on her list, and it was time to go home!

⚔ ⚔

Sylvia Brown pulled up in the darkness, next to the stable where David continued to stable *El Capitan*. After fleeing the pandemonium of Homecoming, David had dropped her unceremoniously at her apartment. She had told him to call her. So far, he hadn't! She was about to lose patience. She had warned people! If she couldn't have him! Nobody would! But she intended to have him. That religious-stuff his dad pedaled had him mixed up, but she could straighten him out. She needed to show everyone she meant business! She planned to show the ABI and FBI agents who got in her way a thing or two!

With a couple of hammer blows, the wood gave way around a hinged lock, and she was inside. About ten stalls stretched before her; she paused confused. Five equine residents all looked alike to her. The small office, locked more securely, didn't invite further intrusion. If she could get in, she wasn't sure she would be able to find the records, indicating which stall David Anderson rented. Her plan was to get David's attention by injuring his 'precious' horse. Now, she just moved silently through the darkness, aiming a small flashlight around, advancing cautiously. The light fell on something intriguing! Something that might come in handy. Grasping several, she hurried back to her car, driving away without headlights.

The owner of the stable, alarmed by the break-in, reported the incident to the Sheriff's office. Since there didn't appear to be any vandalism or theft, the lock was replaced, and the incident forgotten.

⊰ ⊱

Mallory was busy. Calvary's choir was performing a Christmas musical, and there were extra rehearsals. She liked it, although now she didn't see Callie at all. Callie was married and busy making plans to move to the foreign mission field. Mallory was worried about that. Most of the time Callie wasn't even committed enough to be in church. She kept her reservations to herself, then finally felt convicted for criticizing her friend rather than praying for her. Africa needed the Gospel; God was able to strengthen Callie to be the help Park would need.

Packages wrapped, she wrote a few extra checks! One to the general account for both Calvary and Faith Baptist, and personal gifts for both pastors and their families.

Those items cared for, she headed for one more Tuesday evening with the Faulkners and lessons before Christmas. Her hands and neck sparkled with the jewel encrusted *Nativity Scene* pieces.

The Faulkner mansion shimmered with more Christmas trees than Mallory had ever imagined. She only had one. In her den, since being rich was new to her. Diana seemed to have a tree in every room except the bathrooms. Each one was themed, always different every year. Take it down! Give stuff away! Get something new!

The soup was chili, delicious in the cold. Fresh, hot cornbread. Fritos, cheese, onions, sour cream.

The lessons were fun, too. Mallory and the Faulkners presented the teacher with a gift. She was getting a feel for violin, too. Her new instrument helped the quality, but she still had lots to learn to get it to resonate like it did in the hands of *the Maestro*. They played Christmas music, then joined a group from their church going Caroling. They visited nursing homes and the hospital, then sang for some of the shut-ins, finishing back at the Faulkner's for hot chocolate. She loved her life! It was fun! She could remember dreading coming to Tulsa once a week. Now, that was one of the high-lights! Xavier was one of the things making the weekly excursions even better. He was growing, changing every time she saw him. He was adorable. Of course, so were Alexandra and Jeremiah. As much as she missed Cassandra, she figured it must be nearly unbearable for Daniel and Diana!

She was awake early, brewing coffee in her suite from a cute tea table. She needed to include the same special feature in her other areas at home. She opened her Bible, where her reading was pretty far along in the book of Psalms. One of her chapters was Psalm 119, the longest chapter in the Bible. Since beginning in Genesis in June, right after the trip to Turkey, she had steadily advanced through, marking in her new Bible, verses and phrases that she linked to, either Geology, or her newly-acquired wealth. A verse jumped out at her! Rather than rushing through the long chapter, she decided to underline the verse, stop, meditate on it, and study its meaning.

Psalm 199:14 I have rejoiced in the way of thy testimonies, as much as in all riches.

She looked up 'testimonies' in the dictionary: 1) Evidence given by a witness in court; oral or written, detailing what the witness has seen or knows about a particular case. 2) Proof; something that supports a fact or claim. 3) The Ten Commandments. 4)Public avowal of Christian faith.

Wow! Awesome verse! The Psalmist, David, said he loved and rejoiced in everything God testified about Himself! Amazing God! Amazing Creator! Amazing Savior! Revealing Himself through his Inspired Word! All too good to be true! But true, nevertheless! And the 'man after God's own heart', comparing his joy in Biblical revelations to the joy of having wealth. Evidently, possessing wealth wasn't a wrong thing as long as you remembered to rejoice in God for everything!

She was still humming when she went in search of Diana.

"Morning, Mallory, did you rest well?" Diana was in the middle of the floor in the den, playing with the baby with a brightly colored toy. He was cute, bright eyes following the form, lips pursing, little mobile features going through myriads of adorable faces, arms and legs jerking in excitement. He had on a cute outfit with a farmer by a strange-looking antique tractor.

"I slept great. I'm glad he got over his cold right away."

"Me, too. You still have a cough, though. You know, if it doesn't clear up in the next few days, you should go to the doctor. It's really time for you to find a doctor to get started with. You could go back to Dr. Kincaid, though, since she saw you for your lungs. It'll be easier for you to get pneumonia now. I need to ask you a question," Diana plunged in.

"About Christmas!" Mallory guessed correctly.

"Yeah," Diana was amazed.

"What about it?" Mallory was on the floor, too. 'Thank you for not minding my having my own Thanksgiving. We did split up our crowd. I didn't have as much fun as when you guys are around. Do you want everyone to come up here? You have all these gorgeous trees."

Diana's countenance looked troubled. "Oh, you want everyone to come to Dallas!" Of course! Christmas without Cassandra! She should have thought about it. She was already dreading the Holiday without her jovial, Santa Claus daddy. She definitely needed the Faulkners around! "Oh, that will be so much fun. When are you coming? Are you going to come to my Christmas musical? Who all should we invite?"

They worked together on the menu and plans for the big Christmas celebration before Mallory left in the early afternoon.

≒ ≒

Lilly was in a particularly wretched mood. Cassandra's showing up at *the Church of the Holy Sepulcher* in time to serenade American Christians had created all kinds of grief for the Diamond Council executive. Pictures of the dirty, rag-tag child were all over the internet with attacks against the Faulkners and the Israeli government. A phone call reamed her out. Since then, she was aware of every school break, and the little girl's range was reigned in. Lilly still didn't care anything about her. Just the perception. New clothes, plain and homely, were provided, and an occasional bath thrown in, too.

Christmas presents arrived, to be stashed with the unpresented Birthday gifts. Lilly didn't believe in Christmas!

Daniel Faulkner, evidently did, though, shopping carefully and lovingly for his beautiful wife. Lilly was enraged!

Chapter 30: WINSOMENESS

Daniel Faulkner loved the new way to shop for jewelry for Diana! Herb Carlton was really a super-nice guy. One of the diamonds that had rained out of the ceiling of the little house, cut to just a tick below seven carats, was being set into a gorgeous new wedding set to replace Diana's old set. It was a dazzler! Something beautiful for his beautiful wife.

The more the Lord blessed him, the more determined he was to share the blessing with her. He had a folder of Scriptures he referred to often. He knew men who, even though they were earning money hand-over-fist, tried to keep their wives in the dark about it!. Sharp women who realized they were assets to their husbands in countless ways, not receiving the honor they deserved.

> *Malachi 2:14 &15 Yet ye say, Wherefore? Because the LORD hath been witness between thee and the wife of thy youth, against whom thou hast dealt treacherously: yet is she thy companion, and the wife of thy covenant.*
>
> *And did not he make one? Yet had he the residue of the spirit. And wherefore one? That he might seek a Godly seed. Therefore take heed to your spirit, and let none deal treacherously against the wife of his youth.*

Going to Proverbs chapter five, he read those verses, too, about 'rejoicing with the wife of your youth'. He loved Diana, also aware that the success she helped him to achieve, made him attractive to other women. Daily they prayed for a 'hedge of protection' about them. He didn't want to get her a gift just barely good enough not to make her mad. He wanted the best he could come up with!

The Prescotts settling in near them was turning into an amazing event. Daniel held the veteran missionary in the greatest awe and respect, even though their opinion had been that he was awful! Not beginning to be good enough for their daughter! They had that right. They had reared some wonderful, Godly children. Now, he was glad for their love and influence on his kids. And his mom and dad were really enjoying getting acquainted with Diana's family.

He was relieved to be going to Dallas for Christmas. He wouldn't be able to stand Cassandra's absence, still, but the change of scenery would help. The plan sounded fun. Something Diana had always loved to do, was to stay in the Westin Hotel which adjoined the Dallas Galleria. The plan was for the Prescotts to stay in a suite there, and as many guests as possible crowd in at Mallory's. They would attend the special service at Calvary, ice skate at the Galleria rink, have a big, Christmas Day meal, and exchange gifts.

He stashed his file away to go search for her. They were all getting ready to go finish their family Christmas shopping.

⧎ ⧎

Mallory was finishing some paperwork and some tests prior to her taking a Christmas break. Marge buzzed in that her Pastor's wife, Mrs. Ellis was on line one. She picked up,

"This is Mallory. Hello, Mrs. Ellis, heard the kids made it home from college! You ready for Christmas?"

"Yes, Mallory, I want to thank you for the gift. It means we're all able to travel to Arizona to visit my parents. We haven't been able to be together for quite some time! This is really special."

"Oh, well, that's good. Hope you have a safe trip and a good visit." Aside from that, she wasn't sure how to respond.

"Well, now we plan to leave in just a few hours, but I was planning to speak at the Ladies' Christmas Tea Sunday afternoon I know it's really last minute, but could you bring a devotional?"

Feeling panicked, Mallie missed her dad even more than usual. She and her dad had always had an agreement, that if she really didn't want to do something, or wasn't able to, she could give the excuse of having to check with him. Then, most of the time, he would get her out of becoming too overloaded. It could be hard to say, 'no' to people. Now she wished she could plead the same arrangement with Diana.

"Well, if you can't find anyone else~"

"I can't. Lots of people have already left town. Thanks again, Mallory, so much! Merry Christmas!" The conversation was ended.

"Oh no, Lord, now what am I going to do?" She didn't feel like crying, so much as just at a loss. Christmas Tea! Just tell the Christmas story and explain how to be saved? She should probably call Diana for an idea. She could wear the elegant, multi-gem-set silk sweater with the *Wise Men Still Seek Him* theme.

Marge buzzed in again. "Just signed for a big FedEx box. I think it was delivered wrong, should have gone to Herb."

The news scared Mallory. All the valuable gem-show purchases were supposed to go to the more secure facility. If things had somehow been redirected here, someone could be planning to burst in with weapons in an armed robbery. Since she didn't know for sure, she resisted pressing the silent alarm.

Marge's scissors slashed through stringy tape! Mallory rocked back onto her heels with wonder as she viewed the contents of the crate! Nothing to steal and kill over! But a great idea for a Ladies' Christmas Tea devotional.

"Marge, I'm taking about a hundred fifty of these with me. Order another gross. With the way orders are coming, we'll run out of these too quick, anyway!"

"Thanks, Lord, I'm sorry I'm starting to relay on Diana instead of You," she whispered.

"Marge, send someone out for a little rolling suitcase, would you please?"

⚞ ⚟

The weather was freezing, but David was riding *El Capitan* around the camp property anyway. He was wearing heavy layers, but the wind was still biting at him viciously. His first ride since Sylvia's shells had sent him diving for cover. He was still nervous, realizing she could be watching him now, without his being able to see her. Plenty of cover. He didn't want to hide forever from a girl. After hearing about the strange break-in at the stable, he was more eager than ever to move his horse. It was strange; he had an uneasy feeling that it might have been Sylvia! She better stay away from him, and his horse. He wished for the thousandth time he had never stirred her up again.

He couldn't figure out what to give Mallory for Christmas. The violin was a huge hit with her, but he felt awful now, every time he met with Phil Perkins. Perkins was forced to relinquish his concert violin to help make up to some friends about a business deal gone sour, or something. David had tried to convince himself that his paying top dollar for the instrument was a help to the couple.

Riding back to the stable, he removed the saddle, currycombing *El Capitan,* talking to him, feeding him a Larson apple. He still resented Larson's needing to work so closely with Mallory.

Creepy! An eerie sensation he couldn't shake. Standing in the doorway by the newly replaced lock, he gazed around, wishing for his binoculars. He unlocked his truck, shoving his saddle and the rest of his tack into the back seat. If Sylvia had been uncertain which of the horses was his, that explained why she just left without inflicting any harm. His saddle in the stall would let her know which animal was his. One more glance around the property, he slid the padlock through the catch, and secured the building. Hopping behind the wheel, he pulled out, filled with a foreboding dread.

"Lord, I'm so sorry!" He choked back the sobs. His idea of getting Mallory a horse for Christmas didn't seem like a good one. And she already owned a dog.

⌇ ⌇

The Christmas Musical that Calvary Baptist presented each year was always one of the highlights, bringing in visitors whose hearts were tender during the Christmas Holidays.

After the Sunday morning service, Mallory joined Max and Kerry, and a few other teens and career class members she barely knew. She missed Callie, but the lunch was still fun. Then, she returned home long enough to change and get back for the tea. A pleasant lady named Alvie was overseeing the event, and everything seemed to be in place. Still, Mallie made a mental note to order linens from her grandmother for the church to have for receptions and nice events in the future. Many of the ladies had brought in really beautiful china tea sets, and Mallory was enchanted. She hardly knew anyone, but it was pretty easy to get them to tell the stories of their cute sets. Before time to start, Diana showed up with Alexandra.

They both looked gorgeous in soft, rose, cut-velvet suits and matching suede pumps. Perplexed, Mallie couldn't figure out how Diana could have known about the tea in time to design the outfits. But, they both looked ready for a 'tea party'. Amazing!

"I'm so glad you're here. Why don't you speak?"

"I'm glad I'm here, too; since you didn't invite me." Diana's voice was teasing, tinged with hurt.

"Well, I didn't even sign up to come to this, because with singing in the program this morning and again tonight, the day seemed pretty full. Then, when Mrs. Ellis sprang it on me about speaking, I was thinking I should call and ask you what to speak about! Then, the Lord showed me what to talk about, and that maybe I was starting to depend on you too much. I'm sorry for not inviting you."

Diana laughed at Mallory's jumble. "This all looks very nice. We should do something like this at Honey Grove. Maybe on a day with less other stuff going on, though. They could use some table linens."

There was a prayer, and then some of the ladies brewed their favorite teas, explaining the blends; then, everyone moved into line for tea cakes, sandwiches, and samples of the tea. The group seemed to be mostly older ladies, but there was a nice buzz of conversation. It made Mallory miss Delia! And then, suddenly, her grandmother was there, too. Overcome with emotion Mallory was mixing up telling Delia how glad she was to see her, with placing a linen order for her church.

After a skit, a special number, and a poetry reading, Alvie introduced Mallory.

Mallory moved to the microphone, thanking Alvie, and the ladies who had presented the song and poem.

"Okay, some of you noticed me pulling my little suitcase behind me when I came in. It's because I have a gift for everyone. Before you get too excited, I'll tell you, it isn't Diamond jewelry."

There were good-natured, disappointed groans.

"Sorry. This was the best I could come up with. My friends, Diana and Alexandra, and my grandmother are going to help pass them around." She was handing small cardboard boxes to them to distribute. Inside each box was a jar of jewelry cleaner.

"Okay, Ladies, I know it's so exciting, but if I could get your attention back, I want to speak about something we all know about, but this is an object lesson I hope will illustrate the point.

I John 1:9 If we confess our sins, he is faithful and just to forgive us our sins, and to cleanse us from all unrighteousness.

We know we should come to the Lord daily, asking Him to forgive us and clean us up, once again. We all know we can't lose our salvation, but we don't realize how grimy we get, losing our sparkle for Him. He wants to polish us all up so we can shine for Him, but we don't even realize how much gunk is building in our lives. Pretty soon, you can hardly tell anything pretty's here at all.

Now, for this cleaner! Pearls shouldn't go into it at all. And Emeralds and Aquamarines, Beryls, should be immersed quickly and removed. They are softer and more porous than Diamonds, and Corundum, which includes Rubies and Sapphires. They can soak. When jewelers offer to clean your jewelry for you, don't let them put it under those circular brushes. That takes away your gold, which you may be certain, they collect. My dad used to tell a story about a guy who was a maintenance worker at one of the gold-domed, state- capitol buildings. The guy figured out a way to trap the gold which was washed into the rain gutters, using nylon hosiery. Pretty enterprising, but I guess he still ended up in trouble."

She paused, and the ladies laughed. "You swish your jewelry around, use the little brush around the prongs and into spaces where stuff builds up. Then, rinse in water; here's a bowl, pat dry, and voila! See the results!

"We need to take a few crucial minutes every day, to meet with the Lord. It really makes a difference. If you have never received Jesus as your Savior, please come to me or Diana, and let us show you the most wonderful Christmas gift you could ever hope to receive!"

She prayed, and the ladies began filing out, thanking her for the gift, and the memorable talk, flashing their brightly sparkling gems in the ambient candlelight.

Gathering up the undistributed gifts and her Bible, she glanced around, trying to round up her group. She found Delia in the powder room. Evidently feeling more comfortable with someone nearer her own age, one of the visitors was asking Delia about the 'special gift' mentioned by Mallory! Delia was on cloud nine! Her first time ever to share her faith and lead another person in the 'sinner's prayer'!

With little time between the tea and the evening service, they hurried out for near-by fast food, joined by Daniel and Jeremiah.

"How was Mallory's sermon?" Daniel began his teasing immediately.

"Amazing!" Was Diana's response. "When we get our food you need to hear the story. Look how pretty all my jewelry looks now!" She waved her left hand in front of him.

"Wow! It looks good! Maybe I can take back what I got you for Christmas!" He loved to tease.

"Well, maybe it doesn't look that good," she was reconsidering. "Tell me more about Christmas presents."

"Yeah, Mallory, can you guess her favorite Bible verse?" Daniel was still teasing, but the teen really didn't know Diana's favorite Scripture.

"I Corinthians 13:31a But covet earnestly the best gifts:…"

Mallory dissolved into giggles. The verse out of context was really funny. Diana was giving him her fake-exasperated look. They were so much fun. Orders all placed, they scrambled to fill soft drinks, get straws and napkins. Daniel came, juggling the trays of burgers and fries. After Jeremiah's prayer, Mallory explained about the sudden request for her to speak, and her being overwhelmed with the task.

"I was about to call Diana to ask her to come do it, or at least for a good topic. Marge buzzed about a package arriving for the jewelry company. It was an order we had placed for jars of jewelry cleaner. Diana always gives something away free, with every order she fills; so we thought the cleaner would be a nice gift to accompany jewelry orders. When they arrived right at the crucial moment, it was like the Lord was telling me not to let anyone, even anyone as special as Diana, take His place. I didn't feel like I did a good job trying to connect my thoughts, but at least one lady got saved."

Daniel met Diana's gaze in wonder. The object lesson was more powerful than the words, anyway. It was a great idea!

꡹ ꡺

David attended church with the Perkins for Sunday morning, then treated them to some diner-food afterwards.

"Do you have special plans for Christmas?" Conversation was still strained, but he was determined to wangle his way back into favor with the couple.

"Yeah, we got a special invitation from some friends in Dallas we're real excited about," was Risa's response. "You're Dallas-bound, too, aren't you? When you leavin'?"

"Either tonight after church or first thing in the morning. Last I knew, it was still up in the air."

"You going to your dad's church tonight?" Phil's piercing question made David uneasy. He hadn't returned to Faith since the Homecoming debacle, especially not wanting to face the Haynes, or really anyone. Some of Kyle's relatives visited occasionally. Kyle's car accident wasn't David's fault, but he still didn't know what to say to people. He wasn't even sure he was handling stuff, himself. How could he comfort anyone else?

"You're thinking I should?"

Phil shrugged. "Seems like you can't avoid it forever. The longer you drag it out, the harder it'll get. I guess I'm sayin', 'I think it's time' Your family probably wants to travel tonight, waiting to hear where you're gonna be. What ya givin' that girlfriend of yours for Christmas?"

"What are you doing to me here, Phil? Trying to play twenty hard questions?"

Risa laughed. "I think he's trying to get you to think."

"You may be surprised to learn I've been thinking. She owns diamond mines, and a jewelry business. Her house is furnished and accessorized in every nook and cranny. She doesn't need any gift cards. She has a garage-full of cars. I don't think she has time for a boat, although, I have looked at some."

Risa laughed again. "Yeah, a boat may be more up your alley. What about a handsome-looking photo of yourself on your horse? Big! Nice frame?"

"I'm not sure. My mom might go for something like that. Mallie already calls me *Narcissus*." He sounded gloomy, not trying for laughs at all, but it was ten minutes before the couple could stop laughing-even to catch their breath.

"I checked out the gifts at a Christian store. Some of those are kinda nice, but then, I thought it's just like I'm trying to come across 'spiritual' after I blew it so bad."

"Yeah, well don't beat yourself up forever. As soon as you confess and get a meek spirit back, you're a spiritual man once again. You have to work at keepin' yourself there, though." Phil's contemplative thoughts.

"See, Risa, I really like some of your paintings. I'd like to get her an original oil, but I'm not a decorator to tell if there's even anyplace she could hang one. Do you ever sell any of them?"

She laughed, "Only if I have a buyer."

"Do you guys have time to show me?"

"Not today. We have errands while we're here in town. You'll come up with something. It may be something to think about for another time. Have a Merry Christmas and a fun time, David." They slipped a small gift into his hand with instructions to save it until Christmas Day.

⊰ ⊱

Monday morning everyone convened at the Galleria, many to ice skate; others to sit above the rink, hanging out, eating, and sipping beverages. It was delightful.

Allie, Mallie, Callie, and Tammi were becoming reasonably good ice-skaters. David, Shannon, and Shay were showing off, not surprising to anyone! Parker and the rest of the Prescott kids were pretty new to the ice. Mallory was still trying to remember all their names. Usually good with people and names, this was challenging to her skill. They all looked so much alike, that they needed to be in order by size, for her to tell them apart. They all thought it was funny.

Mallory skated Shannon off to the edge of the rink. "Are you okay?"

"If you mean about Callie, I guess I'll live. One minute Shay was saying Parker's marrying you, and then he's tied the knot with Callie. I guess I was shocked, either way! Were you just trying to get even with David?"

"What? What are you talking about, Shannon? We liked each other, but he was looking for someone willing to live in Africa. I mean, I hope I'm willing to go where God wants me, and do His will. I wasn't trying to do anything to David."

Bransom gazed around the expansive shopping mall, concerned. He figured Oscar and Otto, wherever they were, were still gunning for the two cousins. He had been trying to keep them separated. Anyone, from any of the three levels could get a pretty clear shot. To his relief, the skating ended without mishaps, and the party broke up to reconvene at Mallory's for grilled burgers.

Everyone loved her Christmas yard display, and with mild weather, the large party spent time circulating from the outside areas to the interior, enjoying everything the gracious estate offered. Mallory wasn't the only one to love the batting cage. It was getting a major work-out. With somewhat of an awed tone, Kerry warned the guys not to take Mallory on. Once again, the telescope held a knot of people in rapt attention, and the *Bethlehem Star* DVD played repeatedly on the plasma in the den. Burgers, fries, and an ice cream/milkshake bar lured guests back for more than one helping.

330

Delia was laughing. "Next year you can come to Boston for an outdoor barbecue in December!" She was trying not to monopolize John Anderson, but he had been so close with Patrick, and she was hungry to sort out some of her lifelong beliefs from the actual teachings of the Bible.

John was delighted to talk to her, but he also encouraged her to keep plowing through the Bible on her own, explaining that each year, as he read it through, he understood it better. Laughing, he explained to her, the same thing he was trying to get David to see. No shortcuts; just staying at the business of knowing Him more. 'Line on line; precept upon precept; here a little; there a little.' Gaining more glimpses, until someday, Face to Face, He would be entirely revealed!

On Tuesday, the fun continued. More shopping! More ice skating! Traipsing in and out of the Prescott's suite, hospitably furnished with appetizers and soft drinks! Whispers about surprises!

At eight, they all filed into Calvary Baptist for a Christmas Eve service. A choir, numerically depleted by Holiday travel, sang beautiful Christmas Carols, some joined by the congregation. Carmine was next to Callie, and Donovan showed up, quite unexpectedly, to slide in beside her. The assistant pastor told the Christmas Story, asking the question, 'Do you worship the Babe in the manger?' It was probing; explaining how it wa socially accepted to recognize the Baby, more than the Crucified Savior! Mallory was assenting, thinking she should add 'the cross' to her display before next Christmas. Without an altar-call, communion was served, and nearly everyone reverently received. Then, in the jostling to make their exit, many in the group failed to notice Donovan Cline remain behind. Callie and her new husband took him quickly through the plan of salvation, and Donovan Cline received the greatest Christmas gift of all!

Back at Mallory's, sandwich makings, chips and dips, slaw and potato salad were spread in profusion. Desserts were adorable little ice cream snowmen, sprinkled with coconut. In the music room, they sang more Christmas Carols, accompanied by Mallory on the piano, and the Faulkners on their strings.

At eleven, the party was still gong pretty strong. "Okay, I'm headed for bed! Stay as long as you want and party without me." Mallory's announcement. "Be back by ten in the morning!? G'night everybody."

Phil and Risa finished loading Risa's best artwork into their aging sedan. They were excited about their Christmas plans. Saved for a long time, they had allowed life's trials to nearly sweep them under. That was before a newly rich, egotistical brat had answered an ad for violin lessons. The big, handsome, talented kid presented the disillusioned couple an amazing study in contrasts, bringing a fresh vigor to their existence and their Christianity. He kept life from being dull, as they found themselves reveling in his triumphs, groaning with him in his failures!

Before a call from Marge, their Christmas plans were pretty much like they had been for at least the past ten years. Read each other cards at the card shop and roast a chicken with stuffing and Holiday trimmings. Not bad. They still had each other.

They headed toward Dallas from central Arkansas by six. Christmas brunch was scheduled for ten.

"You have that address with you?"

She assured him she did!

⚥

Mallory was awake by five. Even surrounded by friends and fun, it was hard not to think about Christmas without her dad. She kissed the photo in its place of honor next to her bed.

"Thank you for doing all this. I still wish you had used some of it to get medical treatment."

Knowing, he wasn't particularly hearing her, she directed her voice to the Lord.

"Please don't let me be sad, today. I have so much to think about that's so lovely and good, and perfect, and true. Make today a wonderful celebration of Yourself. She read in Luke, about the angel's appearance to Mary, rather than her place in the Old Testament. She was trying not to be sad about Parker and Callie's departure the next day. Kind of an amazing time to be a missionary, linked by cell phones and internet. She considered missionaries of bygone days, sailing away on unreliable ships, to places with no mail delivery; possibly never to return home again.

"Lord, thank You for jets, and wireless, and satellites, and everything. Surely with all that in hand, more people should be going, and we should be doing a better job for You."

A luxurious soak in swirling bubbles, make up, hair, jewelry. A sprig of holly, carved of Jade, with red Aventurine berries, attached to gold stem, adorned her lapel. Another jewel from the fertile mind of Carl Faberge, executed expertly by her master craftsmen.

"Lord, thank You for sending Herb to us! And all his family!"

Before nine-thirty, she was in the kitchen, checking on all the brunch preparations, then checking a vivid mountain of gifts spilling beside another Christmas tree she had adorned in the Formal living room. Fire danced in the fireplaces, and Christmas music played softly throughout the lower level. Platters of food radiated from the kitchen into the dining room, and out onto the deck. Poinsettias lent their festivity to the elegance.

⊰ ⊱

Phil Perkins located the address, staring forlornly at the iron gates, and the uniformed security in the gate-house. Before he could get his window to roll down, the gates swung open, and he was waved through. At the circle drive, an elf met them, saying he had a few helpers to take the car around, unload the art, and park the car.

Mallory met them on the step before they could ring the bell. Was she ever something!

No wonder their cowboy was at such a loss! Her warmth put them at ease immediately, as she pulled them into the foyer. A grandfather clock bonged ten deep stokes as they surrendered their coats and made their way in where a crowd was already laughing, talking, and milling around.

"Grandmother, I want you to meet Phil and Risa."

Delia turned at Mallory's voice, meeting the gazes of the two newcomers, shaking their hands, repeating their names. " Hello Phil, Risa. I am happy to make your acquaintance. I'm always so impressed by talented people. I wanted to sneak a peek at the pieces those elves were carrying in. I'm intrigued."

They laughed, and Delia took charge of them, introducing them to other members of the group, where they felt the same warmth and acceptance. The home was amazingly beautiful! David was right. The décor was stunning! There didn't appear to be any sparse walls begging for a 'starving artist' painting. Gazing around the group, Risa figured their homes were all pretty much the same way. Well, it would be an elegant party, anyway! Better than a chicken in their trailer-house.

The Bethlehem Star DVD captured their attention, but then one of the men was inviting everyone to gather for prayer. After which, pandemonium reigned! Mallory stood directing traffic, bouncing a baby to quiet him so

Connie could fill her plate. He was adorable, but teething had him out of sorts at the moment. She didn't have him long before Roger grabbed him.

"Hey, how's your rewiring coming along? Mom told me about the temporary offices and that Sam got most of your data okay."

Roger smiled, "Yeah, all totaled, not as bad as I was afraid of at first. Hey, did Donovan Cline really get saved last night?"

"He really did! I couldn't believe he showed up at the service. But, of course, Callie's leaving tomorrow. Guess he figured he should see her as much as he can between now and then. How come Tony stopped crying for you?"

"Come on, Mallie, you know why! His grandpa's his favorite person."

Connie passed by with a loaded plate. "I let grandpa think that. It's the only way I get a chance to eat. Spoiled Tony!" The way she pinched at his fat little cheeks showed who was one of the ones guilty of spoiling him.

"Hey, Phil, what are you guys doing here?" David's amazed voice.

"Don't ask my guests why they're here!" Mallory was laughing as she shook a finger in David's face. His question might have seemed rude, except that Phil and Risa could tell their violin student was delightedly surprised by their presence.

Making Risa's acquaintance, Herb Carlton, drew the couple aside, amazed at the artistic talent the woman exhibited just by the unique jewelry she was wearing. Herb knew she was a treasure! "I can't wait to see what's wrapped in those blankets!" His voice, warm, enthusiastic, sincere!

"That makes two of us!" Diana's voice chimed in from the doorway. "We're all pretty mad at David for trying to hide you and keep you for himself! We kind of stay mad at him, anyway." That was a lot for the kind Diana to say about anyone, but Phil and Risa smiled agreement.

"The young man people love to hate! However, not without his charm." Phil agreed.

With most of the breakfast consumed, Daniel assembled the chattering crowd into the formal living room, where French doors opened to the manicured pool enclosure. The mild weather was a boon, and people were finding places excitedly. The family groups had already exchanged gift among themselves, but now Daniel, in a Santa beard and hat, was distributing Mallie's gifts, and she was receiving a stack from them. The Andersons were first! A new laptop, color printer, and cam, and a telescope like hers for pastor! Lana and Tammi received gift cards for very nice jewelry of their choosing, within a generous price-range, from Herb's company. Jeff received the archery set he had been wanting, and a range was already completed at the camp site. David received a batting cage, to be installed at the camp. The two little girls got some cute little jewelry and sparkly things for their hair.

After making sure Delia didn't mind, her gift to Daniel and Diana was a trip to accompany them to Hawaii in February, and also for the senior Faulkners. Neither career geologist had ever viewed a live volcano. They were delighted with the gift!

Mallory loved watching the expressions of wonder. She continued through her gift-giving, finally coming to Phil and Risa.

"David, I'm sorry to do this, because I love the better violin." She was trying not to cry. "But I haven't attained a level to deserve an instrument like this! I want Phil to have it back! Do you mind?"

David's turn to fight tears. "Not at all! I want him to have it back, too."

The man was totally overcome by emotion. He was trying to refuse, because, for one thing, he didn't still have David's money. At last pressured by the entire group, he received it graciously. Unbelievable!

Mallory wiped away tears. "And Risa, what an amazing lady you are! I hear you make an awesome carrot cake! We want to make the world aware of your amazing artwork, so we're arranging some exhibits. For now, though, we want a private showing."

The kids, excused to return to games and videos, hesitated, curious, too, about the mysterious blanket-wrapped items.

"I know. Phil, we'll all go take a break, get fresh drinks, and you and Risa can set up and display what you've brought. What do you need? Maybe thirty minutes?"

Half an hour later, the crowd was admiring oils, watercolors, sculptures, and jewelry. Mallory saw an oil she really wanted, but she was trying to let others go first.

"Risa, this is all beautiful!" Diana was truly dazzled. She was always nice, but her tone was way beyond dutiful compliments.

The artistic woman was pleased, seldom receiving enthusiastic responses to her work. Of course the reason for that, was that people wanted to purchase her soul's work for the least amount of money possible. If you said you loved something and really wanted it desperately, the price would rise accordingly. Like the book of Proverbs said, *"It is nothing! It is nothing! And then the buyer goes his way boasting and rejoicing."* (Paraphrase)

This Christian group was different, wanting to lift up the downtrodden artist, purchasing her pieces at fair market value, praising her, promoting her talents to others!

And her subject matter wasn't limited to one style or topic, but vast and deep, showing emotions from delightful to despairing! Mallory's first choice was a large canvas of white on white. White table top, white place mat, white bowl of milk, with the contrast of brilliant red, ripe strawberries sparkling with sugar, just below and to the right of center. Trying to wait, she really felt ready to kill for it.

"Well, we want to give our hostess a hostess gift and a Christmas present," Risa's cute voice. "Please choose whatever you like, Mallory."

"Oh, I want *the Strawberries*, but I want to buy it."

"No," Phil's response was assured. "Maybe we've given the work away before, too much. And we've probably undervalued it. All it has really needed is a chance! And you, Mallory, and your friends, are giving that to us. And my violin back! Please accept it from us."

"Please, Mallory, it just makes me happy to know you like it."

"Well, I like everything! But my bedroom's all white! And I love the white, and then the bright red strawberries! I want to put it in an ornate white frame, get a white, lighted easel, and put it right next to the French doors. You want to come see?"

Daniel chose a watercolor of the seventeenth hole at Pebble Beach. David chose a sculpture of a horse head, carved in beautiful detail from some rich, brown stone. Beth liked the hammered silver jewelry. John and Lana bought a set of two complementary oils: one showed a despondent, miserable crowd of impoverished-looking people; the other showed the same people, happy and lighthearted, going on their way. They felt it was representative of people with and without the Lord. The set would be featured in pastor's home office. Shay chose a watercolor of an antique woody, and Delia chose a still life of a tea table with a lovely silver tea service.

Before the Perkins left with a handful of checks, Mallory and Daniel met with them to go over some business details. They needed to get with an attorney and CPA for getting incorporated and getting their books set up the most advantageously. They needed to protect their assets from the previous sour deal, and have someone design business cards, stationery, web-site, and phone system. They were truly an amazing couple! Literally, generous to a fault, they had both been able to make a fairly decent living. They really were simply poor managers.

Meeting their gazes earnestly, Daniel explained about the Apostle Paul's instructions to the church at Corinth, to *let everything be done decently and in order.* If that was good advice about the order of a church service, it wasn't out of context to figure God gives us the intellect to put our lives in order. An order for tithing, giving, and living. Daniel carefully went over the plan they had in mind for the couple. An infusion of capital for combined art and music studios in Aspen and Dallas.

"We're doing this because you both have what it takes. You'll both have corporate credit cards to use. That helps with your tax receipts, and it provides really valuable perks. We already rented the space in Aspen, which will require some of your input for renovation and decoration. But, you can set up a temporary exhibition in part of it. I'm telling you, Risa, your pieces will go as quick as you can produce! If you have any students or acquaintances, you might include them, so there are lots of pieces, choices. If that makes sense. You can earn a commission from them, while helping them along, like we're doing for you."

"And we're aware of the fact that your work has been hindered by being broke, lacking the mediums and materials you need." Mallory's excited voice! "Like the price of silver is high right now, but your work in silver is beautiful. If you work with Herb, combining your orders, you can both get more of a discount with the larger purchase. Do you ever use, or would you like to use other gems in your works? I know you inlay onyx, and coral and mother of pearl."

"Well, if you're talking about starting me with an open-to-buy, the sky's the limit. I mean, I've wanted so much; it hasn't been fair to Phil. You really can't make money in the arts."

"Well, Risa, we think that's a popularly held myth. You guys have made money. But you haven't kept receipts. Then, you sell one of your pieces for a fairly good sum, but the money gets away, and then you owe taxes. That traps the majority of Americans, not just artistic people. That's why Daniel's the CFO, and if you guys continue to produce, you will have something to show for it." Mallory's confident assertion. "You said, 'I've wanted so much'. What exactly have you wanted and needed that has held you back as an artist?"

"Well, I've wanted a potter's wheel, and a kiln. I love every medium. I should probably settle on one area of expertise. Look how old I am, and I'm still trying to find myself!"

"That's it!" Mallory's excitement! "That's what makes you so fascinating and gives you such an awesome persona! You're still trying to learn and expand yourself, not just as an artist, but as a person!"

"We want to get a recording of Phil on the violin, to play in your studio as people browse through. They may purchase his CD's as well as your art." Daniel's encouraging words to the other artist. "It's a complement of one another, not a competition. When you become successful, you still need to keep your partnership strong."

Phil laughed. "If there's ever been anything we haven't needed to worry about, it was being ruined by prosperity."

"Yeah, but it's a real danger. The main thing is getting busy with all this, and neglecting your time with the Lord. Everything always fights for that time!" Daniel Faulkner was rising as he spoke.

Chapter 31: WAIF

Cassandra Faulkner and her kittens were garnering the hearts of the residents of Jerusalem. The free-spirited wisp, bright blue eyes alight with curiosity and mischief, was hard to miss. Always leaving Lilly's flat as early as possible, to return by eight at night, as long as she stayed out of trouble at school, making acceptable marks, no one paid her much attention. For a little thing, she functioned.

"Morning, Asra," she greeted the lady who owned a bread kiosk. By now, her Hebrew was passable for day to day conversation. She knew Asra's name because the customers always greeted her by name. Cass knew most of the customer's names, too, just from sitting there with her favorite kitten, and watching.

"Go along. You're waiting to steal my bread, street beggar!"

"I'm not. I don't steal. Would you like for me to help you work? I learned to count at school. I can make change, and count rolls to more than a dozen. I know the people's names, too."

Every day, the exchange was the same. Except on Sabbath. Then Asra wasn't at her stand, and Cassandra's freedom was restricted.

Finally, one morning, Asra was waiting for the pesky child to show up. Her child was sick, so she was desperate enough to give the little girl a chance.

"What's your name, girl? Let me see how you can work."

"Cassandra," came the reply. "I know how much everything is. Here comes Mr. Amos now. He always buys five loaves. Do you ever give anything away free?"

"Wash your hands, and let me see you fix the order for him. I am too poor a woman to give anything away. I barely earn a living." She was cross, but not as cross as Lilly.

Cassandra scrubbed up, and had the fresh merchandise wrapped by the time the customer approached.

Barely tall enough to see over the counter, she pushed the purchase across, thanking him for his business, taking his money, and counting it carefully.

Asra dashed up to a nearby flat to check her child, making it back to check on, what she figured was unreliable help, at best. The little girl named off the customers she had waited on, with the total money collected, but with the admission that she sent every customer on his way with an extra, small sugar-roll.

"Go to school now. Here, take one of the small rolls for helping. Come back at lunchtime, so I can leave for a few minutes again."

Eyes alight at the unexpected, sticky treat, Cassandra skipped happily on her way.

Then Asra began to depend on the little American girl more and more. Within a week, she was known as the vendor who gave away something extra. That brought new customers to wait in line at her booth. With her increased business, she expanded to run an additional stand, hiring her sister, Rachael. Amazed at the difference in her profits, she asked the small girl how she knew to give something free.

Wistfully, Cassandra explained her mother did that with her business. By now, Cassandra missed her mother!

Chapter 32: WINTER

After the mild weather, the cold snap that set in a couple of days after Christmas seemed extra dismal and gloomy. Parker and Callie were gone, and Mallory faced the bleak fact that the one year anniversary of her father's death was staring her in the face. She tried to stay busy, focusing on the upcoming trip to Hawaii. It would be fun; she was excited about viewing one of the live volcanoes; she called them 'Hiccups from hell'. Until then, she needed to get far enough ahead in her school work to take the vacation break. DiaMo always kept her busy, too. She was excited about having the Perkins on board.

Still, time seemed heavy on her hands. She spent extra time practicing her music, both piano, and violin. She wished she could sing like Diana, but figured with so much going on, it would be better not to mention that! She wasn't sure if she was supposed to go to Tulsa on Monday night for the Tuesday lesson day, or if New Years Day would put the lessons on hold until the next Tuesday. She called her mom, but with the Sander's Corporation drama, her mom wasn't where she could really talk. In the temporary facility, there was less privacy, not that Mallory really had that much to say. Her mom hadn't loved her dad like she did!

Having never gotten rid of her cough, she spent hours in the batting cage, anyway; slugging away regardless of the chill. After that, she felt sicker than ever. Finally on Saturday, she spent the day in a cute new pair of pajamas her mom gave her for Christmas, sipping chicken broth, and popping over-the-counter cold remedy stuff.

Sunday she went to Sunday School and church. At least by the hacking and coughing going on around her, she guessed she wasn't the only one there spreading germs. She decided that, even if there were lessons on

Tuesday, she shouldn't take her germs around Xavier again. That was a depressing thought. Because, then on Wednesday, January second, the Day, she would be alone.

Kerry caught up with her as she was trying to slip out after the service. "Are you going to be in your office tomorrow?" His voice sounded like he was as stopped up as she was.

"I'm not really sure, why?" was her response.

"I need to talk to you. Why don't you meet me at one in the café?"

"What about?" She still tried not to meet with him if she could avoid it.

"I'm not at liberty to say, here," he whispered.

Mallory gazed around the empty foyer. The church crowd, diminished greatly by travel and illness, was pretty well cleared out. No one was around. His 'cloak and dagger' stuff was annoying her at the moment. She figured it was something about Cassandra. He still kept trying to get her caught in the middle between him and the Faulkners. She thought he should mind his own business. Or at least, leave her out of it.

"Okay, one o'clock," she acquiesced. It wouldn't hurt to go in for an hour or two, just to check on stuff. Everyone in the office was off for the entire week between Christmas and New Year. Maybe she could get some stuff done. Meeting with Kerry was better than spending the whole rest of the week by herself anyway, and he already seemed to have a cold.

Bracing for the cold, she dashed out to the waiting vehicle.

⚔ ⚔

Kerry was in court by eight-thirty. He expected the trial to drag out for at least one more day; maybe two. Judge Davison was the presiding judge, but behind his back, he was known as *Judge Munch*. Always with piles of snacks in his chambers, you could count on his taking breaks from the 'Process'. You could always count on at least a two hour recess for lunch. Kerry was glad the judge was determined to get the case wrapped up. Evidently the opposing counsel wasn't ready, assuming they would get additional time to tie up their loose ends. Kerry's concern was his lunch appointment with Mallory. This had to be a first for Davison to continue through the lunch hour. He didn't even break so Kerry could make a call.

⚔ ⚔

Mallory managed to get some sleep, but her cough was deeper, painful, and less productive. She couldn't figure out why it wasn't getting better. Her opinion was that you could usually ride it out. After all, the body had amazing powers to regenerate itself. She still felt pretty miserable through her devotion time. Aggravated at herself for being talked into an appointment, she got ready, heading downtown toward her office to get in an hour or so of work before the lunch. The minestrone soup was sounding like an excellent choice. Her in-box was empty so she checked her e-mails; empty except for the usual amount of spam.

She e-mailed several of her friends, more from boredom than because she had anything important to relate. No word yet, from Callie. Finally, at five until one, Janice walked with her down to the mezzanine.

"I'll be fine from here. Kerry should be here any minute. I'll have him walk me back." That was her usual routine with her security when she was within the building. Janet nodded, returning to the penthouse office suite to wait until the girl was ready to return home.

⊱ ⊰

The 'munching' judge allowed a short recess from eleven forty-five until noon, then reconvened until four p.m. A jury trial, the jurors were released for a recess before commencing deliberations. Kerry called Mallory, all apologies for standing her up. She didn't answer; her phone seemed to be turned off. He left a couple of voicemails, and a text. When he still couldn't reach her thirty minutes later, he phoned the office. Marge was out all week, and Janice didn't answer. She wasn't a DiaMo receptionist; she let it ring until it went to voicemail.

⊱ ⊰

At six, Janice couldn't figure out why the meeting with Kerry was still going on. Mallory didn't answer her phone, and Kerry didn't answer his. She was puzzled. Surely nothing was wrong within the secured, holiday-vacation-quiet building. At six-thirty, she called Darrell, after neither Kerry nor Mallory answered her calls the second time.

He was immediately concerned, but he didn't want to raise an alarm with Erik or Daniel. He called the building security to have them check the café for the two tenants. The café had been closed for more than an hour. He was trying to decide what action to take, when a call came in from Kerry Larson.

"Larson, where have you been?" he demanded. "Is Mallory still with you?"

"I've been in court all day. I thought I'd be able to keep my appointment with Mallory with no problem, but the most predictable judge of all the judges decided to become unpredictable on me. We finally broke at four, and I called to apologize. I couldn't get hold of her. Don't blame her for being ticked. Then, the jury came back in about five-thirty, so my phone was off again when Janice was trying to call me."

"Well, do you know what her plans were?" A knot of fear was tying itself around Hopkins' heart. Something was wrong! He was already praying for it not to be too catastrophic.

Kerry was experiencing pangs of terror, too. He didn't know her plans after the lunch, but it wasn't like her to disappear and not answer her phone, even for her security.

"We need to let Erik know," Kerry's assessment.

"Yeah," Hopkins agreed. "You need to give him a call."

"Well, you're her security head," Larson shot back.

"Yeah, but you're the one who wanted her to come down here today, and then stood her up. She told Janice you'd walk her back."

Listening to the blame-shifting in disgust, Janice placed the call. To Faulkner! He was her boss. She answered to him. He wasn't happy!

⚜ ⚜

Mallory regained consciousness, but she wasn't sure where she was. Her hands, bound tightly behind her, were looped to her ankles, also encased in heavy tape. The same tape circled her face tightly. She couldn't make a sound. She worked desperately to draw in enough air! Her nose was so stopped up! She tried to remember what had happened. A voice was screaming at her.

"Get in!" a gun cocked at her temple. "Get in, or you die right here!"

She was terrified by the threat, but the tight trussing made it impossible for her to comply. Nor could she speak. Unable to breathe, she lost consciousness.

⚜ ⚜

Daniel Faulkner sat numbly. He couldn't believe Mallory was gone again. He was too numb to cry. He checked his cell. At least he hadn't missed desperate phone calls from her this time. She was eighteen now; so was David. Maybe temptation got the best of them, and they were eloping. He wasn't sure if he should hope that was the case, or not. An e-mail had arrived for Diana, but that was before one. Before Janice had walked Mallie to the café, and left her to wait alone for Kerry. For Kerry, who didn't show up! Or call!

He placed a reluctant call to the FBI Agent.

"Erik, we've lost track of Mallory again." He spoke softly, trying to postpone the inevitability of Diana's finding out! And Suzanne!

Erik, fumbling for the remote's mute button as he answered, was pretty sure he had heard correctly. "Lost track? Where? How?"

He listened morosely to Faulkner's sketchy rundown. "Wow, weather's bad, too. The roads are already slick here. I'll call the Dallas office and get them started trying to track her down. This doesn't sound good, though. I wish I thought she was just running off to get married, but she gave her word. She'd answer her phone if she could. You know she would."

Clicking the call off, he met Suzanne's gaze sadly. "Mallory's missing, again. She showed up to meet Larson, but he couldn't get loose from court to keep the lunch date. No one's seen her since Janice left her at the café. She never returned to her office."

He placed a call to his superior, who could get things moving at the Dallas branch and with the Addison Police Department. Erik needed that office building searched from stem to stern. Mallory wouldn't have left the building for any reason without letting Janice know. If she had been abducted, it was the last place anyone had seen her.

Suzanne followed him into the bedroom where he was pulling into cold weather clothes. Thick socks, work boots, holstered gun and extra clips. Phone and charger, big flashlight! Then the bomber jacket with the sheared mink lining. An ice storm was unleashing its fury, with strong winds, and downed power lines. The advisory said to stay in.

"Listen, Suze, I'm givin' ya a couple of choices. You can stay hear and wait for word, or I can take you to the office, and you can wait there. Agents'll be in and out. I don't think I can get you to Dallas in this weather, tonight, and no one knows for sure if Mallory's still in Dallas."

"Well, I want you to be able to concentrate on finding Mallie without worrying about me, too. Would you prefer for me to stay here and wait?" He knew she was panicked, just trying to stay calm so he could go do his job.

"Yeah, that'd probably be the best thing. The chairs are softer here, you'll be more comfortable. If you think of anything that might be a clue, let me know. I'll keep you in the loop." He was out the door without a kiss.

≒ ⋟

Mallory came to, slightly. She couldn't figure out if she was riding in a car trunk again, or if she just thought she was. Sometimes the nightmares recurred. She dozed, to waken again. Her head felt light, she was dizzy, her stomach churned. She was definitely riding. She was cold, and still barely able to breathe. She couldn't feel her body, at all. She was pretty sure some kind of strong drug was causing her to feel giddy, while at the same time, the motion was making her sick. She vomited, but the tight tape kept her from being able to get rid of it. She was strangling, with it in her nose, eyes, lungs. She couldn't get her hands free to loose the gagging bond. She lapsed into unconsciousness again.

≒ ⋟

Bransom felt like there was a short list of suspects: the Malovich twins and that band of thugs, the Iranians, or Sylvia Brown. He didn't think it had anything to do with Iran. He had never been able to substantiate any of those rumors, although Shay had been really terrified by the prospect, making David obsess about it, too. Ahmir thought the Maloviches might be dead. Erik guessed he had hoped that was the case. They must be responsible. Of course, Sylvia was linked to them. And Sylvia had been uttering all kinds of vague threats. He wished he could get to Dallas to search the building, himself. Everything was moving slower than he liked. Like finding who worked in the café in the afternoon, to interview them. To ask any of the people who had been in the building if they had noticed anything. To begin sorting through security footage for each corridor and exit! He passed quite a few wrecks. What was normally a five minute drive took over thirty minutes. The storm hadn't been overrated. He wasn't going to get to Dallas, tonight. Nothing would be flying. In the small office, he brewed coffee as a few agents filtered in.

≒ ⋟

346

Diana finished feeding and changing Zave, tucking him into his crib, singing softly as she caressed his soft head, smoothing his hair sideways, smiling into his eyes as he grew sleepy. She started to beam a happy smile at Daniel as he appeared in the doorframe. Her smile froze.

"Come in the office," he mouthed the words, turning in that direction.

She followed. Something was wrong. From the anguish on his face, it was either Cassandra or Mallory. She tried to brace herself.

"Okay, Honey, Mallie's gone again." Even as he broke the news, he was struggling with the unreality of it all. They thought they had gotten stuff ironed out. "Kerry made a lunch appointment with her today, then got hung up in his court case, and couldn't make it, and couldn't call. Janice walked her down to the building café at one, and no one has seen her since. As soon as the police in Dallas can locate the café employees, they might know if anyone else was with her. All this ice isn't helping, either. We should pray."

"Yeah, do the Anderson's know? And her new pastor? We need to get a prayer chain going."

"Well, we don't think the Anderson's know. Guess Erik thinks David won't leave him alone to investigate, once he finds out. I still think they might be eloping."

"Well, I'll call David and ask him. No use in having every agency in north central Texas combing through that building for her if that's the case." Diana's voice was practical. It was something to do; there didn't seem to be many other options, but to sit, and pray, and hope!.

David, one of the few people to brave the elements for a New Year's Eve service at Faith Baptist, was back at his parent's home, trying to get warm by the fire. He was surprised to receive a call from Mrs. Faulkner. It was either an accidental call, or it wasn't good.

"This is David," he answered.

"Hello, David?" Have any of you heard anything from Mallory today?"

He could sense the panic behind her attempt to sound nonchalant. He couldn't believe this! He moved to his room, pushing the door to, behind him.

"I don't think anyone here has. I'll go out and ask them after you tell me why you're askin'."

"I'll let you talk to Daniel." Daniel shot his wife a desperate look, but she was thrusting her phone towards him, so he explained the little bit they knew.

Tammi had received an e-mail before lunch; that was all. It didn't seem to be any coded message she was in trouble.

Going to his dad's office, he turned on the computer, drumming impatiently for his fb page to access. Sylvia was still one of his fb friends; and she sent him quite a few messages and comments every day. They were private from his other friends. He didn't want to hear from her, and he wasn't answering back. He was afraid if he removed her as a friend, she would be even more of a wack job! That was scary.

No fresh messages from her. No taunting words that she had Mallory. Surely, Sylvia didn't have what it took to get to Mallory past all her security. What security? Larson stood her up, leaving her vulnerable. She should have sent for Janice to come back down to meet her, but David could see why she would have felt secure enough to walk a corridor and take an elevator by herself in an office building featuring its own security. Sylvia was a lunatic, but she was all talk. So, did that mean Mallie was harembound, again? It would be easy to get her out of the country in any type of shipping container. Maybe the miserable storm would hold up her kidnappers like it was bogging down everything else. He called Shay, telling him not to let Delia know. But Delia wasn't an easy person to keep secrets from. She called Shannon, and he ducked through the pelting ice to stay with his Aunt Suzanne.

⊰ ⊱

Mallory was cold, and a coughing spasm gagged her, causing her to wretch, bringing more bile into her mouth. Once again, she swallowed. Tears streamed down her face, and she struggled against her bonds. Then, she would remember Diana's soft voice, saying her name, comforting her, "You use up too much Oxygen when you struggle, Mallory. Calm down. Don't cry." She managed to halt the sobs, but tears still flowed. Her nose was running, too, and the tape over her mouth was unbelievably slimy. She tried not to gag.

The car stopped, and the engine turned off. She didn't have the mobility now, she had had before, in the Middle Eastern situation No screwdriver in hand. She was helpless.

"Lord, please, help me." a voiceless plea, again, for at lest the hundredth time.

The trunk lid opened, and the cold wind hit her like a lash. She tried to remember removing most of her clothing; she couldn't think, remember. She shivered from cold and shock. How could this be happening?

"Get out!" Sylvia's voice spat the order as she grabbed her prisoner by a handful of hair. "Ride's over."

Somehow, the tormented girl managed to help thrust her weight over the trunk enclosure, to fall heavily onto concrete. A moan escaped, softened by the gag. She lay dazedly while the other girl moved to push a switch, the switch which caused one section of the concrete floor of a shed to rise, revealing a hand-excavated mine-pit beneath.

The tape made communication impossible, or Mallie would have sarcastically said, "Thanks for giving me a ride home, Sylvia!" And she was mad. Sylvia, at some point in time, had taken her clothing. Now, her nemesis was wearing the expensive boots and the luxurious lynx jacket. Probably the Hermes bag, too, lay in the car.

Without saying another taunting word to her captive, the beautician kicked viciously with one of the boots. Mallory smacked down helplessly, hitting each of the hard, narrow ledges before landing in icy water at the bottom of the pit. With hands and feet bound behind her, there was no way to soften the impacts or break her fall!

-ᄏ ᄐ-

Janice Collins met Paul Simpson, the chief detective who responded from the Addison Police Department. She felt like he was a little disdainful of her for losing track of her charge; maybe it was just that she felt so disdainful of herself. She thanked him for responding without the usual rhetoric about waiting a couple of days to file a 'missing person's report'.

"We vary our routes from day to day," she explained. "From the mezzanine, she should have taken the front elevators to six, then the sixth floor hallway, to the private elevator, to the penthouse. Of course, she has a key to access the private elevator. I don't think she got that far."

The detective nodded. "That gives us a starting place." He sent an officer in search of the day's footage for the space in question. He figured with the probable kidnapping, that the Feds would be showing up soon, jostling him aside. But, with the girl's life in imminent danger, he issued orders!

The sixth floor yielded information immediately. A security guard lay, at the top of the stairwell, tightly bound; hands, feet, and mouth! He was dead, with a couple of empty ampoules of horse tranquilizer nearby. It wasn't entirely evident if the purpose was to kill, or just to neutralize the threat. A glance revealed that, had he survived, he would have lost hands and feet to the cruel binding! The M.E. would determine cause of death, to ascertain whether an overdose of the strong tranquilizer, or oxygen deprivation actually caused the victim to succumb. He wasn't a big guy.

Images of the dead guard appeared on the screen in front of Bransom. It was Sylvia! Had to be! Working alone? He guessed she was. A little bit of a thing, if the guard was in her way, she would feel the need to subdue the threat completely. Erik didn't think a man would have been so threatened by a slightly-built, under trained security employee. It was sad! Sad for a man not expecting to die on his shift! Sad, for Mallory, who was still within the clutches of the crazy girl! He called Suzanne with an update, then David.

Ivan Summers stopped by his apartment to throw in his clubs, toolbox, and whatever else was in his garage, to add weight to the back of his Arkansas sedan. He wasn't the only one sliding all over the roads. He didn't stop to assist other motorists out of the ditches. He was cruising the roads of west central Arkansas for anything that looked suspicious. He still hoped to apprehend the criminal element who had escaped his grasp before. He cruised: Kirby, Dierks, Glenwood, Murfreesboro, Daisy State Park, the camp site. Back in Dierks, on his circuit, he stopped at the convenience store. Not an all-night place, they were closing, and had emptied the coffee pots. He pled with the clerk. Evidently, she thought he was cute, because he wheedled his way in. While the coffee brewed, he chatted to her. Small town, he was willing to bet she knew plenty, that she knew Sylvia.

"So, you from around here?" he asked, leaning on a potato chip display, flirting, trying to act like he had time to kill. "Where'd you go to school?"

She answered like she thought he cared, and knew where she was talking about. He guessed she was local. His response to her questions in return were that he was from Little Rock. With the coffee, brewed, he filled four large cups, paying for them, thanking her, with the usual instruction to 'have a good evenin'.'

Back in the solitude of the car, he turned up the heat. That was depressing. A single mom with two kids, she was underemployed and desperate. If she knew Sylvia Brown, he hadn't been able to get the information. At least he had coffee. He circled back through town.

⚜ ⚜

Daniel and Diana were not liking the information that was coming to them! Each new tidbit seemed worse. At least all three kids were sleeping, unaware of a problem. The couple always wondered where Cassandra was, and if she was happy or homesick. Any new emotional load on what they already carried was too much. Daniel paced while Diana sat glued to her phone and computer screen. The wind howled dismally!

⚜ ⚜

Mallory wormed her way out of cold water which had seeped into the excavated space, maybe a foot deep. Pitch blackness surrounded her, and she couldn't get her bearings for which side of the pit led to the open area of the shed, and which came right flush with the far wall. She wasn't certain she could inch her way painfully to the top, but she was determined to try. Cold and wet, she hurt everywhere; the gagging cough and nausea, hampered by the tight tape. Once more, she tried to stretch the bonds that held her wrists and ankles, like if she strained and fought long enough, she could free herself. Somehow, Sylvia had managed to knock her out long enough to undress her, and wrap her in layer after layer of the thick, sticky tape. She tried to remember, but her head hurt unbelievably. She thought her eyes were swelling shut. It didn't matter, she was in darker dark than she had ever experienced. For the first time, the realization engulfed her, that she might never escape. More tears flowed into the tape.

⚜ ⚜

Daniel was shocked to hear about the dead security employee, but hopeful, that since Mallory's body wasn't there, maybe she was still alive. Diana, hearing the details of the tranquilizer and binding, shuddered with a new dread, demanding information about the strong drug, then amount of the dosage. Erik had just learned about the break-in at the stable: the break-in where nothing was reported missing! Just several ampoules of a strong tranquilizer no one had missed yet! Easy way to overcome a victim.

351

Diana voiced concerns about Mallory's already being sick: worried she was on the verge of Pneumonia, and always bordering on dehydration.

⚏ ⚎

Summers drove his route again. This time as he passed through Dierks, he made mental note that Sylvia Brown's car was on the street by her apartment. It hadn't been there earlier, and it wasn't coated with a sheet of ice like most of the other cars on the street. Evidently the girl hadn't heeded the warnings to stay off the roads. Lights were on in the building, although the hour was late. Different lights from his earlier passes. He wasn't sure which unit belonged to his quarry. Maybe she didn't have any connection to Mallory's disappearance. He sat there, with his skin crawling. She had clawed him half to death on an earlier run-in. Too bad she wasn't still in lock-up! He wished he had evidence for a warrant to search the car for evidence regarding Mallory. He drove on.

⚏ ⚎

David couldn't believe that tranquilizers from the stable near Kirby were involved with the death of a man in Dallas. His fears had still revolved around Mallory's being moved quickly out of the U.S. He couldn't believe Sylvia could be organized enough and crazy enough to lash out at Mallory. And succeed! If it was Sylvia, she would probably make a few threats and let Mallie go.

Having viewed crime scene photos of the dead man, Erik thought that was too optimistic.

⚏ ⚎

Dr. Kenneth Wilson surveyed the small trauma center of the Murfreesboro, Arkansas hospital. In a rural area, the small facility managed to stay busy with the usual sprains, breaks, and contusions. Wilson hated being here. Youthful and brilliant, he tried to get the medical personnel company to place him somewhere larger and more important. The night would probably be crazy with car accidents, people without sense to listen to authorities, and stay home. Sometimes he supervised the larger facilities in Little Rock or Ft. Smith, but this week, there wasn't anybody else to

352

run the small E.R. He ordered the staff to make better preparation to receive victims.

⚔ ⚔

Mallory reached the top tier, dismayed to feel the slimy wall of the building. Tears squeezed from swollen eyelids. She would scooch her way on around, but first, she had to rest. Her lungs burned, and she struggled to fill them with air. In just a couple of minutes~she would be free of the pit, surely there was a way to raise the opening from underneath. In just a minute~she'd check!

In the freezing water once again, Mallory panicked. She couldn't tell if she had fallen asleep, lost consciousness to roll down again. Or if the water was rising rapidly. In her confusion, she struggled desperately. Every move brought pain, but she raised herself a level, once again free from the icy knives. Shivering violently, she struggled for Oxygen, desperately trying to remain lucid. Part of her wanted to give up. She was sadly aware that if she survived, her life would be altered forever. She was losing her hands and feet. That was pretty obvious. And apparently, she had never had David. But she could live crippled, if the Lord allowed it, and Parker had shown her that there were still some guys out there that wanted to serve the Lord. That she could be attracted to. Undecided, she clung there. Should she fight her way upward? What? Just to lose consciousness and smack all the way back down? If she lay there, what were the chances of her being found in time? She suddenly wondered if anyone knew she was missing. She wasn't sure, but she thought the pit was deeper. But who would be working it? The company that owned the property wouldn't be hand-digging clandestinely. So, if someone were stealing diamonds, and they showed up for work, they wouldn't necessarily want to help her since she could testify about their activities. Somehow, through the mental fog, it also occurred to her that it was a holiday. If anyone ever visited this site, would it be today?

She was angry at Kerry Larson. Now, the Faulkners would be mad at her for her security slip-up. She should have called Janice back. When she decided to return to her office alone, she shouldn't have checked out what sounded like someone in trouble! One of the oldest tricks in the book! And she fell for it!

Once more, she strove against the tight bonds, trying to stretch the cruel restraints Once more, they cut painfully into her flesh. The strong adhesive holding the tape across her mouth seemed to be degrading, saturated with vomit, mucous, tears, and the stale water. Rubbing her face painfully on the rough, hard step, she was able to force it downward, finally freeing her mouth, while it pulled painfully in her hair.

She passed out!

Chapter 33: WACKO

Erik Bransom prayed desperately as the hours passed without word of Mallory. Another empty ampoule of the potent drug, found in a janitorial closet, indicated that was the area where Sylvia had hidden her victim while she bound her. A night janitor informed them that a large garbage bin was missing. An identical bin illustrated the manner in which the plastic tubs were bolted onto wheeled wooden frames. Plenty of room to stow Mallory, and wheel her from the building. A couple of small plugs of hair appeared to match Mallory's. Lab analysis would tell for sure. Evidently the helpless victim had been yanked around by the hair.

Bransom determined Sylvia Brown wouldn't walk free again after this! He didn't care who her mother was, or what operation was ongoing! If he had to shoot her and go to jail, so be it! No one like this should be loosed on the world! He phoned Summers.

⚔ ⚔

Inside her small apartment, Ms. Sylvia Brown paced in the dark, pausing occasionally to stare out at the icy build-up, and to look for the nosy Arkansas agent. She was wondering callously if the girl in the pit lived through the tumble to the base. She wished now she had finished her off!

She wasn't sure how cold the weather needed to be, and how long the period of exposure, for someone to die of hypothermia. She had thought she would escape being a suspect, and that her rival might be dead for months before the clever spot was discovered. She didn't want Mallory to live. She wasn't worried about her own fate: she had a powerful and devoted 'Mommy' to protect her from serious repercussions for her actions! She turned up her heat! It was cold! And she pulled the lynx jacket more tightly around her!

Every time headlights passed by, she glanced out. Maybe Summers had grown tired of his stupid game. She switched on the TV. A lot of breaking news about the storm, people without power in the cold, lots of bad wrecks. She switched it back off. Two A.M. She glanced at a photo on her phone, smirking wickedly! Mallory O'Shaughnessy deserved everything! And worse! She shouldn't have thought she could end up with David Anderson! Just because she had all that money!

⚞ ⚟

To Bransom's chagrin, word reached the Dallas media about the dead guard in the glitzy office building. He thought someone within the small municipality force must have talked. At least, the LEO's weren't aware of the connection to Sylvia Brown and Arkansas. Dawson clamped down on any further communication with members of the press. They weren't ready yet, to name Sylvia as a suspect, counting on her brazenness to help them apprehend her. Obviously, she thought she was untouchable!

Bransom's call to Summers was highly informative! Sylvia's car was gone all afternoon and evening. Finally, around one, she had returned home, but hadn't retrieved her children from the babysitter. Summers had crept along the street to force his way into her car, popping the trunk, making sure Mallory wasn't hidden there. Agents and local agencies were combing hundreds of square miles between Dallas and Hot Springs, searching for signs of the missing victim!

⚞ ⚟

Sylvia gave the image on her phone another satisfied glance, then accessed her facebook page. Quite a few messages from David. He should be sleeping soundly at this hour of the morning! Now, she had his attention! Finally! Now, he wanted to 'get together'! She gloated. "All in good time, 'My Pretty'!" She kissed his image. She still had lots to do! And she was growing hungry!

❦

Ivan Summers, not totally convinced that Sylvia was the instigator of Mallory's disappearance, had started checking on her, because, from his place as an Arkansas agent, that was the closest he could get to the investigation. Maybe he could prove this incident didn't involve the crazy beautician.

His hasty check of the car's trunk didn't prove conclusively that Mallory had been in it. At least he didn't find her body. As soon as Sylvia was in custody, the car would go to impound. That would yield answers, one way or another. He swung up her street, once more, lights off. Her car was gone again! He hated having lost her, even temporarily, but at least her erratic activity didn't show she was having a normal night, sound asleep in bed. She had been up to something! Was still up to something! He phoned the Federal agent again.

❦

Suzanne and Shannon spent agonized hours making and receiving phone calls and responding with blanket e-mails. Of course, everyone involved wanted every detail. Details agonizingly sparse! People all over the world were praying! Hoping against hope for a good outcome against woeful odds. From Park and Callie in Nigeria, to Col. Ahmir in Turkey, the churches in Tulsa, Dallas, And Murfreesboro. Even Lilly Cowan, who had spent countless hours arguing with Mallory about why people shouldn't pray, paced her flat, trying to keep petitions for the girl from crossing her lips.

David sat by the computer, following updates, trying to get Sylvia to spill some information, relaying every thing he could think of that might be even a remote clue to Erin's whereabouts. He called her phone once more.

❦

Sylvia drove back-roads to reach the stable, meeting quite a few cops, who were trying to circle traffic tie-ups on the main arteries to reach fresh accidents. At least they were too caught up to pay much attention to her. She fishtailed and skidded but managed to avoid landing in the ditches.

She was in a hurry! After forty minutes, she slipped up behind the stable. The sky was lightening, almost imperceptibly. The ice storm was forecast to keep up for at least the next twelve hours. Stopping momentarily, she placed the elegant handbag down by the weathered building. Driving to the edge of a large, nearby, stock-pond, she leaped free, sending the small, economy car into a watery grave. Slushing back through icy mud, she gazed at the boots which were proving fortuitous. Too big, she had stuffed the toes to keep them on.

A few hammer blows splintered the wood around the newly replaced lock. This time, she knew which stall housed her target. She still opened each gate, freeing every other horse, before pulling herself onto *El Capitan's* bare back. David had started keeping his saddle with him, like she could have saddled his horse by herself anyway!

⚓ ⚓

Tammi Anderson slipped from the oppressive atmosphere of the Anderson household, allowing tears to flow as she headed her yellow mustang through the gates toward town. Everyone was furious with Kerry! Then, Agent Bransom had him arrested for collusion in Mallory's disappearance. It wasn't fair. Mallory was one of the main clients for the law firm; Kerry would never purposely do anything to her. Sobs burst free. An arrest was bad on anyone's record, but for an attorney. Especially one who had such a good reputation! And if he got convicted of anything! She didn't blame people for being upset about Mallie's disappearance! Mallie was her good friend, too. Kerry would be in trouble, too, that his statement to the agents relayed the common gossip about a judge. At the least, he would get sanctioned for that. Respect for the legal system was a given.

She was on her way into town for a coffee at Sonic! To get away from everybody, and listen to her gospel group, and think. She ignored a phone call from her dad. She finally had earned the privilege again, of having a cell. He'd probably take it again, for her not answering. A text came for her to get back home.

The roads were slick, and she wasn't an experienced driver, but she made it the five miles into town, pulling into the drive-in, where a couple of other cars had gotten out in the bad weather. Pushing the red button, she ordered a coffee drink, then texted her dad back that she would get back as quick as she could; that she was fine! She opened her Bible in her lap.

⚘ ⚘

Mallory was once again submerged in the frigid water. Shocked back to consciousness, she gasped in another mouthful, once more inundating her lungs, swallowing more of the sickening garbage floating on the surface. Her thoughts were more and more confused. She couldn't remember if she had actually climbed to the top numerous times, or if she just thought she had. Exhausted, she wasn't sure she could escape the freezing fingers another time. Fumbling weakly, she managed to lift her face onto the bottom ledge. That was all she could muster. The remainder of her body-heat was ebbing away. And she was sleepy!

⚘ ⚘

Summer's cruising wasn't locating Sylvia's car. When her apartment went dark, he assumed she had decided to sleep. He had driven on, to circle back and find her gone. He radioed a BOLO for the car, but by the time he did that, the little car had already disappeared. Bransom was livid with him!

⚘ ⚘

At Sonic, Tammi received her beverage and paid for it. Trying to focus on her Bible was hard, reading through tears, even concentrating! There was no need for Bransom to arrest Kerry! Cars were pulling in, despite the pleas for people to stay in. Tammi gazed around, and a startled cry escaped her lips. She couldn't believe what she was seeing!

⚘ ⚘

Daniel Faulkner was on the phone by five a.m. The storm had let up in Tulsa. His chopper pilot was pretty certain he could get airborne within an hour, once they got some kind of word. Surely they'd hear something soon. Wouldn't they?

Diana was ready, her nurse's bag filled with as many supplies as she could assemble. She had no idea what might be necessary! If there would be anything anyone could do, by the time Mallory was located! She tried to force the fear back! Mallory had been missing for over twelve hours. What was she enduring?

⚔ ⚔

Erik Bransom was furious to have lost eyes on Sylvia Brown (aka Silver Beret). His phone rang with an unknown caller. The office phones were set up for a tip hotline. He didn't want to deal with any calls he didn't have to. The third time the same caller jangled, he responded irritably, "Bransom! Who's this?"

"Agent Bransom, this is Tammi Anderson! I'm at Sonic in Murfreesboro, and you'll never believe who I'm looking at!"

A lot of stuff went through Bransom's head. He didn't care much about guessing games, any time! Looking at Mallie? Had Mallory just awakened to show up at Sonic, not knowing she had been a 'missing person' all night? He was too annoyed to take a guess.

Tammi's words were spilling out in a jumble. Sylvia Brown, according to the frenzied teen, had ridden up to one of the spaces at the drive-in, on horseback, to order some breakfast! That was a little nutty, in itself. Tammi's words were that the girl was dressed in Mallory's fur jacket, saddle-leather boots, and was carrying the designer handbag. Sylvia had boasted to the horrified carhop that, "Mallory would never see the light of day!"

Bransom couldn't believe the sudden new twist! "I'll call Summers. He shouldn't be too far away. Don't expose yourself to danger, Tammi. Do you think Sylvia knows you're there? I have fifty miles of icy roads, but I'll get there as quick as I can. You're sure the stuff's Mallie's?"

He broke the connection to get Summers back in the hunt.

Tammi backed cautiously from her space. Fifty miles of icy roads! And Summers might be clear up in the north of the county? Sylvia had a lot of nerve to ride into town in stolen clothing, riding a stolen horse. Tammi knew her brother's animal as well as she knew her own; pretty much nerves of steel. Car traffic, nothing made him skittish. Still, he wasn't used to Sylvia, or being ridden bareback. A smile crossed her face as she formulated a plan. "This is for Mallory! And this one's for Kerry!" Pulling up behind *Cap'n,* she laid on the horn. The big horse danced nervously, but didn't rear. Still, Sylvia lost her grip on her beverage and the handbag. Racing the engine and honking loud and long again, Tammi prayed for the mount to lose his rider. Sadly, Sylvia was regaining the upper hand, sneering in her direction.

Unnoticed by the two star players in the unfolding drama, Summers, closer than anticipated, had circled the drive-in the opposite direction of the painted arrows. A burst of lights and siren launched the powerful horse upright, to shudder, riderless, before racing away through an opening in the traffic.

The dazed Sylvia was cuffed and in the back of the agency vehicle, before she could inflict one scratch!

Bransom's next call was to John Anderson.

"Any word, Bransom? Tammi's gone now!" Anderson's agonized tone as he responded to the agent's call.

"Tammi's fine! She gave us a lead. Listen up, Preacher. I think I know where Mallie is. You're the closest to her of anyone. You have to leave without David's knowing it."

"I don't know why nobody likes David–" Anderson's frustrated interruption.

"Okay, John, listen to me! No one has a problem with David. I wish I had someone from law enforcement to check this out. You may not be ready for what you're gonna see. Get out without David, and beat it to the O'Shaughnessy place. Brown told a waitress at Sonic that, 'Mallie's never gonna see the light of day'. Mallie may be down in that mine pit. Timing's critical here; get movin'!

Still dazed, John Anderson slipped into his suit coat and tracked down his car keys. As if in a daze, he pulled onto the icy road that led to Patrick's old acreage. As he pulled beneath the protection of the shed, his phone rang again. Bransom's anxious voice wondering what he had discovered.

"Stay on the line!' Erik's terse order. 'Get that switch hit, 'fore the power goes out from all this ice!"

John Anderson was moving a little quicker now, but everything was surreal, and his body could hardly follow the tense orders. With the section raised, he gazed around the murky space. Even with dim light from within the shed filtering down, he couldn't see anyone.

"Hey, Mallie, you in here?" His voice echoed back eerily.

"She's not here, Erik."

Boiling inwardly with pent-up worry and frustration, Bransom agonizingly wished even one of the Pike County deputies had been available. Forcing his voice to show more patience than he was feeling, he responded.

"Do you have a flashlight? Did you turn on the lights in the shed? I need you to climb down and make sure she isn't down there, unconscious!" He forced himself to say 'unconscious' although the fear gripping him was that Mallie could very well be dead. "If her mouth's bound like that guard's in Dallas, she won't be able to respond! Hurry, John! Talk to me! Tell me what you're doing! What do you see?"

"Okay, no, I don't have a flashlight, turning on the shed lights now. Still don't see any signs of Mallie. I'm kind of in my good clothes."

"Ask me how much I care about your clothes! She's down there! Get her! Before she freezes to death!"

The pastor began picking his way cautiously down the tiers. His eyes were adjusting to the gloom, but he still wasn't seeing any signs of life.

"Mallie, you in here?" He repeated her name again. If she couldn't answer, maybe she could at least respond in some way.

"Erik, she's not here. Maybe Sylvia has her stuck into one of the cave systems around here. Maybe 'not seeing the light' doesn't mean she's underground.

"She's there!" Calm certainty. "Wish I had thought of it earlier. Are you all the way down?"

Agonizing seconds ticked by with no response. "Down as far as I can go without getting wet! It's flooded."

Bransom groaned. "How deep?"

"I can't really tell."

"Well, stick your arm in, and see if you can touch the bottom. What part of 'hurry' do you not understand?"

⚑ ⚐

Word reached the Faulkners about the possibility Mallory was in Murfreesboro. Without waiting for confirmation, they were on their way. Diana hated to burst her husband's optimistic bubble that they had located Mallory, and everything would be fine now. She thought the news was pretty devastating. She had already phoned Helenne Kincaid, the Dallas lung specialist. They had all dodged the bullet before, with Mallory's recovery from the 'strangling' attempt by Oscar Melville, and then Sammy's quick rebound from a nasty blow to the head, Mallory's coming out with only a wrist injury in Turkey. Maybe they were out of chances to 'get it right' with Mallory's security. She had to hold herself together!

Suzanne didn't answer their frantic call for an update, and John Anderson's phone was busy. Lana, just realizing her husband had left the house; wasn't sure where he had gone. It seemed as if the chopper, kicking against the wind, would never arrive. They were in some danger themselves. Diana called Alexandra to let her know there was no further word yet. The two kids, pretty unhappy to be left with the Prescotts, were also worried.

⊰ ⊱

Mallory was dimly aware of the ceiling rising above her, of a voice saying her name. Praying for her mother, she was mortified to hear Pastor Anderson calling to her. Her worming around on the rough levels of the pit had shredded the remaining items of clothing left her by her captor. She was huddled beneath a black garbage bag, the one which had lined the garbage bin from the sixth floor. Sylvia had thought using it would prevent trace evidence's transferring to her car.

Mallory prayed weakly for her pastor to leave and her mother to appear! With lots of warms clothes and blankets. She passed out again.

John Anderson was certain Erik Bransom was mistaken. Still, he picked up a stick to plunge into the dirty water. To his surprise, it wasn't deep; not deep enough to conceal Mallory.

"Okay, water's about ten inches deep. I'm at the bottom. There's lots of garbage floating around." The pastor walked along the muddy tier above the water level, still poking at junk with the stick.

Bransom's patience was past the limit, even as hope soared that Mallory was, indeed someplace more sheltered from the wintry elements. Then, an awful sound ushered from Anderson's lips, an involuntary sound of revulsion. Bransom's heart plummeted. He waited.

Finally, "There's a dead woman. It isn't Mallory, though."

"John, it's Mallie. Get her out of there. You gotta do it. You're the only one there. Just pick her up and climb out."

"No, whoever this is, she's been down here a long time."

"Yeah, twelve hours, at least. You sure she's dead? No pulse? Whoever it is, get her up top! Snap out of it!"

Driven by the order, Anderson stepped into the muck, scooping up the body, and the dripping bag. She was kind of heavy, and he was out of shape. The bound limbs made her doubly awkward to deal with. Whoever it was, she was covered in the nasty muck, swollen, bruised, and gashed. He still thought it had to be some transient. Not one thing about her resembled Mallory O'Shaughnessy! Praises be for that!

⊰ ⊱

Kenneth Wilson, M. D., disappointed with the slow night in the Murfreesboro Hospital emergency room, listened forlornly to news of the overcrowded conditions of all hospitals along Interstate 30. He couldn't figure out why he was stranded at such an inconsequential outpost. Everything here was in readiness. Evidently the locals were heeding the warnings to stay in. All the action seemed to be to the south. The stormy night had brightened ever so slightly into a gloomy morning.

⊰ ⊱

Summers transported his prisoner to the Pike County jail. She was whining about injuries she was claiming to have sustained when *El Capitan* threw her. Not in a sympathetic mood, he put her in lock-up. All medical personnel were stretched to the max with weather-related injuries. She'd have to wait. He was sure her mother would be coming for her, anyway.

"Where's your mommy, now?" he taunted.

"She'll be here. Don't worry. I'll be back out before you know it. You'll be in trouble for making that horse throw me!"

"Oooh, I'm all atremble! We're all counting on you getting out. We can't wait! The second you walk out that door, it's open season on you, Honey! At least ten guys are waiting to put a bullet in your head. Then, since it will be impossible to tell who fired the kill-shot, they'll all get off! You want to call your mom again?"

His words hit her like a hammer. If he was playing 'Good cop/Bad cop', the 'good' one was nowhere to be seen. For the first time, fear gripped her! Summer's turn to smirk!

⊰ ⊱

Finally stepping up onto the concrete floor of the shed, Anderson shifted his awful burden, and the painful jarring caused her to choke and vomit up more water. Her movement was a shocker, to say the least.

John Anderson's stomach churned in sympathetic response to the girl's violent retching!

"Bransom, you still there? I guess she's alive; she's throwing up and shivering. Tell me an ambulance is on the way!"

"Every ambulance in Arkansas is tied up. Just wrap her as warm as you can, and get her straight to the hospital there in town. Falkners are almost there now, for Diana to take care of her. I'm online with a Coast Guard

364

medic about hypothermia. You need to be as gentle as possible. Any kind of roughness might put her in cardiac arrest."

Anderson's head was swimming. It seemed like he had unearthed a science fiction monster of the deep. The trip to the surface had been far from gentle! He thought he was carrying something dead, dead and heavy! He had shifted and juggled her pretty callously. But, the orders from here out were pretty simple. Just throw her in the back of the vehicle, deliver her to the ER. In no time, they would establish this victim's identity, and get back looking for Mallory.

⊰ ⊱

Daniel Faulkner burst into tears of relief at Bransom's news. "John's on the way to the hospital right now with her. She'll be there before we get there."

Nodding, Diana reached for the phone. "What else do you know, Erik? What kind of shape's she in?"

"Bad, I guess," his honest admission. "She looks so bad, John doesn't think it's her. Bound tight; at least he didn't have anyway to undo it. That's a good thing. She had managed to free her mouth, but she's been breathing in cold water, and immersed in it. I'm not sure for how long. This Coast Guard guy thinks it sounds critical."

Diana handed the phone back, numbly aware of the softened rotor noise in the luxurious cabin. She wasn't sure if she wanted to get there in time to say, 'Good-bye'. They had failed! Failed themselves! Failed Patrick's trust! And failed Mallory! "Lord, you decide," she whispered.

⊰ ⊱

Mallory once again regained consciousness. She wanted her mother, but knew she was wrapped in John Anderson's suit coat, and riding in the back of his SUV. She was mortified! Through the fog, she was acutely aware of her state of undress, of ruining the suit, the car's interior. When she saw her mom, she would ask her to make sure the suit and the vehicle were both replaced.

Pulling into the 'ambulance' lane and stopping, John Anderson raced around to the rear to remove his cargo. Then, remembering Bransom's warning for gentleness, he ran inside to request a gurney and assistance.

365

A security guy came to tell him to move his car so ambulances could use the lane.

"There's not an ambulance within a hundred miles of here. I have a woman who's real hypothermic here. I thought she was dead, but then she's been sick. She needs help."

ER staff raced into action, getting the victim transferred to a trauma room, paging Dr. Wilson. The pastor stood awkwardly outside the space. He had been so sure it wasn't Mallory! It didn't look like her; it didn't look like anybody. But now, just before being wheeled away, she had called him by name and asked him where her mother was.

On the phone once more with Erik, he was relieved the Faulkners were close. "A doctor's in with her now. I'll leave my phone on while I find out what he thinks-"

"Hello, doctor, I'm a pastor from here in town."

"Dr. Kenneth Wilson! You bring in the Jane Doe? She's not gonna make it. We have a team coming in to harvest her organs. If you're here to pray over her, last rites, or something, make it quick.

"Well, she's not a Jane Doe. Her name's Mallory. She disappeared last night, and we just located her. All her friends are on the way here. Like this nurse, Diana Faulkner, she should be here in fifteen minutes, or so."

"She came in with no ID! Makes her a Jane Doe. Unless you have her Driver's License or something on you."

"Okay, no I don't, but I've known her since she was little. She's a member of my church. Her purse was stolen by the girl who threw her down into that mine. Her dad was against organ transplants, and I'm sure Mallory is, too. Especially since she's still alive, and in need of all of hers, herself. Would you please administer aid to her? Mrs. Faulkner was thinking she would need fluids, and treatment for Pneumonia."

John was sure his words would have some meaning; this was unreal. The most unreal of any of it, yet. "Why don't you get in there, or have someone hook up an I.V.? Get that tape cut off her so she can stretch out. Please, tell them to try to help her. Aren't you bound by law, or something? I can call her attorney. She doesn't have an advance directive not to use 'heroics'. She's barely eighteen; she has her whole life ahead of her."

"Come in here." Wilson's order, as he ripped the suit coat from the girl. "Her skin's shot! Skin's a vital organ. She's been in mess with her skin torn to pieces. You have no idea the bacteria that have already invaded her body. Look at her veins. Compromised by the trussing and the severity of the dehydration. No one could get a line started, if they wanted to. You're right about the Pneumonia. And her core temperature is ninety-six. She'll go into Atrial Fib as soon as she starts to warm up. She doesn't have enough skin left to attach a heart monitor! Her life isn't ahead of her. It's over! You can't stop us from harvesting."

"My name is Mallory, and I refuse to allow my organs to be donated. I want my mother, and could I please have a blanket?" A swollen, disfigured mouth moved, as the voice came, barely audible.

Kenneth Wilson pulled a blanket up over her from its folds at the foot of the bed. "Confused, rambling speech! One of the symptoms of Hypothermia."

"John! JOHN!" Bransom's voice from the phone Anderson still held. "Erik are you hearing this? This is unbelievable."

"Yeah, let me talk to that guy!"

Dr. Wilson refused to discuss anything further with anyone.

"I've told you more information that you're entitled to, as only the woman's pastor. I'm in charge of this facility. Please leave before I notify security."

⊰ ⊱

Summers met the GeoHy chopper as it touched down at the site of the ministry headquarters building. He was the only one available to get the Faulkners from the chopper to the hospital. He was worried about leaving Sylvia in the charge of anyone else. If her mom got her out, there really wasn't a death squad waiting. Only him! He didn't want to miss his chance! He was doubly grim as he transported Daniel and Diana. Hearing Erik briefing the couple wasn't helping his frame of mind. Maybe he could eliminate Sylvia Brown, and this crazy doctor, before they could stop him.

A voice inserted itself. Maybe he was too busy planning to take matters into his own hands to remember to trust God.

"Faulkner, maybe you should pray again. Then, I'll walk in there with you. I can arrest that doctor, if I need to."

Daniel and Diana had been praying, but another prayer, in accord with the ABI agent, couldn't hurt.

They were on their way in as security was ushering John Anderson out. Summers showed his badge, and the hospital guard backed away.

367

Escorted by Ivan, Diana gained access to Mallory. Trained to deal with gruesome sites, it still took every fiber of discipline instilled by her training, not to gasp in revulsion. Tears flowed down her cheeks.

"Mallory, Mallory, it's Diana. How are you doing? Here comes some Oxygen. It will help you feel better. We can't do too much for your pain until we figure out how much tranquilizer's still in your system."

The only response was the barest movement, followed by another weak attempt to gag and cough the sickening sludge from lungs and stomach. Diana deftly turned the girl's head to the side.

"That's the way! That's the way. Cough it up. Get it out. Okay, here we go." An Oxygen mask settled onto her face. A face, raw, bruised, and swollen. Diana's scissors chopped away the tape that had lodged beneath the girl's chin. Most of it was stuck hopelessly in the mass of filthy hair.

"My hands--"

"Sh-h-h, don't talk Mallory. Just breathe the Oxygen. We need to get fluids started, then we'll get to work on some of that tape. Get your hands freed. I know you're really uncomfortable." Diana's gloved hand patted the dirty head.

Periphery veins for an I.V. were out of the question. Running a line into her chest seemed like the best option. Diana actually had no authority, and the ER staff seemed hesitant to go against the orders already issued by Dr. Wilson.

"Is there anyone here who can get a drip started?"

"I can do it, Miss Diana. You taught me, remember?" A beautiful young black girl was by their side.

"She can't! She's just an aid!" From the nursing shift supervisor.

Diana's blue eyes met the gaze of the brown eyes shining from a lovely, coffee-hued face. She had trained some of the nursing students in Nairobi. She was sorry she didn't recognize the name on the ID badge. Many nurses arriving from third world countries had trouble getting opportunity to take State Board exams and be certified as RN's. The 'aid' status didn't bother Diana.

"I can do it." Calm, dignified, self-confidence.

"Okay, let's get a spot scrubbed off." Diana was already dousing an area on Mallory's chest with strong antibacterial soap. She seemed unconscious once more, although her body continued with the involuntary shivering.

"Mallory, can you hear me?"

A stir of response, swollen eyelids tried to open.

Diana was cutting pieces of tape as her protége placed everything else in readiness.

"Honey!" Daniel's voice from the doorway. "Suzanne and Erik are here." His first glimpse of Mallory! He nearly knocked the newcomers down, in his attempt to bolt away. They managed to enter the room in spite of him.

"Mallory, I'm here. I got here as quick as I could. Shannon's here, too. He's been staying with me while we waited to hear. The roads are real bad." If Suzanne was repulsed by her shattered daughter, her performance was world-class.

Tears slid onto the disfigured face. "Mom." Mallie wanted to discuss the ruined suit and messed up car, but the weak, "Mom" was all she could manage

"We're getting ready to start a line. It's going to hurt. We need to find someone to help hold her." Diana's breathless voice. Finding a vein was going to take a miracle. Mallory couldn't jerk!

"I'll help." Mallie felt Bransom's iron hands clamp onto her head and one of her shoulders. "Hold real still, Honey. Don't move. This is gonna hurt some, but then you'll feel better."

The cold of alcohol, with the strong smell. The room tensed! A howl of pain erupted from Mallory, but she stayed amazingly still. The bore slid in, then back slightly. Tape! Tape! Tape! The room relaxed. It was a victory! A small one; but a victory all the same!

Chapter 34: *WITHSTANDING*

With the hydrating drip going, the nurses requested orders for strong I.V. antibiotics. Dr. Wilson, extremely reluctant to order the drugs, once again pointed out the hopelessness of the situation.

"Miss O'Shaughnessy has excellent insurance, and enough money for additional costs. Please, can we do everything possible?" Usually Diana could get her way. She knew the doctor was right about the prognosis; she still couldn't understand his attitude. She was shocked when John confided that Wilson had actually spoken about harvesting Mallory's organs in her hearing.

At an impasse with the ER doctor, they held a prayer meeting in the small chapel. Diana continued to tend her patient, turning her attention to the massive tape job, compliments of Sylvia. Diana's first concern wasn't for the condition of Mallie's hands and feet. She was pretty sure she wouldn't survive at all. Warmed blankets were bringing her body temp up, and they had managed to attach EKG probes to monitor her heart.

The tape wouldn't pull loose from itself, or from the skin. Of a brand specifically designed for repairs needing a powerful bond, the label cautioned against its making skin contact.

Malahna chopped Mallory's dirty mop of hair short, to remove the impossible tape still circling Mallory's head, then dropped the mass into an evidence bag supplied by Ivan Summers.

Diana, using a scalpel, was slitting the thick tape layers with vertical slits, in an attempt at restoring circulation. Finally, she loosed the bonds slightly which connected hands and ankles behind the patient's back. With hours of pressure on joints, tendons, and ligaments, it was actually better to let them ease back to normal gradually. Peeling the tape away, bringing skin with it, wasn't an option; too much skin was already compromised.

"Are we going to get any antibiotics started?" Malahna's soft question to Diana.

⊣┤ ┟⊢

Dr. Helenne Kincaid and a physician assistant managed to reach the tiny town of Murfreesboro. Concerned after Diana's calls to her, she had braved the storm to see what she could do for Mallory O'Shaughnessy. When she and the assistant entered the trauma center, they were shocked by the sight before them.

Her trained eye immediately took in the I.V. bag. "You don't have antibiotics and painkillers going, Diana?"

"Dr. Kincaid!" Tears of relief filled Diana's blue eyes. "We don't! It's kind of a long story. What do you recommend for both lungs and wounds?"

"Brought the latest and best for lungs. It should help fight other bacteria." Dr. Kincaid's words, as Jerry, her assistant began piggybacking it into the drip.

"Do you remember me, Mallory?"

An agonized movement in acknowledgement.

"She been scanned yet? Bet she has some rib fractures. Her pressure's amazingly good; surprised she doesn't have internal injuries. Looks like every bone in her face must be broken, although she might sustain swelling like that from soft tissue injuries. She really bounced around with no way to protect herself. We need to get a good plastic surgeon to stitch these lacerations. Dirt's really ground in everywhere, isn't it?"

Diana frowned slightly. "Yeah, I'd like to get her soaking in an antibiotic whirlpool. Maybe this tape soaks off. We don't want to get her in water yet, in case she arrests and we have to shock her. We need blood work, too, so we can tell if the horse-tranquilizer's out of her system."

"Horse tranquilizer! What on earth happened?"

"Well, we're not sure about everything. This girl used tranquilizers she stole from a stable, to overcome Mallory. Then she applied these yards and yards of tape while Mallie was helpless. At some point in time, Sylvia took Mallory's jacket, boots, some of her other clothing items, and shoved her down into a mine pit. Mallory was in there for hours, in and out of this

371

icy swamp water, evidently trying to climb out, but bouncing back down. I hope her Tetanus vaccines are current."

⧓ ⧗

Terrified and in agony, Mallory hovered on the edge of consciousness. She was aware of her mother and Diana. She could remember Erik's holding her down, and telling her to hold still for the I.V. She couldn't remember seeing Daniel. She was worried again that he would be mad at her. For not calling Janet to walk with her; for checking what she thought was someone in distress! And, it wasn't like she just totally dummied in. Her drawn pistol was in her hand. Then, something stabbed into her lower leg, and her gun clattered from her hand as she sank into oblivion.

Tears rolled down her face. She was worried about David. When, she had come, to slightly, she was still in the janitor's closet with Sylvia, bound and with her valuable clothing removed. Sylvia's words seemed jumbled. Something, that they had to stay hidden where they were until the hallway cameras turned off at nine. Sylvia had used the moments of her victim's lucidness to inflict mental torment along with the physical. Claiming she and David were in love, but now David wanted to stay in Mallory's good graces because of her money. On and on she had ranted. David said this; David said that.

But some of the time, Sylvia was also threatening to 'get even' with David. She was going to do something to his horse. Then, while he was still suffering over that, she had 'plans' for him, too.

Mallie wanted to say lots of stuff. To apologize to Daniel, to get Pastor's suit and car replaced, to warn David, to make hasty provision for a will. She thought if she died now, everything would go to her mom. She had to stay alive and keep everything going the direction of her daddy's plan. Besides, she didn't want Dr. Ghoul-little to get her organs. Whenever she attempted to speak, her dry, swollen mouth wouldn't cooperate. Everyone kept shushing her, ordering her to rest.

⧓ ⧗

David, acutely aware of the happenings at the nearby hospital, was staying in the loop via Shannon. Shannon was warning him to stay away because Mallie looked so hideous, but David was staying away because his childish stupidity had caused the whole thing! He never should have brought Sylvia back out of the woodwork. He should have insisted the break-in at the stable was important. He should have stopped what was coming, since he was the one who started it!

Now, Tammi was at the stable with him. *Capitan* had returned to the stable from the Sonic, and *Star* hadn't gone far after Sylvia opened each stall. Tammi told him the whole saga of Sylvia and the Sonic, of his horse's not rearing when she honked, but that Summers lights and sirens had done the trick. She was trying to be funny, describing Sylvia's plummet to the pavement. His heart was too heavy. She could afford to be giddy; Kerry was off the hook.

⚔ ⚔

The FBI took Sylvia off Summer's hands. Kidnapping was their jurisdiction, and the abduction crossed state lines from Texas into Arkansas. The roads were being sanded along some of the worst stretches. FBI agents were at the mine pit, searching the crime-scene there. Actually, Anderson should have photographed where Mallory was and exactly where and how he found her. The pastor had objected to the photos that were necessary at the hospital.

Still, Mallie's underground torment was being reconstructed, blood, tissue, strips of fabric, revealed exactly where the girl had tumbled twice to the bottom, the route she had laboriously ascended, other indications of her pulling herself up a layer or two to escape the water. The effort hadn't gained her freedom, but maybe the exertion had helped combat the hypothermia. It was tough to tell.

The Federal Judge, Antoine Martine had called Erik, explaining, "This was my idea, to try to set a trap and snag some of the leaders in an Eastern European gang. Ryland O'Shaughnessy, the Malovich twins, Merrill Adams; were all players in the Boston area, doing the bidding of others. Your Col. Ahmir has been invaluable, and we have made amazing progress. I feel like Sylvia is doomed now, because they'll get to her, whether she's in prison, or on the outside. I never intended to involve her, but she's been drawn to dangerous types. I guess when she was such a willing player, they involved her to use as leverage against me. I let Oscar and Otto out on bond so they would flee the country. They did mess up for leading us to people in the next level of the organization. I wouldn't be surprised if they've both been eliminated, but I have no proof that they have been."

Erik came back in, "I can't tell what you're asking me to do for your daughter. Where's her dad, if ya don't mind my askin'."

A sad sigh. "I'm one that thought with my savvy, and my education, I would set the world on fire as a single mother. I had a good income, so I had a baby. I know nothing about the guy. I thought the clinic had a good screening process. Do you think it's a genetic tendency people have to do the things Sylvia's doing?"

"Well, I know as a Federal Judge, you deal with criminals from across the spectrum: criminals come from every socio-economic background, every race. I believe the Bible. That every person has been born with a sinful nature. It takes training from the time a child is very small, to teach them about caring for others, teaching them to get along, not be totally self-centered. Unspeakably evil!

Ms. Martine didn't agree with the Bible and sin-nature stuff, but she left her daughter in custody.

Niqui arrived to relieve Diana, and Dr. Kincaid left Terry to oversee the patient. The two women left together for the Anderson's, to rest and clean up before returning to keep their vigil. Mallory was stable, for the time being, but both medical professionals acutely aware that her condition would continue to deteriorate. The Pneumonia, already evident before the abduction, was a serious concern. Then, the aspirating vomit and swampy water in the intervening hours. No one was certain why the girl's brain wasn't swelling faster than it was. Maybe the cold had slowed the swelling.

᛬ ᛭

John and Daniel talked softly in a corner of the cafeteria, sipping coffee, receiving updates on the patient. Bransom, off the phone from the Federal Judge, poured a cup of coffee, joining them.

"Well, Ms. Martine's letting us book her daughter into custody. She's pretty shocked her daughter went so far. She's afraid, too, Sylvia's at risk for a gangland execution. She's probably right about that."

He was about to cry, and his two friends looked like they'd been drug through a knothole backwards.

His voice filled with raw emotion, "Sorry, you had to be the one to go find her, John. Sorry to take my frustrations out on you. Good thing Tammi was at Sonic when she was. Then, when it dawned on me about that mine, you were just the closest. And, I didn't want David with you when you found her."

"Well, I didn't have lightning-like responses! It was like, I didn't believe you, just this sense of unreality! I'm glad that's not my job on a daily basis. I don't know how you do it. Then, I got her here, and I thought, well, she'll be alright now. I can hand her over to professionals that know how to take care of her. They'll get her untied and warmed up. I didn't even have a knife or anything to cut her loose with. And you were telling me just to hurry and get her transported here! No ambulances were available." His voice broke into sobs. "And that Dr. Wilson didn't want to do anything for her. He thought she was just some *Jane Doe*. Maybe he didn't realize Mallie was still as aware of everything as she was. Mallory told him her name, and that she didn't want to donate her organs, and he said that was 'incoherent rambling due to hypothermia'. Does that sound like incoherent rambling, to you?"

"No," Faulkner's agreement. "Kerry has a court order, now, for everything possible to be done medically. All heroics, resuscitation, life-support. He thinks maybe with the pressure of the media and society to donate organs, that we should make a counter-offensive. 'If you prefer not to be an organ donor, it doesn't mean you're an awful person.' As a nurse, Diana sees both sides. Wonderful outcomes that sound light and bright. But, there's an evil side to the story. I mean, this morning, Dr. Wilson was the self-appointed judge and jury, condemning Mallory to death, just because she looked like a mess."

"Well, I think a patient should be able to walk into a 'care' establishment, expecting aid to the full extent possible." Erik's thoughts, measured carefully. "I know it's expensive though. Many hospitals and clinics turn people away if they can't prove they can pay, with insurance, or some way. I wouldn't have wanted Mallory turned away. I don't want some creep licking his chops for a set of eighteen-year-old organs, either. That's macabre. There are laws in place against this happening, but not always enough oversight. I wonder how many doctors, who know their patients who are waiting for organs, would be willing to sacrifice someone they don't know, someone who looks bad, someone who shows for treatment, not looking to be a functioning member of society. 'This one should slip away, so the one I know to be worthy, can live.' Pretty powerful position to be in."

"It's scary." Anderson hadn't recovered yet. "I still shudder to think what would have happened if you and Diana hadn't showed up when you did. He did not want an I.V. started!"

"Well, Diana's still trying to be fair to him. He didn't think one could be started! Usually if anyone can get one to go in, it's Diana. I don't know if we still might not lose Mallory, but that line in; that girl who got it; that's a miracle!" Daniel swiped at tears.

"Well, you and Diana are more charitable than I am, and I'm a pastor, and being charitable is part of my job. But, when the I.V. was started, he wouldn't order any antibiotics. He's trying to self-fulfill his prophecy that Mallie won't make it. Diana explained that Mallie has insurance and money, but Mallie's just getting antibiotics because that respected Pulmonary specialist showed up. I guess that's another miracle, but I still just want to go punch that so-called Dr. Wilson."

Lana joined them, managing a light laugh. "Discretion might be the better part of valor, John. Remember, this is a small town. You pastor the townspeople; preach self-control; you're a hospital chaplain here."

He laughed in response. "Aside from that, give me one good reason why I can't."

⚔ ⚔

Mallory's temperature reached normal, then continued rising. Fever due to the infection. A fever reducer joined the other intravenous meds.

⚔ ⚔

As word spread and the icy roads improved, people thronged the little hospital. Dr. Wilson was shocked. Maybe the disgusting-looking female really was a person! With friends and family. He retreated to the Administrative office, tuning in CNN. The story of Mallory was top-of-the hour, Headline news. The picture they were showing of the CEO, was of a ravishingly beautiful young woman. How could he have been expected to tell that?

Friends and relatives arriving at the hospital joined various impromptu prayer groups, but none were allowed to see Mallory. She remained critical. And Diana could be ferocious with her protectiveness. She passed updates to Daniel, who passed the information along. Mostly, there was no change! The beautiful patient looked like a hideous mess! Swollen, bloated, covered with deep bruises, oozing serum through a coating of muck! Her lungs sounded awful! The fever continued creeping higher!

⚔ ⚔

David cleaned up at his parents' house. No one was home. Even the little kids were at the hospital, keeping vigil. He shaved again, and pulled on freshly creased jeans with a black *Niagara Falls* sweatshirt. He tied the laces of some new boots received for Christmas. He was relegating his cowboy boots to work clothes for the construction jobs, and riding. He tousled his hair around, surveying the effects. He knew Mallie was way too sick to care what he looked like, but he was hoping to pass inspection with the Faulkners, Bransom, and his dad. He fought tears! He knew he wouldn't be allowed to see her! He had no right to ask!

He stepped out into the frigid night air. The wind had finally died down, at least. In his truck, he turned on a CD, and started to back around to pull out forward through the gate onto the highway. Starting to hum along with one of his favorite songs helped him remember something. He threw the truck into park and raced back into the darkened house. Back in his truck, he was in the hospital parking lot within minutes. A crowded parking lot! Everybody loved Mallory! She was hard not to love.

The small, hospital gift-shop was locked, with the usual sign, a clock, set with the projected opening time. Didn't mean a thing! The shop was always locked. No place in town to get flowers or anything. It would be lame, anyway.

Knots of people stood around, weeping, eyes swollen. A pain stabbed through his heart that she must be gone! His last update had been that she was the same; but she was so critical!

His dad strode toward him. "Where have you been all day? Good of you to show up! Tammi said you were out earlier, checking on your horse! Are you ever going to get your head on straight?"

David shoved his hands into his jean pockets and shrugged, hoping he could do better with Erik and Daniel. He had kind of figured whatever he did would be wrong! Being eighteen wasn't easy. By the time you figured one thing out, something new cropped up. At least he could always count on his dad's yelling at him. He hung his head. He hadn't been anywhere! Just driving, listening to his music, praying, and checking updates. He hadn't come earlier because he figured they'd kick him out, just like they were about to do now.

377

Faulkner emerged from the corridor that led to patient rooms; evidently with another report, joining John and signaling for Bransom to join them.

"Well, they think she's been warmed up long enough, that if she was going to arrest or go into atrial fib, it would have happened by now. That's good news. I can see the relief on Diana and Niqui's faces. They can't decide whether to try to clean her up a bit now, or not 'rock the boat'. Nausea and vomiting are still a problem: hurts her real bad, keeping her a little dehydrated in spite of the fluid replacement. Dr. Kincaid thinks the vomiting might be helping her, though, to get the tranquilizer out of her system.

David heard the report, but the three men moved away from him like he wasn't there, conversing among themselves. John still noticed when his son left.

⊰ ⊱

Between coughing and vomiting episodes, Mallory lay quietly, listening to whispers. She couldn't see. Her eyelids were so swollen by now, that she couldn't force them to open at all. Tears squeezed out, rolling freely. With her hands still bound to her ankles, she had no way to dab at the stream. Her entire face, bruised, swollen beyond belief, looked monstrous! The pain was awful if she attempted to speak, or even to smile. Vile odors assailed her nostrils, and she knew she reeked of vomit, waste, and muck. She had heard that people with poor hygiene managed to become insensitive to their own odor. She wished that would happen; she was pretty sure the smell was contributing to her feeling so nauseated.

⊰ ⊱

The hour was late as David drove toward Sonic. The town didn't offer much for amenities. Without his realizing it, he pulled into the slot Sylvia had pulled into on *El Capitan*, earlier in the day. He pushed the red button and ordered: "Lots of whatever they could get out to him quick, before they closed." The 'closing' shift usually hated last minute stragglers, in their eagerness to close on time. Now, they realized David was here for Mallie's friends keeping anxious vigil at the hospital. They turned all the fryers back on high, filling large bags with anything edible they could throw together. They didn't even both totaling it to charge to David's card. With bags and bags of sandwiches, burritos, fries, and tater-tots, he headed back to the hospital. Loading up with as much of the stash as possible, he made his way through the automatic doors just before the front entrance closed for the night. Bransom relieved him of the bags, and he jogged back out, pulling around to the ER entrance to ferry in another armload. Daniel met him, gathering up the remaining bags from the passenger seat.

"Wow, David, thanks for thinking of this. Great idea! I guess Hope's the closest place for food, once Sonic closes. Everybody's been too worried to think of food. Now it smells great!"

David nodded. He never knew what to say to the guy.

In the lobby, many of the prayer warriors were refusing the food. Alvie and her two friends were leaving for Hope to get a hotel room. They were from Mallie's new church in Dallas. They planned to come back in the morning, and didn't want to eat the food that people needed who were staying. The Haynes, Sanders, Watsons, were all heading home, too, after securing promises of updates.

Niqui sat by Mallory's bed while Suzanne and Diana broke for some nourishment. Erik and John pumped change into vending machines to supply coffee and soft drinks. David sat alone, hungry, but waiting to see if any of the food was left. Daniel and Diana, arms filled with wrappers of whatever they could grab, joined him. Nervously, he waited for them to tell him to hit the road.

"Here, David, here's some kind of Super Sonic cheeseburger. You want fries or tater-tots? I like either, so you pick." Diana proffering the food. "Are you okay?" She unwrapped a breakfast burrito, taking a bite.

"Yes, Ma'am, I'm fine." Beyond that, he didn't know what to say.

Daniel stretched, unwrapping a burger slowly, deliberately. "David, there's no way you could have seen this coming! I mean, when you invited a girl to Homecoming. I was mad at you about that; but the girl's being such a lunatic isn't your fault. When you heard her threats, later, you passed them along. We all blew it! Again! Summers has her phone and laptop; we didn't ask, but he volunteered the info that she was more into you than you are to her."

David guessed he was glad that they were being so nice! He felt so horrible about everything that he almost wished they'd tell him off and order him to get out!

"Mallory's worried about you. I guess part of the time when she was conscious, Sylvia did plenty of ranting and raving," Diana's voice, covered at the end by a yawn.

Paula Rae Wallace

The teen still couldn't believe the whole twenty-four hours. He wished it was him! Wished it was his horse! It shouldn't be Mallory.

"Can I see her?" his voice broke.

"No." He had asked Diana, but Daniel answered. "Believe me, you don't want to see her tonight." Daniel's anguished eyes reflected his horror of catching a glimpse her.

David's eyes met Diana's pretty blue ones. "I think she wants to see you, but I know she doesn't want you to see her like she is. We decided to wait until morning to even start cleaning her up. I'll tell her you're here, waiting. David, it's bad, though. She's pretty shattered! Emotionally, as well as physically. She might never again be the girl you've known. You need to prepare yourself for that." Diana's voice broke, in spite of her professionalism.

"You're trying to warn me she might lose her hands and feet?"

"I'm trying to warn you that we just do not know."

"I brought an iPod. She might enjoy listening to her music."

Nodding, Diana took the device. They finished eating in silence before Diana disappeared back down the corridor.

Chapter 35: WAIKIKI

The Faulkners were forced to admit that David knew Mallory! The close bond between the two since early elementary, would become evident, time and time again. Her favorite songs playing softly through the iPod, almost immediately soothed her distress. Her pain was still terrible, and infection raged, but her improved emotional state gave everyone hope that the girl could overcome the physical problems they feared she would deal with for the rest of her life.

Morning brought an assault on the filth and grime. A cosmetic surgeon trimmed dead skin from four or five of the nastiest gashes, making repairs with fine, internal stitches, using local anesthesia. Deep gashes on chin, forehead, upper arms, and torso, which were already oozing from infection, cleaned and repaired.

When they were able to get a body-scan, it revealed rib fractures and a fractured jaw. Taping her, to strengthen the ribs, and ease discomfort, was out of the question! No way to apply tape to the raw flesh! Other breaks in some of the smaller facial bones would probably mend without too much disfigurement, but they explained the swelling and pain. Diana and Dr. Kincaid asked that a feeding tube be inserted. No way their patient would be able to eat any time soon. Dr. Wilson questioned the advisability of it, explaining that such life-saving methods were easy to put into place, but complicated to terminate.

He was making everyone mad, except for Diana. The nurse in her, respecting the authority and knowledge of doctors, could relate to his opinion. He was young, lacking tact and experience.(No bedside manner, whatsoever). But he had a valid point. Surely, Mallory's brain would still swell; the injuries couldn't just be facial! Could they? It didn't seem likely.

So, if they inserted a feeding tube, and Mallory wound up brain-dead, her body might survive, draining everyone who was involved with caring for such a burden.

The friends and relatives who were assembled held another prayer meeting for wisdom. The doctor seemed to think they were engaging in some *Middle Ages*-type superstition. He was furious when they planned to go ahead with the nourishment.

It wasn't the first time Pastor John Anderson had heard his beliefs ridiculed, but he was tired, hungry, and he still smelled like a swamp! In spite of Lana's warning of the previous day, he delivered a jab! Wilson hit the floor!

Erik Bransom was shocked. It was probably his job to step in, get John arrested for assault, do something! But, he was tired, too. It wasn't enough to rescue Mallory from the 'bad guys', but now the supposed 'good guys' posed a threat. It was like a training exercise, where targets pop up, and you make lightning-fast decisions whether to shoot or not.

The head nurse rang for security, but Bransom's Federal badge sent them back to the break-room. He and Faulkner lifted the limp doctor onto an empty gurney in one of the trauma rooms. In a few minutes, Wilson started to come to.

Once again, the thought crossed Bransom's mind that he would lose the privilege of being an agent. He went ahead, anyway. Hanging Wilson's stethoscope around his own neck, he surveyed him studiously, using his most doctor-like stance. "Nurse, this guy looks in bad shape to me. Pretty sure he won't make it. Why don't you order a team to come harvest his organs? He can probably save lots of good people. Get an O.R. ready, and stand by."

Evidently, Bransom was the only one who found himself amusing, so he gave it up. Dr. Kenneth Wilson got the point, though!

Mallory was glad for the sponge-bath. Diana's soft voice alerted her to each touch, each procedure that was coming. The iPod helped, but she was enraged by the limitations! She couldn't see, couldn't talk, couldn't free her hands and feet of the bonds! Each time the bond between her hands and feet was loosened, it brought fresh pain, rather than the relief she craved. Tears continued to slide into her hair, soaking her pillowcase. Tears which washed more dirt from beneath the swollen eyelids. The dirt was ground in everywhere. Dr. Kincaid was eager to relocate the patient to Dallas. Most of the lab work they needed had to be farmed out. The small facility, better than nothing for trauma, was still lacking. She called in an ophthalmologist from her Dallas office-complex, concerned her patient might lose her vision. Strangely, the pressure inside Mallie's cranial cavity, though elevated slightly, had leveled off. Kincaid, an agnostic, noted to herself that miracles were happening. Probably coincidentally to the prayer groups' petitions.

"Mallory, would you like for David or Daniel to shop for more songs?" Diana's inquiry, as the same menu played and replayed.

"Mm-mm!" barely audible from a face immobilized with swelling and pain. "Psalms!" Croaky-sounding, barely intelligible. Communicating wasn't worth the effort.

Diana patted her on the shoulder, causing her to jerk at the unexpected touch.

"I'm sorry I keep startling you. You want the book of Psalms installed? I'm sure we can get that done for you, and get you hooked right back up."

She could feel Diana's gloved hands, pulling the earpieces free. Every time her hair was disturbed at all, the stench wafted to her nostrils. At least, she hadn't thrown up in awhile. She understood why they preferred not to touch the nasty mess for a shampoo! If she could just get her hands free, she could do it for herself. More tears!

⊰ ⊱

Delia and Shay arrived. Shay still got panic attacks from hospitals. Staying in communication with David, he was aware that Diana wasn't allowing many visitors in to view the gruesomeness that was his cousin. He was praying to be banned, himself. He couldn't stand the thought, let alone the reality! He didn't want his grandmother to see Mallie, either. It was all too much!

Daniel Faulkner greeted them with a hug. "Diana went back to the Anderson's house for some rest and then to get cleaned up. She hasn't been allowing too many visitors in." His voice was emotional and apologetic.

"Daniel Faulkner, I came to visit my granddaughter!" Delia O'Shaughnessy was a sweetheart, but she could get feisty!

"Grandmother!" Shay's soft tone. He knew he never won in arguments with her; well, she was usually right. But he hated to see her throw a fit now, to be able to see something she could never erase from her memory!

He figured if she barged in there, he should go too, offer his strong arm! But, he'd probably faint, and she would have to drag him out. His stomach was churning, and he was only as far as the lobby.

Something in his stricken face silenced her, and she allowed herself to be led to a seat, a Styrofoam cup of tea urged into her diamond-sparkled hands.

⚜ ⚜

Kerry's eyes scanned the group of people in the hospital lobby. A happy grin spread across his face as his eyes met Tammi's, in spite of the gravity of the situation. Having worked out some of the requested legal necessities, he was quite perturbed to hear about the clocking of the physician. He guessed he should be grateful for job security.

Tammi was tragically beautiful! She had spent the night at the hospital, then gone home to shower and change. In less than an hour, she was back. Of course, she had known Kerry was on his way, too.

After his broad smile of acknowledgement, he joined the group of men: Eric, Daniel, John, David, Shay and Shannon, who still encircled Delia.

"Okay, here are the advanced directives." Kerry proffering the documents. "Hopefully, everything makes it plain enough that we all want medical treatment, and aren't eager and willing to have our organs up for grabs! Am I still in the United States?"

"No! You're in Arkansas!" Delia's turn to be cryptic.

"Are you sure Boston's better?" Daniel's repartee.

"I hope so, but to be on the safe side, let me see the directive about me. Someone may see my age and mistakenly think I'm old! I might not have much of a chance, even in Boston, without everything spelled out! Do I need to sign it in blood? Do you think that would be macabre enough?"

A chuckle erupted from the group for the first time in over thirty-six hours.

Delia was glad to add some levity to the somber group, but her mother's heart hadn't forgotten! One year ago today, she had received the inconceivable news that her younger son, Patrick Shay O'Shaughnessy, had passed away in Murfreesboro, Arkansas!

⚜ ⚜

Psalm 121:1&2 I will lift up mine eyes unto the hills, from hence cometh my help.
My help cometh from the LORD, which made heaven and earth.

Mallory continued to lie as quietly as possible, listening to the comforting words of the Psalms. There had been some interruptions. A feeding tube's being placed: an eye exam, after which irrigation and eye salve were prescribed She continued to cry, from the irritants to the sensitive eye tissue, and from the blows she continued to receive. For someone who tried to be nice, and do what's right, and please the Lord, it didn't make sense. More tears, accompanied by sobs that came, even though they intensified the pain in her ribs! And everywhere else!

⊹ ⊹

Daniel picked Diana up from the Anderson's where she had napped and showered.

"Where are you taking me, Daniel Faulkner? I need to get back to Mallory."

He kissed her hand. "Mallie's okay for now. You have once more, performed heroically. Niqui's there, and Kerry has all the legal stuff filed. He talked to Wilson to stave off a lawsuit from him. I'm taking the most beautiful and amazing woman in the world to McKenna's for a steak. Don't argue, Beautiful and Amazing Woman!"

Her laughter bubbled up. "Guess it's settled then. A steak does sound good! You care if I order the *Lumberjack Special*? I guess I am starved. I never knew Drive-in food could taste so good until David showed up with bags of stuff last night."

He cut her a sharp, sideways glance. "Is that the last time you've eaten? You worry me. Your folks and mine are coming later with the kids. Maybe you shouldn't keep nursing Zave."

"Well, it wasn't my idea, necessarily, not to eat today. But when I got to the Andersons, I was more tired than hungry. I hate to just help myself, at someone else's house."

"I know! But, they wouldn't have the house or the groceries without Mallie, and you were here, again, to help keep her alive!"

"I wish Pastor hadn't punched Dr. Wilson." Diana changed the subject.

Her husband coughed to stifle a laugh. "I know! I wanted to do it! Everybody else always gets to have all the fun!"

⊣ ⊢

Mallory, aware of the date, the anniversary of her daddy's death, was pretty overcome with the recent trauma. She remembered, vaguely, her worry about spending the day alone. She couldn't remember why that prospect had created dread. Now, she wished she could be whole, and well, able to function on her own. She didn't want to lose her hands and feet, making impossible demands on the Faulkners from now on. She tried to pray, or concentrate on the Psalms playing softly in her ears. She kept falling asleep, only to jerk awake, sending fresh spasms of pain throughout her body.

"Mallory, it's Niqui." Gentle hands touched her, checking the I.V., the feeding tube, rubbing lightly on her hands and feet. "Your extremities don't have good color, but better than we really expected. I need to work some more on cleaning and treating these skinned up areas. I know it hurts. I am so sorry."

She was right about that! Howls and moans escaped from Mallory, despite her attempts at bravery..

Niqui paused. The hardest part of Mallie to look at was her mouth. Swollen from her biting it, and bouncing against the hard, mine levels, her lips were barely discernible.

Scabs and ground-in dirt made the gaping orifice look even more hideous. At first, they couldn't tell if her teeth were knocked out, broken off, or just obliterated by the intense swelling of her gums. The agents combing the mine pit hadn't found any teeth; the scan didn't reveal that she had inadvertently swallowed a tooth or two. Niqui studied the scan once more; something they hadn't looked for earlier. Her teeth were still in place. If they were chipped and damaged when the swelling absorbed, implants and veneers could easily restore the beautiful smile. For the moment, though, everything seemed hopeless.

A soft rustle and hint of delectable fragrance alerted Mallory's senses that Diana was back, even before she heard her voice. "I'm back, Mallory." She checked everything for herself, recently checked by her sister. "Dr. Kincaid returned to Dallas, but she's keeping eyes and ears on you. I was afraid to suggest something to her that I knew for sure Dr. Wilson would be against. Most doctors are. Surprisingly, Dr. Kincaid has studied it, and feels it's the best option for your treatment. You are of legal age to decide, so I'll explain it to you. Then you can just *Mm-hm,* or *hunh-uh.* Can you understand me?"

"Mm-hm."

"Okay, it's an age-old remedy, and a Biblical remedy. Many folk remedies get accepted when people recognize their effectiveness; still, conventional medicine often opposes. Dr. Kincaid and I both want to treat you with honey. Applied to your wounds, and by mouth. I know Niqui's for it, because she's seen it be effective in Africa. We want to bathe you again, then place honey-soaked gauze all over you. The honey creates a barrier that inhibits infection, and somehow, it reacts with your plasma Promise to be as careful as we can."

Rivers of tears squeezed from her swollen eyes. Tears of relief! It was actually something she had heard of before on the History Channel. About Ancient Egypt and honey in the tombs, how honey resisted microbial action. That kept it from spoiling! Even when it was centuries old, it could be reconstituted to be edible, once more. The same ability to keep germs from growing, made wounds resistant to infection. "Mm-hm," she agreed readily. "Just keep the bears away." She tried to be funny, but trying to talk was excruciating.

Their attempts to cleanse the areas created unbearable pain.

"We may be grinding more germs and dirt in." Niqui finally broke the silence. "Let's just honey up the bandages and lay them on."

To Mallie's relief, Diana agreed. The bandages settled onto her almost imperceptibly.

"Did they put the drops in her eyes again yet?"

"No, they keep forgetting. Since all of her other meds are I.V., they have to keep being reminded about her eyes. Do you think we should use the honey in her eyes?" Niqui catching on.

"Okay, Mallory, do you like honey? I'm giving you a teaspoonful. Just let it go down. Now, I know your eyes feel bad, but I'm putting a little honey in them, too. It can't hurt them, and it is said to be a useful eye remedy. It's supposed to clear up *Conjunctivitis,* and even treat cataracts."

Mallory fell sound asleep, sleeping four hours before jerking awake. She slept through the Psalm she was specifically listening for. Diana restarted the Book. Mallory settled in; she could listen for chapter 121 again: she was going to be here awhile.

Helenne Kincaid was eager for every update, as she dealt with the health needs of her Dallas patients and fulfilled her responsibilities as a staff physician at one of the larger health-care institutions. On Saturday morning, she missed her country-club brunch and round of golf, in favor of returning to Murfreesboro to check Mallory O'Shaughnessy's progress, for herself. She wasn't eager to see Dr. Wilson.

The small-town medical fiasco was creating a national, medical circus. Wilson had attacked the highly esteemed pulmonologist for her part in the decision to try the "quack" treatment on her patient.

Dr. Kincaid refused to respond to the attack. She was hurt that, evidently, Diana had implicated her in the controversial treatment. Still hard, though, for her not to follow the opinions and updates. Finally, there came a medical opinion which brought a triumphant smile to her face. A senior faculty member of a highly esteemed medical school! Part of his response read:

"...One thing we can be certain about, is the fact that, undoubtedly the patient's treatment with honey did her far less harm than the harvesting of her organs would have! I suggest that doctors use every medical means at their disposal, to save the patient before them. When reasonable care has been administered, and a patient has expired, organ donation becomes a possibility....but not a demand."

She was already feeling better about the situation before entering Mallie's room. Dr. Helenne Kincaid was a tough woman, but she fought tears. Her patient's improvement was–phenomenal! She was trying to avoid the word, *miraculous.*

Mallie lay sleeping peacefully. At last rid of all the tape, her arms and legs still splayed out strangely. The Oxygen gurgled softly, but the girl's breathing sounded like music to the doctor's trained ear. The facial bruising and swelling created a scary, Halloween-mask effect. Still amazing how her face had swollen so, and her brain hadn't!

A tall, handsome, young man rose courteously as the doctor entered the room. "Hi, I'm David Anderson." A shy smile. He was trying to slip out past her. In case she needed to examine the patient.

She offered her hand. "Nice to meet you, David. She looks unbelievably better, don't you think so?"

Expressive brown eyes flashed Mallory's direction before returning to eye contact with the physician. A haunted, anguished expression distorted handsome features.

"I guess so. This morning's the first time I've been allowed to see her! If this is 'better', I'm glad I didn't see her before. I'm gonna go get a soft drink; can I bring you anything?"

"Give me about ten minutes; then maybe you can scare me up a cup of strong black coffee."

"Hello, Mallory?" She spoke just loudly enough to rouse the patient.

A weak attempt to stretch swollen lips into a smile of recognition. "Hi."

"Okay, I'm gonna listen to your chest." A sheet covered the girl lightly, beneath it, a hospital gown. An amazing thing. Wednesday afternoon, the girl couldn't bear for anything to touch her abraded flesh.

A nurse entered, greeting the doctor, offering information and assistance. Kincaid checked the I.V., asked about temperature and other vital signs. Amazing, amazing improvement in a short time. Hands and feet looked bad. The color, as well as the odd positioning. At first, everyone assumed the loss of the girl's limbs was a certainty. They were so sure she wouldn't survive at all, that the probability of amputation was hardly a concern. The extremities actually looked good now, considering! Could they be saved? Even one hand, or one foot salvaged, could be a tremendous boon. She listened carefully to the improved lungs, then to the pulses of the damaged extremities.

"Dr. Kincaid!" Diana Faulkner's joyous voice! "Don't you think she looks amazing? I want to promise you that neither Monique, nor I, mentioned your name in connection with the decision about the honey. I read Dr. Harmon's response to Wilson's rantings to Daniel.

He thought it was funny, but he still wants to finish what John Anderson started with Dr. Wilson."

"He is still a doctor." Kincaid's reprimand came stiffly.

"Yes he is," Diana agreed quickly. "And a member in good standing with the AMA!"

"There needs to be an organization like that!"

"Yes, Doctor." Diana didn't have any desire to quibble with the respected woman who was going beyond the call of duty to help Mallory. Probably the AMA was necessary; but sometimes it seemed too powerful, protecting those who should be exposed. Similar to the Catholic Church's Hierarchy protecting its people. Sometimes, there should be a reasonable limit.

Kincaid met her gaze suddenly; determined gray eyes hardened with resolve! "I guess I'm about to climb out on another professional limb. I don't care who you mention it to. What do you think about putting her in a hyperbaric chamber? If we only save one hand, or one foot, it's better than not trying! Like with the honey, there's nothing to lose by trying. Maybe there will be something to gain. It may help speed her overall healing, anyway.

Before the startled Diana could respond, a muffled voice came from the bed. "What~are~we~waiting~for?"

Diana's delighted laugh bubbled infectiously. "Where's David? He's supposed to be sitting with her. I need to get everything in place to transfer her to a better facility and get the chamber set up. Do you think Monday will be too soon?"

"Well, the rest of the weekend will tell. Provided no complications, she should be strong enough to transfer on Monday. You mean to Dallas?"

"I'm really thinking Honolulu! Can you manage to take a working vacation?"

Kincaid couldn't help a bemused chuckle. "You must mean chartered jet; hospital equipped. You know she can't handle a commercial jetliner yet, for that distance! Even in first class!"

Mallory's eyes, finally able to open, sparkled with tears and excitement! The volcano! She hadn't forgotten, but had been worried that everyone else had.

David returned, carrying a can of Dr. Pepper and large steaming coffee. "Mrs. Faulkner, can I get you something?"

"No thanks, Hon, I'm going out to the cafeteria for some lunch and to make some arrangements. Are you going to stay awhile longer? Stay out here a few seconds more while I make sure she'll be okay for awhile. Then, the nurse is still right here to help with anything she might need, and I'm a phone call away." She closed the door, checking on Mallie's personal needs, then encouraging her to drink more water and swallow another dose of honey.

When Erik and Suzanne relieved David of his watch, Mallory actually relaxed. Still not having seen what she looked like, she knew it wasn't a pretty sight. David wasn't much of one to sit still. She couldn't visit, and there was still a rift between them. A huge rift, that wasn't totally David's fault. One planted by hours of her lying helplessly bound, being forced to listen to the spouting of Sylvia Brown!

David switched her iPod from repeating the book of Psalms, to her music, with more of her new favorite songs added. Some of the songs, recorded the previous Easter Sunday evening, brought more tears. She loved the Faulkners' music, but the selections increased her longing for word about Cassandra.

Erik talked softly for a few minutes, updating her on the case, sharing new information. He told her about her Lynx jacket's being taken into evidence; something, that it would have her DNA, proving it was hers, and Sylvia's, proving Sylvia had taken it. She listened with mixed emotions. It was the first, cutest thing she had ever owned! And it was a gift from Diana! She had absolutely adored it, thinking Dallas would never have a day cold enough for her to wear it. But, now, she didn't care where it was! Or what happened to it! She certainly never intended to wear it again! Visitors kept telling her the story of Sylvia's arrival at Sonic that morning, wearing Mallie's stuff, riding David's horse. It was such a nightmare to her! Still so real, that she couldn't see anything humorous in it at all. Eriks' voice continued, sounding reassuring by its characteristic gruffness. Kerry and the Justice Department were intervening to prevent her jewelry's disappearing into "evidence". When he had remembered it, and started tracking it down, Summers was no help at all. Mallory's jewelry, taken by her captor, had never occurred to the Arkansas agent. At that moment, one of the ABI secretaries had brought in their coffee, sporting the fabulous nine carat Diamond ring. However innocent her 'trying it on', might have been, Erik arrested her. She had no right! Amazing how so many people seemed to think everything was up for grabs!

Then her mom's turn to talk, trying to update her on all the gossip. Suzanne told about the internet scandal between Dr. Wilson and Dr. Kincaid, and the crazy *Honey* course of treatment; about the prestigious doctor's comments that smearing honey on a patient would be more helpful than taking her organs.

Her mom's gossipy tendencies got on her nerves in the best of times. Now, tears and sobs broke free. Easy for her mom to laugh! She wasn't here! As usual! It wasn't funny! Sylvia wasn't funny; the creepy doctor with his terse assessment about her prognosis wasn't funny!

"Okay, Suzanne, maybe we should go. I think we're wearing her out. I'll sit with her while you let Diana know we're leaving." Erik's voice.

Diana lined up the trip for Hawaii: chartered jet, hospital bed, the usual emergency equipment. She hoped not to need it. The last thing she wanted was a setback. She was certain that Hawaii would be a good spot to continue the healing process. She was refilling her coffee when Dr. Kincaid returned, a newcomer accompanying her.

"Diana, this is Dr. Mel Copeland. Wilson's been reassigned. Dr. Copeland, Diana Faulkner."

"Nice to meet you, doctor." Diana offered her hand.

He shook it warmly. Nice direct gaze, older, more experienced than Wilson. "Same here, Mrs. Faulkner. We got the chamber delivered; it's being set up in one of the ER trauma rooms. We have the best space there. If you could you get your patient cleaned up from the honey and into these one hundred percent cotton duds, then we'll begin her treatment."

"Right away, doctor." She took the set, making a beeline for Mallory's room, practically in a daze! It was usually hard to get anything special done in a hospital on the week-end. Getting the chamber delivered! And Wilson banished! Her hope was to get Mallory checked out here, transferred to a major Honolulu hospital, and then begin the HBOT (hyperbaric oxygen treatment). That way, only one set of doctors would be around to laugh their heads off. She hoped Kenneth Wilson would never find out. Removing the honey and changing the patient wasn't easy, but she managed to complete the task before a couple of orderlies showed up.

⚔ ⚔

Sunday morning, the crowd was up again at Faith Baptist. Sitting in his office, torn apart in the remodeling and expansion, tears filled the pastor's eyes. He sat in his big chair, tapping his fingertips together. Maybe he shouldn't pray for his church to grow. Seemed like the only time his crowd was up, was when something calamitous was going on with Mallie. A bunch of kids from the high school were there, besides, Delia, Shay, Shannon, the Faulkners, Cline, a bunch of Prescotts and the senior Faulkners.

Since Diana was busy getting Xavier checked in at the church nursery, Daniel answered her cell. It was the charter company, wanting him to pass the word to his wife that everything was ready for the Monday flight.

"Honolulu?" His incredulous voice.

Innocent blue eyes met his. "Well, I think we've all earned another vacation!"

⚔ ⚔

The passengers of the private jet whooped with amazement as the pilot circled over the big island, Hawaii, making a pass over Kilauea Volcano. The joy from the friends surrounding Mallory was enough for the moment.

She couldn't sit up enough to take in the view, without agonizing pain. Hearing the excitement of the others was enough for now. She was tired; although, really she hadn't done anything to exhaust herself so completely. Still, within the past week, the Lord had performed some amazing miracles. Just a few hours beyond one week, since Dr. Kenneth Wilson, looming over her, had made the prediction that she could never survive!

After arrival in Honolulu, an ambulance transported her to the waiting hospital. Mallie didn't get much chance to experience the Island Paradise. But she would, and she could still be busy on her academics, be able to view the astounding volcanoes.

In her heart she repeated her verses, about God's being her Help. Her _Wealth_ was in knowing Him! Assurance of Eternal Life. Assurance of Eternal care and provision.

In her hospital bed after receiving an hour of HBOT, the nurses swathed her in honey-soaked bandages, once more. The edges of the massive bruises were fading into yellowish greens. She could open her eyes, to take in everything around her; smile a little better; make short responses.

She faced uncertainty. About whether her limbs would ever be useful again! And about David. Sylvia's taunting words continued to play and replay in her mind. She tried not to think about him. She would gird up her mind, take possession of her thoughts. Stay them upon the Lord. She would focus her attention upon Him and His _Magnificence_!